BLEEDING HEART

By
John Avanzato

KCM PUBLISHING
A DIVISION OF KCM DIGITAL MEDIA, LLC

CREDITS

Bleeding Heart by John Avanzato

ISBN-13: 978-1-7340941-2-1

First Edition

Publisher: Michael Fabiano
KCM Publishing
www.kcmpublishing.com

KCM Publishing
a division of KCM Digital Media, LLC

Dedication

This book is dedicated to the brave and valiant men and women of the United States Marine Corps and especially to my good friend Robert B. Tierney Gunnery Sergeant, USMC, retired.

Tierney was born in Chattanooga Tennessee and raised in New Jersey where I first met him at the tender age of sixteen. Two years later, he graduated Marine Combat Training School and never looked back. Gunnery Sergeant Tierney, call sign Chainsaw, has served his country with distinction in multiple theaters throughout the world and his list of accolades is almost too long to recount.

The highlights of his career include tours in Panama, Germany, Africa, Iraq and Kosovo. In 2003, Tierney participated in Operation Iraqi Freedom. He was a member of 2nd Battalion 25th Marines and was assigned to the 15th Marine Expeditionary Unit as part of Task Force Tarawa, a name given to the 2nd Marine Expeditionary Force during the 2003 invasion of Iraq, and most notable for its ground warfare in Nasiriyah, Iraq. Tierney served as a platoon commander where his advanced technical knowledge greatly enhanced the successful completion of his platoon and company missions.

Following retirement from the Corps, Tierney has continued to serve his community honorably in law enforcement and is now a decorated detective. From the halls of Montezuma to the shores of Tripoli, first in and last out, Gunnery Sergeant Tierney has served his country well and is the embodiment of what it means to be an American patriot and a United States Marine.

Semper Fi, Gunny

I first met my wife, Cheryl, at a dinner party in the Bronx thirty-five years ago. She was wearing cowboy boots. I don't think I've ever fully recovered.

Other Novels in the John Cesari Series

Contents

"If my doctor told me I had only six minutes to live,
I wouldn't brood. I'd type a little faster."
--Isaac Asimov

BLEEDING HEART

Chapter 1

The sparsely furnished room was dark and smoky, lit by a single incandescent bulb hanging from an exposed wire. At the small wood table in the center of the dank room sat three large men, brothers, swarthy and rough with bulky shoulders and broad chests. The older two were hardened by a difficult life and their faces were set with permanent scowls, a reflection of their underlying ill temperaments. They all smoked unfiltered cigarettes and drank strong mud-like black coffee from small, dirty cups. An unopened bottle of vodka with three empty shot glasses sat on the table begging for attention. Except for their age differences, the men's resemblance to each other was undeniable. They spoke with thick Romanian accents.

The youngest of the group was approaching thirty and appeared to be the least corrupted by life's twists and turns. He was handsome in the extreme with a full head of dark brown, wavy hair, and thoughtful, sensitive features. His large blue eyes were more inquisitive than the others; some would have said dreamy. He asked, "Why all the secrecy, Yorgi?"

Yorgi was the biggest of the three men, his head completely shaven, the oldest by almost ten years and clearly in charge. A menacing tattoo crept up the back of his collar to just reach the lower part of his occiput. It was the tip of a spear bearing the head of a fallen enemy. The writing across his back not visible beneath his black shirt read, *I am Death*. He sat opposite his younger brother and replied, "Because, Tibor, the walls have ears, and what we are about to discuss is best not overheard."

The brother sitting in between suddenly stood and flung his coffee cup at a small shadow scurrying along the wall. The coffee splashed, the cup shattered, and the rat squealed as it ran to safety.

"Do you feel better now, Ivan?" asked Yorgi in a soothing yet sarcastic tone.

"I hate rats, Yorgi. You know that. Why did you have to pick the basement of the most vermin infested tenement building in Manhattan to call a meeting? Wouldn't the penthouse suite at the Four Seasons in midtown have served a similar purpose?"

"Do not knock tenements, Ivan. They are one of things that make us wealthy. There is no better way to launder money, and the penthouse of the Four Seasons would not be safe. You never know who might see us and question what we are doing, and in our line of work, that kind of question is usually answered with a bullet to the back of the head."

Tibor said, "You mean Shlomo? Always you worry about that old Jew. He has one foot in grave and yet you always worry."

"How naïve you are, Tibor. That old Jew has nine lives, maybe ten. Even at his advanced age, he could drink us all under the table and then have a go with two whores at the same time. Remember, my brother, he survived the Nazis, the Russians, and then the Arabs. I have no desire to test his resilience and see if he will survive us. He has put more people like you and me prematurely into our own coffins than you can imagine. So do me favor and do not underestimate him."

"But Yorgi, not only is he old man, he seems to be growing feeble-minded. Don't you agree? Half the time he talks nonsense and seems confused."

"I agree with you. His mind wanders, and that is why we meet. It is time to act decisively and rise from beneath his shadow. But we must be careful. He is not that old and he is not that feeble-minded. And he has people watching...all the time...and he has people watching the people who watch. He is, not unexpectedly, extremely paranoid."

Ivan looked interested. "So what is plan, older brother?"

"I thought you would never ask. Shlomo has recently decided to get into the healthcare business as a way of diversification of his assets. This is where he has over-played his hand. He has talked others from the council, even more rich and even more powerful, into investing with him."

"Healthcare? Why would he do that?"

"It is not one hundred percent clear to me. Perhaps, he is preparing for his declining health and wishes easy access to a complicated medical system or perhaps he is seeking redemption for all the misery he has heaped upon this world in the last eighty years."

Tibor and Ivan chuckled at that. Tibor said, "I somehow doubt that last part."

Yorgi added, "There is always the possibility that he sees it as another way to launder his money. Most hospitals are doing very poorly financially these days. They would welcome the cash infusion and the money would return as legitimate income. Combine that with an army of overpriced lawyers on retainer who could push millions of tainted dollars around until they finally return clean. Multiply that by five or six hospitals and over the course of even one-year tens of millions could be laundered clean, and in addition, Shlomo would be hailed as a humanitarian. He may even be nominated for the Nobel Peace Prize."

Ivan raised his eyebrows, "You have got to be kidding?"

"I do not ever joke, Ivan. You know that," replied Yorgi. "The communists beat any sense of humor I may have had out of me. But his plan to buy his way into hospitals presents us with great opportunity if we can show the other members of the council that Shlomo has made a big mistake with their money."

Ivan countered, "But what if it isn't a mistake? What if it works? And all those filthy rich animals become even more filthy rich. What if they all win the Nobel Peace Prize?"

Yorgi grinned. "Trust me, brothers. That, I will not allow. We will make sure that his plan fails. We will expose Shlomo to the others for the doddering old man he is and then our time will come. Once in charge, I have big plans myself. The time is ripe for new blood and new ideas. New York will be ours, brothers. I promise you this."

"What you mean, Yorgi?" asked Tibor.

"I mean we Romanians have been settling for scraps thrown to us from table for too long. It is time we sit at table and throw scraps to others."

Ivan and Tibor sat back, contemplating his meaning. Ivan finally said, "You mean the Italians…the mafia."

"Yes, of course is what I mean. Where does it say they should have exclusive rights to illegal gambling, prostitution, drugs, extortion and protection? I have read the American Constitution. It says nothing about this."

"But the mafia, Yorgi? Seriously? We have always been at peace with them."

"Am very serious. Shlomo and the others are too complacent. They do not even see what is happening all around them. New York has changed. There aren't even that many Italians in Manhattan anymore. They are paper dragon. All these tenements we own on First and Second Avenues are filled with eastern Europeans…our people. Thousands of them. We have an army right here."

The younger brothers looked dismayed. Tibor said a bit skeptically, "And you think the Italians will just roll over and disappear?"

"Of course not, Tibor. There will be bloodshed, naturally. Perhaps lots of it, but in the end, I am confident we will prevail. We will offer them a truce. We get Manhattan and Bronx and they get Brooklyn, Queens, and Staten Island where they are still strong. Think of it, Tibor. Ivan and I will split up Manhattan and you will be in charge of all Bronx. They will call you, King of Bronx."

Tibor gasped, "But Bronx is shithole. I don't want to be in charge of shithole."

Yorgi very patiently explained, "You will need to be in Bronx at least for short time because of other part of plan. It will be safer there."

"What other part of plan?" Tibor asked visibly shocked.

"Before we can do anything, we must first ingratiate ourselves with Shlomo. We must gain the old devil's confidence in a way that places us above reproach or suspicion."

Ivan said, "And how do we do that?"

Yorgi cleared his throat and continued, "Old man Shlomo begins to worry about things only old men worry about. He married late in life and has only one child. He worries about what will happen to her when he is gone."

Yorgi paused for a moment to open the bottle of vodka that was on the table. He poured three shot glasses and passed them around. Then he raised his glass and waited for the others to follow suit. When they had, he said, "Let us toast to our younger brother. Tibor, you are lucky man."

Ivan looked confused. Tibor looked alarmed and said, "Lucky? How?"

"I have decided that you are to marry Shlomo's only child, the beautiful Drusilla."

Tibor angrily slammed his shot glass down on the table, spilling its contents. Ivan laughed. Tibor jumped to his feet. "Drusilla is the homeliest woman in all of Romania. I would rather marry a goat."

Yorgi rose to his feet as well, clearly exasperated. At six feet four inches, he was nearly a head taller than his brother and twice as intimidating. Years of weight-training and a grueling decade in the Romanian Special Forces had left him with a permanently dangerous aura.

"Sit down, Tibor," he said calmly. "I will not tolerate disrespect. When our parents died, did I not take care of you? Did I not make sure that both you and Ivan were well-fed and clothed? Did I not make sure that the communists did not break up our family and send you to orphanage? Did I not make sure that you were educated and did I not make sure you come to America with me? Did I not get you and Ivan good jobs with Shlomo? Tell me what wrong I have done you that you would speak to me this way?"

Tibor bowed his head, chastised, and slowly sat down. Yorgi sat too and continued, "It is crucial to plan that Shlomo trust us and after you make baby with Drusilla, he will be like butter on toast."

Tibor opened his mouth in horror but said nothing.

"There...that is better," said Yorgi as he refilled Tibor's shot glass. "America is the land of opportunity my brothers, but one must know when that opportunity presents itself and be prepared to seize it. Furthermore, once you seize it you must hang on with every ounce of your strength because right behind you there is always someone else ready to take it from you. Now let us drink to health, happiness, and great success."

Tibor reluctantly downed his shot and finally said, "What if Drusilla does not wish to marry me?"

Yorgi smiled. "Is all arranged. Have discussed with Shlomo who approves. Drusilla is very excited, already picking out wedding dresses."

Ivan laughed. "If they can't find one her size, I know good tent-maker from circus."

"Quiet, Ivan," admonished Yorgi.

"I am sorry, Yorgi," said Ivan, even as he continued to laugh.

All the blood drained from Tibor's face as he felt the walls closing in. Yorgi went on, "Now you see why you must go to Bronx. Stay out of harm's way to raise family. Make love to beautiful wife."

Ivan added, "You are lucky man, Tibor."

Tibor shot him a nasty look. "And what happens when Shlomo is gone or if your plan should fail?"

Yorgi strummed the sausage-sized fingers of one massive hand slowly on the table as he thought about it. Even his fingers were muscular and powerful as if he worked them out individually and as each one tapped the table it sounded like a hammer pounding on a nail. Eventually he said, "If plan fail, then I have no doubt we will all be dead, so I will address only first part. Shlomo gone could mean one of two things which may be out of my control. The council may allow him to retire and live out his days in peace or they may insist he die. I cannot predict. There is much loyalty between the elders. In either case, it will be up to you what you wish to do with Drusilla. She will be your wife, after all, not mine. I do not have the right to tell a man what to do with the mother of his children. Although, if plan succeeds and somehow Shlomo lives, it would probably not be a good idea to anger him. After all, he is still Shlomo."

"Great," Tibor practically spat the word out. "So I may be stuck with her?"

"Don't look so glum. If all goes well, you may not even reach altar with Drusilla. The important thing is to convince Shlomo you love daughter and want to be part of family. If something should happen to Shlomo before big day, then it is quite possible that you would be so upset you might even call off wedding."

"Well, at least there is hope."

"Yes, there is hope but not much. Drusilla is very eager to tie knot quickly before you change mind. She might be homely like cow in field, but she is no fool."

"Once again…great."

"It is all settled then. First thing is to send Shlomo a message."

Tibor shook his head and rolled his eyes. "Message? You give me to old-maid daughter to make children? What more kind of message?"

"Yes, Yorgi. Tell us. What kind of message?" asked Ivan.

"The kind of message that only someone who grew up in small village in shadow of *Castelul Bran* at the foot of the Carpathian Mountains would understand. The kind of message that will shake the self-confidence of a doddering, superstitious old man."

Ivan asked hesitantly, "You don't mean?"

"Yes, Ivan. Is exactly what I mean."

Chapter 2

"Arnie, at what point can we say enough is enough? Things are starting to get way out of hand," Cesari said more or less politely in contrast to his current level of irritation.

Arnie Goldstein was the medical director of St. Matt's hospital on Third Avenue in lower Manhattan. He was a hematologist by profession but had been a practicing bureaucrat for the last fifteen years and Cesari doubted he even knew which end of the stethoscope went into his ears anymore. He was a tad over sixty years old, and with all sorts of health issues, was just biding his time until retirement. His initial plan when he entered medicine was to stick it out until he was a hundred, but he knew that wasn't going to happen anymore. He was personally crushed when the hospital had passed a mandatory retirement age at sixty-five for all employed physicians. They had been friends for a long time and were sitting in Arnie's office on the tenth floor of the hospital chewing the fat. Arnie sipped small batch bourbon that he kept in the lower drawer of his desk to steady his constantly frayed nerves.

"Settle down, Cesari. New CEO's have a right to do things their way and hire the people they feel are right for the position."

"Agreed but laying off ten percent of the operating room nurses without even a discussion seems a bit arbitrary and counterproductive. I know the hospital's strapped financially but the less nurses, the less cases, the less income for the hospital. See my point?"

"I see your point and offer no defense other than the one stated. He's new and has to get his feet wet in St. Matt operations and politics, and we need to cut him some slack."

Arnie finished his drink and planted the glass down on his desk's ink blotter. He went to pour himself another one and for the third time offered Cesari some, but Cesari glanced at his watch and shook him off yet again.

Arnie said, "C'mon, Cesari. It's five o'clock somewhere."

"No, thanks. I'm on my way to the emergency room to see a consult and for the record, it may be five o'clock somewhere, but right here it's not even three. Isn't this a little early even for you?"

"Three you say? I'm surprised I was able to hold off until this late in the day. As you may have noticed this new administration has everyone on edge, not just you. My nerves have been worn thin too. Every day I have to open yet another email from the new boss instructing me on improved ways of tormenting the employees."

"Who is he anyway? It seems like the hospital rushed into hiring him without a whole lot of thought behind the decision."

"Money talks and bullshit walks, Cesari. That's the way it has always been and that's the way it will always be."

"What's that supposed to mean?"

Arnie hesitated briefly, resigned himself and then said, "I'm not supposed to tell you this, but a large donation was made to the hospital by a group of philanthropists. The only catch was that we hire this guy and his people. The offer was too good to turn down and we were looking for a new CEO anyway so…"

Cesari nodded. "Okay, I get it. How much did you sell out for?"

"We didn't sell out, and suffice it to say, it was a lot. It will keep us afloat for at least several more years."

"Is he somebody's nephew or dim-witted son who dropped out of school?"

"Stop...He's qualified for the job. We checked his references."

"Well, he's only been in charge eight weeks and has already pissed off the entire hospital with his policies and how come we haven't met him yet? Isn't that unusual?"

"A bit quirky perhaps but not that extraordinary. He's been busy putting a transition team in place and had to wrap up loose ends at the hospital he's leaving. I've met him briefly on a conference video call with the board members. He's flying in from Los Angeles tomorrow morning and told me to arrange for a meeting with the staff at 5:00 p.m. in conference room C in the basement. So make yourself available. My secretary should have sent you an email about it this morning. In the meanwhile, how have you been getting along with his chief of staff?"

"You mean that goon, Feinberg? Where'd you dig up that storm trooper?"

"Now, now... He's just doing his job, Cesari. And try to be a little more respectful. After all, he's a doctor just like you."

Cesari snorted, "Doctor of what, veterinary medicine?"

"Take it easy, Cesari. He doesn't make policy. He just implements it."

"Yeah well, somebody ought to introduce him to the hospital's policy on sexual harassment."

Arnie raised his eyebrows. "What's that supposed to mean?"

"The OR nurses have already started making noise about him. You know Melissa?"

"The one with the ass?"

"Yeah, well I guess your boy Feinberg noticed it too."

"What did he do?"

"I wasn't there but she says he copped a feel in the break-room after luring her in to discuss OR procedures."

Arnie let out a deep breath. "Is she going to file a complaint with HR?"

"Melissa? Are you kidding? You don't know her very well, but if he does it again there will be blood and those are her words not mine."

"That's not good but right now everybody's feeling a little threatened. Is it possible she misinterpreted his actions?"

"Spare me, Arnie. I know a dog in heat when I see one and it's not just Melissa. Besides, we're talking about OR nurses. The bar is set pretty high when it comes to offending that particular group. They're not shrinking violets. Half of them are dating or married to cops or guys in the military. You want to talk about tough women? And they don't just take it. They give it too. When they want a guy, they'll just as soon throw him down on the floor and take him. Trust me, I've been on that end. If Feinberg is giving them the creeps, then I would be concerned."

Arnie blinked. "Duly noted. Should I talk to Melissa?"

"I wouldn't. Not yet. She can handle herself. If she wants to escalate the situation, she knows how, but I would keep my eyes and ears open with Feinberg. Sooner or later he's going to push the wrong person's buttons and World War III is going to erupt."

"Fine, but right now my hands are tied. We have to let things play out a little more and see where the dust settles. I mean there's a new sheriff in town and that's always going to ruffle feathers."

"All right, but you've been warned. There's a fox in the hen house."

Arnie took a deep breath and let it out as he nodded. "I got it, but you never answered my question. How are you personally getting along with him?"

"Are we having trouble communicating, Arnie? He's a gorilla getting paid six figures to make me and everyone else here miserable. He looks like he stepped off the pages of a bad guy comic book and he's annoying the women I work with, which puts them in a bad mood, which in turn puts me in a bad mood."

"Look, these are hard times, Cesari, and sometimes the cure can be as painful as the disease. As a physician, I'm sure you get that. St. Matt's is entering a period of austerity and it's the mission of this new administration to root out waste. That means someone has to take a serious and objective look at operations. That is neither a pleasant nor fun thing to do. Feinberg is just the tip of the iceberg. There's more to come once the new CEO gets here so brace yourself for more pain. I should let you know that it's already been hinted that the GI department may be running fat."

"Nice, so I may be heading for the chopping block too?"

"You or one of your colleagues, but nothing's written in stone. I'm doing my best behind the scenes to be a calming influence, but you coming in here making wild accusations isn't going to help. I know you can be a bit hot-headed but a little patience on your part might go a long way here."

"Wild accusations? Do you really want to be on the wrong end of a sexual harassment lawsuit?"

"Of course not, but if I'm to do anything then the individual involved needs to speak to me or HR directly. You weren't even an eyewitness, and you are, I might add based on this conversation, just a teeny bit biased. If a judge ever asked me to assess your nature, I would freely admit that you are one of the best gastroenterologists I have ever worked with, albeit slightly prone to hyperbole."

"Easy with big words, Arnie. Remember, I'm from the Bronx. Besides, I'm not being hyperbolic about anything and how am I biased?"

"Cesari, you and I have known each other both professionally and personally for about ten years. Am I correct?"

Cesari nodded slowly, thinking about it. "Sounds right."

"In that time period, roughly how many nurses have you dated, hooked up with, or made nooky with in the backseat of their cars in the hospital parking lot in between colonoscopies just to blow off steam?"

Cesari was quiet, not liking the sudden change in trajectory of the conversation.

Arnie continued, "As I thought... Your silence speaks volumes. Let's just say that the answer to that question is... lots. Now suddenly there's a new fox in the hen house and just to play devil's advocate, isn't it possible that the old fox might be feeling a little bit insecure?"

Cesari stood up stiffly. "I'm glad you're taking this seriously, Arnie. I have to go to the ER now. Call me when you snap out of your coma."

"Calm down. I didn't mean for you to get your panties in a bunch, and I am taking it seriously."

"Great, but I still have to go to the ER."

"Fine, but don't slam the door like you always do when you're in a mood."

Cesari turned and walked out of the room closing the door gently behind him, thought better of it, reopened the door and slammed it hard. He heard Arnie curse from inside and that made him smile as he meandered toward a bank of elevators in the central corridor.

As he arrived on the first floor and exited the car, he bumped into Harry Givelber, the senior of four pathologists at St. Matt's. Harry was fifty, overweight, had a scruffy beard, and was wearing a white lab coat with a large coffee stain on the right lapel.

He slapped Cesari on the back and said jovially, "Cesari, long time no see."

"Hi Harry. You're right and I apologize. I haven't been down to the lab in quite a while."

"I'm glad I ran into you. I was sharing a glass of port with Herb Jankowski last night and your name came up. He told me you took some time off last fall to write a book. I didn't know that. Is it true and if so, how'd it go?"

"Yeah, it's true. Herb was leaving St. Matt's for greener pastures at about the same time I went on sabbatical when I bumped into him, and it went well. I have a rough draft sitting on my desk. I've been meaning to get back to it. So how is Herb? Last I heard he was setting up shop at Columbia."

"He was heading to Columbia and almost made it there when the NIH snatched him up and he is now up to his eyeballs in viral research in Bethesda. He's in town for a couple of days presenting a paper at a meeting. Apparently, he's publishing like crazy."

"The NIH? That's very impressive."

"As he mentioned to me several times over."

Cesari grinned, "Rubbed it in, did he?"

"Yes, he did. In a good-natured way, of course. But they're such alarmists at those research institutions. He claims there's a new virus they've isolated in some remote part of China and that if it ever makes its way here, it will be like the Black Death all over again."

"No kidding? He used those words?"

He nodded, "He said to buy stock in disinfectants, antibiotics and tissue paper."

"Tissue paper? Like for sneezing?"

"No, tissue paper as in toilet paper."

"Toilet paper? Does this new virus cause diarrhea?"

"He didn't say."

"Well, if it's the end of days, I might just sell everything I own and go on a bender. Until then, I'll probably just keep doing what I'm doing. In the meanwhile, if you see Herb again tell him I said hello and to keep up the good work."

"I'll tell him. That's great about the book, Cesari. Kudos to you. I hope you follow through with it. What is it? I hope it's a salacious tell-all about St. Matt's."

"No, pure fiction. It's a murder mystery."

"I'll tell you, Cesari. I could write a book about the things I see every day in our department and with each year the stuff coming in gets even more outrageous. People think of new ways of killing each other all the time. You should come down to the lab more often. There's some great fodder there for murder mysteries. Just last night a guy came in…" Harry glanced in both directions furtively as people walked by, and then lowering his voice to a whisper, he continued, "I'd rather not talk about it right here in the middle of the hallway if you know what I mean. It could be construed as being unprofessional. What are you doing right now?"

"I have to go the ER to see a patient, but it shouldn't take more than an hour."

"Come by the morgue when you're done. I'll tell you all about it. You won't be disappointed."

Cesari was amused. Harry was one of your more even-keeled people and wasn't prone to drama. What he said about the pathology department being filled with fodder for novels was probably accurate though, so maybe a trip there wasn't such a bad idea.

"All right, Harry. Give me an hour."

Chapter 3

The morgue in the basement of St. Matt's was similar to any other. Cold, metallic, and maintained at a constant thirty-six degrees, it was like a giant refrigerator. Cesari watched his breath steam up as he shivered and hoped this didn't take too long. There were ten drawers built into one of the drab green walls, a steel table parked in the center, and industrial strength fluorescent lighting blazed overhead. The place reeked of formaldehyde and death. Autopsies were performed in an adjacent room that housed all the necessary equipment including a drain built into the middle of the floor and a garden hose to clean up. Cesari had sat in on a number of post-mortems in his day but could never quite get used to the idea of fileting open a human being. He found the sound of the saws slicing open a chest cavity or the top of a skull extremely unsettling. It was a nasty job, but someone had to do it.

The day in, day out intimacy with the dead and mutilated caused many pathologists to develop peculiar self-defense mechanisms. Some became hardened and inured to the experience, a sort of detachment from reality. These types frequently had difficulties with socialization and tended to be loners. Others embraced the life with gusto and sidestepped the psychological and emotional horrors of what they were doing by developing overly ebullient personalities and mind-numbing black humor. Harry was of the latter ilk.

He met Cesari promptly and was very excited to display his case. "You're going to love this one, Cesari," he beamed as he approached one of the drawers. "The NYPD brought him in around midnight. They found him in an alley over on First Avenue. I'm doing the autopsy in the morning. Are you ready?"

"Let's keep it moving, Harry. I've had a long day."

"Sure thing. It's just that we don't get many cases like this. Usually it's pretty obvious what the cause of death is. You know; a bullet hole in the head, a chef's knife in the heart, a rope around the neck, but hey, you're Sicilian, you probably know all about this stuff."

"Harry…"

"Okay, here we go."

He reached out to a drawer about three feet off the ground and pulled on the handle. The drawer slid out quietly on its well-oiled sturdy slides until the entire body was in view enclosed in an opaque plastic bag. Harry unzipped it from head to toe and stood back for Cesari to get a good look.

It was a naked Caucasian male, average height, and medium to slender build, no more than a hundred and sixty-pounds lying face up. At one time he was probably in reasonably good physical condition. He was over twenty and under forty, with a full head of dark brown hair and three days growth of beard. There were no obvious signs of trauma to his head, chest or abdomen. He was white as a sheet and Cesari didn't see any signs of lividity, but he would have to turn him over to check. He didn't like to be judgmental and knew it was impossible to determine such things after the fact, but the guy didn't look like he had been very intelligent. His large muscular hands and shoulders suggested manual labor.

"Was he found just like this…naked?"

"Very much so," Harry nodded.

"Is it safe to assume there's no evidence of trauma on his other side, Harry?"

"Yes, and his backside is just as white as the front."

"No lividity?"

"None whatsoever."

Cesari thought about that and said, "How is that possible? Where would his blood have pooled if not there?"

"We'll get to that. I estimate the time of death to be no more than four to six hours before midnight. The police said there were no traces of drug paraphernalia at the scene. They received an anonymous tip about him, and he was found lying next to a dumpster in an alley between a Ukrainian restaurant and some slum buildings over on First Avenue."

"Do we know who he is?"

"His name is Andrej Petrović. He's a thirty-something-year-old Serbian national. We don't know much else yet. A local crowd gathered at the scene and someone identified him to the police, but they didn't know him real well. I don't know yet if they've been able to contact any friends or family or if he even has any here in New York."

Cesari got within inches of the body and scanned him up and down carefully. He said, "I give up; poison, heart attack?"

"I don't think so. The full toxicology will take a couple of days, but I can tell you the initial narcotics and cocaine screen were negative, and you don't usually undress and lie down in an alley after a heart attack."

"You don't?" Cesari grinned.

"Here look," Harry was positively giddy with anticipation of the big reveal. "I've been withholding something from you."

He reached down into the drawer and twisted the head toward Cesari revealing an aspect of the neck on the side that wasn't clearly visible from Cesari's angle. He now noticed two very obvious small puncture wounds in the man's throat but no blood. The wounds were separated by an inch and there was a purplish halo around each one suggesting that the trauma had occurred during life and was not some kind of post death injury. Cesari studied the holes with great interest.

Eventually he looked up and said, "That is interesting, Harry. What do you think?"

"Now you understand….I don't know what to think yet. I'm going to cut him open first thing in the morning."

"Is it a snake bite? Some people keep them as pets."

"The thought crossed my mind and as dumb as it might be it's quite true that people keep them as pets, even the profoundly dangerous ones like Copperheads. I even read a case where a guy kept a Black Mamba in a fish tank. It escaped one day and killed him, his girlfriend and his dog. They died so fast, they didn't even have a chance to call 911. People are nuts."

"That they are. These wounds look pretty fresh, Harry."

"They are fresh so if he did run into a snake or some other type of fanged reptile it must have been before he died or close to it. It's going to take a couple of days to figure out if he has any snake poison in him. There are a number of immunologically-based assay systems that we use to detect specific venoms and venom antibodies, but it's a relatively slow process."

Cesari nodded. "Did you clean him up? Why aren't there any blood stains?"

"Good question, and no, nobody here cleaned him up unless it was the police or paramedics who brought him here, but even they wouldn't have been that stupid. Apparently, there was no blood at the scene in the alley either."

"How deep do you think the holes are? Maybe they have nothing to do with his death."

Harry smirked, "The holes are an inch and a half deep. I took the time to measure that when he came in and from their location, they would undoubtedly have hit either his jugular vein, or possibly even his carotid artery."

"That should have made a bloody mess, Harry."

"Quite, and that my friend is the source of my consternation. His pallor is disproportionate to someone who recently died with the exception of one cause."

Cesari said, "Exsanguination…"

"Exactly, and people who exsanguinate don't usually do so until every drop of their blood is gone. You exsanguinate until your heart gives out and can no longer deliver blood to the site of hemorrhage. The point where the heart fails will differ from person to person depending on circumstances and underlying medical conditions."

Cesari digested that and said, "I guess I never thought about it."

Triumphant, Harry took a moment to swagger. "Of course not. You GI guys are the jocks of healthcare but it's the lab rats like me who do all the heavy lifting."

Cesari glanced down at the corpse as Harry got whatever grievance he had out of his system. He said, "You're right, Harry. Pathologists are definitely underappreciated, but back to our friend here."

"Yes, indeed. So, if an elderly male with heart disease suddenly decides to exsanguinate, his already compromised cardiovascular system would collapse much sooner than our healthy young buck's here."

"So the older guy wouldn't have to bleed that much before his heart stopped."

"And therefore, he would have that much more blood residual after he died."

"But the young guy would just gush and gush until almost nothing was left."

"Now you're catching on Cesari. And that is why he is pale as a ghost and there is no noticeable lividity along the dependent portions of his body. No blood to pool with gravity, no lividity."

"Okay, Harry, I understand that part, but then where's the blood? A guy this size would have close to ten pints of blood in him. If he bled out most of it, that would have made an absolutely horrific scene. He and everything around him would have literally been submerged in it."

"Unless he bled out somewhere else, was cleaned up and then dumped there."

Cesari furrowed his brow in thought and conceded, "That's the only possible way for him to have been found like this, but why?"

"Why drain him of all his blood or why clean him up?"

"And why kill him at all?"

"That, Cesari, is for the detectives to sort out."

"Do we know anything else about him other than he's a Serb?"

"I don't, but the police might know more by now. They'll be coming at eight tomorrow morning to watch the autopsy. I told them I would call them with the results, but they insisted on seeing for themselves. The detective in charge was a bit of a hard ass. You're welcome to join us."

Cesari's curiosity was more than a little piqued. He hesitated for a moment and then said, "I'll have to reschedule my morning, but I think I will."

"Ha, I knew I'd suck you into my world. It's great stuff, huh? I bet you're regretting going into gastroenterology already?"

Cesari smiled, "I've been regretting that since the day I graduated medical school."

Harry zipped the body bag up again and pushed the drawer closed. "Are you going to that get-together tomorrow to meet the new CEO?" he asked.

"Do I have a choice?"

"You could quit now and save yourself some aggravation."

"This guy's not playing ball, is he?"

"He already told us a hospital this size doesn't need four pathologists. He was nice about it and let us decide who, but one of us has to leave quietly or he'll do the picking for us. He gave us the good news via email and a registered letter."

"You're kidding?"

"I'm not. I haven't even met the guy and I already hate him."

"I'm sorry to hear that, Harry. I really am. Have you guys decided who?"

"It'll probably be McDermott. He's only been here a couple of years. We talked it over. He's from Rhode Island and most of his roots and family are still there. He thinks he can swing a job up there without too much fuss. It's a shame because I really like him, but he seems okay with it. Ah, modern healthcare. Isn't it grand the way physicians have devolved into mere pawns on a multi-trillion-dollar chess board?"

Chapter 4

Cesari left the hospital at 7:00 p.m. and walked casually along the north side of Washington Square Park towards his apartment building on the corner of Waverly Place and Avenue of the Americas. It was a beautiful evening in late June and the city was alive and well. Throngs of people milled about in and around the park eating, drinking and listening to street musicians. Cars piled up at red lights honked their frustration. The summer sun was still high in the sky and not a cloud anywhere to obscure its radiance. It momentarily crossed his mind how differently things might look if a plague such as the Black Death suddenly swept across the city; deserted streets, empty parks and businesses, no traffic, maybe a body here or a body there and most eerily of all…dead silence. He shook himself and hoped it would never happen.

His apartment was a massive loft on the third and top floor of a former sauerkraut factory. The first floor at street level was a Polish restaurant and delicatessen. The second floor was storage space for the restaurant. The basement of the building housed massive smokers which ran night and day preparing the kielbasa for the family-run eatery. Cesari ate there often because the food was so good and the ambience uniquely charming. Although, Piotr, a fifty-year-old Polish immigrant ostensibly was in charge, it was his wife, her mother, and her sisters who actually ran the place. Cesari made the mistake of strolling uninvited into the kitchen once following the aroma of something exquisite and ran into a sea of babushkas all holding rolling pins in self-defense at his intrusion. He never did that again.

He stopped in tonight, picked up a ring of garlic kielbasa and sauerkraut-stuffed pierogis for dinner and then trudged up the three long flights of ancient and irregular steps to his apartment. Cesari was in good shape for a guy with a white-collar job in his late thirties. He was six feet and two-hundred and twenty pounds of mostly lean Italian sausage and he intended on keeping it that way. He had spent many hours in his younger days picking up heavy objects of metal and putting them down again in any grimy gym in the Bronx he could find. He wasn't fond of running but kept his cardiovascular conditioning sharp with extreme devotion to workouts with a heavy bag and endless sessions with a jump rope. To keep his fists in shape for the real thing, he frequently pounded the bag bare knuckled, until bleeding and pain made him stop. The skin over his knuckles was permanently rough like sandpaper.

It was an obsession of his to always be ready. Cesari was from a part of the Bronx most people only vaguely knew of from news reports and movies. Certain neighborhoods in certain cities were truly jungles in their own right and just like on National Geographic, survival of the fittest was the only rule people lived by. You had to hit the hardest, duck the fastest, and bleed the least if you wanted to make it. A part of his brain was always on alert from years of living in the war zones of street gangs and organized crime. His medical training and lifestyle had done nothing to tamp down his instincts for survival. A therapist had once told him he had post-traumatic stress and needed to be on Prozac. Cesari had told him that if he ever wrote that down in his chart, he would beat him like the batter for a meringue.

It was for this reason, that when he reached the top floor and stood before his apartment door, he knew something was off. He heard nothing and saw nothing unusual as he scanned up and down the corridor. The old wood door stood expectantly before him, but all was not right. There were two locks and one was a deadbolt. There was no damage to the doorjamb to suggest someone had forced their way in but there was something about the locks that seemed different. They were old and worn and Cesari had looked at them unconsciously thousands upon thousands of times.

He put his face close and studied them. There it was… small almost imperceptible fresh scratch marks on the metal of both locks. Did someone try to pick them open? It might work with one of the locks but not with the deadbolt. He quietly placed his package on the floor to one side of the entrance and knelt down, gently lifting up the door mat. Underneath was a loose floorboard which Cesari gingerly removed. He reached down into the space and came out with a black, snub-nosed, hammerless, .38 caliber Smith & Wesson revolver loaded with five hollow point rounds. Completely inaccurate at more than ten feet but up close it could really ruin your day.

The serial number had been scratched off, but the weapon was totally illegal anyway for a variety of reasons starting with private ownership of handguns within New York City limits was so highly restricted they were essentially banned. Secondly, Cesari was a convicted felon and wouldn't be allowed to own a handgun under any circumstances in New York State. It was a nonviolent felony conviction for lying to a federal investigator, but a felony was a felony. The serial number being erased would simply be icing on the cake for any cop who caught him with it.

After much consideration, Cesari had decided he'd rather be a live ex-felon arguing his case before a judge than a dead ex-felon who followed the rules. He kept the pistol outside his apartment under the floorboards just in case law-enforcement ever felt the need to search his place for whatever reason, and he always wiped his prints from the gun when he stored it away. His argument in court would be that since he didn't own the building and only rented the space within the apartment, they couldn't necessarily claim it belonged to him should it be discovered accidentally. He knew it was lame but hoped that New York's liberal judges with their lenient positions on law enforcement would save him.

Now armed, he felt his confidence surge and tested the doorknob with his left hand, the pistol ready for action in his right. The door was unlocked and slid forward with a mild creaking sound. Cesari stepped across the threshold and was surprised by what he saw.

On his couch sat Beauregard, "call me Beau" Feinberg, the chief of staff for the new CEO who had been sent in advance to begin implementing changes and softening the beaches for his boss. He was six feet two inches tall and two hundred and seventy pounds, most of which was in his huge beer belly spilling over his waistband. His head was just a click too large for his body and he had thick curly salt and pepper hair. Forty years old, fat and lazy was how Cesari appraised him but he had the power and that was all that mattered.

Feinberg was amused as he watched Cesari enter his own home gun drawn and apprehensive. He said, "I hope you have a permit for that thing, Cesari."

Cesari glanced in all directions to see if there were any other surprises waiting for him. He said, "How'd you get in here?"

"You left the door open."

"Bullshit."

Cesari put the gun in his pocket and faced Feinberg who sipped an expensive scotch from Cesari's liquor cabinet.

"Sit down, Cesari. I don't want to fight."

"You break into my apartment, drink my best scotch and then tell me you don't want to fight. What planet are you from? Better still, what exactly do you want?"

But he sat down nonetheless in a plush leather chair opposite his unexpected visitor who said, "Dear God, I hope this isn't your best scotch. In fact, I hope it's not even your sec-ond-best scotch. If it is then you need to get out more."

"I repeat. What do you want?"

"First of all, for clarification, I didn't break into anything so let's take it easy with the accusations. As far as the scotch is concerned, I just assumed that since we work together you wouldn't mind me having a drink while I waited for you."

"The last guy that came in here without an invitation wound up with a six-inch screwdriver in his left eye. I can be territorial like that. That's not a threat, mind you. Think of it more as a history lesson."

"Duly noted and I read your file. I'm impressed. I mean I read your police file. Your hospital file is squeaky clean."

"You read my police file?" Cesari was torn between want-ing to pistol whip this guy with the Smith & Wesson and pat-ting him on the back for his ingenuity.

"It wasn't that hard. I have friends on the force. I like to know who I'm dealing with and boy am I glad I read your file; assault, obstruction of justice, loansharking, ties to organized crime, six months at Riker's Island. How the hell did you get into medical school? Break somebody's arm?"

Cesari was astonished and angry that he was having this conversation. "That's all in the past."

"Is that why you came into the room waving a gun?"

"The real question that you still haven't answered is how'd you get in?"

He reached into his pocket and came out with a set of keys which he tossed to Cesari. "I had them made from the set I found in your OR locker. Before you have a hemorrhage, that's not against the law. Your locker is subject to search and seizure at any time according to the bylaws of the hospital and is not considered your private property."

Cesari raised his eyebrows in disbelief. You went into my locker and copied my keys? That has to be in violation of some law."

"Not really. I'm allowed to search your locker if drug use or theft of hospital property is suspected and I'll just say I received an anonymous tip to that effect. The copying of the key thing is interesting. There are no laws against it because no one ever anticipated anyone would do that. So unlike you, I haven't actually broken any laws. You on the other hand are an ex-felon in possession of an illegal handgun which you have been brandishing at an unarmed houseguest."

"You know what, Feinberg? Forget about the screwdriver in the eye thing. I'm tempted to throw you out a window to see if the laws of gravity have been compromised by climate change."

Feinberg chuckled, "And I thought we could be friends."

"Okay, we're back to square one. Why are you here?"

Reaching into his briefcase, he came out with a bulky 8x11 manila folder which he tossed onto the coffee table separating them. He said, "It's your new contract. Sign it and I'll be on my way. There are two copies; one for you and one for me."

"My old contract still has two years to go."

"That's why you're going to sign this one. We're renegotiating."

"I don't get a chance to read it?"

"Flip through it all you want so long as it's signed by the time I leave. I'm in charge of trimming the fat and unless you want to be trimmed, you'll cooperate. Your buddies have already signed so take comfort in that."

Cesari opened the envelope and pulled out two thick stacks of paper. The contracts were thirty pages long and contained mostly unintelligible legal jargon. On page ten, he saw that his salary was being cut by twenty-five percent. He nearly gasped as he glanced upward at Feinberg who was refilling his glass with scotch.

"Take it easy with my spirits, Feinberg. I may not be able to afford top shelf anymore after this."

"Times are tough for everyone, Cesari, and you're dreaming if you think this swill is top shelf."

"Times are tough? Even for you and the new CEO?"

He just smiled at that as Cesari's mind raced. If he didn't sign, he'd be out of work. If he signed, he'd be agreeing to a significant cut in pay and only God knew what other draconian clauses were in the contract. But if he signed, he could stay and try to fight these guys from within. Maybe he'd ultimately lose the battle, but it was worth a try. He was sure that the others on staff would appreciate his gesture.

He flipped through the rest and on page twenty-five something caught his eye. He remarked sarcastically, "You've got to be kidding? A nondisclosure clause?"

"We need to protect ourselves, Cesari. We live in a litigious society."

Cesari read the paragraphs and rolled his eyes. "I can't say anything that is deemed negative or critical of the hospital, its practices or the administration not only for the duration of this contract but for the rest of my life or I will be subject to punitive damages up to half a million dollars? Are you people crazy?"

"You're the one with the gun, Cesari. No one's forcing you to sign it. Look, I've done my research on you. You're one of the people everyone at St. Matt's look up to. If you play your cards right, we might be able to use you on the management team, but you'd have to show us that you're on our side first. You know, sort of a demonstration of loyalty. A good start would be for you to sign on the dotted line."

Frustrated and feeling trapped, Cesari took in and let out a deep breath and then signed both documents. He handed one over to Feinberg, saying, "I'm flattered, and I'll be sure to keep that in mind."

Feinberg walked out the door without a goodbye, leaving Cesari with the unmistakable sensation of having just been shaken down. He knew the feeling because he had spent a lot of time in his previous life shaking people down. Plus, Feinberg didn't seem at all fazed by Cesari's criminal past or the fact that he had casually pointed a lethal weapon at him when he had entered the room. Feinberg was no ordinary hospital bureaucrat. This guy had balls the size of Wisconsin. Cesari was starting to believe that he was up against something far more sinister than a simple change of administrations.

He collected his kielbasa and pierogis which were still lying outside in the hallway and placed them in the refrigerator. Deciding to shower before he ate dinner, he went to the bedroom. Opening the door, he flipped on the overhead light and stepped back, startled. A beautiful blonde girl lay on his bed under the covers and if he had to guess, she wasn't wearing much. She smiled at him seductively.

Recovering, he asked, "Who are you?"

"My name is Bambi."

"And you are?"

"A present from your friend."

He wasn't in a good mood and said, "Get out, Bambi… Now."

After she left, Cesari changed the sheets and showered. Afterward, he sat down on the edge of the freshly made bed and sighed deeply.

Who are these guys?

Chapter 5

Later that evening, Cesari was restless and a bit unnerved by Feinberg's unorthodox visit so he took a cab over to the Kit Kat Klub on Second Avenue. The Kit Kat was one of lower Manhattan's more notorious and well-attended gentlemen's clubs. It was pricy but well-worth it because of the quality of the entertainment. He arrived at 10:00 p.m. and appraised the entrance. The massive oak doors with brass handles were guarded by two proportionately-sized, enormous but well-dressed bouncers with closely cropped beards and buzz cuts. Cesari nodded at one of them politely.

"Hi, Gaetano. I'm here to see the boss," he said in a friendly manner.

"He's in his office, Doc. Is he expecting you?"

Cesari nodded. "He should be. I called an hour ago."

"Give me a sec and I'll let him know you're here. He's finishing up his physical therapy."

"Thanks."

Gaetano spoke into a hand-held radio and then waved Cesari in. As he passed through a metal detector to enter the club, pulsating music overwhelmed him. Appearing from out of nowhere, a tall brunette in a thong, high heels and matching pasties dangling from large breasts slipped her arm through his and whispered in his ear, "You look lost, handsome. Can I show you around?"

"I'm fine, thanks."

"Are you sure?" she asked, leaning in close.

"I am."

She stepped back into the shadows and he navigated his way past the bar and leather booths and was almost blinded by the flashing purple fluorescent lights that lined the room. Well-dressed men sat hunched over drinks ogling voluptuous women twirling around poles on a central stage. Various other women in similar costumes as the one who met him at the door sauntered around delivering drinks or dancing for men in private booths as tens, twenties and fifties were stuffed into their G-strings.

At the far end of the bar was a staircase guarded by a guy with a bulging neck and biceps. Wearing a black suit and matching turtleneck, Cesari could see at least one pistol protruding out from a shoulder holster and guessed he probably had a second one in the small of his back which would have been standard operating procedure. There were probably multiple other armed men in the room. Vito was always big on security. The man in front of him ignored the mostly naked girls as he surveyed the room for troublemakers and anomalies. Cesari was an anomaly but not a troublemaker. Word had already reached him from outside.

He said, "Hi, Doc. Turn around and put your hands behind your head."

"Really, Bobby?"

Bobby tensed ever so slightly but outwardly was unconcerned. "You know the drill, Doc. Don't make me say it again."

Cesari sighed, turned around and clasped his hands behind his head as the large man patted him down. When he was done, he said, "He's upstairs."

Cesari skipped up the staircase and was met at the top by yet another two guards, only these guys were more normal sized albeit armed with short-barreled submachine guns. They looked like Heckler & Koch MP5s, an older model for sure but very fine and reliable weapons. Both guns were pointed at his torso as he was directed to turn around and lean against the wall. They frisked him again and then pointed to a door at the end of the hallway. Cesari went there and knocked politely.

"C'mon in," barked a familiar voice, deep and throaty.

He opened the door and entered. Vito Gianelli, his best friend since the first grade was naked and lying belly down on a professional massage table. He had propped himself up on one elbow and was pointing a large revolver at Cesari's chest. It looked like a .44 magnum and it was cocked. When Vito confirmed it was who he was expecting, he relaxed, uncocked the weapon and put it away under a towel and positioned his face back down into the donut hole at the head of the table. A partially clad Asian girl, who had had been hiding behind a nearby pool table, stood up, came forward, and began wrestling with his huge shoulders and upper back, attempting to massage the knots out of his brawny sinews. She looked fatigued, like she'd been going at it hard for quite some time.

Without looking up, Vito said, "Make yourself a drink, Cesari. We're almost done."

Cesari looked around the big office. There was a large wood desk on the other side of the room with a liquor cabinet and all the accoutrements. He poured himself three fingers of Johnnie Walker Blue into a crystal tumbler and sat down in a leather chair watching the girl work up a sweat.

Despite all the firearms, Vito was probably the only person in the world he felt he could truly relax around. He knew Vito felt the same way about him. Fighting your way up from the streets of the Bronx together made people close in inexplicable ways. Although why his friend felt the need to own a strip club was beyond Cesari's ability to comprehend. Vito had his hand in so many underworld enterprises in lower Manhattan both legal and illegal that the income from the Kit Kat was inconsequential to the big picture of things. They had talked about this many times and the answer always sounded strange to Cesari's ears. Places like the Kit Kat were where Vito had started out in the business. First as a bouncer, then as a bartender, then a bodyguard, and so on and so forth, eventually manager and owner of several clubs. He had graduated to much bigger and better things, but he had a soft spot for these kinds of businesses. Being in places like this brought him comfort and security, perhaps even peace of mind. It was, for him, like going home for Thanksgiving or Christmas was for everyone else.

The masseuse finished her thing and Vito sat up to thank her. He thanked her with a long kiss on the lips, a pat on the bottom and several crisp one hundred-dollar bills. She scampered away and Vito put on a luxurious, embroidered, white terry-cloth robe, poured himself a scotch and sat down behind his desk. On the desk was a pack of cigarettes. He shook one out and lit it with a metal lighter lying next to it. He then sat back, took a sip of scotch, blew a smoke ring at the ceiling and let out a deep, contented sigh.

"So what do you want, Cesari?"

"I just happened to be in the neighborhood, so I thought I'd check in."

Vito laughed. "I thought you didn't approve of gentlemen's clubs?"

"Not quite what I said the last time we talked about it but I can understand the confusion. I don't have a problem with gentlemen's clubs per se. It's the men who frequent them I disapprove of. They're mostly sleazebags, present company excluded of course."

"Of course. So what's going on? You've been laying low for weeks."

"I've got some problems at the hospital."

"What kinds of problems?"

"We've had a change in management and the new guys are giving everybody grief.

"And this required a trip here…why?"

"I needed to talk it out with someone who understands where I'm going with it. These guys aren't your typical pencil necks if you know what I mean. They're using the kind of strong-arm techniques I would expect from you. One of them broke into my apartment earlier tonight in an attempt to intimidate me. When I surprised him with a gun in his face, he didn't even blink, like it happened to him all the time. Then he twisted my arm to sign a less than favorable contract and left a hooker for me to ease the pain of my humiliation. If that doesn't sound like you, I don't know what does."

"I see your point. What are their names?"

"The one who who's been running around the hospital for the last few weeks is an ape called Beauregard Feinberg."

"Beauregard? You've got to be kidding?"

"I wish I was. He goes by Beau, but I call him Feinberg because it irritates him. The new CEO is flying in tomorrow morning. I haven't met him yet. His name is Tiberius Acevedo."

Vito raised his eyebrows. "Beauregard's bad enough, but Tiberius? What kind of name is that?"

"Tiberius was the name of the second emperor of ancient Rome. Other than that I once knew a guy who called his great dane, Tiberius. Either name ring a bell? They're both from L.A. I don't know much else about them. They have a paper-thin presence on the internet. I already checked."

Vito thought about that and shook his head. "No, I've never heard of either one of them."

"Okay, can you put out feelers? You have many more contacts than I do. If these guys are connected, you might stumble onto something."

He nodded, "I can do that. Anything else?"

"Yeah, do you have any advice?"

"Yeah, quit while you can. Why make yourself miserable? You're marketable. I'm sure you'd have no problem finding a job somewhere else."

"Thanks, but I think I'll stick around. I don't like these guys."

Vito chuckled. "There it is. You could never say no to a good fight, could you, Cesari?"

"These guys are bullies and they're pushing the wrong guy around."

"Fine, I'll let you know if I dig anything up on them. Would you mind if I sent one of my guys over to take a look at them and maybe snap a photo? I'd need you to point them out to him. It might help."

"Be my guest. Say, I couldn't help but notice your security seems a bit thick for a Thursday night. What's going on?"

"The usual. Nothing major. There are some Bulgarians or Romanians or something over on First Avenue making noise. Apparently, they consider Second Avenue contested territory and don't think the Kit Kat ought to be on their turf."

"Do they have a problem with the Kit Kat or with you?"

"Since when do eastern Europeans have a problem with naked women?"

"So it's you?"

"Of course it's me."

"What are you going to do?"

"What do you think?"

Cesari snickered, "You never could say no to a good fight, could you?"

Vito grinned from ear to ear. "I told them to bring it on, and just to rub it in their noses, I let the word slip out that I may be setting up permanent headquarters here."

"You sure you have enough men?"

"Oh yeah. In addition to what you saw. There are two more guys in the room next to this one with AR15s and another four guys downstairs armed to the teeth pretending to be guests. The bartenders all have access to semiautomatic shotguns and Uzis hidden behind the counter. And if that ain't enough, I've made sure all the girls spend time at a shooting range once a week in Westchester. There's a box filled with loaded pistols in their dressing room."

"This should be fun."

Chapter 6

Cesari showed up in the morgue promptly at 8:00 a.m. for the autopsy. He wore a long sleeve dress shirt under a sport coat not so much for the solemnity of the proceedings as to protect himself from hypothermia. Harry was there with two white-coated assistants, and a big guy wearing a dowdy, brown, three-piece tweed suit and red bowtie. He was well over six feet, lean and hard, clean shaven with closely cropped hair. He looked to be in his mid-to-late forties. He had dark, brooding eyes and when he moved slightly to appraise Cesari, he revealed the bulge of a shoulder holster and gold chain of a pocket watch. Cesari was fascinated by his appearance and instinctively glanced around for the man's bowler derby to complete the image. He spotted it on a nearby counter. It too was drab brown with a black band.

The body of the Serb lay on a metal table in the middle of the room and all sorts of equipment stood at the ready on a table next to Harry, who picked up a saw and gave it a test buzz. Cesari tried not to cringe at the unnerving whirring.

Harry put the saw down and said, "Good morning, Cesari. Glad you could make it. You already know my trusted assistants Randy and Sheila... And this is Officer Tierney of the NYPD. Officer Tierney, this is Dr. Cesari."

The big man stepped forward with hand outstretched. "That's Detective Tierney. Pleasure to meet you, Doctor."

"Mutual and it's just Cesari. No one calls me doctor to my face."

Detective Tierney allowed himself a half-smile at that and resumed his somber appearance. He was a serious guy.

There was a knock at the door, and everyone turned to see Arnie in the company of a much older gentleman albeit robust and in good health. He was just shy of six feet, overweight but solid, a circular patch of short gray hair covered his pate like a naturally occurring yarmulke. He carried himself well and the diamond encrusted walking stick he used seemed more of an affectation than a necessity. He was smartly dressed in a custom-tailored suit, crisp white shirt and blue tie. He might have been eighty or he might have been fifty. It was hard to tell. He was vigorous and exuded energy and self-confidence. The most striking thing about him, which immediately drew Cesari's attention, were his eyes.

Arnie said, "I hope you haven't started yet."

"No, but we were just about to," replied Harry.

"Good, because I have someone here who can positively identify the body. This is Mr. Markov. He's the owner of the restaurant next to the alley where the body was found and thinks this man was one of his wait staff."

Detective Tierney suddenly seemed very interested and took a step toward Arnie and the older man, introduced himself and whipped out a small pad and pen to take notes.

Arnie said, "May Mr. Markov examine the body, Harry?"

"Of course. Please step closer, Mr. Markov."

The old man stepped toward the head of the table and examined the face. It didn't take him long. He nodded and said in a thick eastern European accent, "Is him."

"Could you be more specific, Mr. Markov?" asked Detective Tierney.

"Is Andrej Petrović, one of waiters at my restaurant. There is no doubt."

Detective Tierney asked, "How long have you known him?"

"Is more than one year. He was good worker."

"Does he have family here in the U.S.?"

Markov shook his head, "No, he live by self in apartment over restaurant I rent to him. Send all money back to family in Serbia... How he die?"

Harry said, "We're not sure yet. The only signs of violence are these wounds on his neck."

With that he turned the Serb's head so Markov could get a good look at the neck. Everyone crowded forward including Detective Tierney.

Markov suppressed a gasp but Detective Tierney was unable to mask his surprise. He practically shouted, "What the hell is that?"

"We don't know. Did the deceased own a pet snake, Mr. Markov?" asked Harry.

"Snake? I don't think so. You believe that is snake bite?" Markov was starting to turn almost as white as the corpse.

Harry said, "We're not sure of anything right now. We'll need to proceed with the autopsy to know more, and we're still waiting for the results of toxicology, which could take a couple of days to see if he was poisoned. Besides the wounds to the neck the only thing that has come back as abnormal was his hemoglobin which was measured at 1.5, the lowest possible recording for our lab."

"What this mean?" asked Markov.

"It means he had almost no blood left in him at the time he was found."

Cesari thought he detected a slight shudder from the old man. Detective Tierney said, "Mr. Markov, after the autopsy I'd like to interview you more thoroughly as well as the other employees at your restaurant who knew him. It would also be greatly appreciated if you would give me access to his apartment."

"Of course. You want for me to wait here?"

"I would prefer that, if you don't have any pressing reason to leave."

Harry said, "The autopsy should only take an hour."

"I will stay."

Arnie said, "You can sit with me in my office, Mr. Markov. I'll have a pot of coffee sent up from the cafeteria."

Cesari raised his eyebrows in mild surprise. That was an awfully friendly gesture for Arnie to have made. Markov said, "Thank you, Arnie. You are too kind to old man."

Arnie?

Now Cesari was completely baffled. Did they know each other? Arnie said, "Dr. Cesari knows where my office is, Detective. He'll show you there when you're done. That okay with you, Cesari?"

Cesari replied, "I'd be happy to."

"Then we'll be on our way."

Cesari watched them as they left, and as soon as the door closed behind them, Harry pointed to a counter and said, "Detective Tierney and Cesari please don protective eyewear and masks. It's state regulations. You'll find what you need over there."

They fitted themselves as Harry picked up a scalpel and began dissecting the tissue around the neck wound. Detective Tierney and Cesari waited patiently as he dictated his findings into a microphone.

Within minutes he looked up and said, "The puncture wounds definitely pierced through the internal jugular vein and carotid artery. There's quite a bit of incidental soft tissue trauma in the surrounding area but that's to be expected."

Cesari said, "Could an animal such as a cat or a dog have done this Harry?"

"Unlikely. First of all, there would be another set of injuries from the lower teeth to match the upper wounds and there isn't. Secondly, I don't think I've ever heard of a dog or a cat sinking its teeth in so deep as to penetrate the internal jugular let alone the carotid artery of a human being. The truth is,

Cesari, even big cats such as lions and tigers don't go after the jugular or the carotid. That's a common misunderstanding."

"They don't?"

"No, they don't. They generally grab the throats of their prey in order to crush the larynx and suffocate them."

"Seriously?"

"Very much so."

"Okay, let's move on. I shouldn't have started there but I couldn't help myself."

Harry took a few photos of the neck wound and then began dissecting the abdomen while humming merrily to himself. Before long the intestines, spleen, kidneys and liver were being weighed, photographed and sliced open.

Harry said, "He must have drunk quite a bit of alcohol. His liver is enlarged and grossly fatty. There are a few nodules so he may have had an early stage of cirrhosis but there are no signs of bleeding into his GI tract. I'll know more about his liver when I look at it under a microscope. Other than that, there's no evidence of cancer or trauma and the peritoneal cavity isn't loaded with blood which would have been the only other place that large a volume could have gone. His last meal appears to have been some sort of cabbage preparation from the smell of it. His abdominal aorta has some signs of atherosclerosis, but his kidneys look good."

Detective Tierney glanced briefly at Cesari before asking Harry, "Doctor, is it possible that his blood count was naturally low to start with and that maybe he didn't bleed to death at all?"

"A hemoglobin of 1.5? Not a chance that could be his baseline. Some people do have naturally occurring anemias and or medical illnesses, but 1.5 is simply not compatible with life. A normal hemoglobin in an adult male is anywhere from thirteen to fifteen. A chronically ill patient on dialysis will typically run about nine or ten. 1.5 would be unheard of."

"I understand."

Harry waved an arm at them. "I would stand back boys. This is where it gets a little messy."

They took a few steps back to a healthy distance as Harry picked up the saw and cut through the sternum, spraying a fine mist of bone and tissue in the air. The odor was sickening. The screeching of the saw reminded Cesari of a dentist's drill. After he was done, Harry pried open the chest cavity with a cracking sound and then deftly removed the heart and lungs.

"He smoked too much. His lungs are a mess," Harry commented matter of factly. "There's evidence of obstructive pulmonary disease. I'm guessing two packs a day minimum for many years but grossly no evidence of cancer."

The rest of the autopsy was uneventful, and after it was over, they regrouped in Harry's office for a recap. Detective Tierney said, "I know you still have some histologic work and toxicology pending, Doctor, but what's your best guess?"

Harry strummed his fingers, relishing the moment. "Let's work our way backwards and start with what it's not. It's not death by heart attack, pulmonary embolus, pneumonia, cancer or spontaneous hemorrhage into his brain or peritoneal cavity. There is no evidence for strangulation, suffocation, gunshot wound, knife wound or head trauma. All we have are those two puncture wounds to the neck and no sign of where the blood might have gone. At the present time I must conclude that he bled to death from the wounds to his internal jugular and carotid artery. How it happened I can't say yet nor can I comment on why there was no blood found at the scene. One possibility that I mentioned to Cesari yesterday is that he may have bled somewhere else, was cleaned up, and then brought to the alley."

Detective Tierney wasn't happy. "I don't like cases like this."

"Why?" asked Cesari.

"They're too hard," was the honest reply. "And bizarre homicides like this are almost always some sicko playing with our heads which means there are usually more fun and games planned ahead for us."

"So it's definitely a homicide in your mind, Detective?" asked Harry.

"Unless you think he stuck himself in the neck with a fork, waited for all his blood to drain, then took a shower and walked himself down to the alley."

"Probably not," replied Harry soberly.

Cesari said, "This doesn't sound good."

Tierney replied, "It's not. Now how about taking me to the old man?"

"Let's go…Say, Detective, do you ever do ride alongs?"

"What alongs?"

"You know, let non-police people accompany you on investigations?"

"Are you some kind of freak, Cesari?"

Harry found this exchange amusing and burst out laughing but Cesari persisted, "Not at all. I find this case extremely intriguing, mostly because what I do every day is try to figure out where people are losing blood from. Usually it's from some part of their intestines."

"Let him tag along, Detective," Harry interceded on Cesari's behalf. "At the very least you're bound to find him singularly amusing."

"I don't find anyone or anything amusing, Doctor."

"Worst comes to worst, he can fetch you coffee."

Harry was on a roll and it worked. Tierney suddenly mellowed a bit. "I do like coffee."

Cesari smiled. "I'm a great fetcher."

"Fine, but piss me off even once and I'll drop you like a brick, understood?"

"Cream and sugar?"

Chapter 7

"It's a condition known as heterochromia iridis, Dr. Cesari. It's a benign hereditary condition. I'm told my parents had it as well as my grandparents and their parents. My daughter has it as well. I hope it doesn't disturb you."

Cesari shuffled his feet embarrassed, "No, of course not and I didn't mean to stare. Forgive me."

Markov's right eye was a brilliant green and his left an ordinary brown. It had caught Cesari's attention down in the lab, and when he entered Arnie's office, he couldn't help himself.

"Think nothing of it. I have been getting odd looks and worse because of it most of my life. I suppose I should consider myself lucky. In the Middle Ages, an anomaly like this might have gotten me burned at the stake."

After the exchange, the old man moved off to stare wistfully out the tenth-floor window down onto Third Avenue and was soon lost in thought as he gave his statement almost mechanically to Detective Tierney who was sitting nearby. Arnie sipped coffee as he took in the situation.

Markov answered all of Tierney's questions to the best of his ability but his mind was thousands of miles away. He had always been fascinated by the great size of this nation and its masses of diverse people. He was an eighty-year-old survivor of the merciless nazis, the rabid communists and the psychotic jihadists. His was a tale as bold and exotic as any story ever told, from Beowulf to Sinbad to Marco Polo. He had lived through much adversity during his life and there was little that caused him concern…until today.

He was barely a year old when the German horde swept across Europe rounding up the Jews from every town, city and walk of life. For two years he wore a yellow star as his parents toiled and sweated on their small farm. It was a small, quiet village in Romania hundreds of miles from the capital, Bucharest. The farmers had no television or radio nor any concept of what was coming their way. The Jews there were used to periodic pogroms, prejudice and injustice. The yellow star, they thought, was just another passing lunacy of the local bureaucracy.

Little did they know the seismic scope of the terror just on the horizon; pain and suffering on a hitherto unknown scale with smoke billowing day and night from crematorium chimneys turning millions of innocent human beings into so much ash. Even worse for these peasants was that the Romanians weren't just casual bystanders caught in the path of the German war machine and unable to resist its ferocity. Rather, they were fully indoctrinated, supportive and complicit with all of Hitler's worst policies in regard to the final solution. Tens of thousands volunteered to serve in the German army. Many happily betrayed their Jewish neighbors and sent them to their deaths. They were all in as the saying goes.

Thankfully, Markov was not present the day his parents were dragged from their bed and shot in the garden outside their home. Nor did he witness his house being burned to the ground, torched by the other villagers as the SS watched and laughed. He had been lucky that day. His mother had been forewarned of their coming by a friend in a neighboring village, a christian woman who had the foresight to understand the evil of what was happening and the courage to act. She took the young Markov and fled to raise him many miles away from the place of his birth. Their immediate bloodlust appeased, no one cared that he had escaped their murderous clutches. After the war, those who survived the Russian invasion had all escaped justice by becoming good communists.

Well that wasn't entirely true.

Markov grew up to be strong both physically and mentally. On his twentieth birthday his adoptive mother told him the truth of who he was and what had happened, and he had burned incandescent with rage. He returned to the village of his birth and one by one discovered the identities of those involved... and there were many. It wasn't hard. Most were still alive, and behind closed doors, still proud of their service to their führer. Blood flowed once again in that little farming community in the foothills of the Carpathian Mountains only this time no one escaped.

To spare his adoptive family any fallout from his actions should he be discovered, Markov moved to Bucharest to live in the shadows and for the first time, to live as a Jew among his own kind. What he found was that the communists treated his people only marginally better than the nazis and that anti-semitism in Romania was both alive and well. As a result, wave upon wave of Romanian Jews emigrated to Israel in the years after World War II until the brain drain and economic damage from the loss of some of Romania's brightest and most productive citizens forced the communists to rethink their policies on emigration and slam the door closed. Trapped on the wrong side of the iron curtain, Markov thrived in Romania's underworld; trading in the black market, muscle for hire, gun-running, drugs, women and all the while developing close ties with a clandestine network of ilk-minded individuals throughout Eastern Europe.

As time passed, he grew restless and eventually escaped Romania to Israel arriving just in time to be conscripted into the army and thrown inside a tank in the in the middle of the Sinai Peninsula during the Six Day War. To him it was just another pogrom, but at least now he was permitted to fight back. He enjoyed killing the enemies of his people so much that he kept on doing it long after the war ended. He convinced his tank crew that hospitals, schools, grocery stores, apartment buildings and any random person on the street were adequate substitutes for actual military targets. But all good things must come to an end and so it was with his time in the desert. His atrocities were eventually discovered leading to a summary court-martial of him and his men. To avoid an embarrassing public trial which could have damaged the country's already fragile international status, it was decided to disown them. Their identities in the Israeli military were scrubbed and they were transported to the United States with phony diplomatic papers where they resided in the embassy in New York as they applied for student visas.

Once released into the public, they were advised never to step foot on Israeli territory again or they would be shot on sight. Being a practical and resourceful man, Markov returned to his old ways, and using his contacts in Romania, soon thrived in his new home importing drugs and women and exporting contraband. As his illicit enterprises flourished, Markov's star ascended in the criminal underbelly of Manhattan and he soon became a leader of the growing Eastern European community on the east side of lower Manhattan. He made many men rich both in America and back in Romania. He also made many men dead, but over time he legitimized his interests by buying up properties and local businesses throughout Manhattan. He was hailed in the press as a product of the American dream.

He told Detective Tierney the white-washed version of his difficult life in Romania and of his brief time in Israel minus the sordid details. He explained how a series of lucky investments had sky-rocketed his fortunes and personal wealth and how grateful he was to live in such a country as this and how he tried to give back to the immigrant community by providing inexpensive housing and decent paying jobs to those in need.

The deceased in the morgue was a case in point. He had come to the restaurant with no skills, no education and no money. Out of the goodness of his heart, Markov had let him live rent free for a few months, trained him in the restaurant business and even sponsored his green card. Although he didn't know the man extremely well, he was personally saddened by his death.

Detective Tierney was moved by the man's rags to riches story. He said, "When was the last time you saw him alive, Mr. Markov?"

"Was two nights ago. He did not show up for work and was assumed to be not well? Restaurant manager make call but he no answer. Restaurant not that busy last couple of nights so no big deal."

Tierney had been jotting down notes as they spoke. "Was he any trouble for you or anyone else at the restaurant?"

Markov shrugged. "No, I don't think so. Andrej was quiet man. Keep to self."

"And you can't tell me anything more about him? Who his friends were? Did he have a girlfriend? Did he have any bad habits such as drugs or gambling? Did anyone want him dead?"

The old man shook his head. "I cannot say for sure what Andrej do in his spare time but as far as I know he was good boy. No trouble for Markov. I am sorry but is all I know. The restaurant manager will know him better. I will tell him you come. He will also show you apartment."

"Sure thing. What's his name?" asked Tierney.

"His name Yorgi. Restaurant open at noon for lunch. He will be there. Is sad day."

"Yes, it is. Does Yorgi have a last name and a phone number where I can reach him?"

"His full name is Yorgi Romanescu and he is always at restaurant, *Ukrainian Heaven*, number 75, First Avenue. Can't miss or get lost, but I always call restaurant to speak. As I say, he is always there."

"Well, I guess that will be all. Thank you for your time Mr. Markov. If I have any more questions, I will call you."

"Is no problem. Always happy to help police."

Cesari cleared his throat and said, "Mr. Markov, I'm confused about something?"

Markov looked at Cesari with a curious expression. "What is?"

"You said the deceased didn't show up at work for two days and didn't answer his cellphone and no one from the restaurant thought to go to his apartment to check on him?"

"Is not what I say. I say he no answer phone or call. Yorgi go to room but he is not there. Was thought maybe he stay with friend until better. Andrej was grown man. Maybe he no longer like job or apartment. We decide to give time. Is not unusual, Doctor, for immigrants to sometimes behave in ways not in accordance with our own practice. One gets used to it."

"I see. I'm just curious. You're Romanian, but you own a Ukrainian restaurant."

Markov gave him a big smile. "Is America, Doctor. Is melting pot of opportunity, no? I see opportunity and buy restaurant. Just for record, I own Chinese restaurant too."

"Fair enough," Cesari said and turned to Tierney. "Well, Detective, if the deceased possibly owned a dangerous snake, and it somehow got loose, we should probably not waste any time and go to his apartment immediately to assess the situation. Don't you think?"

"That's probably a good idea, Cesari. We could always talk to Yorgi afterward if he's too busy to accompany us right this minute."

"Is no problem, gentlemen. I call Yorgi now and tell him to meet you outside apartment. He has key. In addition to manage restaurant, he manages apartment building for me. Is most trusted employee."

While Markov turned to make his call, Arnie said, "You're going to the apartment building, Cesari?"

"Detective Tierney is graciously allowing me to accompany him. I'm rather curious about this case."

"What about your patients?"

"All taken care of. I called my office on the way over here and they're being rescheduled to tomorrow morning."

Arnie raised his eyebrows and said, "Tomorrow's Saturday, Cesari."

"What's your point?"

"I can't believe the secretarial staff agreed to it. There are union considerations. I don't need anybody filing grievances right now. We have enough problems."

"Let me worry about the staff. They love me."

"Please spare me," Arnie shook his head in frustration and glanced at Detective Tierney. "I hope you know what you're getting into, Detective."

"I think I can handle him, but thanks for the warning, Doctor."

Cesar said, "It's just one morning, Arnie, not even a full day and the staff volunteered. I promised to buy them breakfast. A little quid pro quo action and we'll talk more about grievances when I get back. I was paid a little visit by your boy Feinberg last night to renegotiate my contract and I'm not overly thrilled with his attitude."

Arnie was taken aback by that bit of news and said, "I didn't know that." He glanced at Markov who was still on the phone and then at Detective Tierney, who had turned his attention back to his notepad. He added, "Okay, we'll talk later."

"We sure will."

Detective Tierney glanced at his watch. "We should get going. The more I think about this snake thing, the more it makes me nervous."

Markov finished his call and turned back to everyone. "Yorgi will meet us at apartment. He would like me to be there. Police make Yorgi nervous. He scared that if something wrong in apartment, he get blame, so I come. "

Tierney smiled, "Thank you Mr. Markov. You've been very cooperative."

"Please, call me Shlomo."

Chapter 8

The apartment building was old, very old, built at the turn of the twentieth century and contained very few modern amenities. The lighting was dim, the paint peeling and the smell musty. There was a small elevator installed in the 1950's and the three men squeezed in. Shlomo pressed the button for the sixth floor and they rode in silence as the ancient pulley system creaked and groaned upward. The car shuddered to a stop as they arrived, and Shlomo pulled the metal gate open for them to exit. The carpet was faded and worn and Cesari tried to guess how many thousands, maybe millions of people had tramped across it before him. He wondered how many of those succeeded and prospered in this land of plenty and he wondered how many didn't and what might have happened to them.

Yorgi was waiting for them outside of apartment 6G and Cesari was taken aback. Yorgi was an inch taller than Tierney but about a foot wider in the shoulders. Wearing a tight black turtleneck and black dress pants, every muscle in his body swelled and rippled as he moved. His neck was particularly thick like a football player giving him a formidable appearance. Cesari shot Tierney a quick glance to see if he was equally impressed, but if he was, he didn't let on. Yorgi greeted Shlomo warmly with a hug and introduced himself to Detective Tierney and Cesari who he eyed with curiosity, not quite sure what his role here was.

He said, "I wait here for you. I no go inside."

"Is all right, Yorgi," said Shlomo reassuringly. "You are not under suspicion."

Detective Tierney said, "That's right. We're just looking for clues. Has anyone been in the apartment since you first realized Andrej was missing?"

"I cannot be sure if Andrej made copy of key for anyone, but I doubt it. Is against rules. I have not been inside is all I can be certain of."

Cesari said, "We were told you checked his apartment when he didn't show up for work."

"I knock on door is all. Healthy young man might be drunk or at whorehouse is what I thought at first."

Detective Tierney said, "How well did you know him?"

"From work is all. He good worker."

"You never socialized with him?"

"What is socialize?"

"Have dinner together, watch a football game or go to a bar for a drink?"

"No, never. I boss of Andrej. No good to socialize."

"Why not?" asked the detective.

Yorgi shot Tierney a glance as if he was mentally challenged. "Because what if I have to fire or evict? Cannot do if friend with Andrej, no?"

"Of course not," replied Tierney who clearly knew the answer but was just assessing the man's temperament. "Well, why don't we go in and look around? And everybody, watch out for snakes."

Yorgi produced the key from his pocket, unlocked the door, reached in and flipped on the overhead light. They entered in single file with Detective Tierney in the lead and Yorgi bringing up the rear.

The collective shock at what they witnessed brought an audible gasp as if from one set of lungs. Yorgi made the sign of the cross, Cesari's jaw dropped, Shlomo was speechless, and Tierney uttered, "Jesus Christ…"

The walls from floor to ceiling were plastered with pages torn out from a bible. Not an inch remained uncovered. They walked slowly through the small living room, their mouths agape staring in all directions at the spectacle. The kitchen and bedroom were in the same way adorned, but in the bedroom in addition to the unusual wallpaper were dozens of wooden crucifixes hanging on the walls and even more candles burnt down to varying degrees on the night tables, dresser and on the floor in front of the bed. All of the crucifixes had their bottom edges whittled into sharpened dagger like points.

Cesari whispered to Tierney, "I guess he was a religious man."

"You think?"

"Or he was worried about something."

"More likely, but what?"

Shlomo turned pale at the sight, whispered something to Yorgi, and then left the bedroom. Cesari asked, "Is he all right?"

"His stomach is upset. He went to sit down in living room."

Cesari then followed Tierney into the bathroom where they saw more of the same. The entire tub was filled with candles. Cesari looked at Tierney and said, "Is it safe to assume this isn't going to be one of those open and shut cases?"

Tierney grunted as his mind raced, trying to decipher the meaning of it all. Finally he reached into his pocket and came out with plastic gloves. As he put them on, he said to Cesari and Yorgi, "Nobody touch anything."

Cesari said, "I'll go check on Shlomo."

Yorgi added, "I come too."

In the living room, they found Shlomo sitting dejectedly on the small sofa staring at the walls. He was white as a sheet and sweating. Yorgi asked, "I get water for Shlomo?"

Shlomo thanked him and the big man went to the kitchen. Cesari asked, "Are you all right, Shlomo?"

He nodded, "I will be fine. I am tired, very tired is all."

Cesari glanced around. "This is unsettling for us all."

"Is very much unsettling. Are you a spiritual man, Dr. Cesari?"

"That's a difficult question. I was raised catholic but have never been a big fan of organized religion, any of them to be honest. But the answer to your question is yes. I can't help shake the feeling that we're not alone and that there is some greater design for all of this."

He nodded. "I was raised catholic too. At age of twenty I discovered that I had been adopted and was actually Jewish. The people who raised me were friends of my parents and did so to protect me from the nazis. From then I embraced my true religion with the hope of understanding who I really was. It has given me a unique perspective on the traditions of both faiths though I have never truly bought into any of the...how do you say...smoke and mirrors."

Cesari smiled. "I understand. I guess Andrej was really into it."

"Apparently so. It is intimidating to come across someone whose faith is so strong."

"It does make you wonder, doesn't it?"

Yorgi came back from the kitchen with a glass of water and handed it to Shlomo who immediately took a big gulp. "Is good. Thank you, Yorgi."

Detective Tierney came out of the bedroom with a stack of books some of which seemed quite old. He said, "Yorgi, did Andrej seem eccentric to you or have any odd habits?"

Yorgi thought about it. "No, not really. He come to work, do job and leave. At work, we talk sometime about usual things. He wanted to be plumber someday. Was good with such things back in Serbia. He like soccer. He smoke a lot. Too much I tell him."

Tierney handed Cesari, Shlomo and Yorgi some of the books. He held onto three. The books he gave them were of various sizes and pedigree. Three of the books were travel guides for Romania. A fourth book was devoted solely to Transylvanian folklore.

Tierney said, "Was he planning on a trip?"

Yorgi and Shlomo glanced at each other and shook their heads. Yorgi said, "Not that I know of."

"Nor I," added Shlomo.

Tierney handed them one of the books he was still holding, and they passed it around amongst themselves. It was a copy of Bram Stoker's *Dracula*. The most famous horror story ever written. It singlehandedly put Transylvania on the map, but it was a complete fabrication of the author's imagination. Everyone knew that.

Cesari allowed himself a smile, "You've got to be kidding. Please tell me you're not going there, Detective?"

"Do I look like the comedic type, Cesari?"

"Not particularly."

"Good, now look at this," he said and passed them the last two books in his hands. They were underground manuals. One was a fifty-page instruction guide on how to kill a vampire and the other on how to survive an attack by one.

Cesari looked at them and said, "Too bad. I was hoping you'd find a snake."

"So was I," Tierney said flatly.

Yorgi seemed confused. Markov really looked as if he was going to be ill. Tierney said, "I've called the forensics people to take pictures and collect evidence. This is officially a crime scene now so please don't touch anything more and don't let anybody into the apartment until further notice."

"What means all this, Detective?" asked Shlomo.

"I'm not sure but Andrej was obviously into something bizarre, perhaps the occult, which means that all bets are off as to what happened."

Cesari said, "But vampires? Seriously? Please tell me we're not having this conversation."

"Look, Cesari, just because you don't believe in vampires doesn't mean the victim didn't. Look around you. He was scared of something and somebody may have used that fear against him. His death may have been a ritual killing. It's hard to say." He turned to Shlomo. "I'll need a list of his known acquaintances including all the employees he worked with at the restaurant. I haven't found any ID yet such as a driver's license, so I'll need to see any employee information you have on him."

"Of course," Shlomo said. "Yorgi will help you with all these things."

Yorgi nodded in agreement.

Tierney added, "I just want to search the kitchen and we'll be done. Yorgi, you and Mr. Markov can leave. I'll meet you both downstairs in the restaurant to collect that information I need and begin interviewing the employees. Does that sound like a plan?"

Shlomo said, "We will meet you there, Detective. Come, Yorgi, help an old man up."

Yorgi assisted him to his feet and they left the apartment. Cesari followed Tierney into the kitchen which was small by any standards. A three-foot-long trestle table was pressed against a wall with two wood chairs.

Detective Tierney looked around at the cramped living conditions and said, "Be thankful for what you have, Cesari."

"I am. Believe me."

Tierney walked over to the refrigerator and opened the door. From bottom to top, row upon row of garlic bulbs were wedged tightly inside, hundreds maybe thousands of them. As Tierney stared at the scene, one of the bulbs came loose and tumbled down to the floor in front of him.

He glanced at Cesari and said, "Having fun yet?"

Chapter 9

At 5:30 p.m. the crowd was beginning to fidget. The new CEO was half an hour late for his scheduled introductory meeting and the growing impatience of the room was palpable. There were more than a hundred physicians sitting or milling about in the large conference room in the basement of the hospital, all of whom had mountains of paperwork to do and unfinished patient care responsibilities. The chairs had been arranged in rows of ten separated by an aisle down the center and facing a podium with a gigantic flat screen TV behind it which splashed screensavers of hospital services and smiling staff members merrily at work in the happy halls of St. Matt's. In the back of the room was a ten-foot-long table upon which was set a coffee urn, paper cups, sugar and creamer. Several trays of cookies had already been savaged by the attendees including Cesari, who sat in the first row next to Arnie. In his lap, he cradled a cup of black coffee.

Arnie said for the third time, "I can't believe you're not going to tell me what you found at the guy's apartment."

"I told you Arnie, Detective Tierney warned me against discussing it with anyone. He doesn't want anything leaking to the press that might affect his investigation. If I betray his trust, he'll cut me off from any further involvement."

"Fine, but I don't keep secrets from you."

"Oh really?"

"What's that supposed to mean?"

"Let's start with that guy Markov. Since when does the medical director of a hospital personally entertain persons of interest in a homicide in his office waiting for the police to interview them and how is it that you and him are on a first name basis?"

Arnie seemed puzzled. "What are you talking about?"

"Markov, the guy with the eyes. Remember him? This morning you personally escorted him to the morgue and then back to your office. He addressed you as Arnie both in the morgue and then again in your office. What was that about?"

"Oh that. I should have told you, but we were kind of distracted at the time. Mr. Markov was the representative of the business consortium that donated the big bucks to the hospital. I've met him several times before and even had lunch with him and other board members on several occasions. You were on sabbatical writing your book during that whole wining and dining period."

"Seriously?"

"Oh yeah, he and his friends are rolling in it."

"Interesting…"

"So the guy who's holding us up here is his boy?"

"I really don't know what their relationship is other than we were told to either hire him and his crew or no deal."

"Well so far, I'm not impressed. Nor am I with Feinberg and I still have to tell you what happened."

The door in the back of the room swung open loudly, slamming into the wall as if it were the stopper. In walked Feinberg, scowling and somber, followed by a much smaller middle-aged man in an ill-fitting suit. He wasn't just small; he was diminutive in stature, barely reaching five feet in dress shoes with a full head of jet-black hair and a thick mustache. He didn't say anything and proceeded directly to the podium. Feinberg grabbed a chair and sat facing the room like a sergeant at arms as the CEO tested the mike for feedback. The little guy sized up his audience in a clockwise fashion, adjusted his horn-rimmed glasses and just stood there. The alpha dog had arrived, and he was letting it sink in.

Eventually in a high-pitched, squeaky voice he said, "My name is Tiberius Flavius Acevedo and I am your new CEO."

He waited for a full thirty seconds before continuing, "I was brought into this organization to shake things up and that's exactly what I intend to do. The financial sheets of this hospital are in a shambles and that's why your last CEO is somewhere on a street corner in this city selling pencils from a cup. As far as I am concerned, each and every one of you is dead wood until proven otherwise. Those of you who have not already received new contracts will do so within the next few days. From now on, you will be judged by your work productivity and I don't want to hear any sad stories about how hard life is and how many kids you have enrolled in school. From this minute forward, you eat what you kill. I hope I am making myself crystal clear. There will be no more freeloading in this hospital. I have been given cart-blanche to hire and to fire as I see fit and I will exercise that authority liberally. I will be meeting with each and every one of you in the coming weeks to discuss your shortcomings and ways that I see you can improve your performance. So get your affairs in order and spread the word to those who didn't make it here tonight that there's a new sheriff in town. Are there any questions?"

The silence in the room was deafening. People were astonished to the point that even those with cookies in their mouths had stopped chewing. For two months, they had put up with Feinberg's reign of terror but now they were shocked to find out he was just the carrot and not the stick.

Cesari had noticed in his travels, that CEOs of hospitals came in two flavors, either super-sized or miniature and always with great hair. He preferred the large ones. They tended to be more fun. The little guys usually had Napoleon complexes. He didn't think he was going out on a limb thinking this guy fell into the latter category.

"Well, as long as no one has any questions, let me start the presentation."

A slideshow began on the screen behind him outlining the history and evolution of healthcare in general. Then specifically the timeline of St. Matt's until present day. It's past successes and current failures and at the end there was a graph plotting the trajectory of where it was headed based on his vision. He droned on for more than an hour and just when Cesari thought he couldn't take another minute, he finished.

"I call this the three-year plan," he said with confidence. "Three years to turn this ship around. We will all pull together, see more patients, order more tests, cut the waste and drink from the wine of our prosperity. New equipment for the radiology department, the OR and the emergency room has already been purchased and is on its way. New CT scanners, MRIs, gamma cameras, SPECT scanners, ultrasound, mammography and x-ray machines will be installed within weeks not months. Construction for a new interventional radiology suite and cardiac catheterization lab will begin immediately. That's just the start. Renovations begin this weekend throughout the hospital and will continue around the clock until I am satisfied that we have emerged from the Stone Age. We must expand services in order to compete on a more even footing with the other hospitals. I expect everyone to fully cooperate. There will be no Debbie-Downers in this institution. One big, happy family. Am I clear? By the time I am done, St. Matt's will be the premier health system in all of Manhattan."

In utter silence, he left the room with Feinberg close behind. It was a solid two minutes after they left before anyone spoke or moved. Then, there was the scrape of a chair, a whisper here and a whisper there, and people slowly filed out in deep contemplation.

Finally, Cesari said, "Well that was interesting."

"It certainly was," Arnie replied.

"After that little speech, I doubt there's any point in telling you what happened with Feinberg in my apartment last night?"

"At this point, there's little that would shock me. We live in trying times, Cesari."

"I guess there's not much we can do other than to press forward and hope for the best."

"You have choices, Cesari. You can leave and start over somewhere. I'm too old. There's nowhere for me to go. This is the end of the line for me. My wife and I are this close to retirement."

He pinched the edge of his thumb and index finger together as a demonstration of how close he was to the end of his career. Cesari was surprised at his pessimism.

He said, "You sure have changed your tune since our last conversation, Arnie. What happened to all that, *give the new guy a chance*, stuff?"

"I did give him a chance, and he just blew it right in front of my eyes. There was also this. It came by registered mail an hour after you left my office this morning."

He reached into his sport coat's inside pocket and handed Cesari a folded piece of paper to read. It was from the new CEO. Cesari perused the page's one paragraph and handed it back to him.

"That was pretty cold, Arnie. You're being demoted?"

"He says everybody's going to see patients and lots of them. Nobody's going to be allowed to drag ass including me. The kicker is I have to give up my office to that piece of human waste, Feinberg. I have until Monday to clear my stuff out. Nice way to treat a guy after thirty-five years."

"I'm sorry. I can't imagine St. Matt's without you as the medical director. You're the heart and soul of this place."

"Well, you better start imagining it. Starting next week, I'm just one of the grunts seeing patients in the medical office building. I haven't examined a patient in ten years. Can you believe this?"

"It didn't say anything about your pay."

"A ten percent reduction. The budget office was notified a week ago. I checked right after I received the letter. It's unfathomable. Some guy with a high school diploma in the payroll office found out I was being demoted a week before I did."

"That's better than I made out."

He raised his eyebrows. "Really?"

"Twenty five percent cut."

"Jesus… No wonder you're pissed."

"At least they didn't tell me I'm not pulling my weight."

"That's something of a compliment, isn't it?"

"I guess… Are you going to do it? It's been a long time since you rolled up your sleeves and sweated through a long day in the office dealing with patients, their families, their insurance companies, and the bureaucratic red tape that comes in triplicate with each patient encounter."

"Thanks for the inspiring words but I have to. I'm not quite ready to retire, Cesari, either financially or mentally. And there's no way I'm going out without a fight. I intend on sticking around long enough to see these guys choke on their own piss."

"Good for you, Arnie. Welcome aboard the Titanic."

Chapter 10

The Romanescu brothers convened in the rat-infested basement of the same tenement building again to discuss that day's events. They raised their dirty vodka glasses and toasted their success. Yorgi was particularly pleased.

Gleefully, he told the story, "Worked like a charm, brothers. You should have seen Shlomo. White as ghost. I almost have to carry him down to restaurant."

Ivan slapped his glass down and refilled it with Stolichnaya. "Is good day for sure, brother. I never doubt you again. Is hard to believe man as hard as nails like Shlomo so easy to frighten."

"Every man has his weaknesses, Ivan. Remember that. Shlomo grew up in tiny village, no electricity, no telephones, no schools. All they do is work all day in fields and tell scary stories to each other at night. Is easy to become brain-washed even after you leave and should know better. The myths, the legends, the nightmares get under your skin."

"Good for us."

Yorgi turned to his youngest brother and asked, "And how goes it with you, Tibor? You are very quiet. Wedding in two months. You must be very excited. I know it will be beautiful day. Eastern orthodox priest and rabbi together performing ceremony. Good fortune will shine on you and bride for sure."

Tibor wasn't quite as elated as his brothers, his mood being tempered by other matters. "Forgive me for not being overly enthusiastic, Yorgi. I share your happiness in our success of course but cling to hope that Shlomo will fall before big day."

Ivan said, "Never mind him, Yorgi. He is just upset. Drusilla has been after him for demonstration of his love… before wedding night."

Yorgi raised his eyebrows. "You mean…?"

Tibor nodded glumly. "Is hard to fight off. She is very persistent. I tell her is tradition in my family to remain virgin until after union of man and woman has been blessed by God. Would be bad luck to…"

He didn't have a chance to finish. His brothers broke out in howls of laughter. When they finished, Yorgi who was still chuckling said, "Brother mine, most men would give anything to have such problems."

"Is because most men have not seen Drusilla."

"Perhaps, Tibor, but I have been thinking through this situation from different perspective and have come to slightly different conclusion than before."

"And what is this different conclusion?"

Yorgi poured himself some more vodka and placed the bottle down on the table. He said slowly and deliberately, "News of your wedding to Drusilla has been well-received amongst the other members of the council in Bucharest. They approve. Very much so, in fact. They see it as a sign all goes well with their investments here in America. That Shlomo manages their money and interests well."

"Until we prove otherwise, that is," argued Tibor.

Ivan added, "Where are you going with this, Yorgi?"

"Initially, I think it would be okay for Tibor to abandon Drusilla or perhaps even worse after Shlomo gone but now I realize it would be bad idea. The council are old-fashioned men. They know Shlomo long time from days behind iron curtain after world war. There is unbreakable bond. Sentimental fools they are."

Tibor was growing increasingly anxious, "And what means this to you, Yorgi? Please tell."

"It means that if something were to happen too soon to Drusilla after Shlomo gone, or if you abandon her before wedding, they might not support us. May suspect we planned everything or that perhaps your intentions were insincere."

"You mean I have to marry her no matter what? Even if Shlomo were to fall tomorrow?" asked Tibor, alarmed.

"And stay married to her, brother," Yorgi stated definitively. "But not necessarily forever, Tibor. Maybe just few years until everything settles down and council learns to depend on us. Then maybe you go on vacation somewhere with Drusilla and babies and she no return; get eaten by sharks or something."

"A few years...? Impossible for me to... I cannot, I just cannot..."

"Relax Tibor. You can do for sure. There is no law that says you can't have girlfriend on the side to lift your spirits. Is how olden day kings do."

Yes, Tibor," Ivan snickered. "You will be like olden day king. I am already envious."

"Shut up, Ivan."

Yorgi said, "Stop bickering you two. We still have long way to go. The seed has been planted. There can be no doubt that Shlomo was shaken by what happened to Andrej. Old man very superstitious. We did great job in apartment. Even policeman and doctor's eyes go wide."

"Who was doctor, Yorgi?" asked Ivan.

"I am not sure. His name was Cesari. He seemed to be friend of Detective, maybe working with him as consultant. He was very skeptical even more so than Detective. Not enough to calm Shlomo down but he seem very smart. Maybe too smart. I want you and Tibor to investigate. Find out who he is. Shlomo say he work at St. Matt's. Start there. You have Andrej's clothes and wallet?"

"Yes, and cellphone. They are in large plastic garbage bags. Blood all over them. We were very sloppy."

"Don't worry, Ivan. We will get better. Practice makes perfect. Next time we undress victim before we bleed him. What is plan for clothes?"

"As we discussed, I bring to furnace tonight when no one around."

"No, hold onto them. I change mind. His belongings might be useful. Keep in safe place for now while I think it over."

Ivan and Tibor glanced at each other, somewhat confused but nodded. Yorgi was older and wiser. Ivan asked, "How do we proceed from here, Yorgi?"

"Is good question. Next week, first shipment arrive at hospital from Romania. Shlomo excited but nervous to see if his plan work. He is on edge about Andrej but this will soon pass. We need to get to boxes before anyone else. Is important to keep pressure on Shlomo until he break. So most important thing is to find where boxes arrive and when. That we do this weekend. There will be many construction workers around and much distraction. No one will notice."

Yorgi poured another round of vodka. The three men raised their glasses high and saluted themselves with a loud chorus.

"Noroc!"

"I don't mean to change subject, Yorgi. But what about the Italians on Second Avenue?" Ivan asked. "They show no signs of leaving the Kit Kat Klub. In fact, just the opposite. There is word on street that their boss is spending even more time there."

"The big one, Vito?"

"Yes, Yorgi. Rumor is that he welcomes a war with us... or anybody. He is said to have a belligerent and unyielding personality."

Yorgi nodded in thought. "Is delicate problem for sure. We are not quite ready to start fight with them but couldn't hurt to send even stronger message than last time."

"What you have in mind, brother?" questioned Ivan. "Last time, we put one of them in hospital and then they put one of ours in same hospital."

"Yes, it was just a test of their resolve. I wanted them to know we are here and now they know. I think this time we try something new and yet not that new. We have a girl inside the club, do we not?"

"Yes, Yorgi. Is Sofia. She is dancer. She sleeps with bartender there."

"Does she love him?"

Ivan shrugged. "I don't know."

"Better question is will she miss him?"

Chapter 11

Saturday morning office hours were generally unsatisfying, a necessary evil at best. No one was into it; not the secretaries, not the nurses, not the patients and most of all not Cesari. It was ingrained in our society that Saturday was a day of leisure, especially Saturday morning. As a kid, you got to sleep in, hang out in your pajamas, and watch cartoons while you got a buzz eating some sugary cereal. As an adult you did the same thing only it was the news and black coffee. If you were real ambitious you went to the gym or hit the links for a round of golf with friends. Cesari hadn't been real ambitious in several years. At his age, he figured he was in pretty decent shape, a nice balance between muscular perfection and a nightly and almost overwhelming desire to eat spaghetti alla Bolognese with a nice red wine. He didn't watch TV but he did like black coffee, especially French roast and especially when it was made with a French press.

Today was a day of compromise. In between patients, he sipped black coffee made from a French press he kept in his office using water heated in a microwave and nibbled on one of the two dozen cannolis he bought on his way to work. He hadn't forgotten his promise to feed the staff who appreciated the gesture and would take any leftovers home. The cannolis themselves were a work of art from Giancarlo's Bakery on Mulberry Street. Everything was made from scratch including the shells fried fresh that morning and stuffed with home-made ricotta, chocolate chips and candied fruit. He savored the moment and was in no particular rush because it was his experience that the last patient on a Saturday always showed up late, if at all, and today was no exception.

He stepped into the hallway, glanced at his watch and called out to his nurse, "Hey, Mona, where's my eleven-thirty appointment?"

She looked up from her computer screen, took the cannoli out of her mouth and said in a faux Italian accent, "What's a matter for you?"

Cesari always laughed when she did that. "Is she here or not?"

"She just called. She's running late and got caught in traffic. She'll be here in about fifteen minutes."

"Great."

"She's a new patient by the way and has quite the accent. Just letting you know in case you want to brush up on your Russian before she gets here."

"Even better."

"Thanks for breakfast by the way but my butt really didn't need another cannoli."

"Your butt is perfect, Mona. In fact, I'm going to bring more pastries in on Monday."

"You better be careful who you flirt with, Cesari. I'm a married woman." She laughed and turned back to her laptop.

Cesari went back into his office to complete the morning's medical records on his laptop, punch in billing codes and electronically sign all the digital paperwork created in the process. When he was done, he swung his legs up on his desk, played with his tie for a minute and then with his phone. He saw a missed call from Detective Tierney and hit the redial button.

"Cesari, meet me at Muldoons on Ninth Street at twelve sharp for lunch. I want to pick your brain. Do you know the place?"

"I know Muldoons. Can we make it one o'clock? I'm waiting for a patient. Anything you'd care to talk about on the phone?"

"See you at one."

Detective Tierney was one of those guys who didn't like to use extra words, but that was okay. After he hung up, he speculated about the murder while he passed the time. At five minutes after twelve, Mona poked her head in the doorway.

"She's in room 1 waiting for you... Head's up, Doc, you got a live one in there. She's the short one. You can't miss her and try not to act surprised. All her paperwork's on the door. There's not a whole lot and she brought a friend with her."

"Thanks for not being dramatic, Mona."

He walked over to the exam room with a yellow legal pad for note taking and his stethoscope wrapped around his neck. He picked up the thin stack of papers outside the door resting in a plastic holder and flipped through a few of the ones on top with the patient's demographics. She was twenty-nine, Romanian, unemployed, single, no children...and then he gently knocked.

He entered and saw two women sitting in leather consultation chairs. They couldn't have been more different. One was tall, brunette, and strikingly beautiful, wearing an elegant dress, stylish shoes and oddly, dark over-sized sunglasses. Her full lips were pouty and seductive. They taunted him to the point of distraction. The other wore baggy blue jeans, a flannel shirt, and a thin, nearly transparent veil across her face that did little to hide how hideously, even appallingly unattractive she was. Cesari did his best not to cringe. It seemed to go against the laws of nature that anyone could be so unpleasing to the eye. He had trouble looking at her and couldn't even imagine the sight unveiled. Short and fat, she had one thick furry eyebrow spanning her forehead and one of the worst cases of facial acne he had ever seen in an adult. In his heart of hearts he prayed that she would refuse to remove the veil on religious grounds.

He glanced at her chart, cleared his throat and said, "Hello, my name is Dr. Cesari. And you must be?"

The short one said in a deep, masculine voice, "I am Drusilla."

Her Romanian accent was very pronounced. Cesari tried to smile but realized he was actually grimacing as he held out his hand toward her. "The pleasure is all mine, Drusilla. My nurse must have forgotten to enter your last name in the record."

"I no give last name. I hope is not against the law?"

Cesari hesitated and then said, "No, I guess not. Is there a reason why?"

"Of course there is," she replied but didn't explain.

Cesari stared at her for a few seconds before realizing that was all he was going to get. He said, "That's all right but we won't be able to schedule any tests or examinations without your full name. The same for billing your insurance."

"I pay cash, no insurance, for visit. If I need any further testing, we will discuss options."

Cesari nodded apprehensively. He wasn't thrilled with the way she had taken control of the process. It wasn't a good harbinger of what was to come, but rather than argue, his curiosity got the best of him.

He turned to the pretty one. "And you are?"

"I am friend."

"Is that your name?"

"Is all you need to know."

These two were being unnecessarily difficult but he supposed they had their reasons. Tough opening for a Saturday morning consult but he determined that he would just have to let them proceed at their own pace. They would warm up eventually.

"Okay, let's get started," he said and sat down at a small desk. "So what can I do for you today, Drusilla?"

She turned slightly toward her friend who answered for her, "Stomach hurt…all the time."

Cesari tried to hold back his annoyance and said, "It would be best if she answered for herself."

Drusilla shook her head vigorously. "She speak better than me. Please to listen."

"All right, could you be more specific? Where does it hurt? Point with your hand and could you describe the pain a little better. Is it a burning, stabbing, or cramping pain? Does it come and go? Does anything make it better or worse such as eating or position? Has there been any vomiting, fever or jaundice?"

The friend went on to describe the pain in nonspecific terms noting some association with nausea. She offered no other symptoms and was otherwise well, without significant impairment other than worrying about her pain. Cesari asked several more pertinent questions concerning her past medical and surgical histories. When he finished his review of systems, he looked up at the wall clock. The consult lasted thirty minutes and was abbreviated because she declined to allow a physical examination.

"Without an examination or further testing," he explained, "…it will be difficult to determine exactly what is wrong with any degree of accuracy, Drusilla, but we could try a few simple things. Go to any supermarket or pharmacy and pick up an over the counter antacid and take it as prescribed for a few days. I'll write the name down for you. Try to avoid eating greasy, fried or spicy foods as well. Keep an eye on the types of foods that exacerbate the pain and don't eat late at night like right before bed. You really should have an ultrasound to make sure you don't have gallstones and some bloodwork but if you get better, we'll call it a day. If the symptoms persist, I'll need to know. We might want to reconsider further testing and possibly even an endoscopy to see if you have an ulcer. I'll give you my cellphone number. Please call me if you have any further problems."

Drusilla said, "Thank you, Doctor."

"There is one more thing. Any woman your age presenting with abdominal pain really should have a pregnancy test."

"Pregnancy test?" she asked.

"Yes, it's kind of routine. It would be a terrible thing to miss. You can pick up a home test at any pharmacy. They're simple and easy to use. If it comes back positive, give me a call and I'll arrange for you to see an obstetrician. That's about all I can do without your last name and billing information."

"Is good enough for now. I will do as you say."

"Good, I'd like to make a return appointment for two weeks so I can re-evaluate you. In the meanwhile, you have my number."

"Thank you again, Doctor."

"Yes, thank you, Doctor," added the pretty one.

He walked them out to the front desk and had Mona make their return appointment. After they left, Mona and the secretaries started laughing.

Mona said, "Didn't I tell you?"

Cesari grinned. "That was interesting to say the least."

"What a bunch of whack-a-doodles."

"Okay, let's tone it down a little. They're my patients, at least one of them is."

"Do you think they'll come back?"

"I have mixed feelings about that."

"The friend could have been a model," Mona added with a knowing wink.

Cesari said, "Really? I hadn't noticed."

"Yeah, right...," she said sarcastically. "You noticed my fat ass, but you didn't notice her?"

The secretaries giggled loudly at that. He said, "I'm all business when I'm on the clock, Mona. You know that."

Glancing at his watch, he thought about Detective Tierney. He was running behind and said, "I have to make a call."

He returned to his office and dialed Tierney as he powered down his laptop and hung his lab coat on a hook behind the door.

Tierney was very annoyed. Clearly, he was one of those habitually punctual types. He said, "Cesari, you're five minutes late."

"I know. I got stuck with an extremely ill patient, struggling for his survival on life support. It was tragic. He had five kids all crying and everything."

"Cut the bull. When I say meet me at thirteen hundred, I mean thirteen-hundred sharp, not thirteen-o-five. I have a murder to solve. Now if you want to run with the big dogs, you better have your shit wired tight. Are we speaking the same language, Cesari?" Tierney growled.

"I'm on the way, boss. I promise to be a better protégé moving forward."

"Hurry up. I'm hungry."

Chapter 12

Muldoons was dark and dank, the smell of beer-permeated floorboards almost overwhelming to the senses. It was a classic Irish cop bar on Ninth Street with lots of wood, ceiling fans, and guys in blue standing around, some of whom casually glanced in his direction. Cesari found Detective Tierney in a booth chomping on a greasy cheeseburger from a plate mounded high with fries. A half-empty mug of beer was next to him. Across the table was another plate with the same food and drink order waiting for his arrival.

Cesari sat down. "Sorry I'm late, Detective. Say, do you have a first name?"

"Yeah."

Cesari waited but no further information was forthcoming, so he started eating. The burger had cooled off, the beer was stale and the fries soggy. He asked, "Do you eat here often?" But the way he phrased the question it sounded more like he was asking why.

Ignoring his query, Tierney swallowed and said, "I'm having trouble understanding how all the blood escaped the victim."

"You don't think the two large holes in his neck are enough to explain it?"

"Maybe."

"And your reluctance to accept that as an explanation stems from...?"

"Experience, Cesari. I've seen bigger bullet holes and knife wounds that managed to clot off successfully on their own and prevent the guy from bleeding out like that even when arteries were directly hit. I'm not saying he should have survived but it's the nearly complete loss of blood I find troubling."

Cesari thought about that. "I guess it's possible the artery could have clotted off preserving some of his blood volume, but I have no experience with wounds like that. A vascular surgeon would probably know more about that than I would, but I suppose it would depend."

"Depend on what?"

"On whether the victim was anticoagulated or not and whether he was impaired at the time of injury and couldn't compress the wound adequately."

"Expand on that for me."

"Well some people have medical conditions that we treat with anticoagulants to deliberately interfere with their ability to form clots."

"Name a few."

"Atrial fibrillation is probably the most common condition. The heart's natural rhythm is disturbed and without normal contractions, there is a tendency to form clots which can dislodge and embolize to vital organs such as the brain and kidneys, frequently with catastrophic consequences. We use anticoagulants such as warfarin to help prevent the formation of those clots. There are numerous other situations where it is similarly necessary to do so. If the victim was on an anticoagulant, he would have bled much more than would have been expected had he not been on one."

Tierney nodded. "The deceased didn't have any medical history requiring anticoagulants?"

"No medical conditions at all that we know of, but he did have one finding on autopsy that possibly could have contributed to a condition of auto-anticoagulation."

"Auto-anticoagulation?"

"Yes, a condition where the body has impaired synthesis of coagulation factors. To properly form a clot several proteins have to work synergistically with other components of the blood stream. When a blood vessel is injured, platelets aggregate at the site as a first step to prevent bleeding. This is called a platelet plug. This is followed by a sturdier and more resilient fibrin clot organized by a series of interacting proteins called clotting factors produced in the liver. If the liver is not functioning well for any reason, then an individual might have impaired clotting ability which theoretically could lead to excessive bleeding from even a small wound."

Tierney finished his beer. "And what was the condition of his liver at the autopsy? I was there. I don't remember anything remarkable."

"It wasn't much but Harry mentioned his liver being fatty and possibly cirrhotic. He may have been a boozer. Cirrhosis is an advanced form of liver disease and can definitely impair production of clotting factors."

He nodded. "I remember now. He said he was going to know more after he checked the liver under a microscope. Okay, we're on to something here. So, it's possible he bled excessively due to problems with clotting from underlying liver disease or possibly a medication he was on that we didn't know about."

"It's possible."

"Will Harry be testing him to see if he was on an anticoagulant like warfarin?

"There are several problems with blood tests in that regard. First of all, there's no specific blood test for warfarin and second of all, there are more than one drug out there that can cause bleeding through other mechanisms. However warfarin is one of the most common ones. It works by blocking the formation of vitamin K dependent clotting factors. There's a test called the prothrombin time that is used to measure the effectiveness of warfarin. If it is abnormally prolonged, we could infer that he had a problem with vitamin K related clotting factors, but it wouldn't tell us the exact cause. The other problem is that I don't know how reliable that test is many hours after death and when there is almost no residual blood volume left in the body."

"Still, it's a possibility?"

"Certainly a reasonable theory based on the facts, but I can tell you this; I've never met or heard of a cirrhotic who injured himself and bled to death from the injury. They almost always eventually do clot off save one exception."

"And what's that?"

"Esophageal varices. Those are swollen veins within the esophagus that become greatly dilated from changes in internal pressure brought on from the cirrhosis. When those veins rupture, massive internal bleeding can occur and lead to death."

"Did he have varices? I don't remember the Harry saying anything about that."

"He didn't have varices, nor did he have splenomegaly which is usually associated with end stage liver disease and bleeding of that nature. So, if he had cirrhosis, it would most likely have been in an early stage. But that's not to say he couldn't have had enough impairment of liver function to affect his clotting ability."

"Well you are a fountain of information, Cesari. I'm glad I brought you along."

"I'm not done either. When somebody develops a bleeding injury, Detective, what's the most natural and instinctive thing to do?"

He shrugged, "Compress the wound?"

"Exactly, and compress it hard, almost frantically would be my guess. Wouldn't you agree? Especially a neck wound where your blood is spilling all over the place. Almost anyone would be in a panic and more than likely to overdo it causing some degree of local injury. Yet there was no soft tissue damage to suggest that anyone compressed the wound at all let alone with any significant pressure."

"But I thought Harry said there was soft tissue damage?"

"Yes, a slight amount stemming from the puncture wounds themselves but not in the surrounding tissue where you would have expected it from external compression. The soft tissue damage from desperate hand compression would have been quite significant and encompassed a much greater area than what Harry found."

"What's that mean?"

"That the victim was unable to compress the wound so maybe he was impaired as in unconscious or perhaps drugged or even restrained."

"I guess that pretty much excludes some sort of accidental hemorrhage, but we already knew that unless we believe he fell onto a pitchfork while running around naked on First Avenue."

"Yes, but we're getting closer to understanding the actual mechanism of the crime."

"Except for the most important part like what caused the puncture wounds and where did all this take place?"

"One step at a time. I'll go find Harry and see if he's had a chance to look at the guy's liver yet just so we can close that door." Cesari glanced at his watch. "He might even be in the lab now. It's Saturday and he usually has banker's hours, but he was pretty pumped up about this case. I'll also ask him if there were any signs of incidental trauma anywhere else which is very common in people on anticoagulants. They bleed and bruise all the time and usually don't even know it."

"Good. Get back to me on that. In the meanwhile, I'm going back to the restaurant to finish interviewing the employees. They weren't all there yesterday."

Cesari finished his burger and wiped his face with a napkin. "Did any of them tell you anything helpful?"

"No, not really. Most of them barely spoke English as a second language and they were all scared out of their minds. I doubt if half of them are here legally. But I did get the impression that our victim wasn't much of a social butterfly. Certainly wasn't romantically involved with anybody he worked with. The good news is that no one seemed to have anything bad to say about the guy."

"Well good for him, I guess."

"I suppose. Well, here's some food for thought. Why was our dead friend so worried about vampires and why did whoever it was who killed him try so hard to make it look like he was done in by one?"

"I haven't a clue."

"Start doing some research on the subject and I will too. Are there any local vampire clubs, societies, and the like and did our victim belong to any of them?"

"Vampire clubs?"

"Think outside the box, Cesari. You're a smart guy."

"Okay, I'll do my best. Speaking of the victim, are you going to contact his family in Serbia?"

"That's the state department's job. I notified them yesterday afternoon. I believe the proper channel is for them to contact the Serbian consulate here in New York and then they take it from there."

"I hope he doesn't have any kids. This will be tough on them."

"I hope he doesn't have anybody. Could you imagine hearing how he died?"

"He must have somebody. Markov said he sent all his money back to his family in Serbia. Besides, everybody has somebody."

"Is that right, Cesari?"

"Who do you have, Detective?"

"I have my badge, I have my gun and I have this."

He reached into his back pocket and took out a faded, leather wallet that had seen better days. He opened it, reached inside and carefully placed a five-pointed one-and-a-half-inch wide gold star with an embossed laurel wreath wrapping around a much tinier silver star in the center. The bigger star was attached to a red, white and blue ribbon.

Cesari asked, "What's that?"

"Pick it up and read the back."

The reverse side had the inscription, *For Gallantry in Action.*

"That, Cesari, is the silver star awarded to me by the Marine Corps during my third tour in Afghanistan for service above and beyond the call of duty. You see, Doctor, while you were in medical school learning how to change bedpans and place band-aids on properly, I was dodging bullets and learning how to proposition Kabul hookers in their native Dari and Pashto."

Cesari cleared his throat. "Well thank you for your service. How long were you in the marines?"

"Twenty of the best years of my life. Left as a gunnery sergeant with the silver medal and a purple heart. An IED exploded too close to my brain during my last tour and now sometimes I see double when I least expect it, and then there are the occasional night terrors…"

"Once again, thank you for your service."

"You're welcome. Well what about you? Who do you have?"

Cesari opened his mouth to speak but realized the only person in his life who even remotely qualified for the answer was Vito. Thankfully he was spared the humiliation of saying that out loud when the waitress dropped the bill onto the table between them.

Both men stared at it until Cesari said, "Shouldn't lunch be on the department?"

Slowly Tierney reached for it. "You're lucky I'm in a good mood, Cesari."

"This is a good mood?"

Chapter 13

The pathology department was located in the basement of the hospital not too far from the morgue and autopsy room. There was the sensation of controlled chaos everywhere as the new CEO's construction teams were already working double time to meet his timetable. Men in work belts crawled all over the building with blueprints, electrical cords, and power tools. Palettes of equipment rolled by Cesari as he sought out Harry's office amidst the turmoil. He was impressed at the rapidity with which progress was being made. It was easy to say you were going to do a thing, but it was a totally different animal to actually do it. The door to the lab was open and Cesari let himself in. Harry was planted in front of a microscope and looked up when Cesari entered. On the wall behind Harry was a framed quotation.

Cesari read it out loud, "*If they're breathing, I'm leaving.* That's cute, Harry. Very inspirational. I didn't know pathologists were so funny."

"You should see me after a couple of martinis."

"That's quite the imagery, but I'm not sure I'm ready for that.

"Stick around, Cesari. The best is yet to come."

"I can hardly wait. So I see you're burning the candle late today. This would have been remarkable even in the middle of the week, but on a Saturday? I am truly impressed. It's nice to see my tax dollars hard at work."

Harry glanced at the wall clock. "Damn, you're right. I lost track of time. I've been trying to expedite that case for you. I assume that's why you're here."

"You assume right, and I consider myself extraordinarily fortunate that I found you here so diligently tending to my needs."

"Have a seat and we'll chat… Coffee? There's a pot and cups over on the counter."

Cesari looked at a nearby counter with an industrial strength half-filled glass coffee pot sitting on a burner. He asked, "When did you make it?"

"Not more than three hours ago, four tops."

"I'll pass, thanks. I have a thing about burnt coffee. So what have you got for me?"

"The toxicology results are still pending and won't be completed until Monday. We had to send some of the more esoteric tests out to specialty labs. I've completed the gross and I'm almost finished with the micro. He died of complete cardiovascular collapse. There's no question about that. Massive acute blood loss leading to ischemia in all of his vital organs. There are infarcts in his brain, damage to the myocardium, the kidneys, etcetera, etcetera. But all of it is very fresh meaning that he didn't live long enough to show evidence of severe tissue damage or repair which is consistent with the clinical circumstances."

"What about his liver?"

"There was significant steatosis and cellular changes suggestive of alcohol related liver disease with mild fibrosis but no real evidence for cirrhosis. If he had laid off the hooch for a while, it probably could have reversed itself."

"So his liver function was probably normal?"

"Most likely. Why is that important?"

"We're running down the angle that he may have been anticoagulated either by prescription medications or by poor clotting function secondary to liver disease, and it may have contributed to his exsanguinating so completely. We're having trouble with his having nearly zero blood volume. While we're at it, did the neck wounds show any signs of clotting?"

"I think you can safely eliminate liver disease as having made any significant contribution to his death. It was simply too mild in my view to have caused anything but his physician to wag his finger at him to back off the booze. But it's interesting you should mention the wound. I was puzzled by it all morning because there were no signs of coagulation. None at all. There were no platelet aggregates or fibrin deposits at the site on microscopic examination. Once that spigot opened, there is no evidence the body attempted to close it."

"How were his bleeding parameters?"

"Still running them. As you can imagine, certain tests can be difficult to perform on a D.O.A. close to six, maybe eight hours old, but I can tell you this, the little blood that was left in him was still quite liquid."

"Meaning?"

"It should have been caked like mud adhering to his vasculature. Instead, it was still fluid which means you may be onto something with this anticoagulation angle. I'll know more in an hour. The technicians are running his prothrombin time for a third time."

"Why is that?"

"The numbers that came back the first two times were too off the walls for me to believe. A normal prothrombin time in a healthy individual is about twelve seconds meaning it takes that long for the blood to form a clot. In a patient on therapeutic doses of warfarin it is anywhere from twenty to thirty seconds."

"What was his?"

Harry picked up a piece of paper and examined it. "The first time we ran it, it was too high to be measured. The second time we ran it we tweaked the machine to accommodate much higher results. It came back as over two thousand."

"Damn."

"You see what I mean?"

"Yes, I do."

"I've been trying to rationalize this finding with his having been found lying in an alley for an unspecified period of time and the fact that most of his blood volume was missing. No one really knows for sure what effect such a severe anemia might have on clotting parameters because no one ever gets that low and lives to talk about it. But when you take into account that there was no sign of clotting in the neck wound and that the residual blood found in his body was still unclotted, you begin to get a presumptive picture of an individual who might have been on a very high dose of some type of anticoagulant."

"Well, Harry, I must say that you're doing such a great job, I may never be able to make fun of pathologists again."

"That's good to hear Cesari. I'm glad you're finally developing some respect for us basement warriors."

"I truly am. The next time someone insinuates that you guys are closet necrophiliacs, I swear I'm going to unfriend them on social media."

"Very funny, Cesari."

He chuckled, "I'm sorry, Harry. I couldn't help myself. Seriously though, this was very helpful. Thanks."

"No problem. Anything else?"

"No, that was plenty. Now I just have to understand how this all fits together... On a different note, all this activity and noise must be very annoying."

"Totally, but what can I do? As soon as the meeting ended last night, these guys started pouring in here like a herd of stampeding wildebeests. From what I heard, they've been working all through the night too. They tell me it's going to be like this for weeks, maybe months. Tiberius the Hun wants the renovations done post haste, but this is nothing. You can't believe what's happening on the other side of the building by the loading dock. There are at least ten or twelve semis lined up to unload their stuff. They've been coming and going all day."

"Really?"

"Trust me. I was just there before you found me. You want to talk about noise and chaos. Geez…"

"Well I have to give the little guy his due. When he said renovations would begin immediately, I didn't expect this."

"Neither did I."

"Okay, I'll let you get back to work. Thanks again, Harry. I appreciate you spending your Saturday on this."

"No problem and keep me posted on anything that turns up on your end."

"I'll do the best I can within limits. Detective Tierney doesn't want me blasting every detail of the case out at the top of my lungs."

"He's sort of hard-boiled, isn't he?"

Cesari walked to the door and opened it saying, "Let's put it this way, Harry. He thinks jay-walking should be a capital offense."

"He's that bad?"

"Even worse in person."

Cesari closed the door, and out of curiosity, decided to walk over to the part of the basement where they were unloading the semis to observe the spectacle. The closer he got, the more heavily congested and hazardous the hallway became. In less than twenty-four hours, the basement of the hospital had become filled with dust, drop cloths, and plastic Men-at-Work signs. By the time he reached the loading dock, he felt as if he had placed himself at serious risk for injury by not wearing a hard hat and steel-toed work boots.

The large garage doors leading to a cement outdoor platform were wide open and sunlight beamed brightly in. Two massive eighteen wheelers had backed up to the dock, side by side with their cargo doors fully open. Strong men grunted and groaned under the weight of heavy boxes as they carried them inside. A forklift operator was busy as well with the larger crates. The noise of men and machines echoed loudly in the poor acoustics of the large storage area.

The various markings on the outside of the containers indicated that some of the items were medically related but others were for construction purposes such as stacks of two by fours, yards of electrical wire, sheetrock and the like. One very large wood crate had General Electric written on it and Cesari suspected it was either a new CT scanner or possibly a new MRI. Other boxes were nondescript, and he couldn't tell what they concealed. A few of the boxes had hazardous material warnings stamped on them.

He surveyed the room and was impressed by the manpower present and their industriousness. The CEO was pouring large volumes of cash into this project and he wanted his money's worth. From Cesari's vantage point, he was getting it. As he glanced around, he noticed something out of place, but what? It took him a minute, but he eventually noticed two guys across the room not really doing anything nor were they wearing hard hats. They were walking back and forth observing things just as he was doing. They were in their thirties, slightly above average height and build, with clean-shaven white faces. Nothing particularly memorable about either one, but he was too far away to make out their features clearly.

A forklift carrying a large crate moved in front of them blocking Cesari's view temporarily and when it had passed, they were gone. He searched briefly for them but was interrupted by a worker who tapped him on the shoulder.

He turned and was greeted by big, burly guy in a hard hat. He saw Cesari's hospital ID and very politely said, "You can't be in here, Doctor. At least not like that. I hope you don't mind but there's a lot going on down here right now and it's just too dangerous."

"I understand. I'll be on my way."

Chapter 14

That evening in the Kit Kat, loud music thumped in the background as Cesari held the phone tightly to his ear. Tierney had called for an update and Cesari had just finished telling him about what he had learned in pathology.

"Well that is interesting, Cesari. Thank Harry for me. He's a little quirky but solid."

"I'll pass the compliment along."

"So let's review what we have. Based on the physical evidence and the blood test, the victim may well have been on an anticoagulant. The question is did somebody give it to him to help him bleed to death or was he taking it for some medical reason and accidentally overdosed?"

"That's the problem. It's impossible to know if he was under the care of a physician. There was no paperwork in his apartment and we still haven't found his wallet. My guess is he was uninsured, and if he was, all bets are off as to who he might have sought treatment from. There are a lot of quacks out there taking advantage of the poor."

"Agreed, but at least some things are starting to make sense. He's super-anticoagulated and then gets the major blood vessels in his neck punctured. For whatever reason, he can't call an ambulance or compress the wound and bleeds down to nothing. Somebody cleans him up and dumps him in an alley…why?"

"Am I an official consultant with the NYPD now?"

"Who wants to know?"

"An official consultant would get paid, right?"

"You're unofficial so answer the question…why? And while you're at it what's all that damn noise in the background? Are you at a party?"

"I apologize for the commotion, and yes, I'm at a retirement party downtown. To answer your question, I haven't a clue as to why. Did any of the employees you interviewed today have anything pertinent to add?"

"Nothing at all. According to this bunch, they hardly knew the victim at all except at work and barely any contact there either. Not a one of them can remember ever socializing with the guy, going to his apartment, or even just having a beer to shoot the bull. I don't know how credible that is, but I suppose it's possible."

"Okay, the toxicology results will be in Monday morning and Harry had all but finished the autopsy when I saw him. If any surprises come up, he'll let us know."

"Good, because tomorrow is Sunday and a day of rest."

"I'm glad, Detective. It's been a long week."

"Don't you know sarcasm when you hear it, Cesari? Now are you all in this thing or out?"

Speechless for a second or two, Cesari cleared his throat. "I'm all in of course."

"That's music to my ears. Because I don't need some white-collar, candy-ass slowing me down because he's not committed to the cause. Tomorrow we go door to door in the victim's apartment building and in his neighborhood fishing around. His manner of death has got to trigger a response in somebody."

"What kind of response?"

"I'll know it when I see it. It's usually in their eyes."

"All right. What time?"

"I'll meet you at 8:00 a.m. sharp in front of that Ukrainian restaurant and you'd better have a Starbucks venti in your hands; Sumatran if they have it and black, no cream or sugar, with a cinnamon scone. The coffee better be hot and the scone fresh or my displeasure will be epic."

"I'll be there."

"And Cesari, one more thing. From now on you call me immediately when you find out something relevant. Don't force me to track you down."

Tierney hung up before he could reply. Vito was sitting next to him and asked, "That sounded a lot like you were talking to a cop, Cesari?"

"It was. A detective to be specific. I'm working on a case with him. I'm sort of an unofficial consultant."

"Get out of here. What kind of case?"

Vito took a sip from his Hendricks gin martini with two olives. Cesari was drinking Jefferson's Reserve bourbon neat. They sat in one of the booths at the Kit Kat Klub enjoying the show before heading out for steaks on the west side when Detective Tierney had called.

"The kind I can't talk about."

Vito snorted. "Well don't bring him around here. I don't let the girls give freebies to anyone, especially cops."

"He's not a bad guy. You'd like him."

Vito rolled his eyes. "Just don't do it, all right? I got enough on my plate."

"Fine…By the way, have you found out anything about my CEO and that guy Feinberg?"

He shook his head. "Take it easy. It's only been a day and a half since you told me about them. You act like I got nothing else to do. I made a few calls but so far the names aren't ringing any bells. You were right, there's almost nothing about them on the internet, but I'll keep asking around. One of my guys will drop by the hospital Monday to get some pictures."

"I thought about that and it won't be necessary. I'll just take a few with my cellphone and send them to you."

"That'll work."

"I have one more name for you to look up if you don't mind...Shlomo Markov."

"Shlomo Markov?"

"Yeah, he's one of the big money donors at the hospital. They're the ones who insisted we hire Acevedo and Feinberg. He's connected to the police case I'm involved in. One of his employees was found dead in an alley over on the east side."

"That's a helluva coincidence, isn't it?"

"Now that you mention it..."

Vito furrowed his brow in thought. Cesari said, "What is it?"

"That name...it sounds vaguely familiar, the Markov part not the Shlomo part, but I can't quite place it. What did he look like?"

"An older guy, late seventies or eighty but in great shape. You would have thought he was fifty or sixty. An inch shorter than me, heavy but not fat, mostly bald but for a round patch of hair. Big ruddy cheeks, and the most peculiar eyes. One's green and one's brown. It's a condition called heterochromia iridis"

"Really?"

"It's the kind of thing you wouldn't forget."

He shook his head. "I agree. No, that doesn't sound familiar at all...I don't know... Maybe it will come to me later."

"He owns several apartment buildings and a restaurant over on First Avenue called Ukrainian Heaven. If we go there for dinner, we might be able to catch a glimpse of him."

"And cancel the steakhouse? Not a chance. Maybe tomorrow for lunch."

"What time are the reservations tonight by the way?"

"Eight...Would you look at that."

Vito nodded at the stage where a voluptuous redhead in a thong and high heels had just finished a twirl around a pole and ended in a full split facing their table. She caught Cesari's eye and held on. She was in her early twenties with high cheek bones, blue eyes and a decidedly sultry appearance. It crossed Cesari's mind that this girl didn't give freebies to anyone, detective or not. In fact, there was something in the way she looked that made him think he wouldn't want to make her mad for any reason.

"Is she new?" he asked.

Vito replied smiling at the girl. "A couple of months. Her name's Sofia. She's Russian. Not bad, huh?"

She finished her routine to applause from the audience surrounding the bar and scampered off. Cesari said, "Not bad at all."

Vito glanced at his watch. "We got time. Finish your drink and I'll introduce you to her."

"That's okay. She's a working girl. I don't want to bother her."

"You won't be bothering her, and I want to compliment her on her act. You know, positive reinforcement from the boss. That kind of stuff."

"Can we give her a few minutes to put on a robe first?"

"Jesus, Cesari. This is a gentlemen's club. I think she's used to guys seeing her with nothing on."

"Yeah, but I'm not used to it."

"Will you knock it off. You just watched her dance for twenty minutes for God's sake. Now c'mon, she has to go back on in fifteen and we have dinner reservations."

"Fine. I'll wait outside her room while you give her personalized feedback on her performance."

"Your loss. Let's go."

Cesari downed the remaining bourbon in his glass and followed Vito backstage. The dancers' rooms were behind the massive semi-circular bar and down a short corridor. There were four reasonably-sized rooms with four girls to a room. Given their overlapping schedules, there were usually only two girls to a room on any given night. Dancing like these women did was hard work and involved much athleticism requiring frequent breaks and plenty of hydration.

Vito walked up to a room with the number 4 on it and paused before knocking. Loud voices in heated debate could be heard from within. Vito glanced at Cesari and then knocked politely. The room went quiet and a few seconds later, the door opened a crack. Sofia stood there in a short see-through chiffon robe and slippers, and up close, was even more seductive than when she was on stage just a few minutes ago. She was clearly upset.

Vito tried to see past her into the room. "Is everything all right, Sofia?"

"Everything is good, Vito. There is no problem."

He nodded and said, "We heard people arguing. Do you have company?"

She curled her ruby lips into the phoniest smile Cesari had ever seen. "Oh, is nothing. Baby brother come visit is all. We argue over why he no call mama more often. Is silly thing."

Cesari noticed she made no move to open the door any further than a sliver. Vito nodded sympathetically but he wasn't completely buying it. "Your baby brother, huh?"

"Yes, is brother. He must leave soon. He has date with girl."

"I'd like to meet him. Maybe I'll buy him a drink."

She hesitated, caught between a rock and a hard place. Cesari could see the wheels spinning behind those delicious blue eyes. Finally, she said, "Of course. You are boss."

She opened the door and stepped back into the room. Now in full view was a thick man in good shape with jet black hair about the same height and weight as Vito, which put him at roughly six feet three inches and two hundred and sixty pounds. He was clean shaven with rough, brooding features. He wore a dark two-piece suit with a dress shirt open at the collar. He looked familiar to Cesari for several reasons which he couldn't readily put his finger on.

There were, however, two conclusions that Cesari instantly came to as he tried to avoid staring at Sofia's nipples. One; this was definitely not her younger brother. Unless he had completely lost his powers of observation, the man in front of them was at least ten years older than Sofia and how many men would stand in the company of their sister dressed the way she was? Not many, he thought. At least not many normal men. Then there was conclusion number two; judging from the man's gruff and even formidable countenance, Cesari would've bet just about every penny he had that this guy wasn't too worried about mama's feelings.

Sofia introduced him, "This is brother. Name is Ivan."

Vito looked at the guy and without extending his hand or smiling said, "So you're Sofia's baby brother."

Not a question. A statement of fact. The guy grunted a monosyllable response, "Yes."

"Well, any brother of Sofia's is welcome here. I'll let the bartenders know you can have a couple of drinks for free. I'm Vito, and this is my friend, Dr. Cesari. He works at St. Matt's hospital over on Third Avenue."

Cesari thought the man's eyes flashed as he nodded. Nobody extended hands for shaking, yet somehow it didn't seem as awkward as it should have. After ten long seconds of silence as they appraised each other, Ivan finally said, "I must go now."

Without fanfare, he left the room, and Cesari suddenly realized why he seemed familiar. It occurred to him that he might be one of the two guys he saw in the receiving area of the hospital earlier. Vito turned to talk to Sofia. Cesari hesitated for a moment and then decided to go after Ivan for a better look.

As he was leaving, Cesari heard Sofia say, "I am sorry, Vito. I know I am not supposed to have visitors backstage."

He was too far gone to hear exactly what Vito's response was, but his tone sounded sympathetic enough. Ivan's back was barely visible as he disappeared down the dark corridor returning to the bar area but Cesari hustled after him and picked him up again in the dizzying strobe lights as he made a bee line for the exit.

Cesari made it outside the club just in time to see a brand new, red Ferrari that had been parked across the street make a sudden and dramatic U-turn, pulling up to the curb in front of Ivan. The vanity license plate was bold and unique, ROMANI. Ivan opened the passenger door and got in quickly, but not before Cesari caught a glimpse of the driver.

It was Yorgi.

Chapter 15

Cesari reached for the bottle of wine and poured himself and Vito a second glass. It was a ten-year-old Stag's Leap Artemis Collection cabernet from Napa Valley. Rich, complex and smooth, it was one of Cesari's favorites. It retailed at about seventy bucks but was marked up to twice that in restaurants. Still, it was worth it and considering what they charged for some French wines, it was a steal. He'd been in a French place in Vegas where the wines started at three hundred dollars a bottle and worked their way up to the thousands with no appreciable difference in quality as far as he was concerned.

They were sitting in Wolfgang's Steakhouse in Tribeca, home of the finest dry-aged steaks in Manhattan and undoubtedly the best creamed spinach in the city. The waiters wore black tuxedoes, starched white shirts, real bowties, and sported handle-bar mustaches. They addressed you as *Sir* or *Madam*. Not too far from the dining room was a well-ventilated cigar lounge with plush leather chairs and sofas where you could light up with an expensive scotch or cognac after dinner.

"Do you know what the key to a great creamed spinach is, Vito?"

"Tell me."

"It's the fresh nutmeg; a generous amount grated in at the very end of the preparation. It makes the dish."

Vito chewed on a huge piece of ribeye. He said, "Not to change the subject, Cesari, but are you sure it was him?"

"You mean the guy in the Ferrari? No doubt about it. It was Yorgi. I'd know him anywhere. Why?"

"I thought you said he manages a restaurant and some slum buildings over on the east side?"

"I did."

"Doesn't sound like someone who would own a Ferrari."

"No, it doesn't, but it was him, and I'll tell you another thing. That Ivan guy wasn't Sofia's baby brother. She was yanking your chain."

"I know she was. You think I was born yesterday? It wouldn't be the first time one of the girls snuck a boyfriend into their dressing room. It's against the rules to have any guests back there so she probably thought it would soften me if she said he was family."

"Did it?"

"Of course it did... Cesari, they're women. I can't afford to get bent out of shape every time one of them lies to me. As long as it's just a little white lie, I play along and try not to let my feelings get hurt. Besides, she's turning into one of the best dancers I have."

"That's very mature of you."

"It's just good business sense. I have to pick and choose which battles I'm going to fight with the girls because I can't win them all. Not in that business. Back to you... So Yorgi owns a car way over his paygrade and picked up his friend who's dating one of my girls. So what?"

"It's more than that...a lot more."

"I'm listening."

"I think I saw Ivan in the hospital this afternoon. He was with another guy watching the construction crews unload the trucks dropping off equipment and supplies in the basement."

"Ivan was in the hospital?"

Cesari nodded. "I think so. He was across the room and I only caught a glimpse of him. It was very brief."

"So you can't be sure?"

"No."

"You said you saw two guys there. Was Yorgi the other guy?"

"No, definitely not. Yorgi's much bigger than the guy I saw and Yorgi's bald as a cue ball. The other guy had a full head of hair."

Vito thought about that for minute and said, "Suppose it was Ivan at the hospital. Why would he be there?"

"Your guess is as good as mine, but like I said, I can't be certain."

"So we're back to Yorgi owns a Ferrari and is friends with a guy who's friends with Sofia."

"That sums it up. Not much there, is there?"

"Nothing at all. How's your meal?"

"How's my meal? Let me think about that; a sixty-day, dry-aged twenty ounce New York strip grilled to medium rare perfection, then brushed with melted butter and served with sautéed portobello mushrooms, beer battered onion rings and the best creamed spinach I've ever had... I don't know, Vito. It's almost as if they hate me."

They both laughed at that. Vito said, "As they should, Cesari, but I have something that will save the day. I brought some great cigars to have with scotch later in their lounge."

"I'm down with that, my friend. Here's to living large."

They clinked wine glasses and resumed their meal. An hour later they retired to the cigar lounge and placed an order for twenty-five-year-old Macallan. They took seats in over-sized armchairs, and as the waiter buzzed off to get their drinks, Vito opened up a leather cigar travel humidor and passed a big fat one to Cesari with a stylish cutter.

Vito said, "It's a full-bodied, sixty-ring Nicaraguan, Cesari. One of my favorites."

Cesari read the label, *La Gloria Cubana,* sniffed it, cut the end off and lit it with one of the many lighters placed strategically around the room for patrons. There was seating for about a dozen people but currently there were only five including one woman sitting with two older men on the other side of the room. Tiffany style floor lamps gave the lounge a subdued hue as ventilation fans hummed mechanically in the background.

Cesari took a long draw from his cigar and blew it out, sighed contentedly and said, "So how's the war going with the Albanians?"

"There's no war. It's a territorial dispute, and they're not Albanians. They're Hungarian or Romanian. Maybe. I'm not sure. One of those countries over there. It doesn't matter. Until they declare their true intentions, I'm not going to sweat it."

The waiter placed their scotches down on coasters. Cesari took a sip and said, "I thought their intention was to get you to leave the Kit Kat Klub and Second Avenue?"

"Maybe...I've been in this business too long to accept that on face value. Usually, somebody would have approached me with some sort of deal. You know, quid pro quo. You give us Second Avenue and we'll give you this. The problem is no one has clearly identified themselves to me. I'm getting all sorts of secondhand messages from the people who work for me. Grumblings on the street; that sort of stuff. They roughed up one of my guys a few weeks ago; put him in the hospital with a concussion and a few broken bones. When he woke up, he said he was told to tell me that I should abandon ship or else. We were able to identify one of the guys who did it. We found him and broke the exact same bones. He passed out before we could get a name on who sent him. The problem with the Eastern Europeans is that there's no one person in charge so you can never be sure what the hell is going on."

"So the move on the Kit Kat could be just a rogue group of Bulgarian bandidos for all you know?"

"Could be anybody with a funny accent. My guys aren't exactly linguistics experts. The one we caught was Romanian for sure but that doesn't mean his boss is. Which is why I can't overreact. If I knew who it was specifically causing the trouble, I would of course."

"Of course... So you're biding your time?"

He smiled, "You're getting good at this, Cesari. Anyway a few weeks ago one of the girls heard from one of the customers that the First Avenue guys were planning to move in force on the club. She wasn't sure what he meant but that's why all the security."

"Isn't there someone you could talk to over there to resolve this before it explodes?"

"Not without appearing weak."

"How so?"

"Asking for a truce before the war has started is as weak as it gets, Cesari. Even the French waited for the Germans to come storming across the border before they waved the white flag."

"You've thought this through pretty well."

"Of course I have. In fact, the increased security at the club was designed to bring whoever it was out in the open. You know, I double-dare you kind of thing."

"Like a box of catnip to cats."

"Exactly. How do you like the cigar?"

"I love the cigar... Vito, I've been thinking... In another life you might have been a military genius like Julius Caesar or Napoleon."

"By the time I'm done with these guys, they're going to think I'm the reincarnation of Genghis Khan. He wasn't half as nice as those other guys you mentioned."

"And this is no time to be nice. I see your point. Good choice of role models."

"You're not the only one who reads, Cesari."

Cesari signaled the waiter for more scotch. "I never thought I was... This room is really starting to fill up."

Vito glanced around and nodded. There weren't any more open seats and several guys were left standing next to a high-top table to enjoy their smokes. The noise level had increased dramatically.

"Cigars are becoming more and more popular these days," Vito observed.

"Apparently."

"So without going into details, tell me about this case you're consulting on with the police."

"I guess I can give you some of the generalities. Most of it's been in the news by now anyway. A Serbian restaurant worker was murdered on the east side. His body was found in an alley on First Avenue."

"How was he murdered?"

"He bled to death from a neck wound."

"And why does the NYPD require a medical consultant for that?"

"They didn't at first. I asked if I could tag along out of curiosity but as things are unfolding, I think Detective Tierney is finding my input somewhat useful."

Vito almost gasped, "Tierney?! Bob Tierney? He's the biggest asshole on the force. You've got to be kidding?"

"I gather you know him?"

"To know him is to hate him. He's been a thorn in my side forever. He loves harassing me."

"Any particular reason for this love-hate relationship?"

"You mean over and above the fact that bodies routinely turn up in my wake?"

"I guess that's good enough. Well, I guess I really won't be bringing him around to the Kit Kat."

"You better not."

"Why haven't you tried persuading him to be your friend like most of the other guys in the NYPD?"

"I've tried very hard and twice he arrested the bag men I sent to him with suitcases full of be-my-friend cash. Fortunately, they knew better than to finger me."

"Tierney's a hard man. I can vouch for that. I guess the Kit Kat isn't the place for him. With all those illegal weapons there, I can't imagine how many life sentences you would get as the owner of the club."

"Nice try, Cesari, but I would never be stupid enough to actually be the owner on paper. The real owner lives in Bogota, Columbia, and sadly hasn't been seen in years."

"Real sad, and good luck trying to find him I bet."

"And good luck in trying to connect me to anything that goes on in that place."

"You're too cool school for school, Vito."

"Exactly."

Chapter 16

It was some time after 2:00 p.m. the next day, Cesari and Detective Tierney had knocked on every door in the dead Serb's apartment building, spoken to everyone within a two-block radius of the murder scene and found out nothing. They were standing in the middle of the sidewalk on First Avenue eating hot dogs from a street vendor. The sun shone brightly down on them and Cesari was both hungry and tired. They had begun the day promptly at 8:00 a.m. and they had been going at it hard ever since. He'd decided Tierney must be part bloodhound.

"Isn't it remarkable, Cesari?" Tierney asked in between bites of a Sabrett's loaded with mustard, sauerkraut and onions. "The guy lives here for a whole year and no one knows him, no one's ever talked to him and no one's ever heard of him. Even the people who worked with him every day act as if he was just a vague shadowy presence."

"Not plausible?"

"Not even remotely possible, but that doesn't mean he was into anything bad. Immigrants are like that. They're afraid to get involved, and I can't say that I blame them too much. Where they come from, the police are the bad guys."

"Not like here, huh?" Cesari said with a grin.

Tierney wasn't prone to mirth and didn't find his unofficial consultant even vaguely amusing. He scowled and pinned Cesari's ears back. "You some sort of Italian commie, Cesari?"

"Just joking, Detective. I meant no harm."

"Well zip it, okay? You're here to fetch coffee and not put me in a bad mood, remember? It's hard enough to do my job."

"I guess you guys have to take a lot of shit?"

"Just every day, all day, from everybody."

"I'm sorry to hear that. Well for whatever it's worth, I got your back."

"Oh you do, do you? Let me see your hands, Cesari."

"What?"

"You heard me."

Cesari finished his hot dog, wiped his face and extended his hands, palms up for inspection.

Tierney examined them and said, "Just as I thought, tender and soft, and you got my back. Jesus, I'm in trouble... Well I guess you're better than nothing. At ease, Doctor."

Cesari put his hands down and was thinking of a response when his phone buzzed. It was Vito and he was agitated. "Cesari, we have a problem."

He took a few steps away from Detective Tierney for privacy. Tierney, in turn, decided to purchase another hot dog and walked back to the vendor.

Cesari said, "What do you mean?"

"I mean come down to the club now. It's a big problem and I'm not sure what to do."

Detective Tierney waved at Cesari to see if he wanted another hot dog as well. Cesari smiled and shook his head no. "I'm with Tierney right now. I don't know if I can break away without making him angry."

"What is he, your new best friend all of a sudden?"

"I'll see what I can do."

He hung up and walked over to Tierney who was wolfing down his third hot dog. Tierney said, "Man, I never get tired of New York hot dogs."

"Yeah, they are pretty good. Say, Detective, I was wondering if I could break away now."

"I didn't wear you out already, did I, Cesari? You didn't look like that much of a greenhorn, but maybe I was wrong about that. What do you have to do, a load of laundry or something? I wouldn't want a murder investigation to interfere with something as important as that. It doesn't matter. Sure, we'll regroup tomorrow. Keep your phone on and your nose clean."

He turned and left Cesari standing there wondering what he'd gotten himself into. Cesari shook his head and walked three long blocks up First Avenue and then crossed over to Second Avenue. The Kit Kat Klub was another two blocks north and he picked up his pace. The club didn't open until four, but bartenders, kitchen staff and security usually came at two to make sure everything was at the ready. The girls started to drift in around three to put on their outfits and limber up.

When he arrived, there were the two usual gorillas stationed at the front entrance looking more paranoid and attentive than usual. Expecting him, they waved him through the door without the usual pat down. The club was quiet and dark. Vito sat at the bar with one of his men sipping from a shot glass. A bartender stood at a respectful distance. No one was talking. Cesari had a sense of foreboding as he approached.

Vito turned to him and Cesari saw that he was sipping straight tequila. Cesari glanced at his watch and grimaced at the thought. "What's going on, Vito?"

"You're not going to believe it."

"Try me."

"You might want to have a drink first."

Cesari was warm and thirsty. He'd been on the go since early morning. "Just water. I've been hoofing it in the sun for hours."

Vito signaled the bartender who brought him a tall glass of ice water which he gulped down and said, "Don't keep me in suspense."

"Cesari, this is Rafael, the club's manager and front man when I'm not around. Rafael, meet Dr. Cesari."

He wasn't as big as Vito or the bouncers at the front door but Cesari still wouldn't want to tangle with him. He was in his mid-thirties with a full head of dark curly hair and spoke with a Spanish accent. "Nice to meet you, Doctor."

"Mutual."

Vito said, "Lead the way, Raffy."

Both men stood and Cesari followed them through the kitchen and out the back door to the alley where the garbage cans and club's dumpster were. They passed several wide-eyed kitchen workers on the way. Everyone seemed paralyzed by some as yet unknown phenomena.

In the alley, Cesari soon understood why. The body lay on the ground next to the dumpster, naked and white as new-fallen snow. From where they stood, they were invisible to the street.

He asked, "Who is he?"

Vito replied, "It's Leandro, one of my bartenders."

Cesari sighed, "Do you know what happened?"

"No. First thing I did was to call you."

Cesari crouched close to the corpse and noticed two holes in his neck. Under his breath, he whispered, "Shit."

"What is it, Cesari?" asked Vito.

"Nothing, are you going to call the police?"

"I'm not sure. I don't need that kind of aggravation or publicity."

"Why'd you call me? This isn't the first dead guy you've ever seen."

"No, but a dead naked guy that looks like this is a first for me. Did you see the holes in his neck?"

"You saw that, huh?"

"Oh yeah, and so did half the guys inside. We got a problem here. A couple of holes in his head or chest I'm okay with. Holes like that in his neck not so much. What do you think?"

"Does he have family, a wife, a girlfriend?"

"He's from Chicago and I don't know about family. He was dating Sofia, the girl you met last night."

Cesari looked up surprised. "I thought she was dating that guy Ivan?"

Vito said, "That's what I thought."

Rafael offered clarification. "No, Dr. Cesari. She was dating Leandro. I tell this to Mr. Vito today. I know this for sure. She left the club with him last night after her shift."

"What time was that about?"

"Leandro and Sofia both worked the four to twelve shift yesterday so by twelve-thirty or thereabouts."

Cesari turned to Vito. "So if Sofia was dating Leandro, why was that guy, Ivan, in her room?"

Vito shrugged. "Maybe he really was her brother?"

"Bullshit. I think you better get Sofia here."

"We've been trying. She's not answering her phone, but back to the body..."

"What do you want me to do?"

"You're a doctor? What the hell happened here? Should I be calling the department of health?"

"I don't think they're going to be able to help you and I don't know what happened. Look, you don't want trouble, right?"

"Of course not."

"Wrap him up in a blanket or a tarp and bring him over to St. Matt's. It might be a good idea to get an autopsy on him. The neighborhood over there is usually pretty quiet on a Sunday and they have dumpsters in the back hidden from public view. Drop him in one and then call it in anonymously. They'll treat him with respect. I promise you that. Any of these guys here dumb enough to talk about this?"

Rafael looked offended by the question and said definitively, "Not a chance."

Cesari said to Vito, "You'd better have a talk with each and every one of them and make sure they understand that."

"I'll take care of it. They won't talk about this; not now, not ever. It never happened and they never saw what never happened. Rafael, gather everyone who's here and start talking to them. In the meantime, lock the doors. We're closed tonight. Tell everyone we had a water pipe break or something. Get Gaetano and Lenny and have them pull their Suburban around back with some sort of sheet or tarp and have them wrap the body up and place it in the back of the Suburban."

"I will do that right away, Mr. Vito."

As he walked away, Vito added, "And keep calling Sofia every five minutes until she answers. Come with me, Cesari. There's one more thing you should see."

He followed Vito to his upstairs office. After he closed the door, Vito withdrew an envelope from his jacket pocket and handed it to Cesari who looked at it. It was addressed to Vito. Cesari opened the envelope, took out a piece of paper and read it

When he was done, he looked at Vito. "This isn't good."

"No kidding. Gaetano found it under the door when he arrived earlier. It was sealed and addressed to me so no one else has seen it."

The letter threatened to kill everyone who worked at the Kit Kat in the same manner as Leandro, one at a time, until Vito abandoned the site. He had one week to think about it. As a demonstration of good intention, he was to leave a briefcase with one hundred thousand dollars on the front seat of a black Toyota Camry parked on the street in front of the club tomorrow night. The note was signed, Shlomo.

Cesari was very quiet as he contemplated the letter of extortion. He didn't know many guys named Shlomo. In fact, he only knew the one, but there could be thousands. He couldn't stand coincidences like this. They made the hairs on the nape of his neck stand up.

"You all right, Cesari? You look a little shaken up."

"Do I? So do you know this Shlomo?"

"I don't know any Shlomos. I never even heard the name before you mentioned it last night."

"We need to talk."

Chapter 17

"You've got to be kidding me, Cesari? You mean there's a serial murderer out there draining people of their blood and now he's targeting my club? Does that even make sense?"

Because of what happened to Leandro, Cesari had decided to bring Vito into the loop. They were still in the Kit Kat trying to piece it all together.

"I'm not an expert in deviant sociopathic behavior, Vito. All I know is Leandro looks like he suffered the same fate as that Serbian restaurant worker over on First Avenue. I'm sure I'll get called in for the autopsy as will Detective Tierney, so I'll keep you posted. The fact that the name Shlomo is involved in both cases is the only reason I bring it up. It's most likely unrelated but I've known you too long not to be perfectly honest about something as serious as this."

"I appreciate that but if they are related then Tierney's going to be crawling up my ass like no tomorrow."

"Possibly. Leandro has no identification on him and if his fingerprints aren't on file, they'll have no way of tracing him to you."

"Unless they get a hold of Sofia."

"No word yet on her?"

Vito glanced at his phone to make sure he hadn't missed a call from his men. "No, but I'll send Gaetano to her apartment to find her if she doesn't pick up soon. Anyway, back to serial killers. I don't know much about this stuff either, but it sounds a little odd for one to demand money. Don't they usually kill for pleasure?"

"Pleasure? I don't know about that. Maybe. My understanding was that it was usually out of some sort of compulsion to do so. They get urges that have to be satisfied but I think you're right about demanding money being strange. On the other hand, they're each crazy in their own way so who knows. Maybe we've come across a very poor serial murderer who needs to make a buck."

Vito grinned. "Just my luck...You don't think this is the work of the Romanians that have been hassling me?"

"You know, when I first saw the note, the thought crossed my mind, but I'm not sure how much sense that makes. To go from roughing up one of your guys to this is an uncalled-for escalation and would somebody... anybody, really sign their own name? And what would this have to do with the dead Serb found over on First Avenue?"

Vito thought about that and said, "It doesn't make sense, but there was a threat made to the club a few weeks ago."

"You mean the one your girls overheard from a customer?"

"Yes."

"That's hard to say. Maybe there was a threat made, maybe not. You can't be sure. Some dancer hearing something from some guy she's grinding is not necessarily a serious threat."

He nodded. "True, and this certainly is a strange way to convince me to pack up and leave."

"Exactly, but first things first. I'll check in on the autopsy just to confirm there's a relationship between the two murders. You batten down the hatches here, and please don't retaliate."

"Retaliate? Who am I supposed to retaliate against?"

"That's my point. Don't go out there and pick random targets because you're pissed off. Even worse, don't shoot the first Shlomo that walks through the front door."

"You must really think I'm stupid, Cesari."

"There's no thinking involved."

****

At 8:00 p.m., Yorgi entered the abandoned tenement building that had become the brother's defacto headquarters and made his way down the dark, filthy hallway eventually reaching the stairwell. The rickety stairs creaked and groaned under his weight as he proceeded downward. Light from the incandescent bulb glimmered as he neared their conference room. He smiled when he saw his brothers waiting for him sipping vodka. They looked exhausted and anxious.

"Well done, brothers," Yorgi said. "It was long night but well worth it. There is nothing more satisfying than killing two birds with one stone. Word is the dance club has shut down for the day. Gianelli is telling everyone they have a plumbing problem. I know you are tired, but we cannot rest yet. Is good news, no?"

Ivan said, "Yes, Yorgi, I agree, is good news, but I am not happy that Sofia told those two at the Kit Kat my name last night. I can't be one hundred percent sure, but I think the doctor recognized me from the hospital. He was long way off but still is possible."

Yorgi nodded. "Sofia make mistake under stress. She was not thrilled to cooperate."

"Not at all, brother. Apparently, her feelings for bartender ran deep."

"Still, in the end it all worked out."

"Except for doctor."

"What do you think he was he doing there at the Kit Kat anyway?" Yorgi asked. "Just doing what men do?"

"No, believe it or not, he is friends with that mobster, Vito."

"Seriously?"

"Yes, I am."

While Yorgi thought about that, Tibor asked, "What means this, Yorgi?"

"I don't know yet, but perhaps even better. Perhaps kill three birds with one stone. We save bloody clothes?"

Tibor and Ivan nodded. "Yes, keep with others."

"Good, and Sofia?"

Ivan said, "The dentist is working on her in next room as we speak. He is almost finished. She will be ready in few minutes."

"Excellent, because several shipments arrived early with construction materials and we must remove tonight. Shlomo wishes to meet us there at midnight to perform inspection and inventory. Dentist knows to keep mouth shut?"

"The dentist better keep mouth shut. Not only is he here illegally and practicing without license but Dr. Sundaram is also wanted for crimes he committed in Mumbai."

Yorgi chuckled. "What a world we live in. Okay, as soon as dentist finish, we go to hospital. I have van parked outside with crate."

"What if somebody sees us?" asked Tibor nervously.

Yorgi glanced at his watch. "It is rapidly growing dark. This neighborhood is desolate except for drug addicts. I think we will be fine. Besides, we have no choice. Now show me Sofia."

They all rose and led by Ivan walked over to an adjoining room. Ivan opened the door and they entered a much larger room with an ancient furnace and various other maintenance equipment that had once been used to make the building livable. In the corner near a sink, there was a makeshift table of two carpenter's sawhorses supporting a six-foot by four-foot, three-quarter inch piece of plywood. On the plywood lay Sofia, fully clothed and completely unconscious. Sweating over her was a middle-aged Indian man with a scruffy beard, thick glasses and a blue turban. He reeked of poor hygiene and alcohol. Her head was arched back, and he was scratching at her teeth with some sort of tool.

He stopped what he was doing and looked up at them saying, "I am just now finished. She shouldn't be in too much pain when she wakes, but I can call in prescription for narcotics."

Yorgi asked, "Do you have a license to do that, Dr. Sundaram?"

"No, and the pharmacy I will call doesn't have a license to dispense narcotics. We work well together."

"I do not think that will be necessary, Doctor. She is strong girl and will be fine. Thank you for your service."

He bowed slightly in appreciation. "Thank you and please keep me in mind for future work of this nature."

"Tibor, show Dr. Sundaram out. Ivan and I will tend to Sofia, and Tibor, here are keys to the van. Start the engine and wait there for us."

He handed a set of keys to his brother, and after they left, Yorgi and Ivan leaned over Sofia. Yorgi lifted her upper lip and they studied her. Ivan remarked, "He does good work for a drunk."

Yorgi grunted. "I must say. It is rather convincing. C'mon, let's see if we can get her to walk out of here. It will be easier than to carry her and will look more natural if someone should see us."

With that, he shook her shoulder gently and said, "Sofia, is time to wake up. C'mon Sofia. Wake up sleepy head."

After several attempts of gentle prodding and soft cajoling she began to rouse and slowly opened her big blue eyes, looking around very confused and still quite groggy. The men stared at her large breasts as they jerked upward with a deep inspiration. Her tight blue jeans hugged her delicate waistline and her long red hair somewhat tousled, dangled down around her shoulders.

She whispered hoarsely, "Ivan, where am I? Where is Leandro?"

"You are with friends, Sofia," Ivan replied softly. "Leandro was tired and went home. Let's see if you can stand up. Come now and put an arm around Ivan."

He helped her to a sitting position, and after a minute, she weakly placed one arm around his shoulder and rose unsteadily to her feet. "Why do my teeth hurt so much, Ivan?"

"Last night you drink too much and pass out," he lied. She and Leandro had been given glasses of wine laced with roofies, and for good measure to make sure they remained quiet, he had shot them both up with a healthy doses of heroin. "Not to worry, Sofia, you will be all right. Ivan take care of everything. You remember, Yorgi, my brother? He will help you too."

"Yes, I remember. Hello, Yorgi," she said her voice deeply slurred.

"Hello, Sofia. Is good to see you."

With an arm around each of the brothers, she walked, staggered and was partly carried up the stairs to the front entrance of the building. It was after 9:00 p.m. and dark out. Except for an occasional delirious crackhead meandering aimlessly in the distance, there was no one around. Tibor leaned against a large white panel van parked directly in front of them. On the side of the van was painted *Ukrainian Heaven Catering Service*. Exhaust fumes plumed upward from the tail pipe. Tibor glanced back and forth and then signaled them to bring Sofia out as he opened the back of the van.

As they approached Tibor said, "Hurry, my brothers."

They quickly hoisted her into the back of the van with little resistance or help from Sofia who was still disoriented and rapidly slipping back into unconsciousness. They laid her down on the floor of the van next to a pine box six feet long and eighteen inches deep. In the back of the van close to the cabin were ten massive bags of garden soil stacked high, the kind you might find in any home and garden center. Their classic green and yellow colors were identifiable anywhere in the world. Yorgi and Ivan sat down on the box next to Sofia while Tibor closed the doors and went around to the driver's seat.

The brothers gazed down on the beautiful girl and Ivan said, "Is shame, no?"

Yorgi was more philosophical. "I do not believe one person is any more or less deserving of death than another simply because of their appearance, brother."

"You are right, Yorgi, but you never saw her dance."

Chapter 18

Sunday evening, Cesari was sitting in his apartment unwinding and mentally preparing for another grueling Monday in the OR. Fifteen scheduled cases, mounds of paperwork, dozens of calls to be made, and many asses to be kissed. He was quite certain that if even one person told him how lucky he was to be a doctor, he would slap them silly.

His cellphone buzzed but he didn't recognize the number. He thought it was probably spam and toyed with the idea of simply blocking it. Why they would choose Sunday night to harass people was anyone's guess, but he decided to answer it anyway. Annoying yes, but occasionally these calls were amusing. If someone from Pakistan wanted to help him with his back taxes, why not give him a chance?

"Hello."

"Is this Dr. Cesari?"

"Yes, it is. Who is this?"

"Is friend of Drusilla. We meet in office yesterday morning. You give phone number."

He remembered her very well. The beautiful and exotic if somewhat eccentric companion who did all the talking. He said, "I remember. What can I do for you...? I don't recall your name."

"I no give then but is Zenobia."

"Well, what can I do for you Zenobia? Is everything all right with Drusilla?"

"No, everything is no all right. She very sick. Stomach hurt."

Cesari glanced at the wall clock in his kitchen. "Can you put her on the phone so I can speak to her?"

"She won't come out of bathroom. Say she want to die."

"Is she vomiting or have a fever?"

"I don't know. All she say is call Doctor and tell him come here."

Cesari hesitated and then said, "That won't be possible, Zenobia. I don't make house calls and if she's that ill, she really should go to the nearest emergency room."

"She won't go, Doctor... She just won't."

"Why not?"

"I can't explain."

"I feel sorry for Drusilla, but I can't help her over the phone. We'll need to run tests on her and even if I made house calls, I wouldn't be able to do anything for her."

"Yes, but maybe you could convince her to go to emergency room."

Cesari contemplated that for a minute. It wasn't as unreasonable as it sounded although going to a woman's apartment at night was fraught with all sorts of ethical landmines and could leave him exposed to the ugliest of accusations. But ignoring a patient's request for aid was in direct violation of every oath he had ever taken and ran against his fiber.

He eventually conceded, "That might work. Where are you?"

"347 West 22nd Street in Chelsea. Is four-story brownstone."

"Okay, that's not too far. Which apartment?"

"She own building."

"She owns a brownstone in Chelsea?" Cesari asked, suddenly aware that he was dealing with exceedingly wealthy people. Not that it mattered but he didn't get that impression when he met them yesterday morning.

"Yes, now hurry."

Twenty minutes later, he was in a cab heading toward a swanky part of Chelsea. As he arrived, an urgent call from Harry caught his attention. Leandro's body had been discovered in a dumpster behind St. Matt's and Harry was jumping up and down over it.

"Hey, Cesari. We got a hot one down here. It's a really big guy with two holes in his neck like the Serb. I've already called Detective Tierney who's on the way. He told me to call you."

"I'm tied up with a patient right now, Harry. I'll break away as soon as I can, but I can't promise that it will be any time soon. Keep me posted though, all right?"

"Will do."

Harry hung up just as Cesari reached the brownstone situated in the middle of a tree-lined serene street with expensive cars parked on either side. Their shiny colors glistened under the bright streetlamps. Flowers bloomed in small gardens and window boxes, and in the shadows of the early evening, were very charming.

He climbed the steps to the front door and rang the buzzer. After almost a minute, he heard a shuffling of feet and the unlocking of the door. Zenobia peeked out and then opened the door fully, allowing him entry. She was still wearing dark sunglasses and Cesari was tempted to ask her if she had some type of eye condition. Notwithstanding her odd appearance, she was just as gorgeous as yesterday morning when they met in his office. She wore dress slacks, and matching low-heeled shoes, a silk top, and lots of bling. One would have thought she was about to go out somewhere. He stepped in and admired the home. It was filled with fine woodwork, vases, Persian carpets, plush chairs, and a baby grand piano in the living room.

She said, "Is thank you for coming, Doctor."

"You're welcome."

"May I get you something to drink?"

"Thank you but we should get down to business. May I see Drusilla?"

"Of course. Drusilla is in bedroom on second floor lying down. Follow me."

Cesari followed her up the stairs to the bedroom. Drusilla was lying under the covers on one side of a massive king-sized, four-poster bed with a canopy. Though the bed was enormous in its own right, it was dwarfed in comparison to the size of the room which was easily forty feet by forty feet, complete with its own sofa, two large armoires, a fireplace and chandelier. Cesari had never seen a bedroom that big except in documentaries about European royalty.

On the night table next to Drusilla was a glass of water, a lamp, a bottle of aspirin and a glass ashtray. Cesari tried hard but couldn't smell tobacco. Drusilla was still wearing a veil to cover her face and had the sheets pulled up to her neck. She studied him carefully as he approached her.

He said, "Hi, Drusilla."

"Thank you for come, Doctor."

Her voice was raspy and an even deeper pitch than he remembered. He said, "You're welcome. I'm sorry you're not feeling well… So tell me what's going on."

Her eyes darted to Zenobia who stepped forward. Apparently, they were going to have a replay of the office visit. Cesari turned to Zenobia as she spoke, "The stomach pain much worse today and she has no appetite."

He tried hard to not lose his patience with them and said, "I don't mean to be rude Zenobia, but I really would like to hear it directly from Drusilla."

She nodded. "I understand, Doctor, but Drusilla has requested that I speak to you for her. She is not comfortable talking to strange man. She was raised in convent in Romania and never even see man most of her life."

Cesari sighed, looked at Drusilla and said compassionately, "I'm really not a bad guy, Drusilla. I promise not to hurt you."

She shook her head no and with a fat finger pointed at Zenobia, whispering, "Please talk Zenobia."

He said, "Zenobia, this is highly irregular. I shouldn't even be here. The least she could do is cooperate."

"Please try understand, Doctor."

He was trying very hard but didn't. He took a deep breath and said, "Fine…Do you mind if I sit?"

Zenobia pulled a seventeenth century style gold-painted, red velvet cushioned chair next to him. He sat on that and she sat next to Drusilla on the bed.

He said sternly, "Look, we need to stop playing games. You want to speak for her then fine, but I need to ask some hard questions that she may not like. I took it easy on her in the office yesterday but if she's as sick as you led me to believe then I need straight answers."

"Yes, of course. I know Drusilla as well as I know myself."

"Is she sexually active?"

"No, absolutely not. Is save herself for wedding night like good Romanian girl."

"Great… Well I don't mean to be skeptical, but did you do the pregnancy test like I requested yesterday?"

She hesitated and then said, "Yes, it was negative."

She was clearly lying but he let it go. "Okay, fine… Drusilla, have you been passing any blood or vomiting?"

Zenobia said, "No, I ask before you come."

"Where is the pain exactly, Drusilla?"

"She told me pain is in lower part of stomach on left side. It come and go like cramp."

"Any problems with her bowels?"

"Is irregular when she get cramps and then better."

He turned to Drusilla. "Is the pain there now?"

Drusilla glanced at Zenobia who said, "Yes, not as bad as before when call but still there."

"Drusilla, I need to examine you."

Drusilla shook her head vigorously and said, "No man touch Drusilla."

"But this could be serious. You may need antibiotics or a CT scan or even possibly surgery.

She clutched the sheet around her tightly and repeated even more emphatically, "No man touch Drusilla."

Cesari looked at Zenobia who said something to Drusilla in Romanian. Drusilla shook her head defiantly in response and Zenobia sighed, "Doctor, she will not let you touch her, but I have idea. Perhaps you should examine me while she watch and she will say when hurt or don't hurt. Would that be okay, Drusilla?"

Drusilla nodded her head. "Yes, is good idea."

Cesari almost exploded. "That is the most ridiculous thing I have ever heard. I can't agree to something like that."

Zenobia implored him, "Doctor, I know Drusilla long time. She will do no other way."

"But you don't understand Zenobia. I can't touch you. You're not the patient. I could get in trouble."

"In trouble? With who?"

"With everyone."

"But what if she is sick and needs surgery, Doctor? We must do as she say."

"And what if she does need surgery? Will she let a man touch her then?"

"If she need surgery then we find woman surgeon. There are woman surgeons in America, no?"

Cesari let out a deep breath. "Yes, there are… Fine, but this is insane."

"Is only way," she repeated.

"And just how are we going to do this?"

"I lay on other side of bed and you examine me. Drusilla watch."

Zenobia stood, moved to the other side of the bed and laid down. Cesari followed her passing a window overlooking the back yard of the building. There was a fire escape and he thought about leaving before things got any further out of hand. But he didn't and watched Zenobia adjust herself as Drusilla rolled toward them.

Zenobia looked up at him and said, "And please, Doctor, tell truth. We want to know what you really think."

"I think I'm going to lose my license. That's what I think."

Chapter 19

Half past midnight, the Romanescu brothers pulled the white panel catering van into the back of St. Matt's for the second time that night. Hours earlier and before anyone else had arrived, they had clandestinely dropped off their secret cargo and then retreated to safety. As they came to stop, they spotted Shlomo's Mercedes and a six-wheeled box truck which had preceded them by less than a minute. Shlomo waited for them to exit the van so they could enter the basement of the hospital together in a show of strength. Once inside, Feinberg and Acevedo greeted them in the receiving area with flashlights blazing. Several other large men stood at the ready. There was a lot of work to do and very little time to do it. Shlomo shook hands with Tiberius. Everyone else glanced suspiciously at each other. There were no friends here, only mutual interests and mutually assured destruction should they be discovered.

Tiberius showed Shlomo and his men to the crates and cartons that had been delivered for purposes other than hospital renovations. They were examined and counted carefully by Shlomo who nodded his approval and one by one they were carted away to the box truck idling outside.

As the men toiled in silence, Tiberius came across one last crate and said, "I assumed this one belongs to you, Shlomo. The writing is in Romanian, but it's not like any of the others and it's definitely not medical related. It's not on any of the invoices."

Shlomo said, "Yorgi, my eyes are not what they used to be. What is in this box?"

Yorgi dutifully stepped forward to study the odd-looking wood crate from all angles with his flashlight while the others looked on. Growing impatient, Shlomo said, "Yorgi, what is it?"

Yorgi read the inscription on the top. "I don't know, but it comes from Cluj according the markings."

"Cluj? You mean Transylvania? We don't have business there. We ship from Bucharest, Prague, Moscow and sometimes Warsaw but never Cluj. And what kind of box is this? I have never seen anything like this before."

"I agree, Shlomo. Is strange." He turned to Feinberg and Acevedo. "Are you sure there isn't any paperwork with this one?"

Tiberius replied, "I gave you all the paperwork I had. This one doesn't have any."

Yorgi said with irritation in his voice, "So it just appeared here out of nowhere?"

Acevedo and Feinberg started to grow uncomfortable. One of them hemmed and the other hawed. Shlomo said, "Enough. Yorgi, find some tools and open the crate. We will see what is inside for ourselves."

Yorgi searched and eventually found a crowbar left lying around by one of the daytime construction workers. He inserted one end under the lid and gently worked his way around the perimeter of the box prying the top loose. When he was finished, he lifted the cover off as Shlomo stepped in close with his flashlight.

Inside the crate was soil. Nothing but ordinary gardening soil all the way to the top.

"What means this, Yorgi?" asked Shlomo completely baffled.

Yorgi shrugged and said, "Is mystery."

Tiberius and Feinberg hung back like dutiful vassals, watching and waiting for some cue. Shlomo turned to them and asked, "Is this joke?"

Acevedo's voice quivered and cracked, "Of course not. I have no idea what's going on, Shlomo. I swear to you."

Yorgi leaned into the box with his hand and said, "Wait, Shlomo. There is something in here."

Shlomo, Feinberg, and Acevedo all crowded in as close as they could to peer into the box. Four flashlights pointed in one direction as Yorgi swept away dirt from one end, eventually revealing the visage of Sofia. Even in death, she was a stunning beauty, her red hair sweeping down to her shoulders. Everyone jumped back in shock and then held their breath waiting for the other shoe to drop. They didn't have to wait long.

Yorgi moved quickly and with a sleight of hand worthy of any Las Vegas card sharp, he swept his light across the crate as a distraction and then whispered in alarm, "Look!"

With that he reached into the box and lifted Sofia's upper lip for all to see. Shlomo and the others gasped in horror. Her two incisors were nearly a half inch longer than her other teeth and had been filed to razor-sharp points.

Shlomo staggered back a step but quickly recovered. "Close the crate, Yorgi. Quickly… No, wait. Give me the crowbar," he ordered, becoming increasingly agitated.

Yorgi handed him the crowbar not sure of what was about to happen. Shlomo grabbed it and pushed everyone to the side. Tiberius and Feinberg were too frightened to speak as they watched helplessly. Shlomo then wiped off the earth covering Sofia's chest, and ripped open her garments revealing her bare skin. He placed the tip of the crowbar's straight side in approximation to where her heart was and with a mighty heave plunged it through her skin and through her chest wall as far as it would go. Her collapsing lungs hissed out residual gasses giving those watching the impression she had just now breathed her last.

Acevedo grew faint at the sight and had to be propped up by Feinberg who was turning green himself. Yorgi's eyes went wide but he said nothing. Shlomo turned to the bewildered and now terrified group, saying, "Yorgi, close box and seal it with as many nails as you can find. You must burn the corpse tonight. It is of the utmost imperative that there is no delay."

"My brothers and I will do as you say, Shlomo, though I do not understand the significance of all this."

"It means, Yorgi, that my sins have finally caught up with me. Hurry, get your brothers and take her in your van to the incinerator in Newark. Waste no time."

"I do now."

He left Shlomo to find his brothers for their new task. Tiberius and Feinberg stood there slack-jawed and shaking as Shlomo approached them. He was sweating profusely and breathing hard. His eyes glowed with fear and passion. "You will never speak of this…to anyone or I will cut out your livers and eat them with onions. Do you understand?"

Acevedo managed a nod.

Urine ran down Feinberg's leg onto the cement floor.

A minute later, Yorgi returned with his brothers, hoisted Sofia's coffin and carried it out to the waiting van. As they sped away, they saw the lights from Shlomo's Mercedes come on in the distance.

Safely away from the hospital, they began to breathe easy again. Yorgi said, "Brothers, I am sorry you had to remain outside and miss scene with Shlomo. Old man fell for it, hook, line and sinker. He truly believe Sofia is *vampir*. He even stab body with crowbar like in some old movie. If I hadn't witnessed with my own eyes, I never would have believed it."

Tibor asked incredulously, "He stab corpse with crowbar?"

"Right through the heart, Tibor. Was most horrible sight."

Ivan said, "Is incredible."

"Yes, Ivan, plan work even better than we could have hoped. In wildest dreams, I didn't expect Shlomo to react like that, and the other two nearly start crying like little girls. I tell you, brothers. I never thought I live to see such things."

"Is amazing thing that Shlomo really believes in tales and legends. How could a man like this have come so far in life?" asked Ivan.

"Is not for me to understand such things but I am glad it is so. I had feeling about this. Whenever Shlomo drink too much his inner demons are revealed. He has told me many times that ever since childhood he has feared *vampirs* and things of the night. Still, it would be wise for us not to gloat too much. The seed has been planted and is good. Now our job is to nurture and cultivate that seed until it blossoms into full blown insanity."

"What we do with Sofia, Yorgi?" Ivan asked.

"Shlomo told me to burn body in trash incinerator in New Jersey but I think we might be able to put to good use with the Italians. For now let us store body in spare freezer in basement of restaurant. Keep fresh and thaw out when we need."

"Speaking of the Italians, Yorgi. What is next step?"

"Patience, brother. Let today's events percolate in their little minds. We have given them plenty to think about. You have car ready?"

"Yes, a black Toyota Camry. I have friend in charge of valet parking at Marriott Midtown. He gave me keys to one of guest's cars."

"Gave you or sold to you?"

"Sold for five thousand dollars. He will blame theft on one of his employees."

"Good and you will pay someone to leave car in front of Kit Kat Klub. Do not drive it there yourself. They will be watching. Even better, pay teenager, someone unknown to us to drive car there and leave doors unlocked with keys on seat... And pay him well so he doesn't steal stolen car from us."

"Is it wise to just leave keys on front seat, Yorgi? What if they actually pay the money? Then anyone could grab the car."

"I doubt they will pay, but if car is still there in morning, we will have someone retrieve it for us. My intention was only to let them know that we are confident of victory. Americans like brashness. Arrogance is almost in the DNA of these people. Besides, purpose of note was two-fold. I am sure they are actively trying to figure out who Shlomo is that sign note. Eventually, we will make introduction... Now tell me what you have learned about that doctor who is Gianelli's friend."

"He is gastroenterologist at St. Matt's and apparently in good standing there. Feinberg and Tiberius tell me that he is much liked and respected by the staff. And as I told you already, he is friends with that Vito. What the connection is there, I don't know."

"Why was he down in the basement of the hospital observing the trucks unload?"

"I can't be sure, but I think he was simply curious. The construction has already disrupted almost every aspect of hospital life."

"Yes, that was the idea...Well I guess that makes sense. Still, I don't like that he keeps popping up in the most unusual places in the company of the most unlikely people such as the detective investigating the case and now Vito at the Kit Kat Klub."

Ivan said, "He has a gun."

"What do you mean?" Yorgi asked.

"Feinberg went to his apartment on business. The doctor thought he was an intruder and confronted him with a pistol. Feinberg said that from his demeanor he had no doubt he would be able to use it if necessary. Apparently, he has had some trouble with the law in the past as well."

"Seriously?"

"Yes, Yorgi. Is true. It may be how he knows Vito who is well known to police also."

"Hmm, this is clearly no ordinary doctor."

"What are you thinking, Yogi," asked Tibor.

"I'm thinking that maybe our doctor likes to stick his nose into too many things that do not concern him. Perhaps it is time for him to start having more trouble with the law."

"Our friend, Feinberg, would agree with that assessment."

"What did he say?"

"He believes Cesari is trouble-maker and we would be better off to take care of him sooner rather than later."

"So why didn't he just fire him?"

"He would like to but is reluctant because he is concerned that Cesari's popularity in hospital could cause unrest among the other staff. They are working on plan to discredit him in the eyes of the employees and then terminate him, but I got the distinct impression he would like us to deal with him. It would save them time and effort."

"What kind of plan are they working on?"

"He says they are going to promote him, a purely symbolic gesture as the position will have no real authority, but one which they can lay blame on him for any unpleasant actions they take against the staff. It is good plan but necessarily will take time."

"Hmm, I need to think more on this... So, Tibor, how goes it with the lovely Drusilla? Have you satisfied her thirst for more intimate knowledge of you?"

"Fortunately, that has not been a concern for last few days. She has been having stomach problems."

"What is wrong?"

"I don't know. She go see doctor yesterday."

"On Saturday? I didn't know doctors see patients on Saturdays."

"This is America. Their greed, like everyone else's, knows no bounds."

"When will you see her again?"

"Maybe tomorrow night if she is feeling better. We were supposed to pick out china patterns for wedding registry."

Yorgi smiled and glanced at Ivan. "How exciting, Tibor."

Ivan chuckled and added, "I will buy you and Drusilla vacuum cleaner for gift. There is nothing like a clean house to raise children."

Tibor said, "Shut up, Ivan."

Chapter 20

Cesari yawned loudly. It was way past his bedtime, but he was wound up and confused. When he had examined Zenobia as a proxy for Drusilla, he had found Zenobia to be markedly tender in the left lower quadrant, and was very concerned that she, not Drusilla, may have diverticulitis or some other serious infection or process. After much debate, he insisted that she go to the St. Matt's emergency room, but she flatly refused unless he accompanied her. So here they were. Drusilla balked at the idea of getting out of bed and stayed home. Cesari was now waiting for Zenobia to return from her CT scan. Laura Anzilotti was the surgeon on call and had already seen her in consultation. Zenobia's bloodwork was normal, and she didn't have a fever, which was good.

Cesari stood at the nursing station chatting with Laura while they waited for Zenobia. They drank bad ER coffee from small styrofoam cups. Laura was in her late thirties, her short hair prematurely graying from stress and a recent divorce. She wore blue surgical scrubs and a white lab coat with a stethoscope stuffed in one of the pockets. It was after midnight.

Laura said, "Where'd you find her, Cesari? She's a live one."

He smiled. "Noticed that did you?"

"I did and I also noticed how beautiful she is."

"Really? I hadn't picked up on that."

She grinned. "Am I supposed to believe that?"

"You can believe whatever you want."

"It's okay to acknowledge someone's beauty, Cesari. In her case it's almost ridiculous not to."

"Okay for you maybe, but in case you haven't been watching the news for the last few years, it's not okay for me, and I'm not one hundred percent sure it actually is okay for you either."

"Probably not, so sue me."

"I can't afford to be that cavalier."

"So what's her deal? The sunglasses make me wonder if she's incognito or something."

"I don't know, Laura. It crossed my mind that she may be photosensitive for some reason. Some medications can do that to you."

"Are you sure she's not hiding a black eye?"

"I don't think so. I've been pretty close to her. Even with the glasses I think I would have noticed something, but it's a good thought which I'll follow up on with her."

"How well do you know her?"

"Not well at all. I just met her for the first time yesterday when she came to the office with a friend. Both of them are kind of strange. I just assumed it was some sort of cultural thing. They're both from Romania."

"I guess I'll scratch Romania off my bucket list."

"Probably a good idea. Thanks for seeing her by the way. I know it's late. I hope I didn't overreact by bringing her here, but I was concerned about her reliability."

"No problem, Cesari, and you did the right thing. I doubt that she'll have anything significant but hopefully the CT will help us sort it out. Trouble is, I don't know how far we can go without health insurance or some sort of identification for record keeping purposes. I mean she must have a passport somewhere or something with her last name on it, right?"

"I agree this is unusual, but can't we just treat her like we would any indigent or homeless person that walked through the door? Think about it. We collect people off the streets all the time without any ID."

She thought about that and then said, "I guess we could do that. We're not just going to let her die if she has a surgical problem but what about appropriate follow up and notifying family?"

"I'll take care of follow-up and she assures me she's all by herself here except for the friend I mentioned, who for some reason didn't want to get out of bed tonight."

Laura laughed. "Seriously? Her only friend wouldn't get out of bed?"

"Try to understand, Laura. Zenobia might seem a little weird, but compared to her friend, she's the normal one."

She shook her head. "Sounds like you have your hands full, Cesari."

"I've only known them a day and a half and I feel like we should all be in group counseling."

"You certainly lead a colorful life. Did you really bring her here in an Uber?"

"That I did and we're leaving that way too."

"Is that wise?"

"I'm already in up to my eyeballs, Laura. If she wants to make a false accusation against me, she's already got me by the short hairs. I might as well do the right thing and make sure she gets home okay."

"I guess," she said skeptically.

"So how's the family?"

"The twins just finished kindergarten. Thanks for asking. We're all fine. No romantic prospects on the horizon for me yet, but that's good. I'm still shell-shocked from the divorce."

"I'm sorry, Laura."

"Probably not as much as I am. I find myself lying awake at night trying to decide who I would like to see die more, him or that trollop he left me for." She paused, thinking about it for a moment and added, "Him, I guess."

Cesari cleared his throat uncomfortably. "That's understandable."

"Is it?"

"Absolutely."

"If they were both found murdered, could I use you as an alibi."

He chuckled, "Of course."

"Thanks."

"I don't mean to change the subject, but I hope the new CEO isn't dampening your outlook like he is the rest of us."

"So far, he hasn't come knocking on my door, but if he does piss me off, I'll just mosey on over to St. Luke's or Columbia. I'm not worried. I'm at the peak of my powers. Somebody will take this wench in… Look, they're bringing Zenobia back to her room. I'll go check on the CT scan and meet you in a few minutes."

Cesari entered bay 9 as Zenobia's nurse, Annie, was adjusting her IV. He smiled at Zenobia. She looked tired but smiled back. "How'd it go over there?" he asked.

"Was no problem. Doctor say all look normal," she replied.

"You met a radiologist?"

Annie shook her head. "She means the technician. I hope you feel better, Zenobia. If there's anything you need just come and get me, Dr. Cesari. I have to tend to other patients now."

"I will, Annie," Cesari said and she walked away. He then turned to Zenobia. "Are you feeling any better since they gave you the pain medication?"

"Much better but make sleepy."

"That's to be expected. The surgeon is reviewing the CT scan. She'll be back soon to let us know what she thinks."

"I am worried. I can't stay here."

"Zenobia, I want to help you and Drusilla but you're making it difficult. What's going on?"

She was quiet for a while and drew in a long breath before speaking. "I know you want to help but I cannot tell you. I am sorry. Please to understand. Some things are too important."

He nodded. "I'll try to understand but there are limits to what I can do for you and Drusilla...legal limits."

"I understand."

Just then, Laura entered the room. "I have good news, Zenobia, and maybe not so good news. The good news is that it's not your appendix, so you don't need surgery. You also do not have diverticulitis, colitis, kidney stones, bowel obstruction, ovarian cysts or a urinary tract infection. And just for the record, you're not pregnant."

Zenobia looked puzzled. "Then what is?"

"Your colon and other organs are entirely normal without any evidence for an infection or tumor," Laura added and sat down next to Zenobia on the stretcher looking at her sympathetically.

She asked "Zenobia, have you been under stress lately?"

With some reluctance she admitted, "Yes..."

"A lot of stress?"

"Yes..."

Laura looked up at Cesari who saw where she was going. Laura went on, "Well, there is a condition called irritable bowel syndrome which can cause a great deal of abdominal pain. Dr. Cesari here is more of an expert on that than I am but I can tell you that stress and poor diet can contribute greatly to symptoms such as yours. Eventually, you should undergo a colonoscopy just to make sure everything is okay. For tonight, however, I'm going to discharge you to home. Dr. Cesari will decide moving forward what the next best step ought to be in your care."

Zenobia nodded. "Thank you, Doctor."

"I'll tell your nurse to take the IV out. Cesari...always a pleasure. Stay in touch."

"Thanks for your help, Laura."

It didn't take long for the nurses to discharge Zenobia and while they did, Cesari called an Uber. He saw missed calls from Harry and Detective Tierney, glanced at his watch and resolved to call them back in the morning. By 1:30 a.m. the Uber pulled up to the curb in front of Drusilla's brownstone where Zenobia was staying. He advised her to lay low, drink plenty of fluids and rest. He promised to reach out to her sometime later that day to see how she and Drusilla were doing. He remained in the car and watched her safely enter the building before telling the driver to take him home. As the car resumed its journey, his phone rang. It was Vito.

"Cesari?"

"Don't you sleep, Vito?"

"Where are you?"

"Home in bed."

"I don't believe you. I hear traffic."

"Fine, I'm not home in bed. What do you want?"

"Something fishy's going down over here on the east side at that Ukrainian restaurant you've been telling me about."

"Like what and why are you over there?"

"Sofia never answered her phone today, so I sent some guys over to her apartment to check on her."

"And…?"

"She didn't answer when they knocked so they let themselves in."

"And…?"

"She wasn't there but it looked like there might have been a scuffle, overturned furniture, a broken lamp, that kind of stuff. Her bag with her cellphone were lying on the floor. Nothing major but not quite right if you know what I mean."

"Yeah, I see, but what does that have to do with the restaurant."

"She lives in the apartment building over the restaurant."

"Really? That place is a dump. I was there with Tierney. That's where the Serbian guy lived."

"Yeah, it's a dump but that's not what's interesting."

"I'm listening."

"I decided to stake out the building to see if any suspicious characters showed up with Sofia in tow. She's a dancer but she's been known to turn tricks once in a while. I thought maybe things might have gotten a little out of hand with one of her clients. So my boys were sitting in their car quietly in the shadows of an alley across the street from the restaurant when a white panel van pulls up to the front door and three guys get out. They dicked around for a bit as if they weren't quite sure what to do or how to do it. I was over at the Kit Kat when my guys called me, so I was able to get here in a hurry."

"Why were you at the Kit Kat?"

"Me and a couple of the boys were holding down the fort in case somebody was planning any further actions."

"Fair enough. So what happened?"

"First of all, one of the guys was that Ivan character. The other two I didn't recognize, but from your description, I think one of them might have been Yorgi. He was big, ugly as sin and bald like the eagle. They dragged a large wood crate out from the back of the van and carried it down the side alley. There's probably another entrance there for supplies and stuff."

"A crate?"

"More like a coffin."

"I'll be right over."

Chapter 21

Cesari had the Uber driver drop him off a block away from the restaurant. From there he clung to the shadows of old buildings as he crept toward the alley where Vito and his men were waiting. He spotted the white catering van across the street but didn't see anyone in it or lingering nearby. He found Vito in the back seat of a Cadillac with two of his men up front. The car was parked recessed in the alley facing First Avenue and the Ukrainian restaurant off to the right. Their vantage point was good and with no streetlight near them it was unlikely they would be noticed.

"Got your attention, huh?" Vito asked.

"Yes, you did. So what exactly did you see?"

"It was big wood box, maybe six feet long, narrow, not more than a couple of feet wide and high."

"I'm guessing it's not a supply of pierogis for the restaurant."

"At 2:00 a.m.? Probably not."

"So what is it?"

"I don't know, but I don't like the vibe I'm getting from this restaurant and these guys. Leandro's dead and Sofia's missing. She was arguing with Ivan about something right before she disappeared and he's friends with Yorgi who runs this restaurant and now this. I don't think I'm stepping out on a limb by assuming they're all Eastern Europeans. See where I'm going with all this Cesari?"

"That I do. You think these guys are the Romanians who've been trying to muscle you. I agree, so what do you propose?"

"That's the million-dollar question. I'd love to go in there and interrogate them, although my experience with these iron-curtain types is that they can usually take a punch, and don't rattle easily. So barging in there may not serve any purpose."

"Plus, it really may be a box full of pierogis."

"That would be very embarrassing all around."

"And if it was really nothing more than a late-night delivery of restaurant supplies and we charged in there like a S.W.A.T. team high on amphetamine my employment would probably be terminated by morning light. Yorgi knows me and will tell his boss Markov who's got a lot of pull at the hospital these days. I doubt he would take kindly to an intrusion of this kind."

"And Markov's first name is Shlomo if I recall correctly," Vito mused accusingly.

"I think you're grasping at straws with that one, Vito. The guy's a self-made multimillionaire who just donated a small fortune to St. Matt's out of the goodness of his heart. I doubt he would stoop to extorting you for a hundred thousand dollars and the rights to a strip club on Second Avenue and then sign his name on the extortion letter. More than likely, the name was pulled out of thin air or…?"

"Or what?"

"Someone's making a very clumsy attempt to implicate Markov and set you two at odds."

Vito thought about that and said, "Maybe you're right, but there's a lot of circumstantial evidence floating around."

"Not enough to risk what you're contemplating."

"If you're too soft for this kind of work, Cesari, you don't have to come with us."

"That's good because I have no intention of roughing up a bunch of guys simply because they were carrying an odd-looking box into a restaurant, but may I offer an alternative course of action?"

"I'm listening."

"How about this? Instead of breaking in there and smacking them around for possibly no good reason, why don't we wait for them to leave and then sniff around on our own? This way if that box was nothing but restaurant supplies, we're none the worse for the effort and nobody has to be hospitalized."

He nodded. "I am curious about the box but I'm just as curious about who this guy Ivan is and what he was arguing about with Sofia."

"Agreed, but if we knew what was in the box, we'd have that much more leverage. For instance, if the box is filled with heroin then we could smack them all around as much as we want."

"I guess that makes sense, but suppose we find something illegal in the box and then we never see Ivan again?"

"C'mon, what are the odds of that? He obviously has some connection with Yorgi and the restaurant."

Vito furrowed his brow as he mulled it over. "Fine, but it's already two in the morning. How much longer are we supposed to wait?"

"Do you have a date or something?"

"All right, we wait."

They waited… and waited. After an hour had passed, Vito yawned. "What the hell are they doing in there?"

Cesari's eyes were closed as he spoke. "I don't know."

Vito glanced at his watch. "We have to make a decision quick because I don't plan on sitting here until dawn."

"Agreed. If they're not out by four, we should call it a night and go home."

"Cesari, you don't know me as well as you think. If they're not out by three-thirty, we're going in."

Cesari was too tired to argue. "Fine."

Three-thirty came, and Vito said, "Gaetano, you come with me and Dr. Cesari. Sammy, stay in the car with the engine running and be ready to come get us in a hurry."

"Got it boss," replied Sammy.

"Okay, let's go," Vito added. "Sammy, pop the trunk."

The three men got out and went around to the back of the car where Vito pulled a crowbar from the trunk. Then they looked both ways down the quiet street. The lights of an occasional vehicle could be seen but the neighborhood was otherwise dark and deserted as they hurried across First Avenue to the entrance of the restaurant. Upon arrival, they studied the glass door and tested the handle. It was locked, but was nothing fancy or complicated, just a deadbolt mechanism. They scanned the rest of the windowed facade facing the street searching for weaknesses and security cameras. They found none, but the glass was reinforced like a car windshield and would take a significant beating before surrendering. Like the men inside probably, Cesari sensed.

"You don't want to try the side entrance in the alley?" Cesari asked.

"No, that's where they went in and will probably come out. I'd rather not walk headfirst into them. Gaetano, give the lock a try with the crowbar."

Vito handed him the instrument and stood back as the three-hundred-pound behemoth wedged the crowbar into the space between the door lock and the jamb. He started out slow and gradually built up a head of steam, grunting and sweating with each pull. The door was made of steel, but the jamb was old like everything else in this neighborhood and eventually the wood gave and splintered under his weight. Pleased, Gaetano stood to the side panting as Vito and Cesari entered the dark restaurant.

"Stand guard out here, Gaetano. Cesari, are you armed?"

"No."

"Gaetano, give Dr. Cesari your backup piece."

Cesari said, "Thanks, but no thanks. I'll be fine."

"At least take the crowbar, Cesari...just in case."

"Fine."

Gaetano handed Cesari the crowbar as Vito fished a small flashlight from his pocket. With his other hand, Vito pulled out a .45 caliber Colt with a ten-round magazine from a shoulder holster hidden beneath the expensive suit jacket he wore night and day. The restaurant's dining room was a hybrid between a delicatessen and a classic diner. There were rows of leather booths and small cheap tables with paper tablecloths. Behind that was a countertop with swivel stools that could seat twelve customers. Adjacent to this was a long glass refrigerated deli counter for takeout. It was a fairly sizeable place and Cesari estimated that it could easily seat over a hundred people at a time.

There was no sign of any activity. The place was quiet and dark except for Vito's flashlight darting back and forth as they explored. In the rear of the restaurant they made their way around to the back of the counter and into the kitchen. The tiled floor and steel tables and sinks gave off a decidedly industrial feel but once again, they found nothing unusual.

There were two doors at the far end of the kitchen. One lead to the back alley with garbage cans and a large dumpster. The other opened to a wood staircase leading downward. There were no lights on in any direction to give them a hint, but as Vito scanned the room with the flashlight, he noticed something on the floor.

"Cesari, look at this."

Cesari studied the tiles and crouched to get a better look. "It's dirt."

In stark contrast to the rest of the pristine kitchen, there were splashes of fresh soil by both the door leading to the alley, the door leading to the basement, and the floor in between.

"What's it mean?" Vito asked.

"I don't know. Maybe they were walking in a garden or field before they came here."

"We're in the middle of Manhattan, Cesari."

"I'm just thinking out loud, Vito."

"Well don't think too loudly, they may still be around."

While Vito explored the rest of the kitchen, Cesari stepped into the alley. Using his phone as a light, he tried to see if there was some explanation for the soiled floor. It was dark and his phone light wasn't nearly up to the task, but he didn't see anything obvious. He went back to Vito who was studying the jamb of the basement door.

"What are you looking at?" he asked.

Vito said, "Look at the jamb. It's all scuffed and the paint has just been recently scraped off in places."

Cesari nodded in agreement. "They must have brought the box down the stairs and had a hard time fitting it through the door."

"That's what I think. So maybe they brought the box downstairs and maybe the floor down there is dirty and then they came back up, messing up the floor here. Then they left. That would explain the dirt on the floor but why didn't we see them leave?"

"Unless they're still sitting downstairs in the dark."

"Possibly, but not likely. What would three big guys like them have to be afraid of?"

"Fine, the van out front is a delivery van for the restaurant. Maybe they had their personal vehicle parked in the alley?"

"Wouldn't we have seen them drive away?" Vito asked.

"Not necessarily. In some of these older neighborhoods, the alleys zig zag and can extend all the way to the other side. So instead of coming out on First Avenue, they might have wound up on Avenue A."

"I guess that's possible."

"I was just in the alley, but it was too dark to tell where it led. Let's go downstairs and see what's so important about this box that three guys would stay up half the night for."

"Maybe it's full of gold, Cesari, and you and I would never have to work another day in our lives."

"That would be nice."

Chapter 22

The staircase down was narrow, old and noisy, creaking loudly under their feet no matter how cautiously they proceeded, but they forged on with Vito in the lead, his flashlight illuminating the way. At the bottom, they were convinced they were all alone and flipped on the overhead lights, which were a series of fluorescent bulbs extending the length of the large room.

The basement housed mostly supplies for the restaurant, an oversized refrigerator and chest freezer, stacks of paper products, more sinks, a dishwasher, wine racks and a cache of folding chairs. Again, they saw clumps of soil here and there, both on the steps and on the cement floor.

"What's with the dirt, Cesari? It didn't come from down here. It's a concrete floor and it's mostly pretty clean."

"They must have brought it in from outside."

"And where's the box?"

"Good question."

There was a rectangular four-foot by six-foot-long sturdy folding table in the center of the room with large plastic storage containers lined up on top. Inspection of these revealed a collection of frozen meats such as bacon, chicken thighs and breasts, pork loins, and multiple plastic bags filled with frozen pierogis.

Vito commented, "There's enough food here to feed a small army."

"Yeah, but why's it on the table like this? It'll defrost and go bad."

They both simultaneously glanced over at the chest-style freezer against the wall and walked over to it. At the base of the freezer, was an usually large amount of the soil they had been seeing. A combination lock hooked through a latch on the outside prevented them from opening it. On the lid was a piece of paper telling the employees to not try to open the freezer because of some electrical malfunction which could lead to a shock. It was signed, Yorgi.

Vito glanced at Cesari asking, "What do you think?"

"I'll tell you what I don't think. I'm pretty sure there's no electrical problem here because the freezer's still plugged in."

"It kind of begs the question of what they're hiding?"

"Yes, it does and I'm trying to come up with at least one good reason for all this activity that makes any sense. I mean, what could possibly need to be frozen at two in the morning that couldn't wait until the next day?"

"Should we break it open and see?"

"The only problem there is that then they'll know somebody was down here snooping around and we'll have lost the element of surprise."

They thought it over for a minute and then Cesari said, "Well, they might know somebody was down here but they won't know who, and of course they'll have to be a little concerned that maybe one of the employees broke into it."

Vito nodded slowly and then glanced at his watch. "We're running out of time, Cesari. Just do it."

"Give me your pistol. Is there a round in the chamber?"

"Of course."

"Take it out so we don't have an accident."

After the gun was secured, Cesari placed the tip of the crowbar onto the lock and then using the butt of the gun as a hammer gave the other end of the crowbar three successive and increasingly forceful blows. On the third attempt the lock snapped open. When they lifted the lid to the freezer, Cesari let out a deep breath and Vito muttered a curse.

Vito was the first to speak as they gazed at the corpse of Sofia stuffed in the freezer at an awkward angle with dirt splattered over most of her clothes, face and hair. "Damn! She was a nice kid. What could she have possibly done to these guys to deserve this?"

"Look at her teeth, Vito."

Death and the cold temperature had caused her upper lip to retract back revealing her recent appalling dental work. Vito whispered, "Jesus, what the hell is that?"

"I don't know but we should probably get out of here. It's after four already."

"What are we going to do with Sofia?"

"You don't want to leave her?"

"No, I don't. She deserves better than this."

Cesari thought about it. "I guess it doesn't matter now who broke into the freezer from their point of view. But if we try to lay the blame on one of the employees, they might be the next ones sleeping in there."

"What's your point, Cesari?"

"My point is that unless we take credit for this, there may be a lot of dead restaurant workers taking the brunt of Yorgi's anger."

"So we let them know it was us. That's fine with me. These guys probably killed Leandro too unless you think she did it with those teeth...You don't think...?"

Cesari raised his hand before he could go any further. "Stop it. I don't believe in fairy tales and neither do you. Call Sammy and Gaetano and have them bring the car into the alley and open the trunk. We'll carry her out that way."

After he made the call, they pulled Sofia's body out from the freezer. As they did so her top opened revealing a gaping hole in her chest.

Vito was disgusted. "What the hell did they do to her?"

Cesari shook his head. "I honestly don't know. Looks like she might have taken a shotgun slug. That's a big hole."

"Where's the blood?"

"That's a good point. No powder burns either. In fact, her clothes aren't even damaged." Cesari examined her blouse looking for tell-tale signs of damage but found none. He then rolled her over to see if there was an exit wound and also found none before adding, "It's almost as if they opened her blouse before shooting her. Why would they do that?"

Cesari and Vito glanced at each other. Both could see the other's temperature rising. Vito said flatly, "Somebody's going to have to pay for this, Cesari."

"I agree. I wonder if that was what the argument was about between her and Ivan. He might have known she was dating Leandro and coerced her into bringing him to them. They undoubtedly lied to her about what their intentions were. Maybe they told her they just wanted information about the Kit Kat or how things operated there. She was reluctant but agreed and then the trap sprung with her in it."

"Yeah, so they killed Leandro to send me a message, but why do this to her?"

"I don't know."

"And what's with all this Dracula bullshit?"

"Once again, I don't know. Let's get her out of here, Vito. I need time to think about this."

Sofia hadn't been in there long enough to completely freeze and was easily carried up the stairs by Vito while Cesari remained in the basement toying with ideas. The front door of the restaurant had been damaged so there was no way of disguising the fact that someone had broken in, but they hadn't seen any security cameras. Nonetheless, the break-in itself should absolve the employees from any guilt. So maybe there was another pathway here. Obviously, Yorgi and company were involved in something more complicated than a simple snatch and grab with Vito and the Kit Kat Klub, but was this related to the dead Serbian restaurant worker?

It had to be.

Think, Cesari, think. Turn the negative into a positive. These guys were playing head games for some reason and no one was the master of head games like you. He looked around for something to write with but didn't see anything, so he ran up the stairs to the dining room and found the cash register. He picked up a magic marker and pad that was lying there and ran back down the stairs.

He hurriedly put all the frozen foods back into the freezer and closed it. He wrote on a piece of paper; *Freezer is all fixed now. See you in hell, my darlings.* He signed it, *Sofia.*

Then he bounded back up the stairs to the back alley with the waiting caddie and Sofia in the trunk. Vito said, "Sammy, get us out of here. What were you doing down there, Cesari? I almost left without you."

"Just tidying up the place," replied Cesari as the car lurched forward into the narrow alley. "Wait, wait...Stop the car...Look, there's the box."

Hidden from view behind a large dumpster was the wood box Vito had seen earlier. The car came to a jolting halt and Cesari jumped out to inspect it. He saw the inscription in Romanian on the cover and when he opened it, saw the gardening soil inside.

Vito rolled down his window, "Cesari, C'mon. We need to get out of here. It'll be dawn soon and I don't want to be caught with a body in my trunk."

Cesari hopped back into the car even as it started moving again snaking its way down the alley all the way to Avenue A just as they suspected it would. Cesari thought it through and said, "They must have tried but couldn't fit the crate down the stairs, so they dumped it in the alley and carried the body down to the freezer. They must also have had a car in the alley waiting for them and figured on sending a cleanup crew in the morning."

Vito didn't say anything.

Cesari continued, "I left them a little surprise in the basement to confuse them. Unless they have some sort of secret security system we didn't notice, they won't know who it was."

"I thought we were going to take credit for it, so they don't blame the staff."

"They won't blame the staff. The front door being jimmied will make it clear there were intruders."

Vito didn't say anything.

Cesari persisted, "Did you hear what I said? There's no way of them knowing who snatched the body."

Vito turned to him. "Is that right?" he asked sarcastically.

"What's the matter? I thought you'd find that good news."

"Good news? Two of my people have been hit, Cesari. I don't really care who knows what right now."

"Easy there, big boy. I'm on your side, remember? I'm just saying that without them knowing what happened tonight it will be easier to take counter measures. Plus, we still don't know exactly what's going on or who's involved."

"Well I know Ivan and Yorgi are involved, and we'll find out soon enough who that third guy is."

"I understand you're angry. I'm angry too, but the smart move is restraint. It's always the foot soldiers who get killed while the general's sipping coffee and laughing."

"What are you trying to say? That I should sit on my ass and do nothing while they're picking off my people one at a time?"

"That's not what I'm saying at all. Stay alert but give me time to figure out what's going on. Yorgi and Ivan may simply be following orders and I hate to play devil's advocate, but we don't actually know for a fact they killed anybody."

Vito scoffed, "You've got to be kidding me, Cesari. When did you become counsel for the accused? And what do you mean stay alert? We have been on the alert and this still happened... She was only twenty-one, Cesari. Did you know that?"

Cesari shook his head. "No, I didn't, and I'm sorry."

Vito reached into his breast pocket and took out a pack of Camels, shook one out and lit it up. He blew a puff out the window. "I'm pissed off, Cesari. When I get like this, something's got to give. You know what I mean?"

"I do know what you mean, but if you react now, the game's up and we may never know who's really behind this or what the endgame really is."

"Your assuming it's not just a couple of Romanian punks making a power play on me."

"Let's think about this. The dead Serbian has nothing to do with you or the Kit Kat, right? And, except for the method of death, Leandro has nothing to do with the dead Serbian."

"We don't know that. Leandro may have been into something we're not aware of, and he was dating Sofia. So he may have known these guys or vice versa just from coming to her apartment building. He may have even eaten in that restaurant. In fact, I would guess he probably did."

Cesari thought about that and said, "It's possible, but let's take a step back. Leandro and the Serbian guy were killed in such a way as to make it appear that maybe someone or something with fangs bit them in the neck, and then Sofia shows up with teeth filed down sharp. Someone's trying awfully hard to convince everyone that there are vampires prowling the streets of New York."

"Yeah, but we knew Sofia. We just saw her twenty-four hours ago and her teeth didn't look like that."

"Maybe the person or persons they're trying to convince never met her."

"Who on planet earth would fall for something like that?"

"There are a lot of superstitious and nutty people out there, Vito. Did you know that there are thousands of people who claim that they were abducted by aliens, had probes placed up their asses and then returned back to earth?"

Vito cracked a grin at that.

"And millions more who believe that one day a spaceship with a dead science fiction writer will come and cart them all off to heaven."

"No shit?"

Chapter 23

The next morning, Cesari was dragging. He'd been working on two hours sleep and it was catching up with him despite four cups of coffee and every nurse in the OR wanting to bicker about anything and everything. It was that kind of day. Normally, the frenzied pace of the operating room and cackling of the nurses would get his adrenaline flowing but not this time. He was just too tired. Thankfully, he could see the light at the end of the tunnel. He had already done seven colonoscopies and only had five left. There were two cancellations and the ten o'clock patient was a no-show causing a delay in between cases so he went to the doctor's lounge to close his eyes for a few minutes.

It was a small no frills kind of room with an old worn leather sofa, a couple of armchairs, a TV, bathroom and a coffee machine. He sat down in a plush leather chair and turned on some nonsensical daytime television show more for the white-noise effect than anything else. He wanted to doze a little but not necessarily go into a deep sleep. He texted his nurses where he was and then closed his eyes. A minute later he was out for the count.

An hour after that, his cellphone rang loudly, and he woke with a start thinking he was late for the next case. Feinberg sat opposite him in an armchair, his belly spilling out over his man-spread. His tie was too short, and the tip rested halfway down his protruding abdomen. His tight shirt splayed open between several buttons. He held his phone in one hand and a cup of coffee in the other. Cesari was confused and groggy as he looked down at his own phone. It was Feinberg calling him.

Feinberg grinned at him. "How's that for a wake-up call?"

"Jesus. I got to get going. I have cases to do," he said and started to rise even as he wondered why his nurses hadn't called him.

"Relax, Cesari. I reassigned your cases to Thompson. He wasn't that busy and could use the income. His stats haven't been all that stellar from what I've seen."

"You reassigned my cases? While I'm in the middle of my schedule?" Cesari asked nearly speechless at the unprecedented audacity of the move.

"The only thing you were in the middle of, Cesari, was counting sheep or virgins. You tell me. You were supposed to start your last case forty-five minutes ago. The nurses couldn't find you and I happened to be walking by. I saved your butt. I'm a hero. You should be thanking me for not firing you for dereliction of duty."

"Every nurse in the OR has my cellphone. How could they not find me?" he asked.

"I don't know. Maybe I told them not to bother. It could've been something along those lines. Now freshen up. Tiberius wants to see you."

Cesari stretched and yawned. "What about?"

"If he wanted me to tell you then he wouldn't need to see you, would he? Maybe you should try sleeping at night then you wouldn't be such a hot mess."

"Thanks for the tip."

They both rose and walked to the CEO's office on the main floor of the hospital, dodging construction crews and obstacles on the way. Cesari was a step behind the bigger man and watched him waddle, his long white lab coat flowing arrogantly from side to side. He knew that sooner or later things were going to come to a head between them, but for now, he would play along.

The office was recessed toward the back of the hospital and away from the main entrance. It had a private entrance and exit to the enclosed hospital parking lot in the rear of the hospital. Rumors were already circulating that Tiberius's construction plans included an expansion of his office space to include a sauna and massage room. It was good to be king, Cesari mused.

Whatever Cesari's imagination might have conjured up didn't even come close to reality when they entered his office. Construction was well under way and half the room was covered in drop cloths. Walls had been knocked down and framing had already sprung up. From the scope of it, the space would nearly be doubled in size when completed which would make it a palatial fifty by fifty feet square with plenty of room for almost any amenity.

But that's not what caught Cesari's breath. The little man sat in a leather chair behind his desk dwarfed by a hot blonde sitting on his lap. She was busting out of her blouse with forty-four double-D's and apparently wasn't afraid to use them. She held a yellow legal pad in one hand and a pen in the other. Her legs were crossed revealing very toned and healthy thighs. Cesari suspected the oversized round eyeglasses she wore were just for show, a theatrical attempt to appear smart. The CEO had one arm around her waist and held a martini glass with two olives in the other. Cesari caught the scent of gin and unconsciously glanced at his watch. It wasn't even noon. Almost overnight, St. Matt's was turning into the Wild West.

Acevedo said to the girl, "We'll finish the letter later, Olivia. I have to take care of business now. Hold my calls for the next thirty minutes and be a dear and order me in some oysters Rockefeller for lunch. Unfortunately, I won't be able to take you out like I promised."

She stood up and straightened out her short skirt which was hiked up to nearly pornographic levels as she pretended to pout, "No worries, Tibe. I'll get right on it. You're so sweet."

Tibe?

She swayed and pivoted out of the room precariously on four-inch heels as Acevedo ogled her. After she closed the door behind her, he turned to Cesari and Feinberg, his demeanor changing. "Sit down, gentlemen, and let's chat."

They sat in the two consultation chairs in front of his massive oak desk as he opened a drawer and pulled out two manila folders, one thin and the other thick. He rifled through their contents and sat back taking a sip from his martini.

"So you're the great John Cesari?"

"I'm John Cesari, yes. I don't know about the great part."

"You're being modest. I like that, but according to your personnel folder you're one of the best GI guys we have. The patients love you and the staff loves you even more. No malpractice suits or ethics charges against you on file with the state. That last is impressive in this day and age."

"I try to be nice to people."

"I'm glad to hear that. I understand that you signed your new contract. Thank you. I hope the minor reduction in wages didn't upset you too much."

"Not at all. I felt I was being overpaid anyway."

Acevedo and Feinberg laughed at that. Acevedo said, "I'm pleased you're being reasonable. So let's address the elephant in the living room if you don't mind?" He put down the thin folder and picked up the big one and continued, "It seems you've had some difficulties with the law."

"Water under the bridge."

"Is it? It says here you were born and raised in the Bronx. Parents weren't very involved in your life."

"I think you ought to stop right there."

Feinberg adjusted himself in his chair. "Take it easy, Cesari. We're just trying to understand what makes you tick. You know, see inside you."

"Bring up my parents again and the only thing you're going to see is the inside of an ambulance."

Acevedo grinned. "Let's move on. Tell me what I'm supposed to do about a physician with your sketchy background?"

"Just keep doing what you've been doing. New York State already has all this information and they're okay with it."

"Yes, but we are striving to achieve higher standards than that used by New York State. Sinking to the lowest common denominator could drag us all down. The board of trustees has high expectations for the transformation I intend on bringing to St. Matt's."

"Have I violated any of St. Matt's by-laws governing physician behavior?"

"Not yet."

"Well, when I do give me a call. Until then, I guess I'll be on my way. It was nice of you to invite me to your office."

He started to stand to leave when Acevedo said, "There is one more thing I'd like to discuss with you."

Cesari relaxed back down in his seat. "Yes?"

"According to the staff, you're a real go-to kind of guy. They really look up to you. That quality can be very useful to me."

"In what way?"

"This isn't my first rodeo, Cesari. With any change of management, there are bound to be malcontents stirring the pot, fomenting rebellion. This usually leads to passive aggressive behavior which can be extremely counterproductive. If I can't bring these outliers to heel, then I will have failed in my mission."

"What's this got to do with me?"

"Can I offer you a drink, a martini perhaps?"

"I'm good. So what can I do for you?"

"I'd like to offer you a promotion."

Cesari looked from one to the other in bewilderment. "You have to be kidding? You just cut my salary by twenty-five percent, dredged up ancient history and now are offering me a promotion?"

Acevedo said, "I'll return you to your original salary plus a five percent raise if you agree to my terms."

"And they are?"

"You will report directly to me and Feinberg any subversive behavior you witness, hear about, or simply get a tingly feeling run up your leg. I want to know who the trouble-makers are and what they're plotting."

"You want me to be a snitch?"

"I want you to be the new medical director of St. Matt's."

"You kicked Arnie out and want me to replace him? He's my friend."

"Arnie is a dinosaur. He's lucky he's still got a job. I should have just turned him out on the street."

"Maybe you didn't hear me the first time. He's my friend."

"All right, Cesari think of it this way. Your friend is still making six-figures. If you don't co-operate, I'll be forced to conclude that his continued presence is undermining your ability to think straight and that the only way for you to clear your head is for me to terminate him."

Cesari was getting angry. "If I say no, you'll fire Arnie?"

"If you don't lower your voice, I'll send security over to his office right now and drag him out by the scruff of his neck."

Cesari was momentarily speechless. It was almost impossible to believe that anyone could be so cruel, so insensitive, so base.

Acevedo continued, "Don't look so glum. The job offer has its perks. You can move into Arnie's old office today. I'm building Feinberg a brand new one twice the size of that one."

Cesari looked at Feinberg. "If I take the job, what's that make you?"

"Still your boss."

Cesari slumped in his chair. If he accepted the position, the staff including Arnie would revile him as a kiss-ass. No ifs, and or buts about it. If he didn't, Arnie was out of a job. Great choice.

He let out a deep breath and said, "I'll take that drink now."

Chapter 24

"Cesari."

"Yes, Detective Tierney?"

"Where are you?"

"Let me see. It's the middle of the day on Monday. Oh yeah, I'm at work."

"Funny guy. Did you hear about the autopsy yet on the second victim? That John Doe they found in the dumpster behind the hospital? Harry told me he spoke to you about him."

"He told me about it, but I was involved with a patient in the emergency room and couldn't make it in. I haven't heard any of the details."

"Well I spoke with Harry today. He said it's the same M.O. as the Serb including the blood thinner. He also said the official toxicology from the first guy came back mostly negative except for traces of some type of benzodiazepine and narcotics in his blood stream."

"That is interesting, but he may have been taking prescription drugs or pain-killers or both."

"Maybe, or maybe somebody drugged him to keep him quiet while he bled to death."

"I agree. So where do we go from here?"

"Good question. We're running the second guy's fingerprints as we speak. Maybe there will be some sort of relationship between the two victims. I'll get back to you if something comes up. It's interesting that they dumped him at the hospital. It's almost as if they wanted us to know there's another one. They may be taunting us, Cesari."

"Well, we know a couple of things."

"And they are?"

"Whoever it is must be local, right?"

"Yeah, at least temporarily, although he could be passing through."

"Not likely. He must have a safehouse somewhere in the city where he exsanguinates the victims and then cleans the bodies off. Which means he must also have access to a hose and adequate drainage. My guess is he hangs them upside down to allow the blood to drain better."

"You mean like in a butcher's shop?"

"At least an old-fashioned butcher's shop anyway. Modern ones don't receive full sides of beef anymore. Everything's pre-cut for delivery."

"Well if the victims were hung upside down there should have been bruises around the ankles. Harry didn't mention anything about that."

"No, he didn't but he was awfully focused on the neck wound. It's worth a second look. I'll talk to him… We also know that it's not one guy."

"We do?"

"The Serb was average sized maybe even on the small side. Harry told me the second victim was really big. I don't see how one guy could have plopped him in a dumpster by himself."

"He was a big guy. He weighed two hundred and forty pounds and that's bone dry. I see your point unless the killer was a giant himself."

"Something to think about."

"Duly noted. I'm going to contact Markov to see if he's missing any more restaurant workers."

"Good idea."

"Stay in touch Cesari and let me know about the ankles."

"I will."

After he hung up, Cesari felt a pang of guilt about not telling Tierney about events at the Ukrainian restaurant and what he knew about the latest victim, but that would have implicated Vito who was already on the Detective's radar. Even worse, it would have revealed way more about himself to Detective Tierney than he was ready now, or if ever, to divulge. He sighed deeply at how rapidly complicated things had become.

First order of business was to find Arnie and soften the blow about his promotion to medical director. He wouldn't tell him that his job was to rat out other employees or why he felt he had no choice but to accept the position. Arnie was swamped in patient care and the accompanying paperwork when he found him hard at work. It was only his first day in the trenches and he already appeared haggard and at the end of his rope.

Cesari smiled as he knocked gently on the open door. Arnie's new office was a spartan eight-foot by eight-foot square slightly larger than a cubicle located in the medical office building attached to the hospital. Arnie was so depressed he hadn't even hung up his diplomas or pictures of his family. He sat there in front of his laptop looking much older than when Cesari had last seen him.

He looked up as Cesari entered the room and closed the door behind him. "Good afternoon, Cesari."

"Hey there, Arnie. Mind if I take a seat?"

"Of course not. I welcome the distraction. It's been a rough day so far. I didn't even have time to take a lunch break and I'm still an hour behind."

"You'll get more efficient with time. It's like anything else; eventually through repetition, muscle memory will automatically start clicking the right keys for you."

"I can only hope. At this rate I don't have a chance of making the productivity quota they assigned me. I can't believe this is what you guys go through."

"Every day, Arnie, every day, but seeing how you're holding up is only part of why I came..."

Arnie waited politely and then said, "And what's the other part?"

"I have some news and I wanted you to be the first to hear it. It's hot off the presses..."

"I'm four patients behind, Cesari. I can't for the life of me figure out how to order labs or x-rays and I think my notes are so bad, I'm going to spend the rest of my life in court so if you wouldn't mind speeding things up here?"

"I've just been made the medical director of St. Matt's."

Arnie sat there for a moment, dumbfounded. When he recovered, he said, "I...I don't know what to say."

"I just wanted you to know that I didn't ask for the job and I don't want the job but I took it because I felt that without you there's going to be a void that needs to be filled by someone sympathetic to the needs of the staff. I'm going to do my best to act as a counterweight to Feinberg and Acevedo's boorishness."

He nodded slowly. "And I can't think of a better person to do just that...Well, I guess congratulations are in order."

"Not really."

"Sure they are...Congratulations, Cesari. You finally made it to the show."

Cesari smiled. "Thanks, Arnie. I'll do my best to perform with as much class as you always have."

"I appreciate that, Cesari, and my door is always open if you need any pointers."

"And I have no doubt that I will take you up on that offer."

"So when do you start?"

"Right now, apparently. I move into your old office immediately."

"I thought Feinberg was taking that office?"

"Acevedo's building him a bigger and better one possibly with a hot tub. Those two got quite a bromance going."

Arnie grinned. "That figures."

****

Yorgi tapped his fingers nervously on the table. He and his brothers were sitting in the cellar of the restaurant staring at the freezer with the note Cesari had left them. They were frightened and alarmed.

Tibor asked, "Yorgi, what means this?"

"I don't know, brother."

Ivan said, "Is impossible. There is no such thing as the undead or vampires. Somebody play joke on us."

"I agree, Ivan, but who?" said Yorgi. "Who could have known we put body here? Who could have had courage to break in and steal body? Who would dare make joke with us? Who? Who? Who?"

Tibor wasn't buying any of it. "But what if she really is undead? You said yourself Shlomo believes in such things."

Yorgi admonished him, "Stop, Tibor. Shlomo is old man, teetering on senility. You watch too much American TV. Whole legend of vampires was made up to sell books... Think, brothers, think. There has to be some explanation."

"Is possible one of workers do this?" offered Ivan, referring to the restaurant's staff.

Yorgi shook his head. "No, I do not think so. Most are too scared to take bathroom break without to ask permission. They all think they will be deported at any moment for any reason. No, they would not do this, and why would they? I treat them well, give them job and place to live."

"You are right. Is not them, but who?"

The brothers' mood was dark. They glanced frequently at the freezer and the note as they reflected on last night's activities. Slowly, they simultaneously came to the same conclusion. They raised their heads in unison looking at each other their eyes growing wide. Yorgi slammed his hand down on the table.

"Of course, it has to be," he exclaimed.

Ivan said in agreement, "You don't mean?"

"I do mean."

"Is even more incredible."

Yorgi said, "That old devil, Shlomo. He torments us even as we try to torment him. It has to be him. He must have followed the van when we left the hospital."

"Or maybe he has surveillance on restaurant and saw us arrive, but why wouldn't he just confront us, Yorgi?" asked Tibor reasonably.

"Because this is more fun for him, brother. Or perhaps, he is uncertain of our plans and wishes to lure us out into the open where he will feast on our bones."

"And the reason he break-in front door and not use key?"

"Because we know he has key. That's why. He break door to throw attention away from himself. He put on great show when he stabbed Sofia in the heart and all the while he was laughing at us. He is truly a villain with a black soul."

"So what we do, Yorgi?"

"We play along for now. No one knows anything. Understand? Continue as before. Act as if everything is good but is time to for us to distract attention. Sofia's body is problem. We did not have chance to cleanse like the others. Our DNA is all over her. If she turns up in morgue, we could be implicated."

"Maybe that is why Shlomo steal body? To hold over us with police," offered Ivan.

"Is possible, Ivan. He is shrewd old man. That is why we must act quickly to neutralize that possibility."

Ivan said, "What you suggest, Yorgi?"

"Come closer, brothers."

Chapter 25

By late afternoon Cesari had finished moving into Arnie's old office. He sat down in Arnie's leather chair, adjusted a few things on the desk, glanced around and sighed. Things were changing fast and not for the better. He was now the company snitch or Arnie would be on the subway home holding a cardboard box with his personal effects. Fortunately for Feinberg, he had bigger fish to fry, but his day was coming soon.

He took out his cellphone and dialed Zenobia. She answered quickly, "Hello, Doctor."

"Hi, Zenobia. I'm just checking in on you and Drusilla like I promised. I hope you are both feeling better today."

"Thank you, Doctor. Is very kind of you to call. Yes, we are both much improved today. Is feel silly to have bothered you last night."

"Not at all. I'm glad I could be of help. So just to be clear. No one's having any pain today?"

"No pain at all. Is all good."

"Okay then. Call me if you need anything. I think it might be a good idea if I saw you both in the office for a follow up visit. Like the surgeon mentioned last night you probably should have a colonoscopy at some point just to be safe, and I would like to discuss dietary measures for irritable bowel syndrome with the both of you. If you did agree to a colonoscopy, I would arrange to have a female doctor tend to you if that's your preference."

"Is something I will have to think about. The procedure I mean. I would be perfectly comfortable with you as doctor. Drusilla is different story on both accounts. Will not allow surgery unless life or death. Is possible for you to come to brownstone for follow up visit? Is easier for us and less traumatic for Drusilla. She does not like to go out."

Cesari rolled his eyes and unenthusiastically acquiesced, "Sure, maybe next week. I'll call ahead."

"Thank you."

"Have a good night."

He clicked off, shaking his head. He was getting sucked into their delusion but figured, in for a penny, in for a pound. As he pondered the Zenobia-Drusilla dilemma there was a knock at the door. He looked up as Feinberg entered the room holding a bottle of scotch and two rocks glasses.

He said, "You look good sitting in the captain's chair, Cesari."

"Do I?"

"I hope you like Oban."

"I don't usually drink at work."

"That's probably what's been holding you back all these years."

He placed the glasses down and opened the bottle. Cesari caught the label and saw that it was twenty-one years old. He whistled as Feinberg filled the glasses, "That must have set you back some."

"Not me, Cesari, the taxpayers. Close to six hundred bucks, but that's what expense accounts are for. I figured I owed you one for drinking your scotch the other day."

"Certainly that's not what this visit is about."

Feinberg handed Cesari a tumbler and then took a long draught from his own. Cesari watched him drain most of the amber liquid in one swallow. Afterward, Feinberg smacked his lips, sat down in one of the consultation chairs, adjusted his lab coat, cracked his neck and belched loudly.

He looked at Cesari and smiled. "Damn good scotch... You're right. This visit is more than just about scotch. I thought I would outline in greater detail your role here at St. Matt's now that you're its medical director. Let's start with the chain of command. I am Tiberius's right arm and you are now my right arm. After our meeting, I sent out a mass email to the staff letting them know about your promotion. My understanding is that the word is already spreading rapidly. You answer to me and you will report to me on a daily basis. You will carry out the policies and recommendations of this administration, i.e. Tiberius and myself, to the letter. As part of your daily duties, I expect you to cruise the halls from department to department looking for and rooting out agitators and threats."

"Can I shoot enemies of the people on the spot?"

Feinberg chuckled. "I like the way you think, Cesari, but sadly, no. Just report back to me."

"What about my clinical duties and OR cases?"

"They've been reassigned for the time being. As you become more comfortable in your new role as medical director and I become confident in your ability to function effectively in that new role, I may permit you to see one or two half-days of patients and OR cases per week if you desire to maintain your clinical skills. But that's only after you prove yourself to me. Right now I need you to ferret out the resistance."

"The resistance?"

"You heard me right."

Cesari said slowly, "Okay...but what exactly does that mean?"

"You'll know it when you see it. Just keep your eyes and your ears open." Feinberg tossed an envelope across the desk at him and said, "Here's your first assignment as medical director. In the envelope is a list of employees who have been deemed undesirable. You are to terminate them effective immediately. They will be given two weeks severance, but I want their lockers empty before morning light."

Cesari opened the envelope and took out a piece of paper. There was only one name on it. His jaw dropped and he said, "You can't be serious. Melissa, the OR nurse? Haven't you fired enough nurses?"

"She's a malcontent, Cesari. I want her out of here."

"You can't just fire a nurse because she won't sleep with you, Feinberg."

"Of course not. That would be illegal. She's being fired because I'm dissatisfied with her job performance."

"That's ridiculous and you know it. She's a great nurse. You made a pass at her last week and she shot you down. Everybody heard about it."

"Funny, because I don't remember that. Look, I can't control rumors, Cesari, only facts. And the fact is that she never filed a complaint with HR or her supervisors. You might let her know that if she flies off the handle."

"You're unreal."

"Just do your job, Cesari."

"I won't. She's one of the best nurses we have."

"Let me explain to you how this works, Sir Galahad. If you don't fire her, then I have to resort to plan B."

"What's plan B?"

"Plan B is that I will fire her, along with two other randomly chosen nurses just to keep her company on the bread line. And then I will fire you and your pal, Arnie, and the entire nursing and secretarial staff in your offices. That's what, ten people? And if I have to do the firing, there will be no severance pay at all for anyone. I hear several of them have little kids at home and no daddies. Then there's always the possibility of the police being alerted to an illegal handgun in your apartment. I suppose you could always remove the one you have hidden under the floorboards but then I would just have to dig up another one to plant. Not that big a deal." He reached over to the desk and poured himself another glass of scotch before continuing, "Who knows what else they might find in your apartment; drugs, kiddie porn, whips, chains, cross dressing outfits? A guy with imagination could have a field day with this. You getting the picture? Well, I have to go. You do what you think is best. I'll drop by the OR first thing in the morning to see if we're short one nurse. For your sake, we'd better be. Just for the record, if you tell Melissa or anyone about this conversation, then we automatically go with plan B."

He stood up and left as Cesari imagined strangling him with his belt. As he reached the door, he turned and grinned, "Of course, if Melissa wishes to discuss her continued employment here at St. Matt's with me personally, she can call me tonight. She has my number. I'm always open to negotiations but tell her to call me early. I wouldn't want her to catch me in negotiations with her replacement."

Cesari fumed after he left and gulped the scotch down. This was an absolutely incredible turn of events and one which he hadn't anticipated. Melissa was a firebrand and wasn't going to take this well. She had a notorious temper and was the main reason that he had always kept her at arm's length. He looked at his watch and figured he'd better take care of this immediately, so he hustled down to the OR to find her.

She was just coming out of a cholecystectomy case and was still gowned up with a surgical hat and mask. He signaled her for a word in private and she followed him into the OR lounge. He scanned the breakroom and satisfied they were alone, closed the door behind them.

Melissa pulled her mask and hat off and shook out her shoulder length brown hair. She was in her mid-thirties curvaceous, dangerously cute and of course there was her legendary derriere.

She said, "What's up, Cesari?"

"Can we sit down, Melissa?"

"Sure… Are you okay? You look pale."

They sat at a small lunch table, deserted except for some crackers, paper napkins and plastic utensils. "Melissa, I don't know how to say this…"

She looked puzzled. "Then just say it."

"Did you know they made me medical director today?"

"We were just talking about it during my last case. Congratulations."

"Well, as medical director, I'm the one who has to deliver bad news."

"Cesari, I'm not married, got no kids and my parents died years ago. Just spit it out."

"You've been terminated."

She sat back in her chair, all the wind sucked out of her sails, her pretty smile wiped clean off her face, replaced by stark disbelief. Then she started laughing and punched him playfully in the arm.

She said, "You almost had me, Cesari. I forgot what a joker you could be."

He swallowed hard and took a deep breath. "I'm sorry, Melissa, but I'm not joking. Today is your last day. You'll receive two weeks severance pay but Feinberg wants your locker emptied out tonight."

The laughter changed to anger and her cheeks turned scarlet. "Feinberg… that son-of-a-bitch!"

"Melissa, I truly am sorry."

"On what grounds?"

"He said he was dissatisfied with your work performance. For the record, I tried to talk him out of it."

"Oh, I bet you did, Mr. Medical Director. It must have been difficult trying to talk him out of it while you were kissing his ass over your promotion. So how's it feel to be one of them, Cesari? Pretty good no doubt."

"It's not like that. It feels terrible and I didn't want to do this."

"Then why are you?"

He wanted desperately to tell her the truth but couldn't risk the fall out. "Melissa, believe me. I have no choice. It's not my call."

"So that's it. He comes on to me, I turn him down and now I get fired. And you rubber stamp it."

"I'm not rubber stamping anything."

She stood up and hissed through her teeth. "I thought crap like this was illegal. You tell him that I'm going to sue him, you and the hospital because this is bullshit."

He nodded. "You can do that although you never did file a formal complaint against him, so there's no record of it. He said I should mention that."

She stood there with steam coming out of her ears. "Cesari, I thought we were friends."

"We are."

"Not anymore. You're as bad he is. I can't believe I didn't see that."

"Melissa, please don't shoot the messenger."

"Kiss my ass, Cesari. I have a mortgage on my condo, student loans and credit card payments. I have a cat for God's sake. What am I supposed to do?"

"I'll write you a superb letter of reference. You're a great nurse."

"Yeah, and what if I can't find a job in Manhattan?"

"I can't believe that. There are always nursing jobs available."

Her eyes reddened and a tear slid down her cheek. She choked up with emotion. "But I like it here. It's my home. I've been here since the day I graduated nursing school. All my friends are here."

Cesari said consolingly, "I'm sorry, Melissa. I feel awful and I don't know what to tell you. I'm caught between a rock and a hard place with this... Look, maybe I shouldn't say anything but..."

"But what?"

He slumped back in his chair, defeated and embarrassed at what he was about to say. With his eyes down, he whispered, "Feinberg said to tell you that he's open to negotiations if you are. He said to call him tonight if you want to discuss it."

"Discuss it? What's that supposed to mean?"

"That's all he said."

A knowing look gradually appeared on her face. "Are you kidding me, Cesari? Jesus Christ almighty. You don't really think I'm going to…"

"I'm only telling you what he said."

Chapter 26

After his demoralizing encounter with Melissa, Cesari slunk back to his office with his tail between his legs. He had never been so dispirited and felt like he may never be able to look anyone in the eyes again. Word of this would spread faster than the plague. He'd be lucky if nurses didn't spit at him once they found out, and Melissa made it abundantly clear that they would...and quickly.

He poured himself a scotch and sat there trying to ease his guilty conscience. After he finished the glass, he shook himself and tried to concentrate on the matter of the three murders. He was walking a fine line there. He hadn't told Tierney about Sofia to protect Vito. He'd also been deceptive about Leandro. Neither thing would go ever well at all. He took in and let out a deep breath. He felt like he was in a cage.

He had no choice but to keep moving forward, so he fired up his laptop and began doing research on vampires like Tierney had asked him to. After several minutes of plugging in various internet queries, he came up with nothing but medieval folk tales and absurd legends. There were minor differences from country to country but basically it was all hogwash. It all came to a head with Bram Stoker's novel, *Dracula*, which immortalized the concept of the undead living off the blood of the living. Hollywood took the concept and ran with it with a series of popular movies.

The only organization in New York that even remotely fit the description of a vampire club was something called the Court of Lazarus or Metropolitan Society of Vampires located in Greenwich Village. From Cesari's reading, he gleaned that this was nothing more than a monthly costume party where people wore black gothic makeup and clothes, drank cocktails, smoked weed and listened to punk rock. There was a cover charge if you weren't a member and they even sold prosthetic fangs along with other vampiric trappings at the gate. Totally silly and definitely not serious. Still, he would contact them to see if any of the victims were members or known to frequent the place.

He looked at his watch and decided to pursue it in the morning. He shut down the computer and left his office, deciding to go visit Vito at the Kit Kat. He arrived at 8:30 p.m. and noticed there were no guards stationed outside. Inside was a different matter, and he found a gaggle of large beefy men hanging out just within the main entrance staring outward through peepholes and small windows. They were armed with submachine guns and determined faces. Cesari nodded at Gaetano who was in charge.

"What's going on?" he asked.

"The boss says were closed until further notice. We've been waiting to see if a black Toyota shows up for the cash."

"And then what?"

"Not sure. Boss said to call him but to have plenty of firepower available. No one gets through the door without authorization."

"I'm authorized?"

"You're on the list."

"Who else is on the list?"

"You're it."

"Where's Vito?"

"In his office upstairs."

"Okay, keep up the good work."

The lounge was eerily quiet as Cesari meandered his way to Vito's office finding men stationed here and there at strategic points. Vito was sitting at his desk, the .45 caliber Colt in his shoulder holster, the .44 magnum revolver on his desk and a cigarette hanging out of his mouth. On the pool table was a body bag and two of Vito's men standing nearby. Their sleeves were rolled up and they were covered with sweat.

"Sit down, Cesari. It might be a long night."

"Who's that, Sofia?" Cesari asked nodding at the body bag.

"No, I had the boys bring her to a funeral home up in the Bronx for cremation. One of the guys told the director there she was his sister. They weren't thrilled about not having a doctor's official death certificate but a couple of grand smoothed things over. They even held a little service for her. It was the best I could do."

"Just like that? You mean we could have done that with Leandro?"

"No, I don't like to pull that ace from out of my sleeve too often. There are too many potential problems and witnesses. Funeral homes are overrun with regulations and paperwork just like you guys and there are cameras everywhere to make sure no one messes with the bodies. I took the chance with Sofia because she didn't have any family I know of and I liked her. She deserved better than to be thrown in the East River or a dumpster. I kind of felt responsible for her. Besides, you said you wanted Leandro to have an autopsy."

"I did want him to... So who's that on the pool table?"

"That was the Romanian asswipe we put in the hospital last month. He was part of the gang that assaulted one of my guys. We tracked him down for part two of his interrogation."

"Looks like part two didn't go over nearly as well as part one."

"On the contrary. Grigori was a fountain of information this time around."

"Oh really? And what did he have to say for himself?"

"That Yorgi ordered the attack on my guy. He didn't know why exactly, but he suspected that Yorgi is trying to advance his stock in some Romanian outfit operating out of First Avenue."

Cesari nodded, thinking it over. He then said, "So Yorgi isn't just some ordinary restaurant and building manager and there's some Romanian gang of shall we say, entrepreneurs, trying to muscle their way into your territory?"

"It gets better. Yorgi has two brothers who he shares the heavy lifting with. One is named Ivan and the other Tibor. Their last name is Romanescu. Apparently, these guys are holy terrors in the Eastern European community over on First Avenue."

"Ivan and Yorgi are brothers… That's interesting. Okay, things are starting to make sense. So the third guy you saw at the restaurant presumably was brother number three, Tibor."

"That's what I think."

"Just how big, and even more importantly, how well organized are these guys?"

Vito took a long drag on his cigarette and blew it out unceremoniously. "Grigori was just a street hood. He didn't know any details, save one…"

"You going to keep me in suspense?"

"The Romanescu brothers answer directly to Shlomo Markov. Your Shlomo Markov."

"Take it easy. We already knew that they worked for him."

"Well Grigori said that your boy, Shlomo, is a whole lot more than a landlord and restauranteur. The only thing that strikes more fear in those immigrants than Yorgi and his bros is the sight or mention of Shlomo's name. And now I remember why the name Markov seemed familiar to me. Several times in the last year, the feds came around to hassle me. They asked me if I knew a guy named Markov, but they wouldn't tell me why."

"That is interesting. Can you be sure it's the same Markov?"

"No, they never told me his first name or showed me his picture, but they seemed puzzled that I didn't know the guy since some of my businesses were so close to his on First Avenue. They just assumed we must have crossed paths. Another thing is they always brought his name up in some roundabout nonchalant way like it wasn't really that important to them, but I could tell it was."

"How could you tell?"

"Normally, when the feds bring you in for questioning, there's one, occasionally two guys in the room. You know, the good cop, bad cop thing. Like I give a shit. Well, whenever the name Markov came up there was always a third guy lurking in the background. Now that I think of it, that guy never introduced himself. He just stood in the shadows as if he was supervising."

Cesari mulled over that fascinating tidbit for a minute and then asked, "What do you think?"

"Until today, I didn't think of it at all. But it occurs to me now that a different government agency is interested in our boy, Shlomo."

"Like…?"

"I can't be sure. If it's not the FBI, then who else is there? The NSA, the Treasury, the ATF? To be honest, it could be anybody. I don't know anything about Shlomo except for what you told me and what I just learned."

"When was the last time you got hauled in like that for questioning?"

"That's just it. I didn't recall his name right away because it's been at least six months since I had a visit from the feds.

And you have to remember, when they bring you in like that, you're usually grilled for hours without a break. They ask you hundreds of moronic questions trying to trip you up. It's pure harassment. Plain and simple."

"And they didn't give you any hint what their interest in him was?"

"No, but clearly he's running some racket over there that's got their attention."

"Clearly... So what's the plan if a Toyota Camry shows up tonight?"

He smirked, "We're going to have some fun with Yorgi and company."

Cesari scanned Vito's desk. "I can't wait. Do you have anything to eat? I'm starving."

"I have scotch, bourbon, vodka, rum, tequila and gin. Take your pick."

"No power bars or something like that?"

Vito looked over at his men. "Do you guys have any food on you?"

One of them shook his head no and the other reached into his pocket and tossed a pack of gum to Cesari who unwrapped three sticks and popped them in his mouth for the sugar rush.

As he chewed, he said, "This news about Markov raises all sorts of unsettling questions about his relationship with my hospital and those thugs who were hired to run the place at his behest."

"Yes, it does, but all I really care about is did Yorgi order the hit on my people or did Shlomo order Yorgi to order it?"

Cesari nodded. "I guess that makes a difference, doesn't it?"

"Yes, it makes a difference on how many coffins they're going to need."

"I understand. I'm just confused as to what the hospital has to do with any of this."

"By the way, are these the guys?"

He reached into his desk drawer and handed Cesari a manila folder containing several blown up, high resolution color photographs of Feinberg and Acevedo in various locations of St. Matt's.

"Yeah, the big fat goofy guy is Feinberg. The sneaky-looking runt is Acevedo, also known as the destroyer of hospitals. How'd you get these?"

"I got tired of waiting for you to send me their pictures like you promised, so I sent a guy over there today."

"Sorry about that. Did they run into any problems?"

"None at all. The security guards were happy to help for a little under the table lettuce."

Vito's phone rang and he answered it. It was one of his men from downstairs. He said, "Let the kid go. He probably doesn't know anything anyway. We'll be right down."

He hung up and turned to Cesari. "The Toyota just pulled up with a sixteen-year-old driver who doesn't speak a whole lot of English. Someone paid him to drop the car off here. He doesn't know who. It's probably stolen."

"What was the point of this exercise? They must have known you'd be waiting for the car to show up."

"Who knows and who cares? Maybe they're playing head games or more likely they're just plain stupid... I suppose there's always the possibility they thought I'd cough up the dough."

"Maybe they're trying to show you that you don't impress them all that much."

Vito snorted. "Well then, I'm going to have to do something to change their low opinion of me."

"Such as?"

Vito called to his men. "You guys...Wait until midnight then bring that body downstairs and throw him into the black Toyota out front. Gaetano has the keys. Drive it over to First Avenue and park it in the alley next to the side entrance of that Ukrainian restaurant so they can't miss it. Take the body out of the bag and prop him up in the driver's seat. Have a couple of guys follow you in the Suburban as back up."

The men acknowledged their orders and Vito said to Cesari, "You look hungry. C'mon, let's go eat. I know a place that makes the best porchetta in town."

"I thought you'd never ask."

Chapter 27

The three men sat on one side of the long wood table, glancing around nervously. They had never met each other but they instinctively knew by the way they were dressed this was no ordinary gathering. It was like the beginning of a bad joke; a rabbi, a priest and an imam walked into a bar. But this was no joke and this wasn't a bar. Each holy man had been snatched off the street in broad daylight near his house of worship, hoods thrown over their heads and transported to this foul, dank room with incandescent light bulbs and wet floors. In front of them respectively lay the Torah, the New Testament and the Quran.

A cockroach slowly inched its way from one end of the table to the other, stopping occasionally to assess its surroundings, its long repulsive antennae gently testing the air. None of the men moved to impede its course. None of the men made a comment as the hideous insect climbed on top of one of the Holy Scriptures walked across it and then back down again.

They had been sitting like that for nearly two hours and the stress was taking its toll on them. Beads of sweat dripped down their brows. It was getting quite warm and the rabbi was tempted to remove his yarmulke. The mullah had the same thought concerning his turban. The priest felt like his collar was slowly suffocating him, but no one moved to remedy their situation. They prayed quietly to their maker, one and the same for all three. They pleaded for divine intercession and enlightenment into the nature of their suffering.

The door to the room opened and in walked Shlomo, Yorgi and Ivan. Tibor was absent, having been given permission to visit his fiancée. The brothers took up position behind the three men and Shlomo, dressed in a crisp navy suit and tie, with a dark maroon handkerchief neatly folded in his breast pocket, sat down opposite the clergymen. He leaned his diamond encrusted walking stick against the edge of the table. His strange looking eyes gave him an almost supernatural feel in the glow of the harsh lighting. It was the same room Yorgi and his brothers used for their meetings. Yorgi had suggested it to Shlomo for privacy.

Shlomo looked at the three men and said, "Gentlemen, please forgive me for inconveniencing you. My name is Shlomo Markov and I need your advice."

The three men felt their courage returning. The rabbi was Menachem Weiss of the Temple Beth El on Park Avenue just two blocks from Central Park. At seventy, he was the oldest of the three religious men, wore thick glasses, and had a long gray beard. Sensing one of his own in Shlomo, he spoke, "I am certain that each one of us would be willing to help you, Mr. Markov, but why did you feel the need to kidnap us?"

"Rabbi, if my actions offended you, please accept my apologies," answered Shlomo. "None of you are prisoners here. You are free to go if you wish."

He waved his hand to the door. The three men glanced at each other, but no one moved to escape. Danger hung heavy in the air around them. The rabbi cleared his throat but didn't say anything.

Shlomo said, "Well then, gentlemen, I appreciate your willingness to assist me. Rabbi Weiss, we will begin with you and you may reference your holy book as much as you need."

All three men looked puzzled. The rabbi glanced at the Torah in front of him. "What is it you need advice on?"

"Tell me what the book of Moses has to say about vampires."

"Vampires?" asked the rabbi, confused. "Is this a joke? You bring us here to make fun of us?"

"Please, Rabbi, humor me," replied Shlomo reassuringly. "I assure you this is no prank. Answer question as best you can. You have devoted whole life to your religion and the study of the Torah, have you not?"

"Yes, I have and I can tell you without any hesitation that there is nothing in the teachings of Moses or anywhere else in the Bible about vampires. Judaism does not recognize such entities. They are a mere fabrication of our entertainment starved society like most of Hollywood's monsters."

"And yet the Talmud speaks of the golem. The beast made of clay and mud."

"The Torah is the word of God, Mr. Markov. The Talmud is the codification of oral law by learned men thousands of years after those laws were given to us. Although it too is considered to be of divine inspiration, there can be no doubt that there might have been some human interpretation and bias. Even so, there are but a few passing references to the golem and they most likely represent stories that were over-heard in villages which may have influenced the writers of the Talmud. Modern scholars see the golem as nothing but Jewish folklore like vampires and werewolves."

"Are you certain of this? Do you not wish to glance at the writings in front of you?"

The rabbi scoffed, "There is no need. I have read the Torah many times. If there are such things as vampires there will be no confirmation of that in the Torah."

Shlomo nodded. "And what about your personal beliefs on such matters?"

The rabbi looked at him with incredulity. "I have already told you. Vampires are fabrications of imaginative minds. There are no such things."

"Suppose I told you I had firsthand knowledge of their existence? What would you say to that?"

The priest glanced at the Imam who glanced at the rabbi who was now sweating profusely. He said, "Tell me of your experience that I may understand."

Yorgi and Ivan stood in the shadows several feet behind the three men. They looked at each other and then back at the table. Yorgi suppressed a smile although he was greatly concerned. He had been very worried that Shlomo was on to his little game and was stringing him along. When Shlomo told him to collect the three holy men, he hadn't explained why, but now he knew. The old man was verifiably insane. This was almost too good to be true, he thought. Shlomo had fallen further down the rabbit hole than he would have guessed possible.

Shlomo said, "What I am about to tell you I have never told a living soul before this day, Rabbi. When I was young man in Romania about fifteen years after World War II, I live in small farming village. Many villagers were found murdered, their throats pierced by a fanged creature, drained of their blood, their bodies discarded like so much rubbish. This went on night after night for nearly a month. Twenty-four men and women in all before the carnage ended. An explanation was never found, and the culprit never brought to justice. I saw the bodies with my own eyes, Rabbi. It was widely believed to be the work of a vampire."

Yorgi and Ivan's eyes went wide. This was a story they had never heard before. Yorgi had thought Shlomo was going to tell the rabbi about the dead Serb and Sofia. What did this mean? Is this why Shlomo was obsessed with vampires? Because of some childhood trauma?

The rabbi listened intently, curious and frightened at the same time. Cautiously he said, "Mr. Markov, I don't know what happened to those villagers but that doesn't mean it was the work of a vampire. A psychopathic serial murderer could have done the same thing."

"I have had sixty years to ponder this question, Rabbi. Sixty years to find a rational explanation and have failed to do so. The memory of those villagers has haunted me day and night and I cannot believe any man capable of such horror, such precision and such stealth. After the first death, the small village was on high alert. Everyone armed and ready for what you say, but it did them no good because men cannot fight what men cannot see. And now it is here in Manhattan..."

"What is here now in Manhattan?"

Shlomo was becoming increasingly agitated as he spoke, his face flushed, and his green eye seemed to glow. "Vampires from old country. I have seen them and their victims with my own eyes, and they are coming for me."

All three religious men momentarily held their breath. The rabbi said soothingly. "How may I console you, Mr. Markov?"

"You can tell me that there is something in that holy book of yours that can save me from this nightmare. Consult Moses and your God and help me find salvation."

"I will pray for you, Mr. Markov, but the answers you seek are not in the Torah, and the Lord cannot protect you from that which does not exist. I believe you would be better served by consultation with a mental health provider."

"So you refuse to help me?"

"I do not refuse. It is not within my ability to help you... Not in the way you desire, no."

Shlomo slowly stood up, neither upset nor angry. Simply disappointed, his dispassionate appearance was arguably more terrifying than were he to have expressed white hot rage. The rabbi held his gaze and slowly began to pray in Hebrew as Shlomo picked up his walking stick. In one hand he held the wood leg and with the other he clasped the bejeweled head and twisted it a quarter turn. Then in one smooth motion he withdrew a thin, shiny, razor-sharp blade of steel more than two feet in length, its tip honed to a shimmering point.

The rabbi closed his eyes and the priest stammered, "No, Mr. Markov. Please don't..."

With speed and violence that belied his advanced age, Shlomo leaned across the table and thrust the blade through the rabbi's throat. It passed through his trachea and spinal cord, emerging six inches from the back of his neck. Just as swiftly he withdrew the blade, wiped it clean with his maroon pocket handkerchief and then scabbarded the weapon. His brainstem severed, the rabbi grunted and fell face forwarded onto the table, convulsing uncontrollably as he gurgled up blood and saliva.

Everyone in the room froze at the unexpected spectacle, waiting for Shlomo's next move which was to resume his seat and watch the rabbi die. When the man had finally breathed and twitched for the last time, Shlomo turned to the priest.

"Is your turn, Father Walsh. Perhaps you can help me."

****

Crosstown in Chelsea, in the back seat of an Uber with tinted windows parked outside her brownstone, they held each other tightly. She said, "I cannot stay long, my love."

Tibor looked deeply into her eyes and whispered, "I love you, Drusilla, with all of my heart and soul. I cannot bear being apart from you."

Reciprocating the young man's ardor, she kissed him. "I feel just as you, Tibor. You are my one and only. This deception is making me physically ill from the stress."

"Is that what the doctor told you?"

"Not in so many words, but yes."

"I am glad it is nothing more than that, but how much longer must we go on like this? Five minutes here, ten minutes there in back of taxi…is ridiculous. I burn for your embrace, Drusilla. I burn to know you," he whispered hoarsely, his voice oozing desire.

"And I burn for you, Tibor, but we must be patient. If we were seen together like this it would be very bad. My father and your brothers would be enraged if they knew we deceived them. Each would blame the other. There is no telling what they would do or how much blood they might spill."

"I can't believe they would use us like pawns. We are not cattle to be bartered."

"It is fortunate we are like-minded. But still, we must be careful. I do not wish to spend the rest of my life in Romanian home for wayward women or in hiding from my own family, and neither do you."

"I know. Your family and mine are vindictive in the extreme, and the worse sin they can imagine is betrayal."

"Exactly... Where are they now, your brothers and father?"

"I am not sure. I tell Yorgi you have not been well and need to see me. He was sympathetic and allow me come to you but was tightlipped about what he and Ivan were doing tonight. He and Ivan always treat me like baby who needs to be protected. I am sick of it."

She stroked his hair and kissed him passionately. Their lips locked for what seemed like an eternity as she pressed her warm body against his.

Eventually, she came up for air and breathless said, "You don't kiss like baby, Tibor."

They kissed again and he said, "Nor do you, my darling."

"I must go. I have been gone too long already."

"I love you, Drusilla."

Chapter 28

Cesari spent the next morning walking from department to department in St. Matt's as Feinberg had instructed him to. Most people had heard about his new position and were mildly curious because Cesari had never struck anyone as a company man. He tried to allay their instinctive suspicions with a lot of smiling, optimistic rhetoric and enthusiastic fist-bumping. Relations between the administration and staff had never before been this broken and he was fighting an uphill battle. He could see behind their cautious words and darting eyes that many thought he had been bought off by the enemy.

During a break in the politicking, he called The Court of Lazarus. After many transfers, he was eventually patched through to the Prince of Darkness himself, Hans Broeder, the lead guitarist of a punk rock band called Satan's Knights and acting regent of the court. At first, Hans declined to discuss the identities of any of the court's members. Cesari threatened him with a search warrant and as much negative press as possible and Hans backed down. He had never heard of any of the victims and they weren't on file as members of his vampire club.

After the call, Cesari headed down to the pathology department to talk to Harry. On the way, his phone buzzed with a text from Feinberg congratulating him on his good work with Melissa. Cesari grimaced and sighed but didn't reply.

Harry was in his office leaning over a microscope wearing a protective face mask. Cesari asked, "Hey, Harry. What's with the mask?'

"Are you kidding me? It's not too bad right now but the construction crews have been kicking up clouds of dust to the point that it's actually becoming not only hard to breathe but to see as well. This could become a real health hazard if it continues."

"I'm sorry to hear that. It's not as bad upstairs, but I see your point."

"So what can I do for you? There's a fresh pot of coffee."

"Thanks, but what's your definition of fresh."

"Under two hours."

"Harry…"

"Then don't have any. I don't care."

"Do we have any final thoughts on the autopsies, Harry?"

"Okay, so first of all there was no snake venom present. Let's just get that out of the way. The final toxicology on both victims came up positive for traces of benzodiazepines and narcotics. They couldn't be more specific than that without a larger sample of blood which we can't give them. We were lucky to obtain what we did. However, they did say that they were fairly certain they were the same type of benzodiazepines and narcotics in each of the victims."

"That's interesting. So in addition to the holes in the neck, that would also seem to link the two victims."

"I think so. It appears they were drugged and then bled, helpless to defend themselves. By the way, there were no ligature wounds on the ankles or wrists. I checked like you asked. They didn't need to be bound. They were probably stoned into unconsciousness by whatever animal it was that did this."

Cesari nodded. "I agree and that would explain why there's no evidence of a struggle or any attempts to compress the wounds. They were out cold. Well at least they didn't suffer too much either physically or emotionally. They probably didn't even know or feel anything. Who knows? They might have been at a dinner party having a drink with friends. Someone slips them a drug laced cocktail and they're out, never to wake up again."

Harry whispered, "Jesus...How can be people be so cruel?"

"I don't know, Harry, but it happens all the time. What about the murder weapon? Any thoughts?"

"Yeah, several..."

Harry opened his desk drawer and took out a kitchen towel wrapped lengthwise around something. He placed the towel on his desk and unraveled it. There were three, two-pronged, meat forks of different lengths.

Harry said, "These were in my house. You know ordinary kitchenware for roasting or barbecuing. A well-placed jab from anyone of them could easily have done the job."

Cesari picked up one of the utensils and studied it, trying to imagine the scene. Yorgi drugs the Serb. Maybe he invited him up to his apartment for a drink. Hey, Andrej, you're doing a great job. Let's talk about your future. That kind of thing. He drugs him and while he's lying unconscious, Yorgi exposes his neck, lines up the fork and rams it home. It would have made a horrific mess wherever it took place. Unless Yorgi brought him to the bathroom and put him in the tub first. Then he could just have washed all the DNA down the drain. That would have worked with Andrej. He was a relatively small guy, but Leandro was twice his size. As built as Yorgi was, he would have needed help. So his brothers helped him. They must have, but how did they lure him to his death? Somehow, they coerced Sofia to bring him over to her apartment after work that night. That's what the argument between her and Ivan was about. She most likely didn't know why, but she probably didn't like it. There, they drugged them both. They probably reasoned her emotional attachment to Leandro made her too much of a loose end to leave running free. They put her body to good use nonetheless. The big question that remained was if killing Leandro was meant to intimidate Vito who was Andrej's death supposed to intimidate? And who were they trying to convince that Sofia was an actual vampire?

"What are you thinking about Cesari?" asked Harry.

"Just trying to picture it is all. I think you're on to something with these forks. Thanks, Harry. You've been a big help."

"Just doing my job, boss."

"Boss?"

"I saw the email from Feinberg. Congratulations on the promotion."

"Oh that. When this is all over, we'll have a drink and I'll tell you all about it."

Harry nodded. "You're not one of them?"

"No, Harry. I'm not one of them."

"Are you going to kick their asses, Cesari?"

"You can take that to the bank, Harry."

Harry smiled and for a brief moment, looked like he might cry, before saying, "I knew it."

"Later, Harry."

He left the pathology department and meandered his way to his office in no particular rush. He had a lot on his mind. All he could think about was the barbecue fork, the blood, Leandro, Andrej, and Sofia. Then there was Vito. He knew he could only rein him in for just so long. That was an explosion waiting to happen. And what about Shlomo? Who was this guy really? Acevedo and Feinberg were just minions. He was sure of that. They were too stupid to be anything else. Still, he was going to enjoy beating their brains in when the right time came.

He picked up a coffee in the cafeteria and decided to call Tierney with an update before he forgot and got dragged on the carpet again. He was starting to jump as high as he could even before he was ordered to.

"What do you have for me, Cesari," barked Tierney gruffly.

"A lot...I just left a session with Harry in pathology. First off, the final toxicology report demonstrated benzodiazepines and narcotics in both victims. They're still working on the specific types, but they're the same drugs in both victims."

"Good, so they're definitely linked."

"That's the way I see it. Second, there were no ligature wounds on either victim. My guess is it wasn't necessary to restrain them because of the drugs."

"I agree... Anything else?"

"Yeah, one more thing. I think the murder weapon most likely was a two-pronged barbecue fork."

Tierney was quiet for a minute as he thought about that. Then he said, "So they somehow anticoagulated the victims, knocked them unconscious, poked them in the neck with the fork and watched them bleed out while they sat back with a good book."

"Starting to look that way."

"I like it. This case could punch my ticket to lieutenant... You know, Cesari, if you were just a little smarter you could have been a cop."

"Or a Marine."

"Slow down tiger. You put the cart before the horse on that one. Well if that's all, I got to run. I'm on my way to a meeting."

"Ciao."

A few minutes later, Cesari reached his office and opened the door. As he entered and approached his desk, he caught his breath and gagged on his coffee. Lying on top of the ink blotter was a dead rat, a large dead rat. He was stunned and disgusted by the sight. He studied it, wondering how it got there and how it died. There was no blood and it otherwise appeared physically intact without evidence of trauma. He searched the office for possible points of entry but didn't find any, although rats were quite resourceful. He picked up the wastepaper basket by the side of the desk with one hand and using a pen in the other gingerly pushed the rat to the edge of the desk until it plopped into the trash. He tossed the pen in after it and then placed the basket by the door. Next order of business was to remove the ink blotter and place it next to the wastepaper basket. After that, he breathed a sigh of relief as he called maintenance to remove the items and report the incident. The maintenance guy told him he hadn't heard of a rat problem in the hospital but that he would come up immediately with a crew to investigate and clean his office.

He had no stomach to linger in his office, so he decided to pass through the OR and assess the fallout from his dealings with Melissa. He knew she wasn't going to cut him any slack when she told the other nurses what happened so he figured he might as well face the music and get it over with. The first person he thought he'd check in with was Emily, the head nurse. She'd already left for the day yesterday when he fired Melissa. He should have called her at home but got busy and it slipped his mind. Her office door was open, and he gently tapped on it.

She looked up from her computer and he said, "May I come in, Emily?"

He didn't like the disapproving look on her face. She said, "Are you going to fire me too?"

"No, Emily, I'm not." He stepped into the room, sat across from her and added, "I'm sorry, Em. I meant to call you last night."

"What difference would that have made?"

He sighed. "Not much, I guess."

"So what do you want? A pat on the back? Everything's okay? I still love you?"

"None of the above."

"Look Cesari, you told one of my nurses, my friend, that she should sleep with that disgusting animal, Feinberg, if she wanted to keep her job. You didn't really think that would go over well, did you?"

"I never said that."

"That's not what Melissa said. I had to listen to her cry on the phone for almost an hour last night."

"She misinterpreted my meaning and intention."

"She did, did she?"

"I was simply passing along a message."

"They're making you complicit, Cesari. You better watch out. You lie with dogs, you wake up with fleas"

As they spoke, a group of nurses walked by the open door. Cesari reflexively looked up and saw Melissa with two other nurses. She saw him too and stopped. Her upper lip curled into a sneer, and looking past him, she said, "Be careful, Emily, I heard there are rats in the building, and some are wearing stethoscopes."

He couldn't believe it. Melissa had left the rat on his desk or had someone do it for her. Emily said, "Thanks for the head's up, Melissa."

Melissa continued on her way with the others leaving Cesari confused. He turned to Emily and said, "I don't understand."

"Which part? The dead rat on your desk or the Melissa still works here part?"

"You knew about the rat?"

"Let's just say that's girl talk."

"And she still works here because…?"

"She needs this job, Cesari. What did you think was going to happen?"

"You've got to be kidding me?"

"You're the one who told her to call Feinberg and degrade herself."

"I did no such thing and I didn't think she would."

"You know, Cesari. I wish that you and every guy on this planet could spend just one day in the shoes of a woman. Just then you might understand what it's like."

"I can't believe this."

"Believe it, Cesari. Your currency around here isn't doing so well. Now, if you don't mind…"

He left Emily's office, upset and frustrated. A group of nurses hissed at him as he walked by.

Chapter 29

The afternoon wore on and as word of his perfidy slowly percolated throughout the hospital, Cesari noted that he was greeted with increasing hostility wherever he went. Hamstrung by his inability to adequately defend himself against the accusatory glares of the staff, men and women alike, he retreated to the only safe space he had left, Arnie's new office. At half past five, he swung the door open unceremoniously and let himself in.

Arnie's head peeked out from behind his laptop. He was surrounded by piles of paper charts and both his cellphone and landline were bleating mercilessly at him. "Cesari, I see you more now than when I was the medical director."

Cesari sat down in a consultation chair and said, "This job sucks, Arnie."

Arnie laughed. "It's only been one day, Cesari. What could've happened?"

"I can't go into details. How did you manage to do it for all these years?"

"Here's a trade secret… Keep a bottle of bourbon around at all times. Cheap stuff because you're going to drink it by the gallon."

Cesari snorted, "I believe it. Do you have any here by the way?"

"Always," was the smiling reply as he reached into his desk drawer and pulled out a bottle of Blanton's bourbon and two glasses. He poured a hefty dose in each and handed Cesari one. They clinked glasses and began to ease their pain.

"Thanks, Arnie, but I doubt Blanton's counts as the cheap stuff."

"True, but I'm worth it."

Cesari nodded. "True, in fact, you're priceless."

"Priceless or not, I have hours of paperwork that needs to be completed before I go home so if you wouldn't mind…"

"Can I finish my drink?"

"Be my guest but do so quietly while I work."

Fifteen minutes later, Cesari downed the rest of the Blanton's and left Arnie to his misery. He wandered the hallways of St. Matt's more or less aimlessly. He didn't want to go back to his office. The rat incident was still too fresh in his mind and he was sure the smell of disinfectant from the cleaning people would be overwhelming. He didn't even want to think about Melissa right now. And why hadn't Tierney called him all day? That was a little odd, he thought. Not that he missed the harassment. When he had asked to tag along, he hadn't intended on becoming the detective's girl Friday.

He shook it off and tried to focus. Markov was the key. For some reason, he just knew it. He was everywhere and yet nothing seemed to stick to him. Leandro was killed as a show of force for Vito. The Serb most likely was killed for the same reason but for whose benefit? Markov?

If it was Yorgi and his brothers who killed Leandro and Sofia, and Cesari had no doubt it was, then in all probability they also killed the Serb and decorated his apartment. Cesari pictured Markov's reaction in the morgue and then again in the Serb's living room. He was genuinely sick to his stomach. It was a real, visceral response. Cesari doubted anyone could fake that. Yorgi on the other hand wasn't nearly as affected. He was more concerned about whether he would be in trouble with the law. Interesting difference.

Was the old man the target of this elaborate ruse? It was starting to seem so which would exonerate Markov from any culpability in the murders. But what was the game afoot and what was to be gained by trying to scare the old guy with vampires? And why would they think anyone would believe in that stuff anyway? If it was just a power grab why not just shoot him and get it over with?

Good questions.

He realized that he needed to find out more about Markov and the Romanescu brothers. He also needed a crash course in all things Romanian. There was a distinct possibility that the cultural divide was making this situation that much more difficult to decipher. The trouble was he didn't know any Romanians other than those up to their eyeballs in this mess, and he doubted that they would be forthcoming, especially Yorgi when he found his dead friend in the Toyota.

He instinctively glanced at his watch and thought they must have found the body by now. It was after 6:00 p.m. He put himself in their shoes. A kitchen worker opens the door to the alley and sees the Toyota with the body. He calls Yorgi or Ivan or Tibor or all three. They come flying over and realize Vito is one of those eye-for-an-eye types. They wouldn't call the cops so they dispose of the body somewhere, but now they know that Vito is aware of who they are and where they can be reached. Once that bit of sobering information sinks in they need to rethink their battle plans. While they're sitting around thinking about it, it may finally dawn on them who snatched Sofia's body. They had reached out and touched Vito and he had reached out and touched them back. The crisis was escalating. He had no doubt that they wouldn't back down and would retaliate, but did they have the resources for a full-scale war? And if they didn't have the backing of their boss, Markov, would that be wise? Crazy or not, he'd seen nuttier things happen. Greed and the lust for power made men do the most unbelievably reckless things.

Cesari went down to the medical staff lounge on the first floor. There was no one there and he sat at a computer terminal the hospitalists used to chart their records. He searched the Romanescu brothers and came up empty. Markov queries returned nothing but platitudes for all he had done for the immigrant community on the East Side. It occurred to him to go back to the apartment building and the restaurant to ask more pointed questions about Yorgi and Shlomo. But he nixed that idea as being too provocative and potentially dangerous to the people with whom he spoke.

What to do?

He snapped his fingers. Zenobia and Drusilla were Romanian. Maybe they could help him? They seemed nice enough although their wealth placed them in a vastly different orbit than their brethren on First Avenue. Nonetheless, they could give him valuable insight into Romanian customs, culture and thoughts. It was worth a try, but he thought he should tread carefully. Both women were eccentric in the extreme and would undoubtedly feel threatened. As immigrants they might be alarmed by what may seem like an overly curious interrogation.

He would have to put them at ease and maybe intersperse his real questions with more run of the mill medical follow up. Problem number one was that he told them he wanted to see them next week. To suddenly call them up and say he wanted to come over now would definitely cause them to worry. Problem number two was that he sensed that when the two of them were together they fed off each other and would be less forthright so he would need a way of separating them.

Then it came to him. He would go over there now and say he serendipitously happened to be in the neighborhood and figured he'd drop by to check on them. He was concerned because of the uncertainty of what was going on with them. Just knock on the door and there you go. Would they let him in? If they didn't, he was no worse off, but that wouldn't happen. They trusted him and wouldn't want to be rude. To sweeten the deal he would bring a dozen cannolis from Giancarlo's bakery. The woman who could resist that hadn't been born yet.

It was a few minutes past seven. Giancarlo's was open until eight. By the time he got there and then caught a taxi over to Chelsea it would be between eight and eight-thirty by his calculation.

Perfect.

They most likely would be in the middle of or finished with dinner unless they went out to eat. He guessed that would be unlikely given Drusilla's social anxiety. He logged off the computer and left the medical staff lounge. Near the entrance of the hospital was a young man wearing a long raincoat and sneakers staring at his cellphone with one hand and holding a whipped cream pie in an aluminum pie tin in the other. Cesari was distracted, paid him no mind, waved at security guard sitting at his desk and headed for the exit. The guy in the raincoat glanced at his phone and then at Cesari, sudden recognition lighting up his face.

He stepped in front of Cesari, smiled and said, "You must be Dr. Cesari."

Cesari abruptly came to a stop, looked at the guy and was confused. "Yes, and you are…?"

"I'm a friend of nurses everywhere."

"What?"

The guy mashed the whipped cream pie into Cesari's face and took off at a run, bolting through the front doors before Cesari could even register surprise. The security guard, an old guy named Louie, came running over. Cesari wiped whipped cream from his eyes and face and stood there in total disbelief. Hospital visitors coming and going in both directions stopped to lend a hand and offer assistance. He wasn't hurt and thanked them all. Louie asked him if he wanted him to call the police but he declined. What would be the point?

Louie gave him a paper towel to wipe off. "Are you okay, Doc?"

He said, "Thanks Louie. I'm fine."

"This is awful. Why would anyone do such a thing?"

"He probably had his reasons. Thanks for your concern, Louie."

Cesari took a deep breath and regained his composure. There was a bathroom nearby for visitors and he went there to finish cleaning up. Melissa was on a roll. He hoped she'd get it out of her system soon. Glancing in the mirror, he couldn't help but laugh at himself and the hole he had landed in. Hopefully, she didn't have any firearms.

He picked up the cannolis at Giancarlo's, and at 8:30 p.m. had the Uber driver drop him off a block away from the brownstone in Chelsea just in case the girls were getting some air on their front stoop. It was just starting to get dark. There was a red Ferrari with tinted windows and the engine running, double-parked in the middle of the block facing away from him. It was several hundred feet from the entrance to Drusilla's building. As he got closer, he spotted the unique vanity plate he had seen in front of the Kit Kat Klub the night Ivan argued with Sofia. It was Yorgi's Ferrari, so he ducked behind an oak tree a safe distance away and watched patiently. Why would Yorgi be here?

In a minute, he found out. A young man got out of the driver's side and glanced up and down the street. He was about six feet tall, late twenties, not a day over thirty. A good-looking muscular guy with sharp features and a full head of wavy hair. His resemblance to Yorgi and Ivan was uncanny. This had to be their younger brother, Tibor, Vito had told him about. His memory jogged, Cesari also suddenly recollected that he was the other guy he saw with Ivan in the basement of the hospital where the construction crews were unloading the semis. Another piece of the puzzle just slid into place.

Tibor walked around to the passenger side of the vehicle and politely opened the door to let his passenger out, a shapely woman in jeans and high heels who carried herself with style and elegance. She wore a wide brimmed summer hat but her back was to him so he couldn't see her face. Tibor once again furtively looked both ways down the street and then kissed her. She wrapped her arms around him briefly and then walked away down the sidewalk while Tibor watched. She didn't look back as he closed her door, walked back to the driver's seat and sat there for a minute, presumably watching her. There was something about the exchange that struck Cesari. It was the gentleness of the encounter, the true tenderness of it. He could feel it all the way to where he was standing.

Tibor was in love.

Suddenly, a BMW pulled up behind the Ferrari in the narrow street and honked angrily for Tibor to move his car out of the way. Cesari was distracted by this as he watched the powerful car roar off. When he looked back, the woman was lost to sight. This was a new development and he wasn't sure what to make of it, but he suddenly realized he had overlooked something of great significance.

He needed to explore the storage area of the hospital. Something was wrong there. Why would Ivan and Tibor have been there at all? With everything that had happened, that seeming coincidence had been drowned down to insignificance, but not anymore. He glanced at his watch. It was approaching 9:00 p.m. and he decided to forego his unplanned visit with Drusilla and Zenobia.

He ditched the box of cannolis, took out his cellphone and dialed Vito. "What are you doing?"

Vito said, "Keeping watch. What do you think? I'm waiting for Yorgi to retaliate."

"Can you break away for about an hour?"

Chapter 30

They convened at the entrance to St. Matt's at 11:00 p.m. Vito showed up with a duffle bag in one hand and a cigarette in his mouth. He wore his perfunctory two-piece suit. When he saw Cesari he flung his cigarette onto the sidewalk and stamped it out with his Italian made shoe. They nodded greetings to each other and walked in through the main doors. Cesari flashed his ID at the night security guard and they were allowed passage. As a physician, he could travel freely day or night anywhere he wanted in the hospital, but as medical director, he was given carte blanche of a whole different magnitude. He could say the most absurd thing that came to his mind and it would be accepted.

So when the guard said, "Working late tonight, aren't you, Dr. Cesari?"

"Couldn't be helped, Marvin. Mr. Gianelli here is with OSHA and they requested a spot check of the construction in the basement. There've been reports of safety violations."

Marvin nodded knowingly. Compliance with the department of Occupational Safety and Health Administration was an everyday part of life in any business including hospitals and it affected everyone.

"Then be careful down there, Doc. Do you have hard hats and masks?"

"I have them in my office. We'll go there first. Thanks."

They went to the elevators and boarded, going to the tenth floor where Cesari's office was just in case the guard was watching the elevator's progress. At the tenth floor, they leaned against the elevator doors to keep them open.

Cesari asked, "You brought the crowbar?"

Vito held up the duffle bag. "Two of them, just like you said."

They waited a couple of minutes and then took the same elevator down to the basement.

When they off-loaded, Cesari said, "It's a zoo down here so be careful."

Within twenty paces of the elevators, it was a like a warzone. Vito commented, "What the hell's going on down here? It's almost as if they're trying to kill somebody. This has to be the sloppiest construction project I've ever seen."

As they passed the pathology department, Cesari dodged a hanging electrical wire and said, "Maybe we really should find some hardhats?"

"I'm game for that."

Several workers were busy cutting copper pipes for some type of plumbing upgrade. Sparks were flying freely in the hallway as they approached. When they saw the two well-dressed men approaching without protective gear, they stopped what they were doing.

One said, "Hey, fellas. You really shouldn't be down here, at least not like that."

Cesari replied, "I'm with administration and this is Mr. Gianelli, an agent from OSHA doing a surprise inspection. His office has received several complaints concerning work-related safety issues. I appreciate your concern. Maybe you could provide us with some hats and eyewear?"

The guy glanced at his friends and said, "Sure. Down the hall another thirty feet or so is a bin with extra hats, glasses and face shields if you want."

They thanked him and proceeded to the bin to don hard hats and protective glasses. Now they looked the part, sort of anyway. Vito's silk suit and Cesari's dress shirt and slacks stuck out like a sore thumb to anyone paying attention. However, the clouds of dust, myriad of activity and cacophony of noise provided a distracting background ambience if someone wasn't specifically homed in on them. They just moved along with purpose acting as if they belonged. Cesari found a clipboard with some paperwork on it and picked it up. As they walked and talked, they would occasionally stop to inspect some part of the construction, reference the clipboard, and move on.

The warehouse was crazy busy just as the last time he was down there. Gigantic trucks were backed up to the entrance with their doors open giving access to men and machines. Forklifts buzzed back and forth with their cargo. Vito and Cesari slowly surveyed the room and decided to make their way from left to right, examining boxes and crates. Once on the main floor in the heart of things it was actually easier to stay out of sight. The great size and quantity of the equipment dwarfed them in comparison, and the majority of the workers who were toiling at the semis couldn't care less about two suits in hardhats running around doing an inspection.

"What are we looking for, Cesari?"

"Anything that would explain what Ivan and Tibor were doing down here."

"Can you give me a hint?"

"No, I can't. That's why this is problematic. I don't see the connection."

"So Tibor has a babe over in Chelsea," Vito commented. "Good for him. Funny coincidence you just happened to come along when you did."

Cesari had filled him in on his findings. "I know, but it had to be him. It was the same Ferrari I saw Yorgi driving and he was the spitting image of both his brothers."

"And it wasn't one of the chicks you were on your way to see?"

"I don't think so. He was parked more than half a football field away from their building. Why would he do that? The couple I saw seemed to really care for each other. The normal thing would have been to get as close to her door as possible and walk her up to the entrance. It probably was just a coincidence, although it worked out well because I had almost forgotten about him and Ivan being here."

Most of the crates were well marked with brand names or stamped with some type of easily recognizable manufacturing seal. Stacks of sheetrock, PVC tubing and plywood spoke for themselves. Eventually they came to a store of boxes that were different from the others. Six feet long by three feet across and two feet deep, they were painted a drab green, had sturdy handles and were marked in a strange language. They had been deliberately placed apart from the normal construction and hospital deliveries. There were quite a few of them.

"What's that language, Cesari?"

Cesari studied the crates and said hesitantly, "I'm not one hundred percent sure but it looks Cyrillic...Russian."

"Russian?"

"That's what I think. Look, it says Москва. I think that means Moscow."

They both glanced at the writing on the side of the crate and Vito said, "So what's that word next to it, Russia?"

The word next to Москва separated by a comma was Россия. Underneath that was some type of abbreviation, РПГ-7.

Cesari shrugged. "I have no idea."

"I don't like this, Cesari."

"Neither do I. Let's open it."

"You sure you want to do this?"

Cesari said, "Why did you think I asked you to bring the crowbars?"

"Self-defense?"

"Stop wasting time and hand me one."

Using the crowbars, they pried the edges of the crate open a couple of inches at a time circumnavigating the box. It was laborious work, but they eventually succeeded, and the cover popped loose. Carefully removing it, they peered into the opening and were greeted by a thick layer of protective straw. They dug through this and found a long metal tube which they lifted out to examine. It was a hair over three feet long, about three and a half inches in diameter, weighed about fifteen pounds and had a telescopic sight, handle and trigger.

Vito whispered in alarm, "Oh shit."

Cesari agreed, "Shit is right. It's some type of Russian-made RPG."

He looked at the size of the box and estimated it could hold anywhere from forty to fifty of the weapons. That would put the weight of the box at close to six or seven hundred pounds not counting the weight of the thick wood crate itself. On either end of the box were heavy duty steel handles drilled into the wood and two more sets on both lengthwise sides so it could be carried by up to six men.

"Let's get out of here, Cesari. Arms dealers don't appreciate people snooping around."

"Fine, let's put the cover back on as best we can and then I want to snap pictures of them."

They replaced the cover and while Vito was gently tapping the nails back into their holes with the crowbar, Cesari busily took pictures of the writing on each of the boxes with his phone. Just as they finished, a big guy with a hard hat approached them. Unshaven and sweating, he wore a yellow vest, dirty blue jeans, and well-worn steel-tipped work boots.

"Hey, you guys. What are you doing?" he demanded gruffly in a you-better-have-a-good-explanation tone.

Vito discreetly tucked the crowbar behind his back as Cesari read the guy's name tag. He had quickly decided that the average worker down here couldn't possibly be involved in anything as nefarious as gun-running, but this guy was the foreman and therefore possibly an active participant. More than likely though, he was just flexing his muscle and enforcing rules that had been handed down to him.

With authority Cesari said, "I'm the safety compliance officer of this hospital and this is Mr. Gianelli from OSHA. He's conducting a surprise inspection of the work environment here authorized under both state and federal law. Furthermore, both environmental and employee safety concerns have been filed with the agency. I suggest you fully cooperate, or we may have to shut you down completely pending a full investigation."

The guy was quiet as he digested that and then said, "How come I didn't hear anything about this?"

Vito stepped forward, the crowbar still behind his back. "That's why it's a surprise. There's not much point in warning people, is there?"

The guy mulled it over and said, "I guess that makes sense."

Cesari said, "We were just about finished anyway. So don't fret about it. You guys passed with flying colors."

The guy had a walkie-talkie hooked to his belt and it started crackling. He picked it up and said, "Paulie here, what's up?"

"Acevedo and Feinberg just arrived. They're looking for you."

"Roger that. Where are they?"

"In the driveway by the semis. They told me to get you."

"Okay, I'll be right there."

He looked at Cesari. "Your boss is here. I'm sure he'll want to see you too."

Cesari nodded, "Definitely, and I'll be there in a minute. I just need to wrap up things here with Mr. Gianelli."

"Sure."

He turned to leave, hesitated, and turned back. Vito and Cesari froze. Paulie said, "Just for the record, guys, may I see some ID?"

Before Cesari could intervene, Vito said, "No problem."

With his free hand he reached into his left trouser pocket and handed Paulie a matchbook from the Kit Kat. Studying the image of the naked girl on the cover, Paulie furrowed his brow in confusion.

Cesari saw what was about to happen and said, "Vito, no…"

Too late, Vito slammed the crowbar hard against the side of the man's head. His hard hat went flying off and the big man silently crumpled to the floor unconscious. Cesari let out a deep sigh.

Vito raised his hand. "Don't say anything, Cesari. I had no choice."

Cesari knelt quickly and felt Paulie for a pulse. He had a strong one and was still breathing. The hard hat had saved his life, but he was going to have a wicked headache and a nasty concussion, if he didn't bleed into his head, that is. If he did, then he was going to need a neurosurgeon.

Cesari said, "Pack up the crowbars and let's get out of here before all hell breaks loose."

Chapter 31

"What happened?" Yorgi asked Feinberg.

They were gathered around Paulie, the night foreman, who was just regaining consciousness. The ugly bruise and laceration on the side of his face made them shudder. His left eye was swollen shut and his chipmunk cheek was turning purple with caked blood.

Feinberg shook his head. "We don't know. Tiberius and I had just arrived. One of the workers spoke to him to let him know. He said he would join us and then he never did. When we searched, we found him here."

"Did everything seem okay before that?"

"According to the worker who spoke to him, yes. He said he would meet us right away and didn't mention any problem."

Acevedo and Shlomo looked on as Ivan knelt next to Paulie trying to revive him. They all glanced around in different directions but didn't see anything amiss with the weapons crates or anything else. Paulie's right eye fluttered open for the first time since they arrived but he looked massively dazed and disoriented. He drooled on himself and his eyes darted around without recognition.

"Perhaps he fell and hit his head," offered Acevedo. "There are tools lying all around to trip over."

With that they glanced at the floor and noticed a few carelessly placed hammers and screwdrivers here and there. Shlomo grunted, "Perhaps... Check the crates, Yorgi. Make sure they have not been tampered with."

While Yorgi did that, Ivan helped Paulie to a sitting position and placed a bottle of water near his lips. Paulie was beginning to make sense although he was a long way off and would be for several days.

Acevedo said, "We should call the emergency room to come get him. He'll need proper evaluation and a head CT."

Shlomo nodded. "Yes, but do so after we take cargo away. It would be better."

Acevedo agreed. "Of course."

Yorgi returned after a minute and said, "Everything seems to be in order."

"No more coffins, Yorgi?"

"No, Shlomo. Just what we ordered."

"Good. Too many mysterious things have been happening." He took in a deep breath and let it out before continuing. "And now this."

Yorgi stood over Paulie and asked him, "Do you know what happened?"

Paulie looked up at him with glassy eyes, thought about it and whispered, "I'm not sure. Everything's so fuzzy."

"Think hard, Paulie. Is important. Did you fall?"

"No, I don't think so... wait... There was a big guy. I think I remember now. He was from the Department of Health. He hit me."

Feinberg said, "He's delirious. He probably has a concussion."

"Undoubtedly," mused Yorgi. "You wouldn't have to be a physician to make that assertion."

"I'd bet a million to one he tripped on something and landed headfirst into one of these crates." Feinberg guessed. "Paulie, have you been drinking tonight?"

Paulie shook his head. "No, sir. I stopped doing that years ago."

Yorgi's eyes scanned the floor again until he saw something adjacent to Paulie's butt. He reached down and picked it up. His eyes went wide as he looked at it, and immediately and as discreetly as possible placed it in his pocket.

"What you find, Yorgi?" asked Ivan who had caught the move.

"Is nothing, Ivan," he answered quickly and changed the subject. "Paulie can you describe this big man from the Department of Health?"

"I don't know. I can't think straight...He was big like you only ugly as sin like an experiment that had gone wrong."

Yorgi asked Feinberg, "Are all the workers accounted for?"

Feinberg said, "Yes, they're all waiting outside for further instructions."

"No one heard or saw anything?"

"Not that they'll admit."

Yorgi contemplated that and crouched down close to Paulie. Ivan was kneeling on Paulie's other side. Yorgi said, "Is very important, Paulie. I need you to think hard about everything that happened tonight. Can you do this for me?"

Paulie took another sip of water. His eyes were coming into focus. He said, "Like I said. It was a big guy...mean-looking." He paused to take a breath and another sip. "He said he was from the department of health...no. I remember now. It wasn't the Department of Health. He was from OSHA. That's it. Now I remember...OSHA."

Acevedo and Feinberg glanced at each other. Shlomo owned multiple business enterprises and knew all about OSHA, but he had never heard of an OSHA agent sniffing around the workplace at midnight.

Shlomo asked, "Is this normal for OSHA to come to hospital this late at night?"

Acevedo said, "Absolutely not. I've never heard of such a thing."

Yorgi asked Paulie, "Okay, Paulie. So it was a big mean-looking man from OSHA. Why did he hit you?"

"I don't know. We didn't argue. He said he was finished with his inspection and that we passed. He was getting ready to leave and bam. The next thing I know I'm lying here with the worst headache of my life."

Paulie's voice and demeanor were growing stronger with each passing minute. His story seemed coherent and consistent although outlandish. Yorgi was piecing it together in his head but it still made no sense. Why would an OSHA agent be doing an inspection this late and why would he attack Paulie? Unless he wasn't an OSHA agent and the man knew his cover was blown, but then who was he?

"Paulie, you are doing very well, but try to remember anything else you can about this man. Did he have a name?"

Paulie thought it over for a few seconds before replying, "Yes, his name was Gianelli."

Yorgi tensed ever so slightly, his suspicions confirmed, but how could Gianelli have known what was going on down here? That was a question that would have to be answered at some other time. Ivan looked at Yorgi with raised eyebrows but said nothing.

Shlomo turned to Acevedo and Feinberg, "Does this name sound familiar to you?"

Both men shook their heads no. Feinberg said, "I'll check with the OSHA people first thing in the morning to see if they have anybody by that name and if they knew of any surprise inspection."

"Yes, please do so. Yorgi continue. He may remember something else important," Shlomo said.

Yorgi turned back to Paulie. "Did the man give a first name?"

Paulie shook his head. "No, but he did give me a present."

Yorgi asked, "What do you mean, Paulie?"

"He gave me a picture of a naked girl. She was very pretty."

Yorgi said to the others, "I think he is becoming confused again."

Shlomo said, "Very good, Yorgi. That is enough. I do not think we learn much more from him. We must get started."

"Yes," said Yorgi. "We are already behind schedule. Feinberg, get some men and help carry crates outside. There is mid-sized box truck waiting in driveway. Drivers speak no English so don't talk to them. Ivan will supervise. Ivan, tell Tibor we will be few more minutes but to start van and be ready to go."

"Wait," whispered Paulie hoarsely. "There's something else."

Yorgi leaned over him. "Yes, Paulie. You remember something else?"

He nodded. "There was another guy. It just came to me. Not as big. A good-looking guy. He said he was the safety compliance officer for the hospital."

Feinberg shook his head and said, "We don't have a safety compliance officer."

"What was his name, Paulie?"

"He didn't say."

Shlomo said, "Enough, Yorgi... Tiberius, maybe I am misinterpreting tonight's events, so let me summarize them to make sure that we both understand the same thing. Not one but possibly two men made their way into the basement of your hospital unchallenged, managed to wander around for an unknown length of time for an unknown purpose, attacked one your workers, and escaped unscathed? Is that how you see it also?"

Acevedo's mouth was as dry as cotton. Feinberg began to fidget in place. Acevedo stammered, "I will tighten up security. No one will get in here again. I promise."

"I want armed security not just dimwits with big bellies and handheld radios."

"But we're a hospital. That could be complicated."

"Are you making excuses?"

"No, I'll figure it out. It won't be a problem."

"It had better not be. Anybody that comes into this room without authorization, I want dealt with severely."

Finished, Shlomo turned to Paulie who was again staring dreamily off into space. Shlomo grabbed the leg of his walking stick, gave it a quarter turn and withdrew the gleaming, deadly blade. He placed the point over Paulie's heart and before anyone could say anything, gave a quick shove. In and out. Just like that. Paulie's eyes went wide and he gasped briefly in pain and just as quickly slumped over dead.

Acevedo and Feinberg looked like they were going to be sick. Shlomo cleaned his blade on Paulie's yellow vest leaving a red streak across it. He said, "Yorgi, take him to incinerator in Newark with the others."

"Yes, Shlomo."

Shlomo looked at Tiberius. "You are probably wondering why... Because he was weak and I have no use for weakness. Remember that Tiberius."

"I will."

****

Later, after the weapons had been loaded into the box truck and the drivers sped away, Yorgi, Ivan and Tibor sat in the front of their white panel catering van with the bodies of the priest, the imam, the rabbi, Grigori and now Paulie in the back. It was nearly 1:30 a.m. They were about to drive to the incinerator in Newark to dispose of them all, but first they needed to come up with a plan. They had a big problem on their hands, and they knew it would only grow bigger with

John Avanzato

time. If they didn't deal with it decisively, they would be on the receiving end of Shlomo's walking stick.

Yorgi said, "I don't know how is possible, but that Italian, Vito, from the Kit Kat has turned tables on us. That was him in the hospital tonight, and if my instincts are correct the other man was his friend, Dr. Cesari."

"How can you be sure, Yorgi?" asked Ivan. "The name Gianelli might be very common. This is New York. Italians are like locusts here."

"I can be sure because of this, brother."

He reached into his pocket and retrieved the matchbook Vito had given to Paulie in order to distract him for the sucker punch. He showed it to his brothers. On the cover in miniature was a voluptuous naked girl blowing them a kiss with the name and address of the Kit Kat Klub written at the bottom.

Ivan nodded, "You are right. There can be no doubt, but maybe they were just fishing around."

"No, Ivan. They know what is inside those crates. I am certain. I did not want to say to Shlomo, but one of the crates had clearly been tampered with and then resealed."

"What should we do? If Shlomo finds out we are the ones who provoked Gianelli we are finished."

"Exactly, my brothers. Which is why we need to take care of Gianelli as soon as possible as well as that nuisance, Dr. Cesari. I had hoped to pit Gianelli against Shlomo, but I fear it may be too late for that. Ivan, you and I will bring body of rabbi to back of Kit Kat and throw in dumpster. Gianelli's men will be on lookout, but it is late, and they will be complacent. Most of their security will be sleepy guards peeking out the front door from time to time. We can access alley behind club from side street away from Second Avenue. We will take other bodies to incinerator. After we have accomplished task, we call police with anonymous tip."

"And what about me, Yorgi? You give me no assignment, and who are all these dead religious people anyway that I have

221

been baby-sitting all night?" Tibor asked peevishly, tired of always feeling as if he wasn't in the room while his older brothers planned things.

"Do not concern your pretty head about them, Tibor. The less you know, the better off you will be in the long run. Suffice to say, they got on the wrong side of Shlomo. And you are in error to think I have no job for you. Is very important thing you must do tonight. Feinberg made copies of keys to Dr. Cesari's apartment and gave me set. There is chance doctor may have had locks changed. Feinberg didn't know but doubted it. His assessment is that Dr. Cesari is much too arrogant to worry about locks. I am sure you will be able to master this small task. We will find out. I want you to bring Andrej's and Leandro's bloodied clothes there and place them somewhere discreet as if he was trying to hide them. Wait until morning to call police, Tibor."

"Why wait?"

"If two anonymous tips called in at same time it may raise suspicions, but more importantly, Feinberg would like Dr. Cesari dragged out of hospital in front of employees."

Tibor furrowed his brow in thought and then asked, "How can I plant clothes in his apartment? Won't he be sleeping there now?"

"Create diversion, Tibor. Please to think before speak. You are no longer infant."

"Yes, older brother."

Chapter 32

At 2:00 a.m., Cesari was in his apartment but he wasn't sleeping when his phone rang. He had been googling up the English translations of the pictures he had taken of the crates and was trying to make sense of it. So far, he was confident that there were two boxes of RPG-7s, the latest model produced by Russia, and at least two crates of ammunition to go along with it. There were two crates of AK-12s, the newest model assault rifle, chambering the 5.45×39mm cartridge along with four boxes of said ammunition. There were two whole boxes of hand grenades, a crateful of night vision goggles and so much more. Somebody was preparing for battle. The inventory's black-market price tag was staggering, and he still had a dozen more images to decipher. Nearly overwhelmed by the importance of his findings, he was actually relieved by the buzzing of his cellphone although he was surprised by the identity of the caller.

He said, "Hi, Zenobia. Is everything all right?"

Her voice was stressed and worried, "No, is no all right. There is man outside house watching me."

Cesari immediately tensed in alarm, "Could you be more specific?"

"I went to front stoop to smoke cigarette. Man was in car across street watching me."

"You went outside at this hour to have a smoke?"

"No, was two hours ago, but he still there. I know to smoke is bad habit, but I cannot help."

"Fine, but how do you know he's watching you? Maybe he was waiting for someone and you just happened to appear at your door?"

"No, because I go back inside when I see him watching. I don't like the way he look at me so I peek from inside curtain. Always he stare at house. Please come. He seems very dangerous. I think he is predator."

"Have you tried calling the police?"

"Yes, they say they can do nothing because man has commit no crime. I am very afraid and cannot go to sleep. I hold kitchen knife for protection. Please, Dr. Cesari. I know he is bad man. He wants to hurt Zenobia."

"Okay, try to relax Zenobia. I'll be there in ten minutes. I'll leave right now."

He left his apartment in a hurry and caught the first passing yellow cab. True to his word, he arrived at the brownstone in a hair under ten minutes. The first thing he did was scan up and down the street for a villain. It was two in the morning and he saw no one. He walked back and forth checking all the parked cars on both sides of the street within a hundred-foot radius of the brownstone in case the guy was trying to conceal himself by lying down, but he found nothing.

He then climbed the brick steps to the entrance and was just about to knock when the door opened and Zenobia greeted him. She was wearing a floral-patterned, oriental, short silk robe and stylish, heeled slippers. Her bare legs were toned, tanned and very distracting. Oddly, she was still wearing her dark sunglasses. He was sure she must have some sort of light sensitivity. She glanced past him across the street and then up and down the block.

She asked, "He is gone?"

"I think so. I checked most of the cars on either side for quite a distance and didn't see anyone hiding."

"Thank you so much for come, Doctor. I feel better knowing you are here. Please enter. I already make coffee."

"You want me to come in?"

"Certainly…What if man come back? Please stay just for short time."

He hesitated. This felt very weird, but he said, "Sure."

She led him into the kitchen where she said, "Please have seat. Would you like cream or sugar in coffee?"

The room was large and quite upscale with granite counters and high-end appliances. He sat at the highly polished wood table and watched her walk toward a counter with a ten-thousand-dollar automatic coffee machine sitting on it. It was the kind of coffee machine you might see in the first-class lounge of an airport as you stood behind Bill Gates waiting for him to make himself a macchiato. It ground its own beans, and could make drip coffee, espresso, latte, cappuccino or whatever your heart desired. There was a half pot of drip coffee waiting in its cradle.

"Black, please," he replied. "Where is Drusilla?"

"She sleep. I did not wish to worry her."

"She doesn't know about the guy out there?"

"No, was late when I first see him. She was already sleep. If I wake her up, she would panic. She is not as brave as Zenobia."

Cesari smiled at that as she served him his coffee in a fine china cup with a delicate print, and then sat across from him. As she crossed her legs, the top of her robe splayed open revealing way too much of her anatomy. He was starting to feel uncomfortable. It was bad enough that she was in her nightwear on full display in front of him, but the sunglasses made the scene surreal bordering on bizarre. She was incredibly beautiful and apparently just as nutty. In his opinion these types were the most dangerous to be around. You never knew what was going to happen next.

He said, "Thank you for the coffee, Zenobia, but I'm not sure how long I can stay. I've had a pretty long day."

"Just a few minutes, Doctor. In case bad man return. Who knows? Maybe he went for coffee too?"

Cesari grinned at that and nodded. "You have a point. He may have gotten hungry or thirsty but tell me. Why would anybody be watching you or this house?"

"I don't know. Does sex maniac need reason? Maybe he saw me in supermarket earlier and follow me."

"Another good point... Okay, but I can't stay here all night. I really have to get some sleep. If he's not back in thirty minutes, we'll just have to take our chances. You can always call me back. Does that sound reasonable?"

"I agree. Half an hour should be enough time."

The way she said it sounded strange. He assumed she meant enough time to see if the guy returned, but it didn't come out like that. He said, "If he does return either later to-night or tomorrow, please try to take his picture from your window and also a picture of the car's license plate. By the way, you didn't say what kind of car he was driving. Did you get a good look at it?"

She seemed unsure of herself for a second and then re-sponded, "It was red Ferrari."

Cesari was taken aback by that and said, "A red Ferrari? Are you sure?"

"Yes, very sure. Why?"

"That's a pretty ostentatious car for someone to be doing surveillance work in."

"What mean?"

"Usually when people follow other people or are watching them, they try not to stand out either in their clothes or the ve-hicles they drive. They don't want anyone to remember them."

"Hmm, well I learn something today."

Cesari contemplated that for a minute. There were an awful lot of red Ferraris floating around this part of town all of a sudden. It was almost as if there was a sale on them somewhere.

"Did you happen to see the license plate?"

She shook her head, "No, I couldn't see."

He wondered if maybe Tibor was waiting for his girl and for some reason Zenobia mistook his intentions. He said, "Tell me about the guy you saw, Zenobia? Was he young, old, clean-shaven, white, black, Chinese…?"

She thought about it and said, "He was old man with long white beard and definitely was Chinese."

This surprised Cesari. It certainly wasn't what he expected. "Are you sure? That's a somewhat unusual profile of a stalker or potential robber."

"I very sure. He leer at me with beady eyes and then lick his lips. You think I don't know what I see?"

"I meant no harm. Okay, well that narrows it down quite a bit unless it was some sort of disguise."

"He was evil to look at. I hope I never see him again. Zenobia never so frightened."

"I understand. It's all right now."

Cesari finished his coffee and was halfway through his second cup when he looked at his watch. He said, "It's been more than half an hour, Zenobia. I'll check one more time but if he hasn't returned, I'm going to have to leave."

"I understand and thank you for being so patient."

He walked over to the front window and peered from the side of the curtain up and down the block. He didn't see any red Ferrari or elderly Chinese man with a white beard. The street was well-lit, deserted and serene. The whole thing seemed so absurd he wondered if she was scamming him. Maybe she was on some sort of psychiatric medication… or needed to be started on one. He felt very exposed being in her house at his hour with her dressed as she was. This situation was even more compromising than the last time he was here. He needed to go…now.

He turned to say goodnight and saw her in the kitchen cleaning off the table. He said, "There's no one here, Zenobia."

She seemed relieved, "Good. I will be able to sleep. I come there to let you out."

She walked into the living room toward him and accidentally caught her foot on an irregularity in the carpet, tripped and fell forward landing on her hands and knees with a yelp. He rushed forward to help her up. She wasn't hurt but the impact knocked her sunglasses off onto the floor. She was embarrassed and flustered, feeling very silly. He lifted her up and stood facing her as she regained her composure. Her robe had come nearly completely undone, and she wasn't wearing anything underneath, but that wasn't what caught his attention. He stared at her eyes; the right one was brilliant green and the left was drab brown.

Blushing, she quickly wrapped her robe back around herself and retrieved her sunglasses while he stood there equally embarrassed and unsure of himself. By the time she had put the glasses back on, he had taken two discreet steps back toward the front door to put some much-needed distance between them. He gave no indication to her at all that anything unusual had just happened. It was 3:00 a.m. and there was a beautiful naked Romanian girl with sunglasses on to hide her strange eyes. He was there to protect her from an elderly Chinese man with a long white beard driving a red Ferrari. Nothing to see here. It happened every day. Every nerve fiber in his body screamed for him to get out of there while he still could.

Ignoring the obvious awkwardness of the situation, she said nonchalantly, "Thank you for your help, Doctor. I will call if he returns."

He said, "Yes, please do. I hope that you'll be able to get some rest tonight."

The let's-pretend-that-didn't-happen strategy worked for him.

Chapter 33

The next morning Cesari opened the door to his office hesitantly, fully expecting to find some type of dead life form on his desk, perhaps a fish wrapped in newspaper this time. But there was none, and he breathed a sigh of relief as he sat and looked around for surprises. There was a lot going on that required his full attention and this sideshow with Melissa wasn't helping him concentrate. Nonetheless, he did his best to shake it off.

The hospital was being used as a temporary storage facility for illegal weapons. The question was who was buying them, who was selling them, and where were they going? Were Acevedo and Feinberg in on it or simply stooges for some greater mastermind. Yorgi and his brothers were somehow involved but in what capacity? They were trying to take over the Kit Kat and make a name for themselves but what did that have to do with illegal weapons and vampires? It seemed a little out of their league.

It all came back to Shlomo.

It was his money bankrolling the hospital. Acevedo and Feinberg were two-bit players but they belonged to Shlomo. Yorgi and company also worked for Shlomo. Federal agents were interested in Shlomo. He was the common denominator. Shlomo, Shlomo, Shlomo... He seemed like a nice old guy but Cesari had been fooled before. Outward appearances frequently masked a black soul. He would have to bring this up with Tierney when he told him about the weapons he discovered. Old Shlomo would need greater scrutiny.

Then there was Zenobia and Drusilla. Last night had drained him. Those two were starting to drive him a bit crazy. An old Chinese guy driving a red Ferrari around Chelsea? And he fell for the whole thing...but why? Tibor was in that neighborhood as well. Was Zenobia the girl he saw that night? What were the odds that a strapping young Romanian guy driving a red Ferrari and a beautiful albeit nutty Romanian girl living right there were unknown to each other? And if they were known to each other, why did he not park near her home? Why would he have let her walk such a great distance alone at night?

And those eyes...

It was starting to make sense. He took out his cellphone and dialed Tierney. The call went to voicemail. He tried again without success. He needed to speak to him in a hurry and was afraid that he had already wasted too much time. There were millions of dollars in Russian made weaponry waiting to be transported to destinations unknown and that may have only been the tip of the iceberg. He should have reported it to the police immediately but that was water under the bridge now. He wondered what the foreman would have to say when he woke up. Would the weapons still be there this morning?

As he fretted, Feinberg swung the door open and entered with Acevedo close behind. Acevedo was holding a martini glass half-filled with a clear liquid and an olive skewered by a colored toothpick. Cesari glanced at his watch. It was 10:30 a.m. You could say what you wanted to about these guys, but they had chops. That was for sure. They sat down uninvited opposite him. Cesari put his cellphone away and stared at them, wondering what new form of torment was coming his way. Should he confront them about last night? He decided not to. They would just deny everything anyway.

He said, "Good morning, gentlemen."

Feinberg smiled, "Isn't it though? Great work with Melissa, Cesari. I wasn't sure if you had the stones to carry it off, but you came through with flying colors."

Cesari frowned but didn't say anything. The temptation to leap across the desk and pummel the guy was almost uncontrollable. He would start with a couple of rights to the head just to stun him but allow him to remain conscious so he could register pain while he broke every bone in his body, finishing with a well-placed stomp to the groin.

While Cesari's thoughts roamed to premeditated murder, Acevedo added, "Yes, I must say. You proved yourself worthy of the team, Cesari. In fact, Feinberg has been regaling me so much with tales of the delights of Melissa's sweet embrace that I thought I might like in on the action."

Cesari's eyebrows went up unconsciously. "Excuse me?"

"There's a little number in the ICU that's caught my eye. Her name's Jada. She's relatively new. You can't miss her; thin black girl, boobies to die for. I was thinking to go the traditional route of wining and dining her but after what Feinberg told me I think I'd prefer to try the angry, coerced, completely humiliated path to sexual gratification. It has a certain appeal that I find truly compelling. I'll give you until the end of this week to procure her for me and remember, I saw her first. I understand that you have a quite a formidable reputation with the ladies. By the way, Cesari, she wears funky, cool European style eyeglasses. Make sure you impress upon her that she is to keep them on at all times, if you get my drift."

Cesari said, "I get your drift, but you guys can't expect me to wander around the hospital everyday pimping nurses for you."

They both started laughing but didn't answer the question. Instead, Feinberg said, "C'mon, Cesari, lighten up. Tiberius was just yanking your chain."

Tiberius added, "Of course I was. I meant you can have until early next week."

They both started chortling and snorting again. When they calmed down Feinberg said, "You're hysterical, Tiberius."

Acevedo replied, "Thank you."

Cesari said, "Is there anything more I can do for either one of you?"

Feinberg nodded. "In fact, there is. It's come to my attention that nursing feathers have been ruffled, and I think it would behoove the entire institution if we cleared the air with them before things get out of hand. I've arranged for a lunch meeting down in conference room C in the basement for you to answer questions and allay their concerns."

"And just how am I going to allay their concerns after what just happened?"

Acevedo took a long gulp of his martini and said, "C'mon, Cesari. Grow up and put on your big boy pants. They're women. Not only do they like being pushed around, they expect it. They deserve and require a firm male hand to guide and direct them. Show them what you're made of for God's sake."

Feinberg added, "Jesus, Cesari. I'm a little disappointed by all this pansy-ass whining. You were given a Y-chromosome for a reason. Now learn how to use it. The meeting's in an hour."

Cesari glanced from one to the other, blinked, and said, "Who exactly is going to be at this conciliatory gathering?"

"As many nurses as possible," Feinberg said. "I sent an email this morning to all the charge nurses on all the floors including the OR and ICU to allow as many people as possible to attend without jeopardizing patient care. You should have quite a crowd. I wish I could attend."

"You won't be there?"

Feinberg shook his head. "Negative. For obvious reasons, it could be a little uncomfortable for me. I mean what if Melissa is sitting in the front row with a cream pie or something?"

"You heard about that?"

Feinberg chuckled, "And the rat...too funny. The girl's got spirit. I really like that."

Cesari turned to Acevedo. "What about you? Are you going to be there?"

Acevedo finished his martini. "Do I look insane?"

"Great...So I'm going it alone?"

Feinberg said, "You can handle it."

They both stood up and walked to the door. Acevedo turned around and said, "Remember to tell Jada what I said about keeping the glasses on."

They stepped out and closed the door before he could respond. He just sat there not sure of what had just happened. Whatever this was had to stop. This meeting with the nurses was going to be brutal. He wondered if he should just skip it. It would be cowardly for sure but the idea of trying to stand in front of a room full of angry women attempting to justify the unjustifiable was starting to make him physically ill. They would skewer him.

He fiddled for the better part of an hour thinking of ways to sugar-coat the events of the preceding days, his new role as medical director, and specifically his misstep with Melissa. He was new at his job, he would say, and handled an uncomfortable task with the clumsiness of a rookie. He would promise to learn from his mistake. Mea culpa, Mea culpa. That could work.

As noon approached, he went down to the conference room and grabbed the doorknob to enter, but hesitated. His heart was pounding. Gird your loins, Cesari. How bad could it get? He entered the room and was dismayed at the size of the crowd. There were more than a hundred and fifty people jammed into a room that would have felt crowded with half that number; all nurses, all women and all bristling when they saw him.

The room went quiet except for an occasional hiss as he waded his way to the front where there was a podium. He felt their eyes burning holes into his back and he resisted the urge to bolt before things got ugly. Show no fear he told himself as he stepped behind the stand to face them. Some sat, most stood, a few held signs saying either *#metoo* or *My body, My choice.* His spirits sank as he spotted Melissa in the front row. She was holding a noose made of thick rope.

He cleared his throat. "Hello, everyone."

Quickly drowned out by catcalls and loud booing, he waited patiently for order to return. The ladies were having a grand time and it crossed his mind that he could possibly be in physical danger.

After a minute, quiet came back and he resumed. "I think most you know me. For those of you who don't, I'm Dr. Cesari, your new medical director."

A nurse from the rear shouted, "We're not for sale, Cesari."

"I know that," he said calmly. "And although you all might have heard several skewed versions of recent events, I would like to set the record straight."

Another woman called out, "Are you calling Melissa a liar?"

More boos and jeers followed this and he again patiently let them settle down. He then shook his head, and said, "No, I'm not calling anyone a liar, but I think that there have been a lot of very strong emotions and tempers flaring which may have caused some distortion of the facts."

Melissa stood up suddenly in front of the podium and faced her colleagues. She held the rope over her head and yelled, "Let's hang the son-of-a-bitch! Let's hang him high!"

The rest of the women howled their approval, chanting loudly, "Hang him high!"

Cesari turned pale and flustered and stepped back from the lectern. The crowd started chanting even more stridently over and over, "Hang him high! Hang him high! Hang him high!"

Soon they began stamping their feet to the rhythm of their chorus and the room reverberated with riotous, deafening noise. He had lost total control and was considering his options when the door at the back of the room swung open. Detective Tierney and two uniformed NYPD patrolmen entered and observed with consternation what could only be described at that point as a rowdy mob with violence on its mind. Tierney and the officers marched to the front where Cesari stood sheepishly and more than just a little thankful for the backup although it wasn't entirely clear why they were there. It crossed his mind that someone outside the room had heard the commotion and called for help. Whatever the reason he was glad Tierney had arrived. They had a lot to talk about.

Gradually, the noise died down to a dull roar as the nurses watched the newcomers with curiosity. Cesari's courage returned and he was about to address the unruly crowd when Tierney grabbed the back of his head and slammed his face hard into the podium. Dazed and blood pouring from his nose, he turned to defend himself but felt his arms being roughly twisted behind him as the officers handcuffed him tightly.

Tierney growled loudly for everyone to hear. "I'm sorry ladies, Dr. Cesari and I have a few things to discuss down at the station. You can dismember him at a later date."

The room erupted in boisterous cheering.

Chapter 34

The interview room of the NYPD's Ninth Precinct on East Fifth Street was a ten-foot by twelve-foot bare room with a wood table in the center and several wood chairs. A five by four one-way mirror on the wall and video camera blinking in the corner were the only adornments in the room. Cesari sat in his chair holding his nose with a bloody rag. He was thankful that it wasn't broken and that the handcuffs had been removed. Bottled water sat on the table in front of him.

He hadn't been read his Miranda rights or told why he had been brought down to the station house. After Tierney had given him the head slap to the podium, he was carted away in complete radio silence. He wasn't even sure if he was actually under arrest. Tierney had then gone off in a different direction, and he'd been sitting there for nearly thirty minutes without a hint of what was going on. The bleeding had mostly stopped.

Another ten minutes passed, and the door opened. Vito was escorted into the room by two officers and told to sit in the chair next to Cesari. A bottle of water was placed in front of him. He looked like he had fallen down a flight of stairs. His clothes were disheveled and his hair mussed. His white shirt was half out of his pants and his usually pristinely polished shoes were scuffed. Cesari took the rag off his face to study his friend. He wasn't handcuffed either.

After the officers left, Cesari asked, "What happened to you?"

"I fell down a flight of stairs."

"Tierney?"

He nodded. "And you? Tierney?"

Cesari nodded. "Do you know what's going on?"

"I know why I'm here, but I don't know what that's got to do with you. They found a body in the dumpster behind the Kit Kat."

"A body? What kind of body?"

"That's all I know…a body. I wasn't even at the Kit Kat when they found it. I was in my apartment on Mulberry Street. I'm not even sure Tierney didn't make the whole thing up. I told you he likes to roust me. Anyway, the next thing I know I'm here. What about you?"

Cesari said, "I'm not important enough to give a reason. He picked me up in the middle of a meeting and said he wanted to talk."

"About what?"

"He didn't say. He probably did me a favor though. The meeting was a nursing gripe session and tempers were starting to flare."

Vito looked at the camera and then at the mirror. "They're probably watching and listening."

"Undoubtedly… I wonder what's going on. They hand-cuffed me but didn't formally arrest me. No one read me my rights or charged me with anything."

"The same here."

Five minutes later, Detective Tierney entered the room with a thirtyish year-old Hispanic woman in uniform. They sat opposite them. He opened a hard-shelled briefcase on the table, reached in and took out several manila file folders of varying thickness as she opened a laptop. As the device powered on, she placed a yellow legal pad to one side in order to take notes.

Tierney nodded at them without expression and said to the officer, "Are you ready, Miriam?"

She nodded and he turned back to them. "Let's take it from the top. You tell me what you know and then I'll tell you if you're lying. Even one lie from either one of you and the voluntary question and answer part is over. You both get read your rights, processed, and spend the rest of the night in the tank getting acquainted with the local meth-heads while you wait for your lawyers. Please acknowledge either verbally or non-verbally that you understand."

They nodded and said in unison, "We understand."

"Let's start with you, Cesari, and let me explain the ground rules," Tierney began. "This is not a two-way conversation. I ask the questions and you answer them, not the other way around. Mr. Gianelli keeps his mouth shut until I ask him a question. Now…how long have you been friends with Mr. Gianelli?"

Cesari raised his eyebrows but answered truthfully, "Since the first grade."

"Are you aware of Mr. Gianelli's criminal activities?"

"I am aware of the things that he has been accused of, yes."

"Fine, and have you ever been arrested and or convicted of a felony yourself?"

He hesitated ever so slightly, "Yes…"

When he didn't expand on the subject, Tierney slid one of the manila folders over to him. "Dr. Cesari, please review the contents of the folder and tell me whether they are true or false to the best of your knowledge."

He opened the folder and flipped through his legal history; arrest record as a troubled youth, mug shots, court ordered psychology opinions, felony conviction for obstruction, known associations with underworld figures and much more."

He slid the folder back and said, "Mostly true."

"Mostly?"

"I'm six feet even not five-eleven."

Vito suppressed a chuckle. Tierney scowled. "Very funny. And you failed to mention all this to me...why?"

"I didn't think it was important and you never asked."

Tierney's face colored in anger. "I am a New York City detective investigating a double homicide and a felon with ties to the Cosa Nostra offers to help me and you didn't think it was important? Did your mother drop you on your head as a child?"

"When you put it that way..."

"Shut up..."

Tierney tossed another folder at him. "Do you know what these are?"

The folder contained multiple eight-by-eleven high resolution color photographs of two different sets of bloodied clothes. Vito sat stone faced and quiet but darted his eyes to get a look

Cesari shook his head, "No, what are they?"

"They are what we call in the detective business, evidence, and they were found in your apartment."

For the first time Cesari showed a reaction. He sat forward eyes opened wide in alarm. "My apartment?"

"Yes, underneath your bed in a plastic garbage bag along with this."

Another folder came flying across the table. It contained a photograph of a long-necked, two-pronged bloodied barbecue fork."

Cesari absorbed the information and said, "That's the murder weapon and those are the two victim's clothes. They were found naked."

Tierney turned to the officer. "Miriam, make a note that Dr. Cesari acknowledges that the barbecue fork is indeed the murder weapon and that those are the clothes of the victims."

She nodded quietly and made the entry into the laptop. Tierney relaxed a little. "I'm glad we're on the same page, Doctor. It makes my job that much easier."

"We're not on the same page by a long shot."

"But you just admitted…"

"I didn't admit anything, and you know it. Somebody planted those items in my apartment in an attempt to frame me."

"Now who would want to frame a nice catholic boy like you?"

"The murderers obviously."

"You know, Cesari, you almost had me…all those helpful ideas and theories. It was almost as if you were at the crime scene yourself. But you overplayed your hand when you told me you figured out what the murder weapon was. That was a bridge too far."

"I didn't figure it out. It was Harry in the pathology department who figured it out. I just took credit for it."

"So Harry's in on it too…Well that makes sense. It's always nice to have a guy on the inside."

"You can't be serious. Harry couldn't hurt a fly."

"But you could?"

Cesari didn't say anything.

"Cat got your tongue, Cesari? Let's start over. Where were you on the nights of the murders and can anyone confirm that?"

Cesari thought about it for a minute and said, "The night of the first murder I was home in bed alone, but I had a late dinner at the Polish restaurant on the first floor of my building. Piotr Zielinski, the owner, would probably be able to confirm that. It was a slow night and he sat down with me to talk. We had a lengthy conversation about European politics. I left at close to 11:00 p.m. or shortly thereafter."

"What about the second murder?"

Cesari rubbed his chin and glanced at Vito. "I had dinner and cigars with Mr. Gianelli. We were at Wolfgang's Steakhouse in Tribeca and we left after midnight. There should be plenty of witnesses there to confirm that."

Tierney thought about it. "I'll have to do some math but if the Polish guy at the restaurant confirms your alibi, I agree it would have been impossible for you to have dumped the first victim in an alley over on First Avenue at about the same time. As far as the second murder is concerned, I'm not thrilled that your alibi is some snake-in-the-grass hoodlum but if the staff at Wolfgang's can place you there at the time you say, then you're off the hook on that one too. Miriam, please get on the alibis as soon as we're done."

She answered in a sweet voice, "Yes, Detective."

Cesari asked, "Were there any fingerprints on the fork?"

Tierney scowled. "I ask the questions, remember... No, it was wiped clean or they wore gloves. Both victims' blood types have already been confirmed on the fork by the way. The forensics people are all over this."

"The fork being wiped clean supports my innocence."

"How so?"

"Why would I go through the trouble of wearing gloves or wiping my prints off it and then store the thing covered in the victims' blood under my bed? It doesn't make sense. Besides, I would have soaked it in bleach, run it in the dishwasher, soaked it again and then put it back in my kitchen drawer or disposed of it. Same for the clothes. In less than an hour, there wouldn't have been any trace of anything."

Miriam looked up, impressed.

"Possibly, Cesari, but maybe you just like to keep souvenirs? Happens all the time. Point in case, Jeffrey Dahmer, remember him? He used to keep body parts of his victims in his refrigerator."

Touché, Cesari thought.

"But I'll grant you that it does seem a little farfetched. Too convenient if you will," Tierney continued. "I received an anonymous tip about the evidence at 7:00 a.m. this morning and fifteen minutes later that manila folder showed up at my door with your past history. I like an open and shut case as much as the next guy, but a lawyer would rip this one apart like a paper bag. Seems like somebody has a grudge against you."

"Either that or somebody thinks I've been sniffing around in places I shouldn't be sniffing around."

"I'm still pissed you weren't forthright about your past. It could have tainted the whole investigation not to mention my career."

"I'm sorry."

"No, you're not. You got caught. There's a difference."

"I'm still sorry."

"Shut up...Your turn, Gianelli."

Chapter 35

"I never saw him before in my life," Vito said as he perused several glossy photos of the dead rabbi discovered at the Kit Kat. The gaping wound in his throat was the obvious cause of death. Cesari peeked over Vito's shoulder at the photo too.

"Think hard, Gianelli," retorted Tierney.

"Who is he?"

"He *was* rabbi Menachem Weiss of the Temple Beth El in midtown, and he was found in the dumpster behind your strip club. What happened? Did he owe you money or something and you ran out of patience?"

"I never saw him before or heard his name, and it's a gentlemen's club not a strip club. The girls are professional dancers, not strippers and I told you, it's not my club."

"Well excuse me," Tierney said slowly and sarcastically. "Thanks for the lesson on the finer points of the sex industry. So if it's not your club, then whose is it?"

"How should I know?"

"Don't play with me, Gianelli. Maybe you're not the owner on paper, but you're the default boss of it. You're in and out of that place on a regular basis and everyone there answers to you."

"Do they?"

"Here's another photo for you."

He slid over a manila folder with Leandro's morgue pictures. Vito nonchalantly inspected it before saying, "Can't help you."

"Interesting, because his prints match up with a Leandro DePasquale, a known undesirable from Chicago. He did a little of this and a little of that. His claim to fame was a failed carjacking near the Drake hotel. Since no one got hurt and he squealed on his accomplices, he was able to plea bargain it down to six months in county and five years' probation. If he hadn't scratched the Bentley in the attempt, he might have gotten off with no time at all. Sound familiar yet?"

"Not a word."

"We tracked down his sister who lives quietly in the suburbs of Chicago with her husband and two kids. Nice woman and very helpful. She talked to Leandro a couple of times a year. It seems he left the Chicago area to work as a bartender in a gentlemen's club in Manhattan. Do I have to go on?"

"Go on all you want. I still never heard of him. I don't own the place so why would I know anyone who works there?"

"Look, Gianelli, that's two dead guys who are connected to you. If I were you, I'd start being concerned."

"Can I have a cigarette?"

"Normally at this juncture I would allow the perp the luxury of a smoke to convince him I'm a nice guy, and that he can trust me, but since I don't like you the answer's no."

Vito yawned, "Fine, just how did you come across the rabbi anyway? You never said."

"I really don't have to tell you anything, but I will. We received an anonymous tip at three in the morning."

"Another anonymous tip? Somebody had a busy night."

Cesari fidgeted uncomfortably. "May I interject, Detective?"

"What are you, his lawyer?"

"No, and just for the record, I have no idea who the rabbi is either, but it seems to me quite a coincidence that you received a tip about a body at the Kit Kat just a few hours before you received a tip about the bloody clothes in my apartment."

Tierney said, "Meaning?"

"That whoever has an axe to grind against me seems to also have an axe to grind against Mr. Gianelli."

"Are you saying the same guys who are killing people and trying to make it look like the work of vampires not only hate you but hate Gianelli as well. I don't see the connection and why kill a rabbi for Christ's sake?"

"I don't have an answer to that," replied Cesari reasonably. "But you have to admit, it's a hell of a fluke."

Tierney thought about that and then said, "I agree."

Vito said, "I'm not trying to incriminate myself by saying what I would or wouldn't do should I theoretically kill someone but there's not a chance in hell I would dump the body outside a club I supposedly owned and or managed and or frequented. They'd be in the East river or Jersey, lots of places, but not in the dumpster behind the club, and did you really have to push me down the stairs, Detective?"

"First of all you tripped, and it was only the last five or six, seven steps tops. Second of all, I didn't push you or anyone down a flight of stairs, not now or ever, in my entire career," he said adamantly and turned to Miriam who was taking notes like a court stenographer. "Make a note of that, please."

He turned back to Cesari and Vito, rubbed his hands together and said, "Okay, boys. Let's say that I accept the notion that someone is trying to frame you both. Give me a hint as to what it is that links the both of you in the eyes of the killer that he feels the need to neutralize you."

Tierney's eyes bore into Vito who glanced sideways at Cesari. Tierney turned his gaze to Cesari. With the sudden dawning of comprehension he sat back and chuckled, "Well, I'll be damned, Cesari. You're full of surprises, aren't you? Here I am thinking you're some sort of pink-bottomed, milquetoast college boy when all along you're really some sort of guinea Batman and he's your guinea Robin."

Cesari said, "I don't know about that, but I think I know what ties us together."

"Pray tell, Dr. Cesari."

"There are a group of Romanian thugs over on First Avenue who've been making a move on the Kit Kat Klub in an attempt to increase their sphere of influence and drive a certain Italian businessman out of the neighborhood."

Tierney was interested. "A certain Italian businessman?"

"A perfectly legitimate one."

"I see. Please continue."

"I can't prove it, but I believe that these same thugs are not only making a move on this particular law abiding, flag-waving, Italian-American citizen but are also making a move on their own immediate superiors. I believe the deaths of the Serb and Leandro were performed in a similar manner in the hopes of instilling fear and terror into their intended targets."

"So you think they were hoping this honest, flag-waving Italian businessman believed in vampires?"

"Possibly, although the mode of death was grisly and weird enough that whether he believed in such things or not it might have achieved its desired effect."

"And did it?"

Vito said, "Not a chance."

Cesari very obviously kicked him under the table to remain silent and added, "Our businessman is too much of a believer in truth, justice, and the American way to allow himself to be intimidated."

"Just to play devil's advocate, Cesari, why was the body dropped off at the hospital? Wouldn't it have made more sense for these Romanians to leave it at the front door of the Kit Kat?"

"It's possible that our law-abiding citizen might have found the body at the club just as you say, but because he's had some problems with the law in the very remote past, he might have decided to move it."

Tierney rolled his eyes and looked at Gianelli who looked away. Tierney said, "Fine, so what about the dead Serb? Why was he killed?"

"Once again, it all goes back to these Romanian thugs. I think the Serb was killed to frighten their boss and to give him nightmares. That's why the Serb's apartment was immersed in biblical and vampire references."

"So the Serb didn't decorate his own apartment, the killers did?"

"It's what I now believe."

"Who are these Romanian riff raff and who's their boss?"

"They are three Romanian brothers, last name Romanescu. Yorgi, Ivan and Tibor. Yorgi is the oldest and the one in charge. You met him. He's the one who showed us around the Serb's apartment."

"And the boss?"

"There was only one other person who was at the autopsy and then at the apartment."

"The old guy Markov? You're kidding? He's dirty?"

"Like a ten-dollar whore."

Miriam gave him the hairy eyeball from behind her laptop screen. Tierney asked, "Are you telling me Markov believes in vampires and they're trying to scare the shit out of him so that maybe he'll retire or check himself into an asylum?"

"It's the only possible reason for decking out the guy's apartment to the extent they did. It had to be for the benefit of someone they knew was going to go there sooner or later and who also knew how the Serb died. I can't think of another explanation. Romania is ground zero for people who believe in the undead and that's where Markov is from. That's why there were all those books in the Serb's apartment about Transylvania and vampires. They may have known that he'd be susceptible to their mind game. I think all these events are part a well-orchestrated psychological operation targeting Markov."

Tierney contemplated that for a minute before saying, "Jesus, Cesari. How am I supposed to tell anyone about this? They'll think I'm insane too. Delete that last part, Miriam... One question; why go through all this trouble? Why don't Yorgi and his brothers just push the old guy off a cliff or arrange for a car accident?"

Cesari shook his head. "I don't know. Maybe Markov has friends or partners who may not take an act of violence against him well."

"I need to think about this."

Vito offered, "While you're thinking about it, you might want to consult with the feds about Markov. I'm pretty sure they have an open file on him."

"And just how do you know that?"

"Just check, all right?"

Tierney rolled his eyes. "I'll take it under advisement. So once again, who's the rabbi and how does he fit in to all of this?"

Cesari shrugged. "I have no idea."

"Fine, then what's this business they're all in that's worth all this commotion?"

Cesari thought he handled the story masterfully up until this point. Nobody admitted to anything, and so far, Vito was coming out of it smelling like a rose. Now for the tricky part.

"Promise me you won't get pissed off."

"I'm already pissed off."

"Last night, a certain legitimate businessman of Italian extraction and I performed an impromptu search of the basement of the hospital pursuant to our main goal of seeking out the truth."

"Would you cut the crap, Cesari? What did you and your boyfriend find?"

"Weapons and lots of them."

"Weapons like in guns?" Tierney asked raising his eyebrows.

"Assault rifles, RPGs, ammunition, anti-personnel mines, grenades, night vison gear, a shit load of C4, the Russian equivalent of Stinger missiles…boxes and boxes full of military grade weaponry."

"Stinger missiles?"

"Man-portable shoulder launched surface to air missiles."

"I know what a Stinger missile is, Cesari. They have the Russian 9K38 Igla?"

"Four crates full."

"Do you have any evidence or is this one of those trust me I'm a doctor moments?"

"Let me have my phone and I'll show you. I took pictures so I could translate the Russian markings."

Tierney reached into his briefcase and came out with Cesari's cellphone which he slid across the table at him. Moments later, Cesari slid it back with the appropriate folder opened and Tierney scrolled up and down studying the photos.

After a while, Tierney said, "It's all in Russian."

"Maybe the officer next to you could look up the translations while we chat?"

"Who's the guy in the background with the crowbar? Is that you, Gianelli?"

Cesari answered for Vito. "Yes, that's him."

"What's he doing?"

"We took one of the covers off to see what was inside. He's hammering the nails back in."

Tierney nodded. "How can I be sure these are real, and you didn't stage them or snatch these pics off the internet?"

"You can't be sure."

"Miriam, could you translate these for us please?"

She took the phone, pulled up an online Russian to English translator and started punching keys while they waited. After translating just a few of the inscriptions she turned to Tierney and nodded.

She said, "They're Russian military weapons and ammo crates."

Tierney's mood changed. "These are in the hospital? What are they planning on doing with them?"

"I'm guessing start a war."

Tierney glanced at his watch. "When were you going to tell me about this?"

Cesari said, "It needed to be put into context."

"I'm going to put you into context, Cesari. Miriam, get started on their alibis. Me and Dr. Cesari are going to St. Matt's to check this story out."

"It's unlikely the weapons will still be there. Unfortunately, we were discovered last night and had to beat a hasty retreat. Multiple people saw us and I had to show my ID to the security guard at the hospital's entrance. In retrospect, that's most likely the reason why we were both setup today. They needed us out of the way."

"Nonetheless, we'll go there and see for ourselves. I can't sit on something like this."

Vito said, "What about me?"

"Miriam, put the legitimate, flag-waving businessman in the tank until we return. If Batman here makes a run for it, book his friend for the murder of the rabbi."

Vito said, "This is bullshit."

Chapter 36

Cesari glanced at his watch. It was after 3:00 p.m. and they were walking down Third Avenue with St. Matt's main entrance just ahead of them. The sun shone brightly in the sky overhead. The sidewalk was heavily congested and the street traffic was worse.

He said, "Detective, I know you're eager to go search the place, but might it not be wiser to wait until night fall? My guess is that's when most of the illicit activity takes place."

"Cesari, if there's even the slightest chance that what you say you saw is there, then I can't risk waiting another second. You should have called me immediately."

"I'm sorry."

"Stop saying that and start acting like a man. We're in combat now and I don't have time for pussies. If the whole story weren't so unbelievable, I would have called in the S.W.A.T. team, but as it is I'm risking my entire credibility by acting on a lead from a convicted felon who was about to get lynched by his own nurses. What was that about anyway?"

"It's a long story. I'd rather not bore you with it."

Tierney finally cracked a smile. "Trouble with the ladies, Cesari? Who would have guessed it? I would have thought a pretty boy like you would have been rocking the casbah."

"So would I."

"Take advice from this marine, Cesari. Love them while you can but leave them when you're done. Men and women weren't meant to be together for more than brief periods at a time."

"I'll try to remember that."

They entered the hospital and began walking toward the elevators. The security guard spotted him through the crowd of visitors and came over quickly. Cesari noted the older man's demeanor was stiff and serious.

He said, "Hi, Louie."

"Hi, Dr. Cesari. May I have your ID?"

Puzzled by the peculiar request, Cesari looked at Tierney and then back at Louie. The ID was in plain sight attached to a lanyard around his neck, but he detached it and handed it over.

Louie said, "Thank you, Doc, and I'm sorry but I was told to confiscate it if and when I saw you."

Cesari raised his eyebrows. "Why?"

"I don't know how to tell you this, Doc, but the entire staff received an email an hour ago informing us that you've been terminated and that you should be considered dangerous. Now can you please step over to my desk? I'm supposed to call the police."

Cesari was too surprised to say anything but Tierney stepped forward to intervene. He showed Louie his detective shield and said, "No need for that, Louie. I am the police and Dr. Cesari is with me. I'll take full responsibility"

Louie studied the shield and then Tierney. Whatever was happening was way over his pay grade and he decided that he had done his duty.

He said to Cesari apologetically, "I don't know what happened but I'm truly sorry, Dr. Cesari."

"No worries, Louie. Have a nice day."

They continued on their way to the elevators and as soon as they boarded, Tierney turned to Cesari. "Believe it or not, I'm starting to feel a little sorry for you."

"Thanks."

"Healthcare is a bit more cutthroat than I would have expected. I mean even the police would have waited to see what you were being charged with before issuing a termination. Even then, there would have been some sort of due process, union hearings and stuff like that."

Cesari sighed, "Welcome to my world."

They reached the basement and approached the doors leading into the storage room and loading dock only to be confronted by two of the biggest, fattest, dumbest-looking guys Cesari had ever seen, wearing hardhats and red suspenders. The hospital's new security team, Cesari thought. Last night's escapade had clearly raised the alarm. These guys were a little rough around the collar but with nearly seven hundred pounds of stupid on their side, they would be quite an effective deterrent to inquisitive staff.

One of them said, "I'm sorry gentlemen but only authorized people are allowed inside. We've had safety issues."

He didn't have a clipboard with names and presumably was told to not allow anyone in. Cesari said, "Maybe we're authorized?"

"Sir, you're not authorized."

"You didn't even ask me my name?"

"It wouldn't matter. Unless I get a call from my boss, you're not authorized."

He was relatively polite. Tierney not so much. He showed his badge and said, "Hey, tons-of-fun, do you know what this is?"

The big man squared away, and his partner tensed. The guy looked at it and said, "I don't give a rat's ass what it is. I was told nobody gets past me without a direct order. I get the order and you go in. I don't get the order and you don't. It's pretty simple."

Smoke began billowing out of Tierney's ears and Cesari thought his head might twist completely around and then he might spit green pea soup on the guy. He put his badge away, reached into his suit coat, and came out with a 9mm Glock 19, the preferred firearm of the NYPD. It was loaded with the Speer's 124-grain Gold Dot hollow point cartridge and had a hefty twelve-pound trigger pull to safeguard against accidental discharge. For a guy as strong as Tierney, twelve pounds was nothing.

He aimed the weapon at the guy's forehead and said, "I'm giving you a direct order, tubby. Let us pass. It's a matter of national security and I need to get in there and I don't have any more time to waste. Now get out of the way and give us your hardhats."

Cesari was impressed. So were the two fat guys who handed them their hats, stepped aside and opened the door. Tierney's parting words of advice to the two men was, "If you guys are even slightly smarter than you look, you'll forget you ever saw us."

They glanced at each other and then back at him, nodding slowly. Cesari and Tierney walked in and made a bee line through the hustle and bustle of activity to where the crates were, but they were now gone. In their place was a large empty space amidst a sea of stacked boxes and cartons.

Cesari said, "This is where they were."

Tierney nodded as he studied the now vacant area. "How many crates and how big were they?"

"There were thirty crates and each one was about six feet long by three feet wide, maybe a little less deep. They were painted a drab military green and were stacked here side by side, two at a time in a row of fifteen."

Tierney did the math in his head and whistled. "That's a lot of weapons."

"You believe me now?"

"I'm starting to, otherwise why would there be two behemoths guarding the door and why were you fired so quickly? Somebody's trying to make sure you don't come back and that no one else gets the opportunity to snoop around. Besides, I'm no genius but fifteen crates at three feet wide would take up a length of forty-five feet of floor space. Looking at this empty floor space here, it seems just about that give or take so your description fits what I'm seeing right now."

"What do we do?"

"Let's go somewhere and talk about this. I need to think it through."

They worked their way back to the entrance and from a distance saw the fat guys burst through the doors holding baseball bats and scanning the room for them. They were followed by another two equally big guys. One held a crowbar and the other a massive wrench. Tierney pulled out his Glock and they both crouched behind an idle forklift, temporarily out of sight.

Cesari said, "I guess they didn't like your advice about forgetting us."

Tierney nodded. "Apparently so. Not for nothing, but these guys don't seem to have too much respect for the law, Cesari."

"No, they don't, or possibly upon reflection they might have come to the conclusion we were yanking their chain. Anybody with a TV knows it's not that hard to get a fake badge and bully your way into a place you're not supposed to be. Who knows? Maybe they discussed it amongst themselves and realized we should've had a warrant."

"Whose side are you on anyway, Cesari?"

"The side of self-preservation. May I suggest an immediate withdrawal?"

Tierney grinned. "C'mon, Cesari. You don't strike me as a cut and run kind of guy. This is just a little skirmish. It could be fun."

"True, but we're outnumbered four to two and outweighed by nearly half a ton. And if I recall correctly, we're the ones who waved the guns first. Should we lose the firefight, they could argue justifiable homicide or even self-defense. We don't even have any contraband to prove to anyone what we're doing here."

Tierney thought about that and then said, "You're no fun, Cesari. You know that? All right, tactical retreat, but make sure to remind me to come back here and pistol whip these guys one day, all right?"

"It will be my highest priority."

"Are there any other exits?"

"Yes, the outside entrance to the loading docks is behind us where the semis are lined up. They haven't seen us yet, so we have a chance unless they call a general alarm which they don't seem bent on doing just now. Maybe these guys think they can score some points if they handle it themselves."

Tierney looked both ways, determined the time was right and said, "Let's go."

They reversed their course and slinked along the wall, ducking behind crates, machines, sheetrock, piles of lumber... anything. Two thirds of the way to the exit, they heard a gunshot echo above the routine sounds and they froze in place. Shouting soon followed and they turned to see what was happening. A fifth guy had emerged from the doorway holding some sort of rifle. They had been spotted and he had fired a warning shot in the air. The first four guys were pointing and waving at them to halt. The guy with the rifle was drawing a bead on them. More than fifty yards off, with multiple obstacles in the way, it would take an extraordinary shot to hit them. The guy fired and the round buried itself into a pile of two-by-fours less than a foot away.

Tierney said, "Shit! Run, Cesari...now."

Chapter 37

They took off like rabbits and sprinted the remaining distance to the entrance as men all around them began hitting the floor and running for cover. Another shot rang out and pinged off a nearby forklift. Thirty yards, twenty, ten. They were almost at the back of the nearest semi when a worker came out from deep inside the container. Surprised by the sight of the beleaguered men, he hadn't yet caught wind of the commotion.

He raised his hand and demanded, "Hey, you two. Where do you think you're going?"

The crack of the rifle and the explosion of his head took place almost simultaneously. A cloud of pink mist sprayed the truck behind him and he was dead before his body had time to register the tragedy, so he stood there with a gaping hole in the center of his face for a second before collapsing in a heap. Cesari and Tierney didn't have time to feel sympathy for the man. They ducked into the narrow gap between the truck and loading dock's side wall, and squeezed their way out into the driveway as the last shot banged into the rear of the open truck and ricocheted off the metal walls.

Once in daylight, they breathed a sigh of relief but still needed to keep moving. Both men realized that once the decision had been made to use deadly force, there was nothing that would stop them. It was an unwritten rule of the jungle. They glanced around quickly at the line of trucks five deep idling to the side of the massive driveway waiting their turn to unload. They were facing away ready to back up to the loading platform. The last one was a smaller box truck, maybe a third the size of the larger semis.

Cesari was sweating and short of breath from all the excitement. He pointed to the truck. "Can you drive one of those things?"

Tierney was also winded. He said, "Probably. We all had to have some experience in the Marine Corps. It's probably similar, but I'd rather jack a car. It'd be a lot easier and less high profile."

They looked around for an alternative. There was a five-story parking garage attached to the hospital, but it was uphill and at least a hundred yards away from where they stood. The front of the hospital was at least twice that distance in the other direction and if they were followed, they could endanger civilians on Third Avenue.

Tierney saw where his attention was focused. "Are you up for it?"

Cesari nodded. "Let's go."

They ran toward the garage as still unaware truck drivers sitting in their cabs watched with curiosity as the two well-dressed men bolted by their vehicles. They were soon ducking behind their steering wheels and down into their footwells when the guy with the rifle came charging out searching for them.

Cesari and Tierney were almost there when the first shot hit the cement façade of the garage chipping off a fragment. They slipped around the guard rail and disappeared into the darkness of the enclosed parking lot. They were breathing hard now but felt as if the worst had passed. From behind a pickup, they looked back and saw the five guys hesitating at the boundaries of the driveway. The one with the rifle was scanning around through its scope. It was clear they were out of their depth and unsure of themselves. They already had one unscripted dead guy on their hands. Their orders involved taking care of business in the storage room itself and did not involve hunting down trespassers once they had escaped to the public domain.

Cesari said, "Are you going to call it in? They killed a guy."

Tierney thought about it. "I need to think about it. If I call it in, that'll get us the guy with the rifle but then the one who gave him the order will disappear. It always happens that way."

"Look..."

Tierney scanned back down the driveway where the men were standing. A large white van had pulled up next to them and three men got out. It was Yorgi and his brothers.

Tierney squinted his eyes. "Is that them? I remember Yorgi."

"Yeah, that's him and his two baby brothers, Ivan and Tibor."

The brothers conferred with the security crew who gesticulated with great animation and pointed repeatedly at the parking garage. Yorgi grabbed the rifle and hoisted it to his shoulder as he searched back and forth for them through the scope. After a minute, he stopped moving and seemed to focus in on something. He was looking right at them, and they ducked down behind the bed.

A shot rang out and took out one of the tires. Cesari peeked around the side of the truck and saw Yorgi give an order to Ivan who ran back to the van and opened the back. He returned with an RPG and traded it for Yorgi's rifle.

Tierney had joined Cesari and said, "Is that what I think it is?"

Just as Yorgi hoisted the weapon to his shoulder, they turned and sprinted away. They made it twenty feet when the explosion rocked the garage knocking them off their feet. The back of their clothes and hair were singed as they landed face first several feet from where they started. They were dazed but all right, stood slowly and continued their escape. Cesari glanced over his shoulder and saw the overturned fireball that was once a very nice, shiny pickup truck. He also noticed something else.

He stopped and looked back through the smoke and flames. Tierney called back and said, "What is it?"

The men, now eight strong counting Yorgi and his brothers, were marching up the hill to finish the job and they all were carrying assault rifles. Cesari said, "I can't believe it. They're coming after us and they're loaded for bear. Yorgi must have brought more guns with him."

"These guy are crazy, Cesari."

"I agree. Now would be a nice time for you to pick out a car to jack."

They ran to the far end of the garage and spotted a bright metallic yellow Aston Martin DBS Superleggera convertible with the top up parked by itself near an entrance to the hospital. Both spaces to either side were empty and marked with diagonal white, no-parking stripes. The vanity plates on the high-end car read, TIFLAC, and Cesari guessed that was for Tiberius Flavius Acevedo. As they got close, they could see the sign at the head of the parking space saying, Reserved for Administration.

Cesari smiled and said, "I like this one."

Tierney liked it too. "Is this your boss's car?"

"I can't be a hundred percent sure but it's a good guess."

Tierney looked through the window and said, "Too bad. It's a keyless ignition. You can't hotwire electronic start cars."

"You're kidding?"

"Sorry, computers have taken all the fun out of grand theft auto. Let's find an older model. Where do the employees park?"

"The two upper levels, I think. I'm not sure. I walk to work."

"Well, we better move fast. Once they realize the RPG didn't kill us, they'll probably search the rest of the garage at least until they hear the fire engines and police sirens."

Cesari looked back at the entrance to the hospital and thought of something. He said, "I have an idea. Follow me."

The door to the hospital was locked and required a hospital ID to swipe at the electronic fob next to it. Cesari took out his wallet, found his spare ID and opened the door.

Tierney said, "Seriously? You had a second ID and the security guard didn't think to ask you for it?"

"Leave him alone. Louie's old. What kind of training do you think you need to watch the front door of a hospital?"

"Unbelievable... So where are we going?"

"Acevedo told me they were renovating his office so that he would have direct access to the parking garage. Eventually, this will be made a private entrance and the employees will have to use one of the other access points. There's one on every floor of the garage. Obviously, it's still open to the staff."

Inside the hospital, they were immediately immersed in construction. Tierney asked, "We're in his office right now?"

"Not quite, this whole wing is under renovation. We're actually standing in a hallway that makes a few turns here and there but eventually goes all the way to the main lobby up front. If we dig our way through the wires and scaffolding to the right, we'll find his office in about a couple of hundred feet. He plans on creating a private tunnel from there to the parking lot."

"He's just going to commandeer this entire section of the hospital for his personal use?"

"You're starting to like him as much as I do. C'mon, let's go find his office."

"Why not just walk out the front door?"

"Because I have a better idea."

They meandered their way through a maze of sawhorses and a sea of machinery nodding at workers who largely ignored them. This area of construction was a low security risk and they progressed unchallenged eventually reaching a spacious opening that was in a more advanced stage of renovation. Wallboard was hanging and hard wood flooring was being laid down. Large windows with their factory stickers allowed ample natural lighting. Playful voices could be heard coming from down the hallway less than twenty-five feet away.

As they approached a room whose door was partially open, they could hear splashing with both male and female voices teasing each other. They crept up close to the opening and sneaked a quick look. Apparently, Acevedo's hot tub was a high priority to be installed because he was having romp in it with, Olivia, his secretary. She was bouncing up and down on his lap as they sipped champagne. She was so well endowed and he was so diminutive it crossed Cesari's mind that she might accidentally suffocate him with her breasts.

Cesari and Tierney glanced at each other and moved past the doorway and out of sight. They wound up in Acevedo's main office where Cesari had received his promotion the other day. On a coatrack hung Olivia and Acevedo's clothing. Cesari searched Acevedo's trouser pockets and found his wallet, cellphone and car keys. He grinned, put the items in his own pockets, rolled up all of Acevedo's clothes into a tight ball and tucked them under his arms.

He said, "Follow me."

Tierney did and they retraced their steps back through the construction zone out to the garage. On the other side of the parking lot, they saw two fire engines parked outside and a multitude of firemen inside hosing down the now smoldering pickup. Black plumes of smoke billowed into the air but the danger was over. In the distance, the flashing lights of a patrol car strobed back and forth.

Cesari asked, "Are you sure you don't want to call it in?"

"The only thing I'm sure of is that I want the head of the snake not just its tail… Besides, let's be real. What am I going to say? That I acted on a hunch from a convicted felon and murder suspect that there were armageddon quantities of Russian made military weapons in the basement of a non-profit hospital. And that in my zeal to be a hero, I failed to follow basic procedure and obtain a search warrant, and when an unarmed employee told me I couldn't enter the basement, I threatened to shoot him in the head. And then I didn't find any of the said weapons but don't worry somebody used one of those weapons I didn't find to try to kill me. I don't know, Cesari. Even I would suspend me if I heard that story."

"Cops worry too much about procedure."

"You're telling me? What are you going to do with his clothes?"

Cesari walked over to a trash can and shoved them inside. Tierney laughed and said, "Remind me not to piss you off, Cesari. So why'd we come back to the parking garage when we could just have easily walked out the front door?"

"And walk home when we have a spanking new Aston Martin waiting for us?"

"Jesus, Cesari. It's one thing to requisition a car when you're trying to save your neck but just to do it out of spite? What was the plan if the midget wasn't there or if he still had his clothes on?"

"If he wasn't there and I couldn't find his keys, then we would have gone out the front door. If he was there and still had his clothes on, I would have politely asked him to take them off."

"Seriously?"

"Admit it, Detective, you're having fun."

Tierney cracked a grin. "Truth be told, I haven't had this much fun since I was blasting away on a 25mm M242 Bushmaster chain gun inside a Bradley personnel carrier rampaging through a terrorist training camp north of Kandahar. That RPG heading right at us really brought me back. Man, I can still taste it…"

"I bet those were the days."

"Good times, for sure."

Chapter 38

There were twelve hundred dollars in the CEO's wallet and Cesari declared them the spoils of war. After having been shot at and nearly killed by an RPG, Tierney agreed they were indeed at war and that the normal rules of engagement for police work were temporarily suspended. With that in mind, they decided to hang on to the Aston Martin for a while. Tierney drove the seven hundred horsepower beast while Cesari reclined in the soft leather passenger seat. He reveled in its heated massage feature as it caressed his tired and sore muscles like a familiar lover.

"We need to switch the license plates," Cesari said. "He's going to report the theft."

"One step ahead of you, but the big problem is whether the car has one of those fancy anti-theft security systems that's integrated with the police. They'll track us down in a heartbeat."

"There's no way of knowing or disabling it?"

"Where there's a will, there's a way, Cesari. They're small battery-operated transmitters about the size of a deck of cards. There are a limited number of places they can be installed, and I know them all. As soon as we stop, I'll search for it."

"So if we see flashing lights behind us in the next ten minutes, it's probably not because you forgot to signal a lane change?"

"Relax, Cesari. In order for the device to work, it requires a call from the owner to the police to report the vehicle stolen.

From what I saw, your CEO's going to be tied up with his girlfriend for a couple of hours minimum. Besides, he may not even have had one installed so let's not think negative while we're having such a good time. Look, I'll swing by the city tow pound at Pier 76. It's on West 38th Street & 12th Avenue. They're open 'til ten and I have a friend there who owes me big. I'll pick up a pair of plates from one of the long-term cars. We'll use them until such time as we're inclined to return the vehicle. While we're there, I'll look for a transmitter."

"What are the long term cars?"

"Mostly drug busts or state confiscated vehicles. They could be there a long time while their owners await trial, and if things don't go well, they'll eventually be put up for auction… Man, this baby handles. I'd love to see what she can do on the open road. What do you think, more than a hundred and fifty miles an hour?"

"Let's look it up." Cesari spent a minute googling up the specs of a new Aston Martin Superleggera and then said, "It says here the twin-turbo V12 engine can make this thing haul ass upward to two-hundred and ten miles per hour."

"Really? Too bad there's no place around here to test it out."

By the time they put the new plates on and searched unsuccessfully for an anti-theft transmitter, it was almost 8:00 p.m. Cesari said, "Are you sure we're in the clear, Detective?"

Tierney scowled at him, "Exactly how many twenty-year marine combat veterans have you met, Cesari?"

"I take it we're in the clear."

"Good. Don't ever doubt me again."

"So how about dinner? I'm flush with somebody else's cash."

"Sure, why not? Where?"

"Wolfgang's in Tribeca. Just get on the West Side Drive and you're right there. Best creamed spinach in the city."

"Isn't that where you and Gianelli have your alibis?"

Cesari nodded. "Speaking of whom, is he still at the precinct?"

"I haven't heard from Miriam and she was waiting to hear from me so I guess he is. I'll call her."

He pulled out his cellphone and dialed the officer. He exchanged some pleasantries and asked how her inquiry into the alibis went. After she spoke, he instructed her to release Vito, thanked her and hung up.

He said, "Your alibis check out, but I still don't like Gianelli."

"I understand, but he does sort of grow on you."

"Please…"

Cesari waited five minutes and called Vito. The call went to voicemail and Cesari left a message to meet him at Wolfgang's for dinner and to bring at least three cigars.

Tierney said, "What was that all about? You trying to make me lose my appetite?"

"Not at all, but we're at war, right?"

"What's your point?"

"The enemy of my enemy is my friend, Detective."

"Meaning?"

"Vito has a horse in this race. They killed two of his people and have been hassling him and disrupting his business for weeks if not months. Since it is our intention to skirt some of the rules, we may want to tap into the skillset and resources of someone who is highly experienced in this area of operation, and highly motivated to help us achieve our goals."

"You can't seriously expect me to work side by side with a guy I've been trying to lock up for more than five years? That aside, he's a criminal and you know it."

"May I remind you that we just stole an Aston Martin."

"Commandeered for the duration of hostilities and from what just happened I can easily guess that this car is most likely going to wind up being impounded at some point anyway. Gianelli's unlawful behavior is a whole different animal."

"Think of it another way. Suppose you and your men were trapped in an ambush in Kandahar and were receiving fire from all sides. Air support and reinforcements were hours away. You already lost several guys and things aren't looking good. Would you refuse help from known jihadists who had just switched sides and were now offering to fight with you against your common enemy?"

He thought about the analogy for half a minute. "That's not as dumb an analogy as you might think. Tribal loyalties over there not infrequently trumped religious extremism. Sides switched so often it was sometimes impossible to tell who was who. It was at times a very fluid situation... Okay fine, Gianelli's on board. Now tell me about the two people of his that were killed. I only know about the bartender, Leandro. Who's the other one?"

Cesari told him everything he knew about Sofia and how they had mutilated her teeth to make her look like a vampire. When he was done, Tierney clenched his jaw and had an angry expression on his face.

Cesari misinterpreted Tierney's mood. "I'm sorry. I know I should have told you before."

"I'm not mad about that. What happened to the girl?"

"Vito bribed a funeral home director to give her a small service and decent send off. He was pretty upset at the way she had been used and then tossed away like refuse."

Tierney nodded. "There's way too much of that in this world, Cesari. You wouldn't believe what I saw in Afghanistan. Women there are treated worse than the way we treat our pets. In fact, it's not even a close comparison. It's unreal. That's one of the reasons I kept re-upping and going back. It made me angry... Maybe Gianelli isn't so bad after all."

"I wouldn't go that far."

He smiled and said wryly. "Nice friend. Still, I'll have to take it down a notch when I see him. I can't help but respect him a little more now that I heard that. I would've done the same thing."

They pulled off the West Side Drive onto Vestry, drove two blocks to Greenwich, made a right, got lucky and found a parking space on the street a half block from the restaurant. They walked to Wolfgang's and were seated by the window with an expansive view of the dining room.

"You can smoke cigars in here?" asked Tierney.

"Not in the dining room. There's an attached cigar lounge. The entrance is on the other side by the kitchen. You pass through a short corridor that's more like a wind tunnel to keep the smoke out of the restaurant."

They ordered Manhattans straight up, fried calamari, and blue point oysters on the half shell to keep themselves busy while they waited for Vito. Thirty minutes into the appetizers, Vito walked through the entrance, spoke to a waiter, and soon caught up with Cesari and Tierney who were in the process of ordering another round of drinks. When they saw Vito, Cesari told the waiter to make it three.

Vito was speechless at the sight of the detective and stood by his chair staring at him. He said to Cesari, "What's he doing here?"

Cesari replied, "Sit down, Vito. We're all friends."

"Friends?" he asked glaring at Tierney.

Tierney repeated it, "You heard him."

Vito growled, "Friends don't push their friends down the stairs."

"C'mon, Gianelli, can't you take a joke?"

"That's a joke?"

"Gianelli, I must've pushed a thousand guys down stairs like that and no one ever died, all right? A few broken bones here and there, I think maybe one guy, two tops, got disabled but the majority did just fine. I knew from experience that you'd probably be all right, so relax."

Cesari said, "Yeah, relax. He almost broke my nose and you don't hear me whining. Now sit down."

He sat down, looked at Cesari and suddenly grinned. "Yeah, but you deserved it." Then he turned toward Tierney. "So why are we friends all of a sudden?"

Tierney said, "How about we order first? Me and Cesari had a rough day at the office."

The waiter returned with the cocktails and they placed their orders. After he left, Cesari and Tierney filled him in on their afternoon's activities. By the time they finished, their steaks and sides arrived with an expensive Bordeaux.

Vito took a mouthwatering bite of medium rare ribeye and looked at the detective. "So you pinched the midget's car? I'm impressed, Tierney."

"Don't look at me," replied Tierney. "It was your friend's idea."

"Yeah, but you didn't try to stop him. I believe that makes you an accessory."

"I see where you're going with this, Gianelli, but you're wrong. I'm not like you. Any laws we may have inadvertently broken were done so for the greater good. We're trying to save humanity and we needed wheels."

Vito scoffed, "A Toyota wouldn't have worked just as well?"

"What's the price of the car got to do with anything, Gianelli?"

But Vito was on a roll. "And now you can't go to your own people because you broke so many rules, they'd take your badge."

"No, they wouldn't."

"Sure they would. There's a dead guy now and it's all because of you. I know how your Internal Affairs works. They'd say none of that would have happened if you hadn't menaced anyone with your pistol. You had no right to do that."

Cesari finally said, "Simmer down, Mr. Attorney General."

Vito had a contented look on his face as if he'd been waiting years to dress Tierney down which of course he had. He finished with, "And now you need the guy you've been kicking around forever. There's a certain amount of irony here, don't you think?"

Tierney took it well and chuckled. "You crack me up, Gianelli. All of a sudden you're on the side of law and order... Well, there's an expression that politics makes strange bedfellows, but as Cesari pointed out earlier, so does war. Make no mistake about it, this is war, and yes, I need the guy I've been kicking around forever. So let it be known that all hostilities between Detective Robert Tierney of the NYPD and Mr. Vito Gianelli of Mulberry Street are hereby suspended indefinitely. In honor of the moment, I'd like to make a toast to you, Gianelli."

He raised his glass and Cesari raised his. Vito cautiously and with only minimal hesitation joined them. Tierney said, "Brave, handsome, intelligent, and sexy...but enough about me. Here's to you!"

They all broke out in laughter.

Chapter 39

No one was more surprised by the call than Yorgi. Things were falling into place faster than he had hoped, facilitated by Cesari and Tierney's inept investigation the day before. He had recognized them through the assault rifle's scope. If it had been anyone else, he might have let them escape but he decided they were becoming too much of a nuisance. The fact that they were working together had really roiled him and he shook his head in frustration. He had presented Tierney with a gift of the bloodied clothes and murder weapon. What more did he want? It was, as they say, a slam dunk. In Romania, Cesari would already be in front of a firing squad or more likely be found hanging in his cell, a victim of Yorgi assisted suicide. Nonetheless, he was confident the RPG had done the trick. It would have been nice to have verified the bodies, but the fire was too intense, and the emergency vehicles came too quickly.

He had told Shlomo that no one saw anything; not human at any rate. It was as if an apparition had been swirling throughout the warehouse causing mayhem. He had chased after it into the driveway to no avail but would have sworn he saw only a large bat flying away in the distance. He could not be certain. Afterward, another coffin-like crate was discovered only this time the box was discovered already opened with nothing but soil inside. He had disposed of it immediately. Shlomo's reaction was one of terror and disbelief that whatever it was had gotten away. At the rate the old man was decompensating mentally, Yorgi doubted he would last much longer.

And then serendipitously, the call came. Yorgi smiled, glanced at his watch and fired up his laptop. He was instructed to make himself available at 11:00 p.m. sharp for a video conference with Bucharest where it was now almost 6:00 a.m. He was a few minutes early and nervously adjusted his tie. He had dressed sharply and was wearing a hand tailored silk suit. Never before had a member of the council reached out to him personally. This was a big deal and he assumed it had something to do with yesterday's events. Nothing travels faster than bad news, he mused, unless it was tens of millions of dollars of missing weapons.

The room was dark as he prepared for the big moment. Without turning he said, "Brothers, can you feel the excitement?"

Ivan and Tibor sat behind him in the shadows out of reach of the laptop's camera. They were there to watch, to listen and to learn. It was big brother's moment of triumph.

The camera suddenly whirred and began flashing green. The onscreen message flashed that there was an incoming call. He pressed the receive button and the image flicked on the main screen with a smaller image of himself in the upper corner. It was an old man with thinning white hair and thick glasses. He looked small and frail. Yorgi was tempted to laugh but refrained. He enjoyed life too much. The man spoke slowly, in English. Much better English than Yorgi would have thought. He'd obviously been well-educated or well-traveled or both.

"You may call me, Dimitri," the man said softly. Yorgi knew it wasn't his real name but who cared. "Do you know who I am, Yorgi?"

"Yes, I was informed earlier today by your representative."

"Do you know why I am calling?"

Yorgi shook his head. "No, I do not."

273

"Have there been any problems there, Yorgi?"

Yorgi hesitated ever so slightly. He had rehearsed his lines in the mirror all afternoon in preparation. The hesitation was designed to suggest concern rather than deception. Its delivery required precision and subtlety. The old man did not get to where he was by being stupid.

He stammered, "I...I don't know what to say."

"Just say the truth, Yorgi? Have there been any problems?"

Yorgi hung his head for a second and nodded, whispering, "Yes, there have been problems."

"What kind of problems?"

"There have been people snooping around hospital, but I took care of them."

"What kind of people?"

"I am not certain. Two men gained access to the hospital's storage facility by showing the men on duty a policeman's badge, but it may have been a fake badge. They will not bother us again. I made sure of it."

"Why were they there in the first place? Do they know our business?"

"I cannot see how they could possibly know anything but as I said, they have been neutralized. Unfortunately, we may never know who they were. The method used to rid ourselves of them was extreme."

Dimitri's face was emotionless as he nodded in thought. "I am glad they will no longer be a problem, but I remain concerned, and what can you tell me about Shlomo?"

"I don't know what you mean?"

"Tell me about Shlomo's state of mind and do not lie, Yorgi. I will know if you do."

More hesitation, more concern. It became easier with time he noticed and said, "Shlomo has been...preoccupied."

"In what way?"

He tried to urge a tear but couldn't. He wondered how women were able to do that so easily. He said, "I would rather not say. Shlomo has been like father figure to me and brothers."

"I called Shlomo late last night, Yorgi, midnight your time. Do you know why?"

"No, I do not."

"Because I received a phone call that the weapons did not arrive at their destination and the drivers did not check in nor did they answer their phones. Do you know what Shlomo told me?"

"No, I do not."

"He told me to halt any further shipments of weapons. I asked him why and guess what he says."

"I cannot, Dimitri."

Dimitri's soft voice took on a nasty edge. "He told me that there are vampires in New York and that he thinks they may have something to do with it. Did you hear me, Yorgi? Vampires…"

Yorgi made his eyes go as wide as possible. "No…"

"Yes, Yorgi. We are missing fifty million dollars' worth of weapons and he tells me vampires may have taken them. Two of our drivers are missing and one of them is married to my granddaughter. I was guest of honor at their wedding."

Yorgi was silent and Dimitri continued, "Do you know anything about this Yorgi?"

He shook his head, "No, Dimitri. I know Shlomo has been under a great deal of stress, but I had no idea of this. He never mentioned vampires to me. Is hard to believe, although…"

"Although what, Yorgi?"

"I revere Shlomo. Is very difficult for me."

"I appreciate your loyalty, Yorgi. I also respect the delicate situation you are in now that your brother is engaged to Shlomo's daughter, but I need you to be truthful."

Yorgi hemmed and hawed as much as he thought possible without provoking the old man before saying, "As much as

Shlomo loves me as family, he would kill me if he knew I say anything. It would be interpreted as betrayal."

In a soothing, reassuring voice, Dimitri said, "He will never learn of this conversation, I promise, but is important Yorgi. Half a billion dollars' worth of weapons have just been put on hold and I have to tell my peers that the man in charge of their money in New York thinks vampires may be stealing our assault rifles and land mines. Do you see my dilemma, Yorgi?"

"I do… Shlomo has been behaving erratically of late. He has even been consulting with rabbis and priests."

"Rabbis and priests?"

"Yes, and Imams too."

"What about?"

"I do not know. I thought maybe as he grows old he wishes to know about what comes after. He has asked me several times if I believe in the afterlife…although the way he phrased it seems strange in retrospect."

"How did he phrase it?"

"He asked me if I believed that someone could return from the dead. He used a peculiar word that I never heard of… I remember now. He asked me if I believed in the undead. My English sometimes fails me, but I believe that wasword he used. I thought he was talking about angels or heaven."

Dimitri thought about that. "I agree. That is an odd way of putting it. What else?"

"Little things… He becomes agitated quite easily, especially at night. Sometimes I am not sure if he is aware of where he is or even who he is."

"What do you think, Yorgi? Truthfully."

Yorgi took a deep breath. It was his finest performance. "Dimitri, I love Shlomo. I could not bear if anything were to happen to him…"

"Do not worry, Yorgi. It is precisely why I call you. Is because I do not want anything bad to happen to Shlomo that you must be completely forthright with me. Listen to me, Yorgi. I have been friends with Shlomo since childhood. For that reason, I have not told other members of council, but at some point I may have to. They will not be as forgiving or understanding. I must know what is happening."

Yorgi took a deep breath and exhaled it slowly. He then looked away briefly as if troubled by some inner conflict. Finally he said, "Is for some time, I think Shlomo may be developing some sort of mental illness. I think at first because of his age, he develop Alzheimer's but now that you tell me this about vampires, I wonder if it may be something worse, a breakdown perhaps."

Dimitri sighed deeply, "I agree. Do you think you can get him to seek help?"

"I doubt it. No matter how much he cares for me, I am still his underling not his equal."

"Yes, of course. I will think on this... Do you have any idea where weapons might be or who might have taken them?"

"No, this is first I hear of it, but will investigate immediately. I know all drivers and truck routes. They will not get far. There is limited number of buyers or people who can move such large quantities of this type of commodity and I know them all."

"Good, Yorgi and one more thing..."

"Yes, Dimitri."

"I meet with others today. I must be able to guarantee them that there will be no further delays in shipments of merchandise. Promises have been made. Money has been exchanged. Risks have been taken. The Russian military machine, despite its corruption, is not to be trifled with. Do you understand?"

"Yes, Dimitri. What is it you wish me to do?"

"I am going to recommend to the council that you become acting head of operations for us in New York while we sort out the Shlomo conundrum. From now on our people there will take instructions from you alone, and you will answer directly to me. If you can salvage this situation, we will consider making your promotion permanent."

"Dimitri, I am flattered, but I am not worthy of this honor."

"Nonsense, Yorgi. For too long you have been in Shlomo's shadow doing all the heavy lifting. We are not unaware of this. Is time to recognize your service."

"But Shlomo..."

"Enough! I need you, Yorgi. I will handle Shlomo. Will you do this for me?"

"I am humbled and will do whatever is required of me."

Chapter 40

Two nights later, Cesari and Vito crouched in Vito's Cadillac in the parking garage overlooking the loading dock. They were in the identical spot where the pickup truck had been blown up and the cement floor was singed black from the fire. They were watching the entrance to the hospital's warehouse for activity through high powered binoculars. It was nearly 1:00 a.m. and they had been there since nightfall.

Vito yawned, "This is two nights in a row that nothing's happened, Cesari. What do you think?"

"They're probably just being cautious. Wouldn't you after what happened?"

"I guess, but weapon's aside, won't they have to at least start bringing in supplies for the hospital's renovation?"

"You were there, Vito. There were enough materials to renovate two hospitals."

"What was that about anyway?"

"I think all the construction activity is just a smoke screen to disguise their true business."

Vito nodded. "I agree, but what are they going to do with the excess materials?"

"I'm not an arms dealer. I don't know… Maybe they have another construction project going on somewhere else and this is the main drop-off for all the supplies."

"That's an interesting thought. Suppose they were using more than one hospital."

Cesari pondered that for a minute. "That's a good point. I should have thought of that. There are tons of small hospitals both in and around the city they could have bought their way into. Maybe they just temporarily pulled up stakes here and are using another facility until they're sure it's safe again."

"Which means we could be sitting here pulling pud for a long time and never see anything."

"That's a possibility. For now, we sit tight."

"Where's Tierney?"

"He's on First Avenue keeping an eye on the Romanescu brothers. There's been an unusual flurry of activity the last two nights. Apparently, something big must have happened. It's probably related to the little firefight we had here, but he can't be sure."

"What kind of activity?"

"Yorgi has been holding after hour's court with a variety of unsavory types at the Ukrainian restaurant. They've been coming and going almost non-stop."

"Is Shlomo one of the visitors?"

"That's what's really strange. He hasn't been there once. A little odd since he's their boss although I'm sure he could be directing things by phone or video call."

"That doesn't smell right to me."

"What do you mean?"

"If one of my lieutenants was having late night meetings with all of the people I work with or who work for me without me being present I'd be suspicious he was making a move on my job."

Cesari nodded. "We already suspected that might be the case so maybe you're right. The time may be at hand and Yorgi might be making sure that all the pieces are in place so that there's a smooth transition of power."

"Did Tierney ever ask the feds about Markov like I told him to?"

"I'm pretty sure Detective Tierney doesn't like being told what to do by suspected mafiosi, but having said that, we've all been just a teensy-weensy bit tied up the last day or two so I suspect not."

"Geez, Cesari, do you think you could tone down the sarcasm? I'm just trying to help."

Cesari looked at him. "Aww, did I hurt baby's feelings?"

"Will you shut up?"

By 1:30 a.m., there had been zero activity at the loading dock and Cesari said, "I think tonight's a bust. Let's go over to First Avenue and see what Tierney's up to."

"Wouldn't it be easier just to call him?"

"It would but I want to see for myself."

Vito started the ignition and the caddie sprung to life. The restaurant was just over a half mile away and they arrived quickly, parking on the street well out of sight. They caught up with Tierney a few minutes later sitting in a Subaru Forester positioned obliquely across the street a couple of hundred feet from the restaurant, hidden in a dark spot behind several other vehicles. They piled into his car, Cesari in the front and Vito in the back.

Vito laughed. "Nice wheels, Detective."

Tierney lowered his binoculars a hair to respond, "You got a problem with my car, Gianelli?"

"Not at all. It's a very sensible vehicle. Probably gets great mileage."

Tierney shook his head, refusing to let himself be goaded. He said to Cesari, "Remind me again why he's here."

"He's going to fetch us coffee."

"Like hell I am," barked Vito from the back.

Tierney ignored him. "Anything happening at the hospital, Cesari?"

"No, a total fizzle. How's it going here?"

"Same as last night. Cars coming and going all night, dropping people off, usually just one or two at a time. They go in and an hour later they come out again. The last group should be coming out in a few minutes. It's probably the final meeting because I haven't seen a new car arrive. They usually overlap a little bit."

"What do you think?"

"There's only one thing possible to think. We shook them real good the other day and the instability and uncertainty has given Yorgi the impetus to make his move on Shlomo. Since Shlomo's the only one who hasn't been here, I must conclude that Yorgi is cutting deals with all the other players to gain their support, and they're all here to kiss his ring."

Vito shoved Cesari in the back. "I told you."

Cesari glanced at him and then said to Tierney. "Where's Shlomo?"

"Do I look like I have eyes in the back of my head? It's hard enough keeping track of Yorgi and his brothers. I've never seen such activity. The youngest brother, Tibor, by the way, took off in a Ferrari at around midnight for parts unknown."

Cesari said, "I think I know where he went. He has a girl in Chelsea."

"Well at least someone's having fun tonight."

Vito asked, "Did you ever get to ask the feds about Markov?"

"Oh yeah, in between getting shot at, nearly blown up, stealing an Aston Martin, and following the Romanescu brothers all day and night, I managed to slip in a few calls to the Bureau in my spare time to let them know I'm in the middle of an unauthorized investigation in an area that's completely out of my jurisdiction and would like their help. They very politely told me to tell you to keep your nose clean and to mind your own business."

Vito was miffed. "Jesus, what's with all the attitudes around here?"

Cesari turned to him. "Will you stop horsing around? What could they possibly tell us that we don't already know? They're running guns, isn't that enough?"

"It would be nice to know where."

Tierney found that amusing. "And you think the suits in the FBI will know? Gianelli, I thought you were smarter than that. You know what we call the feds?"

"No, what?"

"The Federal Bureau of Ineptitude. They couldn't find their own asses in a blackout, but to address your very legitimate concern about where the weapons might be going. The answer is almost anywhere; the Mexican drug cartels, rogue countries like Venezuela, Syria, Somalia, Sudan and Afghanistan just to name a few. There are plenty of militia groups right here in the U.S. who would love to get their hands on these types of weapons. And let's not forget about the average American. Nobody loves their toys as much as we do and the more illegal and dangerous they are, the more we want them. Hell, Cesari and I almost got killed by a Russian-made RPG and all I could think about later was how cool it would be to have one of those no matter what the cost. And the markup for black market weapons is incredible. A thousand dollar, easy to mass produce RPG like the one they used on us could easily go for five times that amount, but the real money is in the ammo and you can never get enough ammunition."

"Why send the weapons here if they're destined for places like Syria or Afghanistan?" asked Cesari.

"I don't know where they're destined for, but let's say they were heading back to the Middle East. Maybe whoever the seller is couldn't deliver them directly to the frontlines of those places without being exposed or maybe it would have been too risky. Think about it, if large shipments of Russian-made weapons were discovered in transport directly from Russia to the enemies of the United States to be used against our men in uniform, the political fallout would be horrendous. No amount of spin could alter the facts. It would be a devastating setback in Russo-American relations. And if it wasn't the Russian government directly, then whoever it was would have to be publicly crucified to make amends. So ship them here, recrate them, maybe scrub the manufacturer's identification off, and then ship them out again. Alternatively, the level of corruption in Russia is at an all-time high. These could be coming directly from the manufacturers using duplicate order forms to cover their trails. They may be thinking to themselves: why get the equivalent of five hundred U.S. dollars for a state of the art, brand new, fully automatic AK12 from the Russian military when I can get three thousand dollars or more, from the Mexicans or some schlemiel sitting in his living room watching TV in Michigan? So whenever an order comes in from the politburo, he just duplicates it for the inspectors, pays off this guy here and that guy there to get them on trains, planes and boats to the U.S."

Cesari said, "And the hospital is ordering so much equipment that the quantity of crates with weapons seems insignificant in comparison."

"Except for one thing," argued Vito. "All the crates were marked. Granted, it was in Russian but somebody would have seen it and thought to translate it, don't you think?"

Cesari said, "Not necessarily. Did you happen to notice the size of some of the other boxes and crates, particularly the ones with the CT scanners and MRI machines? They were gigantic. They could easily have put ten or more of those weapons crates inside a box that size and marked it like it was some sort of hospital equipment. When it got here, the workers would have just opened up the one box and removed the smaller ones... Now that I think of it they wouldn't even have to go through all that trouble. Even individual boxes could have been hidden in slightly larger ones and labeled as plumbing supplies or whatever. That whole storage facility could be filled with weapons."

Vito added, "That's why there could be so much extra equipment there, not necessarily to feed another construction site."

Cesari turned to Tierney and explained. "We were speculating earlier why there seemed to be such an inordinate amount of boxes and crates in the storage facility. One theory we came up with was that maybe there was another hospital involved and they were feeding supplies to it through one centralized area, but now we have to consider that there may be dozens more crates of weapons there that simply haven't been unpacked yet."

"You've got to be kidding? More, maybe lots more?" Tierney asked incredulously. "Wasn't what you found enough?"

"It's never enough for him, Detective," chimed in Vito.

Tierney sighed, thought it over and asked, "Do you think the workers are in on it?"

"A few perhaps in key positions but I doubt all. Too many people involved and you can't possibly keep it secret. On the other hand, maybe none of them are involved. They're told to open certain boxes, take the contents out and line them up. The crates have funny writing on them, so what? Ninety percent of those guys wouldn't even have known it was Russian and the rest would have just assumed it was special order items for the construction project. The bottom line is that these guys work hard all day. They don't give a crap what the writing is or what's in the box. Their job is to lift and carry, not to think and worry."

"But one of their guys was shot," Tierney said. "They must have thought that was unusual."

Cesari said, "I didn't say they were smart."

"Fine, but back to matters at hand. This meeting is about to break up and right before you arrived, I was trying to decide what to do about that exit in the alley. It would be nice to have eyes on it in case Yorgi and Ivan decide to leave that way. I already checked. There's no car but you never know. They might decide to hoof it. Any volunteers?"

"If there's no car, then how'd they get here?"

"Yorgi and Ivan were here already when I set up surveillance. Tibor came in the Ferrari."

They both turned around to Gianelli at the same time. Tierney said, "How about being a sport, Gianelli?"

Vito looked at Tierney and then at Cesari before rolling his eyes and getting out of the car. Cesari said through his open window, "Thanks."

Vito grumbled, "This is bullshit."

They watched him walk quickly over to the alley and disappear inside. Twenty minutes later an SUV pulled up to the front of the restaurant and at shortly after 2:00 a.m., Yorgi and Ivan came out of the restaurant with two other men. They shook hands courteously and the men were driven off in the waiting SUV. Yorgi said a few words to Ivan and they went back into the restaurant. A minute later, the lights went out. Tierney started the Subaru's engine and Cesari spoke into his cellphone to Vito.

"Party's over up front. Yorgi and Ivan are still in there. Anything happening?"

Hiding in the shadows behind a dumpster twenty feet from the side door, Vito whispered back, "Lights are out. It's just me and the rodents."

"Okay, just sit tight for a few minutes. Something's got to give."

"What if they come out this way and see me?"

"Lie on the floor and play dead."

"You're a funny guy, Cesari."

"Relax, you'll be fine. We're right here. Just keep your phone on. We got the car running. It'll take us five seconds to get there. Besides, you have a gun remember?"

Tierney said, "I wish I didn't hear that."

Vito said, "Of course I have a piece, but I don't want to shoot them."

"You're growing up, Vito. I like that. Just let us know right away if they come into the alley and then shrink into the darkness. As I recall, it's nearly pitch black where you are."

"Yeah, it is, but what if they have a flashlight?"

Tierney grabbed the phone from Cesari without warning and rumbled into the receiver. "Look, Gianelli, we're in combat now so would you do me a favor?"

"Sure, what?"

"I want you to slide your hand down into the front of your pants and make sure your package is still there. If it is, then I want you to stop your belly-aching and be quiet. Can you do that for me? Because I don't have time for all this girlie stuff you and Cesari seem to enjoy so much. We need to be focused and ready to act. Am I making myself perfectly clear?"

"Geez... Yeah, you're clear."

Tierney handed the phone back to Cesari and turned his attention back to the front of the restaurant. Fifteen minutes later, he said, "Something's wrong. Why wouldn't they come out?"

Cesari said, "I don't know. Having a late night snack?"

"With the lights off?"

"They could be in the basement where we found Sofia."

"Why would they hang out there when they have a perfectly comfortable restaurant to sit in with leather booths? Besides, it's two-thirty in the morning. They've been going at it since seven. I would think they'd want to call it a night."

"I agree, but if they are orchestrating a hostile takeover, their adrenaline might be at a fever pitch."

He nodded. "I guess, but why sit in the dark?"

"Unless they really are in the basement seasoning tomorrow's Borscht. You know, mama's secret ingredient or... there's another exit?"

"Another exit...where?"

"I don't know."

"Check in with Gianelli to see what's going on over on his end."

Cesari raised the phone to his mouth and said, "Vito…?"

"I'm allowed to speak now?"

"Yes. Anything happening?"

"Not a thing. What now?"

Tierney heard him and said, "Tell him we're giving them ten more minutes, and then we're going in. We got nothing to lose."

Vito said, "I heard him, but why?"

"Because I want to see this freezer they put Sofia in for myself. I don't want to have any doubts in my mind what kind of scum I'm dealing with."

"That's really bothering you, isn't it?" asked Cesari.

"Yes, it is."

"Is there a story behind it?"

"Yes, there is."

Cesari gave him a few moments but when he didn't offer any further information, he said, "What if they're sitting there having espresso in the dark?"

"Then I'll arrest Yorgi for shooting an RPG at me and I'll book Ivan for being Russian."

"He's Romanian but I guess that's splitting hairs."

Chapter 41

Tierney was just about to start the engine of the Subaru when Vito whispered urgently, "A light from the kitchen just came on. I think they're coming out."

Tierney leaned over to the phone in Cesari's hand and said, "Sit tight and stay out of sight even if you have to lay on your stomach. I've seen that dumpster, it's enormous. You should have no problem staying hidden."

"That's easy for you to say."

"If they come out to First Avenue, we'll follow them. If they head out down the alley toward you, we'll swing around and pick them up on Avenue A."

"Shh, here they come."

Cesari said, "What about the freezer?"

"We'll come back. I have a sudden urge to see where arms dealers go after a long night."

Cesari nodded and noticed that Vito had ended the call. After ten minutes, the phone buzzed again. Vito said, "Jesus Christ, they passed within a few feet of me. They're heading down the alley to Avenue A."

Tierney said, "Okay, come on out and we'll go to Avenue A together."

"No, I'll follow them on foot in case they double back or something. There's a lot going on between here and Avenue A."

Tierney started the engine and said, "Good thinking."

They pulled the Subaru around the block quickly to Avenue A where the alley opened up almost directly opposite East

Fifth street. They cut the lights and idled the car a block away and waited.

After a while, Vito spoke, "They just entered some abandoned building about halfway to the other side."

"An abandoned building?" asked Cesari sounding skeptical as he glanced at Tierney.

"Yeah, the windows are all boarded up. It looks like it should be torn down."

"Are you sure?"

"I'm standing twenty feet away from when I last saw them. Granted, the lighting's not great but I'm not blind. They went into this building."

Tierney said, "Okay, fine. We'll meet you back at the side entrance to the restaurant. I'm going to drive back to First Avenue rather than navigate the alley and take the chance of attracting their attention."

Five minutes later, they gathered in the alley by the door and assessed the situation. Despite Cesari's last visit, there were still no security cameras. He assumed that was a tactical decision on their part because of their own nefarious activities. Cameras were funny that way. They didn't discriminate who they were recording.

Tierney took out a basic lock pick set from his jacket pocket and played with the lock. It took a minute, but the door opened without difficulty. Using a small but powerful LED flashlight he brought with him, he scanned around the kitchen briefly to get oriented. His attention eventually focused on the basement door and they followed him down the steps.

Once there they flicked on the overhead lights and looked around. Tierney said, "Is the room pretty much how you found it?"

Cesari nodded. "Yeah, it was pretty routine except for the body."

Tierney walked to the freezer and stood there brooding over it. He said quietly, "Is this where you found her?"

Vito answered this time noticing Tierney's somewhat pensive mood. He said, "Yeah, there was a note warning people not to open it."

Tierney lifted the cover up and looked in. It was stacked with frozen meats and pierogis. "What condition was she in?" he asked.

Cesari said, "Partially frozen, maybe two thirds the way there."

"And her teeth had been sharpened to make her look like a vampire and she'd been shot in the chest?"

"Yes, about her teeth but the injury to her chest we're not as sure. There was no blood around it or obvious tissue injury suggesting that she may have incurred the injury after death. It's also possible somebody stabbed her rather than shot her."

"You should be able to differentiate a stab wound from a gunshot wound just by looking at it. Don't you think?"

Cesari hesitated momentarily and said, "With a knife, yes but perhaps not with a spear or...?"

"Or what?"

"A sharpened stake."

Tierney just looked at him dead-panned and asked, "Did you probe the wound looking for a bullet or a slug?"

"No, we didn't."

"What about the funeral home. Did anyone there try to figure it out?"

Vito replied, "Not that I'm aware."

"What do you guys think happened?" Tierney asked. "Give it your best shot."

Cesari said, "We think Yorgi and his brothers killed her and filed her teeth to make her appear to be a vampire and apparently were so highly successful in their endeavor that the person they were trying to convince bought into it to such a degree that he shot or stabbed her in the heart the way they do in horror flicks."

Tierney was nonplussed. "Because that's how folklore says you kill vampires?"

Cesari nodded.

Tierney said, "Shlomo?"

"It's a very short list of people who might believe in such things, and they *are* trying to displace him. Maybe driving him crazy was easier than killing him."

"Killing the boss never goes over well," added Vito knowingly. "It's hard for anyone to trust you when you do that and invites all sorts of retaliation from the soldiers who were loyal to the dead guy."

Tierney thought about that and said, "Okay, so why bring Sofia here?"

"That's the part we don't understand. Unless they were planning on using her again," offered Cesari.

"Like maybe against Gianelli? If the trick with Leandro didn't work then maybe double-down and throw Sofia at him?"

"Something like that...maybe."

Tierney shook his head. "A twofer... Man, they got big ones, don't they?"

Cesari added, "It looks that way."

Tierney looked inside the freezer one last time and closed the lid. The rest of the basement was unremarkable. He then went over to the table in the center of the room, sat down on a folding chair and closed his eyes.

After a minute, Cesari asked, "Are you okay, Detective?"

He opened his eyes again and looked at Gianelli. "I'm fine... You got her a decent funeral, Gianelli?"

"The best I could do under the circumstances. I wasn't there but my understanding of it was that they said a few prayers and treated her like a human being. Her ashes are still up there in a nice urn. They said they'll keep them for a month in case a relative shows up."

"That was a nice thing to do."

Vito didn't say anything and Cesari stood there silently. The feeling in the room had just taken on an entirely different aura. It was if some silent signal had been sent out about who, what, where and why. An invisible bond had just been forged between the men, and their commonality of purpose fully revealed.

Tierney said as if to no one, "I never knew my mother. She abandoned the family unit right after I was born…drugs. My father died from a heart attack when I was fourteen. I had no siblings and needless to say all sorts of issues. I joined the Marine Corps when I was eighteen. I was full of piss and vinegar and couldn't wait to go overseas for God and country to slay the enemies of the republic. It was a dream come true when I was deployed to Afghanistan. God bless the U.S.A. and all that."

Cesari and Vito glanced at each other but didn't say anything. Tierney went on, "My first tour was quite an eye opener for me as it was for almost all of us; roadside bombs, unseen enemies, snipers, RPGs coming out of nowhere, divided loyalties of the people we were supposed to be helping, a shithole of a country, mostly illiterate mob type mentality wherever we went, freezing in the mountains, scorching in the deserts. I wasn't there a full two weeks when four of my company got sent home in body bags from IEDs. It took a while but eventually my enthusiasm started to wane a bit. It wasn't like World War II or the American Revolution where your enemy wore a distinctive or even colorful uniform and lined up across from you on the battlefield. This kind of warfare just sucked. Every rock is potentially hiding a mine, every abandoned vehicle a booby trap, every child a suicide bomber. It gets to you after a while."

He took a deep breath and let it out.

"By the end of my first tour, I had made corporal. Not because I did anything so great. It was more of a last man standing kind of promotion. You know, *"Hey Tierney. Everybody's dead so you're getting promoted,"* kind of thing. By that point it wasn't about democracy anymore. It was about trying to keep the guys in my unit alive. All the while, we're being told to win hearts and minds. But how do you win the hearts and minds of people who don't even know what indoor plumbing is? In America, rural means Walmart, pickup trucks and country music. Over there, rural is goats running down a dirt street and guys being flogged for missing afternoon prayer, and the mistreatment of women..."

He shook his head.

"You can't even imagine what goes in some of those remote villages. Anyway, I had six months left on my first tour. We were doing well on the military side of things but politically, we weren't even close. If the idea was to convince these people that our culture was not only superior but more desirable than their own, we had failed miserably. We were simply an invading army that they knew would eventually just fade away with time and they had every right to think so. No one had tried harder than the Russians and the British before them and both had disastrous consequences."

Cesari sat down on the chest-style freezer and Vito leaned against a metal shelf. They didn't know where this was going but felt it would be very wrong to interrupt. Clearly, the detective needed to get something off his chest.

Tierney continued, "We had occupied some Taliban controlled village north of Kabul called Andarab and things were mostly quiet. We'd been there over a month making daily patrols but mostly trying not to get blown up. By that point, I couldn't wait to get the hell out of there when I met Shahzadi. She was fifteen or sixteen. She might have been seventeen. She didn't know for sure. She didn't speak any English and my Dari was awful. Dari is a variety of Persian used in Afghanistan by the way and they give grunts a two-week crash course before they deploy. It's not nearly enough... I was crouched behind a wall facing the only road leading into that side of town when she came up to me with some hot food in a basket. She wore a traditional dress and was barefoot. She wore a hijab, but her face wasn't covered. She was beautiful and exotic. She sat next to me and was clearly curious. She expressed an interest in learning English so in the interest of that *hearts and minds kind of thing* we embarked on a relationship of sorts much to the amusement of my guys.

She came back the next day and the next and we had long sessions sometimes lasting hours. She was a fast learner too and I became fond of her and our visits. This went on every day for nearly six weeks. Just for the record, there was nothing else going on. Let's just get that out in the open. She came during daylight in full view of my men and always left before dark. I never went to seek her out except on one occasion and that was the day we pulled out.

Eventually the order came to withdraw back to the next largest town, Charikar, which is the capital of the Parwan province. I guess the powers that be decided we couldn't afford to occupy every little podunk village. On the day we left, I found Shahzadi and gave her a present. It was nothing much; an inexpensive braided leather bracelet I wore for good luck. She cried, and in English, said she would pray for me. Do you have any idea how that made me feel? A teen-age girl in that hellhole of a country who had nothing was going to pray to Allah to watch over me. I don't know about you, Cesari, but for me, suddenly everything I was doing made sense again. Within a week of us pulling out the Taliban overran Andarab again. I didn't think much of it until I was on patrol one morning and spotted a body lying in the middle of the road coming down from Andarab."

Cesari and Vito held their breath. Tierney looked at them and sighed. "I can see from your faces you've already figured out this story doesn't have a happy ending. It was Shahzadi. She had been raped, beaten, and her face mutilated with acid by the Taliban when they learned she had befriended me. I found out later, this had been done to her with the entire village present to serve as a lesson to the rest. She had been dropped off on the road they knew we patrolled on a regular basis. They wanted me to know that there was one less heart and mind I had to worry about. I found my bracelet shoved in her mouth."

Tierney had choked up at the end but quickly recovered and added. "Shahzadi means princess in Persian and she truly was. When you told me about Sofia, I couldn't help but see a comparison in the way they had both been brutally treated by men they should have been able to trust and then discarded like rubbish."

Cesari was about to say something consoling but Tierney raised his left hand in protest. For the first time, Cesari noticed the worn leather bracelet on his wrist.

Chapter 42

"There is problem, Ivan," Yorgi said soberly. "After our conference call several days ago, Dimitri and the council summoned Shlomo to come to Bucharest immediately. They did not tell him why, just that they were concerned over the missing weapons and wanted to discuss future security measures. They did tell him that they wanted me in charge in his absence. Shlomo agreed but Dimitri just called to tell me Shlomo never arrived at scheduled time in Bucharest."

"Maybe his plane was delayed or for some reason he had to change flights?" offered Ivan.

Yorgi strummed the table with his fingers. Tap, tap, tap, like small jackhammers. "No, Dimitri called airline. He was supposed to be on flight. He even checked in with airline, was given boarding pass and went through security, but he never got on plane. Now he doesn't answer his cellphone."

"Tibor drove him to airport. How did Shlomo seem?"

"Tibor said he was fine, as if going on ordinary business trip. Did not seem apprehensive at all."

"What does this mean?"

"I hope it does not mean Shlomo knows he has been betrayed, but I can think of no other explanation."

"How could he know?"

"That is the question, younger brother."

"Would he so brazenly defy council of elders?"

"Apparently so."

"But that would mean death for sure."

Yorgi smiled, "How naïve you are, brother. His death was assured the minute he opened up his mouth about vampires to Dimitri. They cannot afford to have a delusional old man who knows as much as he does about their empire running around unhinged. Dimitri did not say it out loud, but I read in between the lines. I still cannot believe Shlomo would say such things even to an old friend such as Dimitri."

"Then is possible he still does not suspect us?"

"Yes, is still possible. He may blame council and friend, Dimitri. Is good and bad for us."

"How so?"

"Is good because we are firmly in control of our own destiny. Is bad because Dimitri is now angry at Shlomo for disobeying the council. Even worse, he is embarrassed because he reassured others Shlomo would comply to his wishes. Now Dimitri come to New York to seek Shlomo out and determine what is going on for himself."

"Oh boy."

"Oh boy is right, Ivan."

"Is time to return weapons?"

"Not yet. It would look too suspicious to suddenly find missing weapons hours after Dimitri announce he is coming here. We must play game just a little longer."

"What about drivers, Yorgi? Can you believe the bad luck that one of them is related to Dimitri?"

"Yes, very bad, but if all goes well, we pin blame on Shlomo. Aside from desperately needing an air freshener, they are not bothering anyone. Let them sit tight for a few more days with the weapons. There is too much risk now for any movement. Too much uncertainty."

"I understand… The same for hospital?"

"For now, yes, but after last of weapons have shipped, we will terminate our relationship with that runt Acevedo and his pet gorilla, Feinberg. They were Shlomo's men and I never approved of them. They are both weak and only care about having their physical needs satisfied. Once they are gone and our business at the hospital has concluded, I will recommend more traditional income streams for council that have been tried and tested over many years by current organized crime."

"You are wise, Yorgi."

Yorgi suddenly looked around, "By the way, where is Tibor? He misses yet another meeting. Is not like him."

"He visits Drusilla."

"Visits Drusilla? Again? I would have thought that with the demise of Shlomo he would have put great distance between himself and that troll. Instead, he sees her even more often. I do not understand."

"Between me and you Yorgi... Is almost impossible to believe but I think he may actually have fallen in love with her."

Yorgi roared with laughter and slapped the table. "Seriously? How is that possible? Not too long ago he was ready to attack me for just suggesting the union."

Ivan shrugged. "I do not have explanation, but he truly pines for her. Almost every day he finds some reason to go see her. His passion runs deep."

"You do not think that they are...?"

Ivan shuddered at the thought. "Please, Yorgi, do not plant imagery before my eyes. I will not be able to sleep if I think baby brother..."

"I agree. Is one thing to carry out plan for sake of family and another to satisfy one's personal desires. Do you really think he lusts for her? Men have done crazier things although sleeping with hag, Drusilla, would be one for the history books."

"Please, Yorgi, stop talking about it."

"I know what you mean Ivan. If Drusilla was lying on bed in front of me naked and someone put gun to my head and order me to do it, I would grab weapon and shoot myself, but first I would shoot Drusilla in order to save mankind... Well, is tough pill for us to swallow, but if Drusilla makes Tibor happy then we must embrace her for his sake."

"Mentally, I will accept her, Yorgi, but I will never physically embrace her, and I don't care if it is her birthday, Christmas or the end of the world. That will never happen."

"Enough Ivan. We must prepare for Dimitri and search for Shlomo. What better proof could we have of our ability to manage their affairs than to provide council with Shlomo's head and the weapons all at the same time?"

"I agree."

"Then spread the word. There will be a one million-dollar reward for information leading us to Shlomo, two million if he is found dead, and five million if it looks like he was made to suffer greatly before death. I want every resource we have at our disposal used to find old man."

Chapter 43

After leaving the restaurant, Cesari, Vito and Tierney headed down the alley to the tenement building where Vito had last seen Yorgi and Ivan. It was a decrepit ancient structure with boarded up windows and crumbling brick. Litter dotted the alley leading up to the entrance. It was hard to believe that this had once been home to thousands of people and that this had been a teeming, thriving neighborhood full of life and vigor. It was after 3:00 a.m. and this portion of the alley was completely black. They were at the halfway point between First Avenue and Avenue A and out of reach of ambient street lighting. There were no people, no cars, no noise, just rats scurrying along the filth looking for whatever it was rats looked for at this hour.

Tierney looked around and said, "It's kind of strange. No addicts, no homeless people. They're all over First Avenue but not here and you'd think this would be a great spot for them."

Cesari thought about that for a moment before saying, "You're right. In fact this whole alley from one end to the other is perfect for druggies and winos."

Vito said, "Isn't it also kind of odd for a building to open into an alley like this?"

"Maybe it didn't always. Back in the late eighteen hundreds when these building went up, there probably was no alley here," replied Tierney. "And the population swelled so fast from immigration, the demand for housing grew faster than the building codes to regulate them. You also have to take into consideration that there were no cars, buses or subways at the time. This ten-foot-wide alley might seem claustrophobic to you but was probably plenty wide during the horse drawn cart days."

Cesari said, "It looks pretty quiet. Do you think they're still in there?"

"It's hard to say," Tierney replied. "Why would they go in there at all is the question?"

"I don't know, but that's what we should find out. It's been well over an hour since Vito saw them. I say we go in. There are three of us against two of them."

"Not that I give a crap, but they have RPGs and assault rifles," Vito observed.

"That's true, Gianelli, but I doubt they're still in there. I mean these guys got to sleep sometime, right?"

"Yeah, I guess, but on the other hand, it would be nice to find them in there so we could slap the snot out of them."

"I agree with the sentiment, but the last thing we want to do is actually find them," Tierney said. "This is a force recon mission."

"Meaning?"

"You can't be serious, Gianelli. Force recon is a Marine Corps special operations unit. They're armed scouts prepared to engage the enemy if they have to, but their main goal is to work deep behind enemy lines and gather intelligence. Don't you watch TV? Everybody knows that."

Vito turned to Cesari, "Did you hear that, I'm a marine now."

With a seldom seen half-grin, Tierney said, "Gianelli, I'm starting to like you. I really am, but if you say something ridiculous like that again, I'll be forced to reconsider my position. No offense, but I doubt you're even Army material."

"No offense taken."

"Good. Now let's keep it down until we're certain we're not walking into an ambush. Although now that I think about it, they could very well have gone in and come back out without us ever seeing them. We were in the restaurant for over an hour." Tierney shook his head in frustration and added, "I should have left one of you out here as a sentry. Damn, I'm getting rusty."

"Or maybe there's another way out of the building. If this is the front, then there must be a back," Cesari said.

"That's very true, and since I'm rather curious about what would possess them to go into a condemned building at this hour, I think we should do it... Okay, saddle up. Gianelli, if you're armed, now would be a good time to make sure you have a round chambered and the safety off. We don't want to have a shootout but better them than us if it comes to it."

Tierney pulled out his Glock and Vito took out his Colt. They all climbed the three decaying concrete steps to the splintered and rotting wood door. The handles were rusted, and the joints jammed tight from humidity but with a little pressure they were able to force their way inside. In the vestibule, Tierney turned on his flashlight and they surveyed their surroundings of cobwebs, decaying wood, layers of dust, and debris everywhere.

"Look at the floor," Cesari whispered, pointing at footprints in the thick layers of dust.

Tierney spent a moment to examine the clue and then led the way cautiously following the trail down the grimy corridor toward the back of the building. At the rear, the tracks abruptly ended at two doors. One led outside the building into an unpaved, unlit parking lot which fed back around the side of the building to the alley. The other was a fairly new door which was locked. They stepped outside and scanned the lot for any activity but found none.

Tierney said, "Interesting."

Cesari added, "They may have had a vehicle parked here."

"Agreed, but why'd they come inside. Were they too lazy to walk the few extra feet around the building? I can't believe that."

"Neither can I."

"C'mon, let's see what's behind door number 2."

They stepped back inside, and Tierney took out his lock pick set. The door was no match for him and swung open in less than a minute. They stared down into the blackness at a set of rickety steps, but unlike the rest of the building they appeared to have had at least some minimal repair work done to keep them functional. At least two of the steps had been replaced recently and were made of unpainted pine. The ancient risers were supported in several places by fresh two-by-fours. There was a light switch at the top of the steps and Tierney flipped it upward. A light somewhere in the cellar flicked on.

Cesari said, "Even more interesting. They've got electricity."

"It certainly begs the question of what they do here that requires utilities," mused Tierney. "Well at least no one's home."

"Are you sure about that?" asked Vito.

"Mostly, I have an instinct about these things. All right, troops. It's show time. Let's find out what's going on in this dump."

With his Glock at the ready, Tierney proceeded with care down the steps with Cesari and Vito right behind. They moved slowly and cautiously but not enough to prevent the creaking and groaning of the old wood. Cesari hoped their combined weight wouldn't cause the staircase to collapse.

At the bottom, Tierney inspected the room and then seemed to relax. He said, "I told you. Nobody's home."

The basement was bare and musty with a cement floor, an old wood table, a few chairs and an incandescent bulb hanging down from an exposed wire. The plaster walls were cracked and leaking. A dead, desiccated rat lay in a corner. Two shot glasses sat eerily by themselves on the table. Tierney lifted one of them and sniffed it. At the far end of the room was another door. Tierney went over, opened it and peered in. It was a large room, quiet and dark. He recoiled from an unpleasant, pungent odor.

He panned his flashlight back and forth and said, "I think it's the building's utility room. From the smell, there might be a lot more dead rats in here."

He was about to investigate further, but Cesari called to him with some urgency, "Detective, you should see this."

On one side of the table, there were dark smear marks where someone had done a poor job of trying to clean something up, something red. On the floor on that side were obvious blood stains only with no attempt at a cleanup. Three separate areas of stains, on the table and on the floor. Tierney stooped low with his flashlight trying to make sense of it.

"What happened here and why didn't they get along?" he mumbled to himself.

Vito said, "Some sort of business deal took a wrong turn would be my guess."

"It would seem that way, but three separate stains?" Tierney added not expecting a reply as he examined the walls for bullet holes. He found none and looked at the table just five feet away. "It must have been a small caliber bullet. It didn't make it through their bodies."

Cesari studied the table and blood stains. "Something doesn't make sense. If three guys were sitting or standing here and one got shot wouldn't the others run or at least try to get away?"

"Not necessarily," Vito said. "Maybe they were shot at the same time by three different shooters or possibly they were restrained."

Tierney nodded, "Very possible."

Cesari said, "So they were shot, and blood splattered onto the table and then oozed onto the floor. It was a low caliber bullet which is why there are no holes in the wall."

"They could have been stabbed or had their throats slit," conjectured Vito. "Suppose they were lined up in row, maybe sitting, maybe tied up? Somebody could have come up behind them with a knife and done the deed. They would have fallen forward staining the table and then leaked onto the floor."

Tierney said, "Or they could have been stabbed through the throat from front to back like the rabbi."

Tierney went to the other side of the table across from the blood stains and sat down in one of the chairs. He stared at the dried blood trying to picture the scene. He said, "Cesari, grab a chair and sit down opposite me."

Cesari sat down and waited. The table was four feet wide. Tierney put his pistol away and took out a four-inch long pocketknife and flicked it open. He stretched his long arm across the table and could barely reach Cesari's face with the tip of the blade while sitting. He then stood up and leaned across the table…better, but still not nearly enough even if the knife was twice the length. The postmortem had demonstrated that the blade was thin and at least long enough to completely penetrate the rabbi's neck from front to back easily. The exit wound suggested that a fair amount of the blade came out the other side, anywhere from four to six inches. If the murderer shoved it through sinews, tendons, muscle and bone and then forcefully yanked it back out, then the rabbi would have been pulled face forward onto the table accounting for the blood stain there. Blood would have continued to ooze and then drip down to the floor, but who were the other two victims?

"What do you think, Detective?" asked Cesari

"I think Yorgi and his brothers are probably the biggest assholes I've encountered since I left Afghanistan. The good news for you, Gianelli, is that I think the rabbi was murdered right here with two other poor souls who as yet are still un-identified so you're officially off the hook on that one."

"Thanks, I appreciate it."

"The bad news is that I think the murder weapon was some type of long double-edged blade anywhere from two to three feet in length and the blow was probably delivered from right where I am. Preliminary autopsy results suggested the blade came in the front of the neck at a slight angle down-ward. I'm guessing Yorgi or whoever stood suddenly and rammed the weapon home. It must have been a savage thrust to slice through his vertebrae and continue on out through the other side."

Cesari said, "Two to three feet long? You're talking about a sword?"

"I think so."

"What does a rabbi have to do with any of this?" Cesari asked thinking out loud.

"I'm going to ask Yorgi that very question when I see him, but right now we need to check the next room. There was a funny odor in there that I wrote off to a dead rat but now I'm not so sure."

Chapter 44

Cesari turned on the overhead lights and they observed a very large room but only the half where they stood was lit. The back half remained in the shadows for some reason and he thought there might be a second light switch somewhere, perhaps to save energy. Peculiar, but since Tierney had a flashlight, they didn't give it much thought. Directly in front of them, in the center of the room was a massive, ancient furnace, nearly six feet high and equally wide with three-foot-wide duct work shooting out of it up toward the ceiling. The furnace received its fuel from a proportionately large oil tank not too far away along with a dilapidated hot water heater. A conservative guess of the oil tank would have put it at a thousand-gallon capacity. All of the equipment was rusted, grimy and covered in dust from disuse. Against a wall to their right, was a large metal bin on wheels positioned close to a four-foot-wide chute coming in from the outside. Cesari judged the chute led out to the parking lot behind the building. They all winced at the noxious scent that Tierney had noticed earlier.

Cesari walked over to the bin and looked inside. It was dirty and there was a dead rat at the bottom with insects feasting on it. Vito came up behind him and said, "Disgusting... What is this?"

"I think it's a coal bin and that chute is how they made deliveries in the late eighteen hundreds. They probably switched over to oil some years afterward. The building was most likely abandoned before they had a chance to modernize to natural gas."

"You think the rat's the cause of the smell?"

"Possibly. Look at the floor."

The space directly below the chute was relatively clean but everywhere else footprints could be seen in the dust and muck, and their travel pattern suggested great activity. Vito nodded, "A lot of people were down here relatively recently."

"I agree. Certainly more than one or two that's for sure. There's a lot of back and forth, and the bin itself is out of place."

"You're right. It looks like it may have been moved recently."

Tierney was studying the furnace, fascinated by all the dials and levers of the old-fashioned device. A five-foot-wide fan connected to the heat compartment delivered hot air to the big duct which eventually branched in multiple directions overhead. Cesari and Vito came over to him and could see him trying to calculate in his mind how well this solitary piece of equipment might have heated an eight-story apartment building or whether the poor tenement dwellers froze their asses off most of the winter.

After a moment, they walked around the furnace to examine the other half of the room. Using his flashlight Tierney scanned the walls for a second light switch and eventually found one. The lights flickered on and the back half of the room revealed several more dead rats lying scattered about on the floor. Along the far wall, there was a large metal sink six feet long with two porcelain faucets and a hose attached below. It was lower than most sinks and Cesari wondered what it was used for. He thought about a coal fired furnace and dirty, soot covered men needing to clean themselves or their tools off.

Alternatively, the building was well over a hundred years old. There could be at least a hundred other reasons in that time frame why the landlord might have installed a sink. On one side of it were two sawhorses stored neatly on each other and next to them a six-foot-long by four-foot-wide, three-quarter inch piece of plywood leaned against the wall. To the other side of the sink were multiple wood crates stacked two deep against the wall in a row of fifteen. There were thirty boxes in all, six feet long, three feet wide, and two and a half feet deep. They all had Cyrillic writing on them. The last two boxes looked as if their lids had been tampered with. The edges were splintered and frayed in places.

Tierney walked along the row of weapons studying them and whistled, "Sweet mother of Jesus, Cesari. We found the mother lode."

Cesari was close behind. He said, "Now that we found them, we can't just leave them."

"I agree, but if I call it in now whoever's in charge may get away. It's the big fish we want Cesari or at least the biggest one we can catch. I think we both agree Yorgi's not the boss here. These weapons are coming from somewhere outside the country and that's who we want too. As much as I hate to do it, I may have to call the feds in on this soon."

As they stood in front of the last two crates Vito commented, "Damn, this is where the odor is coming from."

"We need to open a few of these anyway to confirm the contents so we might as well have at it. Look around for a tool."

They searched for a minute or two and eventually found a small rusted mallet lying on the floor between the furnace and hot water heater and a metal file used for smoothing out pipe fittings. It was covered in muck. They moved the top box and laid it on the floor next to its twin and then Tierney got to work smashing the edge of the file under the lid in multiple places working his way around the perimeter until the three of them together were able to pry the top off.

They were overwhelmed with the putrefying gases of decaying flesh and covered their faces as best as possible as they gagged. Vito wretched but didn't hurl. It was the corpse of a rough-looking, Caucasian male in his late thirties. His clothes were of poor quality. There were no obvious bullet holes or stab wounds but there was an ugly circular bruise around his neck suggesting strangulation and his belt was missing. He had no wallet or identification on him.

They opened the second box and found a male, similar in appearance, with four rats eating his face. They ran in all directions jumping out of either end of the crate. There was an irregularly-shaped hole in one of the sides of the box three inches in diameter from damage in transport and Cesari surmised that's how the rats gained entry. The cause of death was more readily apparent as this guy was still wearing the missing belt around his neck. He too had no identification.

Tierney looked disgusted. "These aren't the guys who were killed in the other room, Cesari. They were strangled and beyond that there's no blood."

Vito said, "How'd they get all these crates in here? I don't see any steps."

Cesari turned around to look at the walls. He said, "I doubt they carried them down that rickety staircase, so it was probably through the coal chute."

Tierney nodded. "I agree. They could have used ropes to lower them slowly with a couple of guys down here to stabilize them and then an ordinary hand truck to move them around."

Vito said, "So where's the hand truck?"

Cesari said, "Maybe they needed it for something else. They probably borrowed it from the restaurant."

Tierney said, "Sounds reasonable... Okay, Cesari, let's check a few more boxes just to make sure what's in them is what we think is in them and then we'll cover them back up.

Cesari nodded at the dead men as they started to unroof another crate. "Dare I ask who they are?"

"I haven't a clue. Welcome to the dark underbelly of the city that never sleeps. These Romanescu boys are racking up quite a body count. They're liable to give you a run for your money, Gianelli."

Vito had wandered back to the sink and sawhorses and was examining them. He turned around in protest. "Me? I'm a legitimate businessman."

Cesari added, "Actually, I believe that's their main goal; to replace my friend over there as the most powerful legitimate businessman in lower Manhattan."

Tierney grinned. "Well I'll grant you this, Gianelli. Compared to these guys, you're a choir boy."

The first crate they opened was loaded with assault rifles and they were in the process of opening a second crate when Vito called out. "Hey guys, you should see this."

They walked over to him and saw that Vito had arranged the sawhorses about five feet apart and had placed the large piece of plywood on top of them with one end close to the sink.

Cesari and Tierney stepped close and saw that the wood was heavily bloodstained at one end. Tierney said, "So this is how and where they did it. The sink is functional?"

Vito leaned over, turned on the faucet and cold water came pouring out. He turned it off again and nodded. "They probably used the hose underneath to clean them off."

There was a large cardboard box on a shelf above the sink. Cesari reached up and brought it down. Inside they found handcuffs, syringes, several large bore intravenous needles, IV tubing and a large box of rat poison.

Tierney grunted, "They brought the victims here, heavily sedated and handcuffed, placed them on this board with their heads over the sink and stuck the needle in their necks. I'm down with that but what's the IV tubing for?"

Cesari said, "Probably to keep the splatter down to a minimum. You stick the IV needle into the jugular or the carotid, attach the tubing and wait. The tubing would help the blood flow directly into the sink."

"So maybe the barbecue fork was used simply for cosmetic reasons to make it look like a vampire bite. Does that sound about right?"

Cesari contemplated that and wondered how difficult it would have been to get someone as big as Leandro down here but Yorgi was a big muscular guy, even bigger than Vito, and Ivan and Tibor were no slouches either. It was definitely possible, and the bottom line was that a gun to the small of one's back or head generally made everyone very cooperative.

He said, "It does, and once down here maybe they force-fed them the anticoagulant followed by an extra dose of heroin to quiet them down before surgery. Then they just let them drain into the sink until the well went dry. To be honest, if things went smoothly, there wouldn't even be that much cleanup. I'd hazard a guess that most of the blood here on the board was accidental spill from when they introduced the IV needle into the neck. If they hit the artery, it would have sprayed like crazy."

Vito said, "They used the rat poison as an anticoagulant?"

"I'm sure of it," Cesari said as he read the side of the box. "For decades the main ingredient in commercial rat poison has been warfarin, a commonly used anticoagulant also marketed for medicinal use as Coumadin. It's extremely common. We talked about that, Detective."

"I remember," Tierney nodded. "So they gave them the rat poison while they were restrained."

Cesari nodded. "I think so. This particular box of rat poison contains warfarin. It's been falling out of favor recently because of newer improved poisons but it's cheap and still widely available. That would explain all the dead rats around here."

Cesari put the rat poison back in the box and was about to place it back on the shelf when he noticed another unusual item. It seemed familiar but out of place. He took it out to show Vito and Tierney.

Tierney took it and held it up for all to see. It was a thin metal stick with a tiny mirror angled at one end. Vito announced, "It's a dentist's mirror. The kind they put in your mouth to see things."

Tierney said, "He's right, but what on earth did they need this for?"

Vito glanced at Cesari and said, "You think they worked on Sofia's teeth down here?"

Cesari replied, "Why not? They did everything else down here."

"Okay, Cesari," Tierney said. "Put everything back and let's put the covers back on those crates. Gianelli put the wood board and the sawhorses back the way you found them. I'd rather not let anyone know we were here until I come up with a strategy."

After they finished, they reconvened in the other room and sat around the same table as Yorgi and his brothers. Cesari said, "You're the boss, Detective, but like I said before I don't feel comfortable leaving those weapons here."

"Duly noted, Cesari, and just for the record neither do I. But if I call the feds now and they swarm the place, we may get Yorgi and his brothers and they may possibly squeal on Shlomo and that's a big if but that will be it. By tomorrow, they will have all been replaced by someone else equally as capable. It's my experience that the guys on the ground getting their hands dirty are almost never the big movers and shakers. Once in a while it would be nice to catch the puppet master."

"Agreed, but it still leaves us with the problem of the weapons in the next room. If we let them out of our sight, they might be gone tomorrow and in the hands of undesirables, maybe even taking shots at friends of yours."

"I hear you loud and clear, Cesari. What say you, Gianelli?"

"Thanks for the vote of confidence. I can put a sentry up on either end of the alley, one on First Avenue and one on

Avenue A. Yorgi will need a truck to get rid of all those crates. If my guys see anything bigger than a Honda Civic going into the alley they'll call immediately."

"That's very generous of you, Gianelli. That would work, but what about the hospital? If Cesari's right and there are dozens more crates loaded with weapons, we'll need more eyes."

"I can spare another guy. I'll place him in the garage overlooking the loading dock. If he sees trucks being loaded rather than unloaded, he'll call."

Tierney nodded. "At which point the party's over. I'll have to intervene because we can't let them move any more weapons." He took a deep breath and let it out. "You know, Gianelli, I'm seriously thinking of taking you off my bad guy list."

"And I may take you off my list too."

"Which list is that?"

"Let's not spoil the moment, Detective."

Chapter 45

It was well after twelve noon the next day when bright beams of sunlight piercing through his bedroom curtains jolted Cesari from a deep slumber making him groan. He wasn't just tired, he was exhausted, physically and emotionally, and he was unemployed. They were in a waiting game at this point and the next move was mostly out of his hands. They had eyes on Yorgi and the weapons, and just for good measure, Vito had stationed a guy in the abandoned apartment building across the street from where the crates were stored to keep an eye on foot traffic. It had dawned on them that there were no addicts or street people squatting in the alley or abandoned buildings there because Yorgi's goons must have forced them out to maintain secrecy. Desperate people weren't necessarily stupid, and they had learned quickly that this particular alley was off limits.

He cleaned up, made a pot of coffee and a pile of scrambled eggs, and was eating when his phone rang. It was Arnie.

"Cesari, where've you been? I heard you got canned. That has to be the shortest tenure anyone has ever held that job. So what happened?"

"It's a complicated story, Arnie. What's the rumor mill churning out?"

"I just want you to know I don't believe a word of it."

"Go ahead, Arnie. I can take it."

"Well there's bad news and then there's not so bad news. Some of the nurses are saying that you used your new position as medical director to sexually harass one of the OR nurses. Some believe it and some don't. It's a real controversy here. You know how women are. They use mob mentality to make their decisions when it comes to these things. Most of them think opinions are facts. All the guys are afraid to open their mouths. Well that's the not so bad news."

"Great, so what's the bad news?"

"That you're under investigation for murder."

"Who'd I murder?"

"Nobody knows and nobody's talking especially administration. You can't even bring your name up around them. There's even a rumor that you stole the CEO's car. Is any of it true?"

"I didn't murder or sexually harass anyone."

"So you did steal the shrimp's Aston Martin?"

"I'd rather not go into that at this time."

"Fine, but do I get a rain check?"

"Yes, as soon I resolve the situation."

"Thanks… Is there anything I can do to help?"

Cesari thought about that and said, "Actually, there is. I could use some quiet time in the CEO's office."

"To do what?"

"Arnie…"

"Fine, what do you want me to do?"

"I just need to know for sure that he won't be there. Invite him out for a drink after work. Tell him you just want to talk about possibly being reinstated as temporary medical director again now that I've been terminated. Stroke him a little. Tell him there are no hard feelings about your demotion and that you just want to do what's right for the hospital. Even better, tell him that you agree with my being fired and that you feel you can smooth things over with the nursing staff and be a good snitch for him."

Arnie laughed. "I can do that. Sounds rather spyish. I like it. When?"

"Tonight, if possible. He drinks like a fish and likes gin martinis. Tell him you're a big martini man. Find common ground. I can get into his office from the parking garage. I still have my spare ID. Security didn't think to ask me for it."

"What if he doesn't go for it or is busy?"

"Then I'll figure it out some other way. Get back to me as soon as you get an answer, all right?"

"I'll call him now."

An hour later, Cesari left his apartment wearing a light windbreaker and a baseball cap. Rain was predicted for later in the day and he wanted to be prepared. He locked his door and wondered how Yorgi was able to plant the evidence in his apartment without breaking in. Just then it hit him that Feinberg must have given him the keys he copied. He kicked himself for not changing the locks. That was a careless oversight. He reached under the floorboard and realized his .38 special was missing. Either Yorgi or Feinberg was trying to make sure he couldn't defend himself. Well that was a mistake on their part.

He made two stops on the way to the hospital. One was at a small clothing store to pick up a black duffle bag and the other at a hardware store where he purchased a six-pound crowbar. He tested its weight and balance and after he was satisfied, placed it in the duffle bag. On Third Avenue, he took a seat in a coffee shop across from the hospital, ordered black coffee and called Tierney.

"Cesari, what are you doing?"

"Deep recon at the hospital."

"You just made me smile. I'm in my car with your boy Gianelli on First Avenue. You're on speaker phone. He says hello. So far, nothing's happening here, but it's early. We might be the only ones awake in the whole neighborhood... How deep is deep recon?"

"I'm going to search the CEO's office as soon as I'm sure he's not there." He glanced at his watch. "It's almost three. I might be here a long time. There are a few other small issues I need to straighten out as well."

"Just out of curiosity, what are you looking for? We already know he and Feinberg are just boot-licking lackeys for Shlomo and Yorgi."

"Probably nothing but this is personal now between me and them. They've hurt my friends and ruined my reputation. I just want to see if I can return the favor."

Cesari heard Vito snort in the background. "You see, Detective. I've been trying to tell you what he's like. No matter what's going on it's always about him."

Before Cesari could respond, Tierney said, "Hey Cesari, I appreciate how ticked off you are, but Gianelli has a point. We have bigger fish to fry, and you better not screw this up with any personal vendettas."

"When did you and my friend over there become Starsky and Hutch?"

"That's not the point."

"I won't screw it up, all right?"

Just before he clicked off, he heard Vito throw more gasoline on the fire. "He's always been stubborn like that. It's an ego thing."

Cesari grimaced and resisted the urge to throw his phone against the wall. He finished his coffee, threw a bill on the table and walked over to the hospital, frustrated that he still hadn't heard from Arnie. At the security desk, he said hello to the guard who knew him and asked him his business now that he was a civilian. He told him that he had left in such a hurry he had never cleaned out his office. He had some pictures and diplomas he needed to get. He also had a few charts he needed to complete, or the hospital might get dinged by the state. His plan was to go to his office for a few minutes, collect the items in question and then head straight to the medical staff lounge. He would obtain a temporary password from medical records, complete the charts and get out as fast as he could. After he concluded his speech, he crossed his heart in the universal *I promise* gesture.

The guard mulled over whether he should call someone for advice but decided that he hated the administration as much as anyone else, and that although Cesari was being accused of all sorts of heinous things, in general he had always held him in high esteem.

Eventually, he nodded sympathetically. "Go ahead, Doc, but please don't do anything to get me fired. What's in the duffle bag?"

"Nothing, it's for the stuff in my office."

"All right, and for what it's worth, I don't believe anything of what they've been saying about you."

"Actually, it means a lot. Thanks. If for some reason, someone asks how I got by you just say you were occupied with a crowd of Chinese tourists whose tour bus mistakenly dropped them off in front of the hospital thinking it was an Italian restaurant."

The guard smiled and then laughed. "Yeah, that should work. Go ahead, Doc."

He walked with purpose down the corridor and hopped on an elevator to the OR. He got off and went to the nursing supervisor's office. Emily was sitting at her desk staring at her computer screen. She looked up when he walked in.

"Hi, Emily."

"Hi, Cesari. I'm surprised to see you here. We're supposed to call security if you show up. They say you might have killed someone."

He cocked his head and smirked. "You don't believe that, do you?"

She shook her head. "I don't. What happened?"

"Somebody who doesn't like me, tried to have me framed, but it was so amateurish even the cops didn't believe it."

"Sit down, Cesari, and tell me what you want."

He sat and said, "I want to sincerely apologize to you and all the other nurses here. I should have stuck up for you guys, but instead, I made a bad choice. At the time I thought I was doing the right thing, but I realize now it wasn't."

"You mean Melissa?"

"Yes, I mean Melissa. It's complicated but I let you, her, and everyone else down and I'm sorry. If I could take it back I would."

Emily sat back in her chair and sighed. "I appreciate you saying that, Cesari, and I think a lot of the other nurses will too."

"I'd like to apologize to Melissa in person, if she'll allow me but I'll understand if she doesn't want to talk to me."

"So you haven't heard?"

"Haven't heard what?"

"She was in an accident."

Cesari raised his eyebrows in surprise and concern. "An accident? What kind of accident? Is she all right?"

"She's got a black eye and a fat lip, but she'll be okay."

"What happened?"

"She says she was home alone on her treadmill and was running fast when she slipped and was thrown off."

"Oh my God. That's awful."

"Certainly would be."

Emily's voice and the way the sentence was phrased betrayed an underlying skepticism and Cesari asked, "You don't seem convinced that's what happened."

"I'm not. I've been around enough battered women to know the difference between a true accident and a cover story that's got more holes in it than Swiss cheese."

"Battered woman? What kind of holes?"

"I asked around and none of the other girls remember Melissa ever saying she owned a treadmill."

"And you think she's lying and that somebody hit her?"

"C'mon, Cesari, people who slip or trip on treadmills usually get thrown backwards and hit the back of their heads. How the hell do you get a black eye and fat lip falling backwards?"

She was right. "Do you know who did it?"

"You tell me."

His eyes flickered with stunned comprehension. "Feinberg?"

"She must have had a bit of a concussion because she forgot she told me she had a session with him two nights ago. The following morning she came in with the injuries. Maybe I should have but I didn't press her. She'll talk when she's ready. That's the way these things work."

Cesari felt his blood pressure start to rise as his face colored with anger. "Where is she?" he asked through clenched teeth.

"I sent her home early because she didn't look good. Don't bother trying to interrogate her right now. She already feels like crap and the last thing she needs is for you to come along and try to push her around even more. I understand your intentions are good, but this just isn't the right time. She's going to be all right, Cesari. She just needs time."

He slumped in his chair. "Emily, I don't know what to say. I'm so sorry."

"I understand and I'll pass it along. I'm going to see her after work."

Chapter 46

Cesari was seething when he left the OR and answered his phone. "Yes, Arnie?"

"I've tried multiple times and can't get a hold of Acevedo. Sorry."

"Don't worry about it, Arnie. There's been a slight change of plans in that regard. I'm afraid the time for subterfuge has passed."

"That doesn't sound good. What are you going to do?"

"Not sure yet, but don't be surprised if you hear I got arrested for murder again."

"Take it easy, Cesari. Whatever it is just count to ten, let out a deep breath and think about something happy."

"I'll try to remember that. Got to go. We'll talk later."

He hung up and went down to the main floor winding his way through the labyrinth of construction going on in the back half of the hospital until he found the CEO's office. He knocked three times, and after no one responded, he entered uninvited. His secretary wasn't at her desk, so he walked past it into the main office. Acevedo wasn't at his desk either but there was a bottle of gin and a tumbler on his ink blotter. Cesari glanced at his watch. It was 4:30 pm. It was close enough to 5:00 p.m. to seem reasonable except knowing Tiberius he'd probably been drinking since ten in the morning. Then he heard laughter and the bubbling water from the hot tub.

The door to the hot tub room was closed and he walked past it into the construction zone. There were a couple of workers there hammering and sawing and he held up his hand to get their attention.

"Hi, guys. I'm Dr. Cesari. The boss is having an emergency meeting in about five minutes with New York State inspectors. He's grateful for all your hard work but he told me to tell you you're finished for the night. He needs it quiet."

One of them looked puzzled and said, "But we're the three to eleven shift. We just got started."

"Don't worry. He told me to tell you he's cleared it with your foreman. You get paid in full for the day. Thanks. You really do have to leave now. We appreciate your cooperation."

They glanced at each other, shrugged and left their tools on the floor. After they were gone Cesari stooped to pick up an industrial strength DeWalt power drill. It was a big thing and weighed at least ten pounds. It had an extra-long quarter inch titanium bit in place, and he gave it a test whir. The thing was so powerful, his hand jumped. Its six foot power cord was plugged into a hundred foot long orange extension cord which allowed the tool to be used anywhere in the expanse of the office.

Perfect.

He carried the drill to the hot tub room, paused at the door, put the duffle bag down and listened. Then he knocked politely and called out, "Room service."

The voices went quiet and then the CEO said, "Whoever you are, you're in the wrong place."

Cesari opened the door and said, "I don't think so."

The CEO was in the hot tub up to his neck and was snuggling a beautiful young black girl with very large breasts bobbing around in the water. She had a strained look on her face as if she couldn't decide whether this was worth it to keep her job. It was Jada, the new nurse from the ICU. Cesari had never met her but remembered the CEO talking to him about soliciting her. Apparently, he must have done his own dirty work. They stared at him momentarily speechless in large part because of the drill in his hands. The humidity in the room and the smell of bromine was almost overwhelming.

Cesari glanced around and found a luxurious white bath towel. He picked it up and said, "You must be Jada."

She nodded, her eyes growing wide and said softly, embarrassed, "Yes, I am."

"I'm Dr. Cesari. I'm sorry we had to meet under such awkward circumstances." He put the drill down and opened the towel for her to step into. "You have to leave now, Jada. I have some business with the boss."

Acevedo was initially in shock at the intrusion but quickly recovered. "Don't go anywhere Jada or you'll be fired. You got some nerve, Cesari. If you don't leave right now, I'll call the police."

Jada hesitated but saw the grim, determined look on Cesari's face and instinctively understood that she did not want to be part of whatever was about to happen. With Cesari's help she climbed out of the tub into the waiting towel, wrapping herself up tightly.

He said reassuringly, "He's not going to fire you, okay? And I promise that I won't mention this to anyone. In fact, today never happened."

"Thank you."

She picked up her clothes and practically ran out of the room. He closed the door behind her wedging the power cord underneath, picked up the drill and sat on the edge of the hot tub looking down at the CEO. The control panel for the tub's jets was right next to him and he turned them off. The room went quiet with the two of them staring at each other. Suddenly, Cesari pulled the trigger and the drill whirred loudly and ominously in the small room for a few seconds.

"Where's your secretary, Olivia?" Cesari asked.

"I sent her home early…for privacy."

He nodded. "Here's how this works. I ask the questions and you answer them, understand?"

Acevedo stammered, "Aren't you in enough trouble, Cesari?"

"Who do you really work for?"

"I don't have to tell you anything and you aren't going to do shit."

If he wasn't already in such a bad mood, Cesari might have admired the little guy's spunk but he was way past that point. Without warning he grabbed the diminutive tyrant's hair with his left hand and shoved him face forward underneath the water. He kicked, fought and splashed water to no avail. Cesari counted to ten, let out a deep breath, thought about something happy and then let him up gasping and coughing.

"Are you out of your mind?" he panted. "They'll kill you, Cesari. I did you a favor by firing you."

"Thank you for that. Now, who do you work for?" Cesari raised the drill and pulled the trigger again and as the tool whined added, "If you don't give me an answer, you're going to start springing leaks."

"His name is Shlomo Markov. You've already met him. I know because he asked me about you."

Cesari was curious and took his finger off the trigger. "Why did he ask you about me?"

"He didn't say. He just wanted to know if you were any good."

"You mean as a doctor?"

The little guy shrugged. "I presume. I told him you were in good standing with the hospital and that everyone on staff thought you were great."

"What is he sick or something?"

"He didn't say, and it doesn't matter because he's probably dead or soon will be."

"What makes you say that?"

"I've already told you too much."

Cesari grabbed his wrist and pressed the drill bit hard against it with his finger just barely grazing the trigger. He glared at him and hissed, "It's up to you what happens next, shortcake."

"Take it easy, Cesari. He's gone missing. We all got word a couple of days ago that Yorgi, his second in command, was taking over for him. I know you know who he is too. There's an all-out manhunt for Shlomo, dead or alive. There's even some big shot flying in from the old country to figure out what's going on and to resolve chain-of-command issues."

"Who's the big shot?"

"I have no idea and I don't want to know. I just do what I'm told."

"So what do you think happened to Shlomo?"

"No one's saying it out loud, but everyone knows it had to be Yorgi."

Cesari nodded. "That would be my guess too. How did you and Feinberg get mixed up in all this?"

"We were working a gig out in a hospital in L.A. Doing the same thing for some Asian mob guys bringing in counterfeit pharmaceuticals when we got the call from Shlomo. We never met him before, but he made us an offer we couldn't refuse. We've got sort of a reputation in this particular area of expertise."

"Reputation for what? Destroying hospitals?"

"Creating chaos so that all the illegal merchandise being imported gets lost in the shuffle. We overwhelm the place with a massive renovation project and create duplicate and triplicate invoices so no one can figure out what the hell is going on. I order one CT scanner and two or three are delivered. Get it? Do you have any idea how much powder can fit into one of those crates?"

"So you knew about the weapons?"

"Yes and no. We had a feeling from the writing on the sides of the crates that they weren't drugs, but we didn't want to know the details. That's not healthy. I'm sure you can understand that."

Cesari mulled it over. "At what point in your career did you get bent?"

"Oh, c'mon. Give me a break. I get paid twenty times what I would as an ordinary CEO and I get me a harem of beautiful women wherever I go. It wasn't that difficult a choice."

"What about Feinberg? Is he really a doctor?"

"Sort of. He graduated medical school but never finished his residency. His drinking and womanizing caught up with him. I found him in Vegas losing his shirt at a craps table. Every hospital CEO needs a thug like him to do their dirty work. We hit it off and have been doing our thing for close to seven years now."

"So what happens when everybody's finished transporting whatever it is they're transporting. I mean the kind of bedlam you've created can't last forever."

"When we're done, we pull up stakes and move on. By that point the board of the hospital is in total free fall panic and can't believe what's happened. They curse us under their breath but can't admit publicly what a disaster they allowed to take place with their approval. The good news is they have tons of new equipment lying around they can either install or sell. They usually just scramble for a new CEO, tell him almost nothing and simply say here, fix it."

Cesari shook his head. "That's quite a plan. Well if I were you, I'd begin considering an alternative career."

"Why, because of you? You've got nothing on me. You're a wanted man without a job. The staff hates you and before long Yorgi's going to take care of you more permanently."

Cesari nodded. "You got some of that right but you're forgetting one thing."

"Such as?"

"The most dangerous guy in the room is generally the one who has nothing left to lose."

Cesari pressed the trigger again and smiled. Acevedo watched him with growing alarm and asked, "Are you going to kill me?"

"Why would I do that when I'm one hundred percent certain Yorgi will? One more thing. Where does Feinberg live?"

Acevedo hesitated only marginally before saying, "424 Fifth Avenue. He has the penthouse apartment... What are you going to do?"

"Did you know he likes to hit girls?"

He didn't say anything.

"That was a dumb question. Of course you did. You've been partying together for seven years."

"What are you going to do?" he asked again.

"I'm going to talk to him about it and if anybody tries to warn him, I will certainly come back and shove this drill up his ass. Remember what I said about a guy who has nothing to lose. Am I making myself clear?"

He nodded.

Cesari tossed the drill to the floor and stood. He searched around the perimeter of the hot tub until he found the drainage spigot. He twisted it off and water began gushing out, rapidly swirling around the outside of the hot tub.

Acevedo looked over the side and asked, "What are you doing?"

Cesari kicked the drill close to the growing pool, stepped away toward the door quickly and said, "You better be careful when you get out of the tub, boss. Death by electrocution is far more common than most people are aware."

The CEO's eyes grew wide and he jumped to his feet, suddenly realizing the imminent danger he was in. Electrical current would travel directly back into the hot tub. He jumped to his feet and clambered onto the sides of the tub. He stood there perched precariously trying to decide what to do. He was naked and whimpering when Cesari left the room, closed the door behind him, and propped a chair up against it for good measure.

Chapter 47

He sat in the back of the Uber contemplating his next move as the car plodded through thick traffic to Feinberg's apartment. There was a chance Acevedo had called ahead but he deemed it unlikely. Cesari judged Acevedo and Feinberg to be every man for themselves kind of guys. Given that assessment, if he was the CEO, he would be planning his exit strategy and not worrying about what happened to his junior, very expendable partner. He could always pick up another Feinberg. Fat, stupid guys like that practically grew on trees.

Cesari was also cognizant that there would now likely be set in motion a chain of events from which there could be no turning back. Acevedo had three choices. He could clear out without telling anyone. Just disappear on the first flight and hope for the best, but that would mean looking over his shoulder for the rest of his life. The CEO would be well aware of that. Or he could sit tight and pretend he didn't know anything and hope that Yorgi would take care of the Cesari problem. But if he did that and Yorgi found out that he had visited the CEO and that the CEO hadn't been forthright about it, then that would be tantamount to betrayal and would incur Yorgi's wrath. The CEO would know that too. Option three, as unappealing as it was, would be to tell Yorgi that Cesari had confronted him and that Cesari knew everything and would be going to the authorities. Then Acevedo could advise Yorgi to remove the rest of the weapons immediately and appear to be a valued servant. The show closes down for everyone, with some hit to the CEO's pocket book no doubt, but at least he gets to exit with his head still attached to his shoulders.

Cesari thought it through several times and finally came to the conclusion that the CEO would probably be on the phone right now with option number three. Therefore, Tierney needed to close down the hospital. He could not really afford to wait any longer. Men would have to be placed at the loading dock in preparation for a rapid response from Yorgi, but could Tierney mobilize his forces fast enough? Democracies don't work that quickly. Tierney would first have to present his case in its entirety to his superiors. If approved, he would then have to go to a judge for a search warrant and demonstrate probable cause which could take days. So far all they had were illegal breaking and entering and unconstitutional searches of private property, not something you really wanted to tell a judge. If he called a contact in the FBI, the same process would be required.

Cesari didn't like the odds. Still, he needed to give Tierney a head's up so while they stalled in gridlock, he took out his phone. "Good evening, Detective. How goes it?"

"What do you think? I've been sitting in a car all day listening to Gianelli tell me how great he is. I'm ready to resign for reasons of mental duress. Don't you Italians understand the concept of humility? I needed a break and just sent him out to get us something to eat. But aside from that nothing's going on. What happened with you and your ex-boss? Did you find anything in his office?"

"Just a naked girl in his lap, but we did have a very positive chat which I'd like to tell you about."

"I'm listening."

It took Cesari about fifteen minutes, pausing periodically to answer questions and clarify points of interest. He didn't leave anything out including what he thought was going to happen next. When he was done there was silence on the other end of the line for about half a minute before Tierney let out a big sigh.

Not happy but not necessarily angry either he said, "How bad did Feinberg hurt the girl?"

"I haven't seen her, but I heard from a very reliable source that she has a black eye, a fat lip, assorted bruises and a possible concussion."

"What is wrong with these people?" Tierney asked.

"And they're not even the bad guys."

"They're bad enough apparently."

"You're not mad at me?"

"How could I be mad at you? I would have done the same thing. I'm surprised you left the little guy still breathing. He was, wasn't he?"

"He should be okay if he was patient. Once the water hit the drill it should've tripped a breaker. As long as he wasn't in the water at that particular moment, he'd be fine. From the looks of things when I left, he wasn't coming down off that ledge for a while. Hopefully he's still up there screaming for help when someone finds him. I may not be so lenient with Feinberg."

"Is that where you're going now?"

"Yeah, I figured I'd take care of him now while I'm still infuriated. I'm more creative that way."

"You going to kill him?"

"Maybe I shouldn't tell you all the details."

"Maybe you shouldn't, but if you do kill him, make sure you do it slow. Guys like that make me so angry my right eye starts to twitch."

"Roger that. What are you going to do with this information about Yorgi?"

"I'm not sure yet. I'll talk it over with Gianelli. In between bouts of braggadocio and egomania, he actually is a pretty good tactician, and as you surmised, it could take days for me to mobilize my troops whereas all he has to do is make a few phone calls. Besides, I'm not a hundred percent convinced your CEO is going to do anything but sit tight at least in the immediate future. I'm sure he'd love to cut and run, but he needs to think through all the pros and cons first. A knee jerk call to Yorgi pressing the panic button when Shlomo is missing and some high up guy is flying in from Romania would be like a wrecking ball on Yorgi's house of cards."

"You have a point. With this guy coming to town, they'll want to keep up appearances that everything is proceeding smoothly in Shlomo's absence and that Yorgi has everything under control... I need to give this some more thought too, but this might actually present us with a unique opportunity."

"How so?"

"Think about it. Acevedo told me that Shlomo is either missing or dead. He believes Yorgi most likely killed him to take over the business, but that doesn't make sense."

"Why not?"

"If Yorgi was going to kill Shlomo, then why go through the elaborate vampire charade? It doesn't add up. Not at all. He didn't do all that just to kill him. Shlomo's an old man maybe with early dementia or some other type of mental problem. Yorgi and his brothers were exploiting that weakness to make him think he was crazy. They were hoping the reins of the operation would be handed to them by default due to Shlomo's increasingly weak grip on reality."

Tierney said, "Maybe you're right, but then where's Shlomo?"

"Good question. Maybe his senility is worse than we suspect, and he just wandered off?"

"You're grasping at straws with that one, Cesari. We met the guy, remember? If he was developing Alzheimer's it would have to have been in its earliest stages. He seemed fine to me."

"You're right. Then maybe he figured out Yorgi's plot and rather than fight a war he felt he was in no shape to win, decided to go to ground. He could be hiding right here in the city or sitting on a beach somewhere."

"That's more like it. Does he have family he could be hiding with?"

Cesari thought about that and a lightbulb went off as the dots started to connect, but not all the dots. Something didn't make sense. He said, "I remember he mentioned a daughter, but he never said how old she was or where she lived."

"I remember that too, now that you bring it up. So he could be with her."

"Maybe. He's loaded so potentially he could be any-where."

"All right, Cesari, so maybe he's not dead. Maybe he's in hiding. How does this present us with a unique opportunity?"

"Think about it. Yorgi goes through all this trouble for what reason?"

"To take over the business."

"Yes, but not just to take it over by force but by guile. He wants this to be a smooth transition, a pat on the back, big smiles all around, total approval from the power brokers back home, but with Shlomo on the loose there's a potential mon-key wrench in the plan. I mean what if he should show up at the wrong time and seem perfectly normal?"

"I see what you mean. So now they would have to kill him, but I thought you said that might not go over well with the ruling class."

"Unless they could demonstrate without any doubt that Shlomo's instability was affecting the bottom line."

"Money talks and bullshit walks. That's true in any lan-guage, so how do they do that?"

"I think those weapons in the basement of that tenement building were deliberately misplaced by Yorgi and his brothers to prove to their bosses that Shlomo is incapable of being in charge and needed to be replaced. But Shlomo's been around a long time and would be given the benefit of the doubt unless..."

Tierney finished his sentence, "Unless he started babbling about vampires. I see what you mean."

"You can thank me later."

"So what's this golden opportunity?"

"We can kill two birds with one stone."

"Hang on, Cesari. Gianelli just returned… Damn, that smells good. What is it?"

Vito said, "Chicken parm on fresh-baked bread. I even got us a bottle of chianti and some plastic cups."

"You're my kind of guy, Gianelli. I got Cesari on the line. I'll fill you in on the whole story later."

"Fine but put him on speakerphone now so I can start piecing it together."

Tierney said, "Okay, Cesari continue. You were about to kill two birds with one stone."

Cesari rolled his eyes as the Uber driver pulled to the curb on Fifth Avenue outside Feinberg's apartment building. He said, "You're going to drink alcohol on a stakeout?"

Vito said to Tierney, "See, what did I tell you about him?"

With a mouthful of chicken parm, Tierney said, "Don't worry about us. Now go ahead with your thoughts."

"As I was saying, I'm suspicious that Yorgi stashed those weapons to put the icing on the cake of Shlomo's ineptitude. I'd bet anything that once this boss of bosses arrives, Yorgi's going to claim to have miraculously recovered them to prove his worth. With Shlomo going off half-cocked about vampires it's a sure bet Yorgi will get the promotion he's after."

"And Shlomo?"

"What usually happens when you outlive your usefulness to any criminal organization?"

"Yet another reason for Shlomo to go into hiding. He saw the writing on the wall. I hope you're listening to this, Gianelli. There are no pensions and retirement parties in your field."

"I hear you loud and clear," Vito said.

Tierney asked, "So what do you propose, Cesari?"

"We wait until dark and then take the weapons. When Yorgi goes for the big reveal, he will have egg all over his face and this Romanian guy will think the whole damn lot of them need to be replaced. You and the feds swoop in when they're at their most vulnerable and willing to cut a deal."

"There sure are a lot of ifs in there, Cesari. Like what if Yorgi has no intention of telling this new guy about the weapons? What if he took them for himself to sell?"

"I don't think so. There's a very limited market for these kinds of armaments and more than likely they've already been paid for. I bet someone is already waiting for delivery and getting a little pissed at the delay. Try to imagine the raucous if some guy on the other end gets stiffed and all of a sudden those same weapons show up somewhere else. It's possible Yorgi might do that but I doubt it. That would be an extremely dangerous gambit. I don't see this going down like that. There's an internal power struggle going on. Why make the buyers angry when you're going to need them after it's all over? Look, if we do this then at the very least, millions of dollars of dangerous weapons won't be lying around waiting to be delivered to bad people. If Yorgi discovers they're missing ahead of schedule he will no doubt suspect somebody betrayed him which could possibly work equally well for us."

"Fair enough, but what happens if Yorgi shows up in the middle of us lifting the weapons?"

"That's easy. You arrest him and his brothers and charge them with international arms dealing and murder and hope they'll cooperate. At that point, you'd have no choice. On the other hand, we could create a diversion to get them away from the neighborhood for a while."

"What kind of diversion?"

"Give me an hour to come up with something. Where are they now?"

"Yorgi and Ivan are inside. I assume Tibor is getting laid. He doesn't seem to like to hang out with the other guys too much. Okay, you come up with a diversion and call me. In the meantime, where am I supposed to get a truck?"

"Vito, tell him."

Vito said, "I'll have one here in thirty minutes."

"You just happen to have a truck lying around?" Tierney asked.

"It's not a big one, but should be enough, and it will fit in the alley. Worst comes to worst, we make a second trip. I have a garage we can store the crates in."

"Why do you have a truck, Gianelli?"

"I use it for various purposes that are germane to my line of work.

"I bet." Cesari had this image of Tierney shaking his head and rolling his eyes before saying, "Nice choices you're giving me, Cesari. Leave the weapons with the Romanian maniacs or steal the weapons to give them to the Italian maniacs."

Vito said, "That wasn't very nice."

Tierney ignored him and added, "Cesari, suppose we pull this off without getting busted. Then what?"

"I haven't gotten that far."

Chapter 48

424 Fifth Avenue was a nice building in a nice part of town, but it wasn't upper tier. This wasn't the Dakota. It wasn't the kind of building you expected movie stars and billionaire bankers to live. Neither would you expect bus drivers or teachers. This was an abode within the financial reach of orthopedic and plastic surgeons, maybe even a cardiologist, certainly not family doctors. Some lawyers would make the cut, but not the public defenders or human right's people. Dentist's specializing in implants and oral surgery but not your run of the mill, drill and fill guys that your mother took you to as a kid. This was a place for the people who might have been rich in any other city on the planet but in New York they were just clinging to the lower end of upper middle class, one recession away from taking the subway to work.

The one doorman was helping an older woman into her chauffeur-driven Mercedes, and Cesari discreetly tucked behind him into the revolving door of the building. There were security cameras which he did his best to avoid but no security guards unless you counted the woman working the information desk bustling with people. Cesari spotted an elevator bank in the middle of the lobby and boarded an open car. It was 7:00 p.m. and he clutched the duffle bag just to be sure the crowbar was still there. It was and he let out a deep breath as the car ascended.

On the sixth and top floor, he got out and walked down the hallway to the one apartment on that level. This floor was fairly posh with nice carpeting, wall sconces and decorative artwork. He arrived at the door and took the crowbar out of the duffle bag which he let rest on the floor. He hesitated momentarily as he thought through his strategy.

Ring the buzzer, let him answer. He'll be surprised to see him unless he was warned by the CEO in which case, he may not answer the door at all. Okay, so if he answers the door, smile and then punch him hard in the sternum. That usually took the wind out of most guys, even big ones like Feinberg. While he's gasping, push him backward into the room and close the door. If he doesn't fall, smash him on the side of the knee with the crowbar. At that point, the fun begins. He'll be cursing and threatening. They always do at the beginning. Explain to him the nature of his sins with emphasis on the fact that his parents should have taught him not to hit girls.

Should he let him live was the question. He wasn't sure. He liked the thought of hospitalizing him for several weeks and possibly leaving him with some disability as a reminder of his poor behavior. Maybe a broken elbow or ankle. They never healed right and could be a source of persistent pain. That would do it.

He pressed the buzzer and heard it screech inside. He waited but there was no answer, so he knocked three times. Again, there was no answer. He tapped the crowbar impatiently into his free hand and wondered if Feinberg wasn't home or possibly hiding under the bed. He glanced at his watch.

He pressed the buzzer again, waited another full minute and tested the doorknob. It was unlocked and he let himself in. The apartment was very large, two thousand square feet easy, and very expensive looking. Granite counters in the kitchen, an enormous wine rack, and glass doors in the living room leading out to a balcony overlooking Fifth Avenue. What more could you want?

Cesari quietly looked around and listened but heard nothing. He began to explore the apartment which had three bedrooms in addition to a full kitchen, living room and formal dining room. A bit much for a single guy, he thought. As he reached the first bedroom, he smelled something odd…cordite. Spent gunpowder. It was subtle but definitely there. It was an unmistakable smell. One that once you've experienced it, you never forgot.

He immediately tensed and gently turned the knob slowly pushing the door open a crack. He was surprised by what he saw. Half off, half on the foot of the king bed was Feinberg lying on his back fully clothed clutching a wound to the abdomen. Blood was still oozing over his hands, staining his shirt and the bedsheets. He was groaning quietly in a semiconscious state. Cesari was still taking in the scene when he heard a soft sobbing sound. He opened the door fully and saw Melissa curled in the far corner of the room, her head buried in her hands, one of which was holding a .22 caliber Ruger semi-automatic pistol.

He called out softly, "Melissa, it's me, Cesari."

She looked up. One eye was nearly swollen shut and was deep purple. The other eye was red from crying. She began to bawl loudly when she saw him. He went over, sat down next to her and put his arm around her shoulder. She pressed her head into his chest for comfort and he laid the crowbar down to hug her with both arms.

He said, "It's all right, okay? Trust me, it's going to be all right." When she didn't say anything, he continued, "Let me have the gun, Melissa."

She handed it to him without resistance and he asked, "Is this legal?"

She shook her head. "No."

"Does anyone know you have it?"

"I may have told Emily about it when I bought it last year, but I never fired it before today. I don't want to go to prison, Cesari."

"I'm not going to let that happen, Melissa, but I'll need your help."

"My help? How?"

"I need you to collect yourself and think hard. Did you tell anyone you were coming here tonight?"

"No, definitely not. I wasn't even sure I was coming here tonight myself. I've just been so upset over what that animal did to me."

"I know and I'm sorry. Emily told me she suspected that he did this to you."

"I knew she would guess as much. She doesn't even know the worst of it. He tied me to the bed and beat me with his belt. It turned the sick bastard on. I got welt marks all over my backside."

He held her tighter. "You've been here several times, everyone knows that, so we won't have to clean up your fingerprints. And just to be certain, you never admitted to anyone that Feinberg beat you, not even Emily? Is that right?"

She said, "No, I just couldn't face anyone about it, so I made up a story about falling off my treadmill. Why?"

"If you stick to the treadmill story no one can say you had a motive to kill him. You do have a treadmill, right?"

"Yes, I've had one for years, but I don't use it. It's mostly just a spare closet."

He smiled. "Here's what I want you to do. Get yourself together, take a deep breath, and wait for me in the living room. I have to do a little work in here. When I'm done, we'll leave together."

After she went into the living room, he leaned over Feinberg. He was still breathing, and his pulse was strong and rapid. Cesari shook him. His eyes fluttered open as he regained consciousness and asked weakly, "Cesari, what happened?"

"You slipped and fell, asshole."

"I did not. Wait…that bitch Melissa shot me. I remember now. She tricked me. Cesari, call an ambulance, call the police. Oh God, it hurts so much."

"I'm afraid I can't do that."

"Why not?"

"Because I don't like you."

"Well if you won't I will. That whore is going to spend the rest of her life in prison."

He struggled weakly but couldn't make it to a sitting position and fell back down. Cesari watched the blood bubbling out of the wound as he thought of a scenario that could work. A gunshot to the abdomen was difficult to make look like an accident. It was possible but would raise eyebrows. Robbery was a classic but then he would have to waste time ransacking the apartment and would undoubtedly leave fingerprints. So far he hadn't touched anything but the doorknob to the apartment and the bedroom.

Suicide?

Not likely. He would have to go with accident. He was sitting on the edge of the bed playing with his pistol and it inadvertently discharged. Lame for sure, but the best he could do.

He grabbed a pillow from the head of the bed, a big fluffy, thing. Feinberg had laid back down, the previous exertion of trying to get up had drained his last energy reserves. His eyes were half-closed and his breathing shallow. Cesari placed the pillow down forcefully over his face covering his nostrils and mouth. He pressed hard as Feinberg fought weakly to save himself. A minute later, he went limp and a minute after that, he was dead. In the struggle, Feinberg's blood had stained the pillowcase and Cesari's shirt sleeves. Not a lot but enough. Cesari removed the pillowcase, folded it into a ball and placed it next to the crowbar on the floor. He went into the bathroom, washed and dried his hands, and then went through Feinberg's drawers and closets until he found what he needed; a fresh pillowcase, sport coat and a handkerchief.

He placed the new pillowcase on the pillow, fluffed it, and replaced it back at the head of bed as neatly as possible. Using the handkerchief, he wiped down everything he had touched including the gun and its magazine. He thought about wiping each bullet but decided not to get carried away. This was the NYPD after all. He then carefully placed the weapon in Feinberg's right hand and positioned his index finger on the trigger. When he was done, he stepped back and thought that he had performed a decent job.

He put on Feinberg's sport coat to cover the bloodstains on his shirt. It was enormous on him but served its purpose. He then retrieved the crowbar and pillowcase, wiped the doorknob and found Melissa.

She said, "Will he make it?"

He shook his head. "I'm afraid not."

She looked distraught. "Then I'm a murderer. I'm going to jail."

"You're not a murderer and you're not going to jail. He might have survived if I hadn't finished him off with a pillow."

"You killed him?" she asked, her eyes growing wide.

"Alleviated his suffering."

"But I shot him."

"Melissa, you hurt someone who hurt you. You were lashing out in anger at someone who physically assaulted you and humiliated you for his personal pleasure. As far as I'm concerned, he got what he deserved."

She thought about it for a moment and said, "I agree with that, but why did you…?"

"I made sure that he couldn't hurt you again by using the law as a weapon. But the less we talk about what happened here, the better. What matters is that you understand tonight never happened. It would serve no purpose. Can you do that?"

She nodded. "I'll try. Why did you come here with a crowbar?"

"I loved Feinberg almost as much as you did. Let's just leave it at that. I think you should take a week off and go somewhere to recharge. No one would blame you for needing some down time."

"That sounds like a good idea."

"Now listen carefully, Melissa. We're going to leave now. You need to maintain your composure and act is if nothing is wrong. The doorman and security cameras saw a young woman with a black eye walk in…"

"No, they didn't. I wore sunglasses."

"Even better. Anyway, it's dark out now, so we'll ditch the sunglasses. They will make you stand out. What people are going to see walking out is an affectionate couple holding each other. You bury the side of your face with the bruised eye into my shoulder. Emily told me she was going to see you to-night. What happened with that?"

"She called me. I thanked her and took a rain check. I told her I was exhausted and planned on taking a hot bath and go-ing to bed early."

"Perfect."

Their last act as they left the apartment was to wipe the doorknob and shove the handkerchief into the sport coat pocket. He folded the pillowcase as tightly as possible and was trying to decide what to do with it when Melissa said, "Give it to me. It'll fit in my bag."

"Okay, but it'll have to be burned or washed in a powerful bleach. It has his blood on it."

As they entered the elevator, Melissa said, "How can I thank you, Cesari? I was losing it in there."

"Thank me? I got you into this mess and I'm very sorry. I hope you can forgive me."

Smiling, she said, "I already have."

"Thanks… Look, if for some reason it comes to it, then I'm your alibi. I was with you in your apartment all night, understand? We had wild, wall-rattling, unforgettable sex. I'll swear to it. Just keep saying that to yourself over and over until it becomes real."

She nodded. "Maybe it will become real one of these days."

He looked at her. "Maybe it will."

"I'm sorry about the rat, Cesari."

He chuckled. "That was a bit over the top, I have to admit. The whip cream pie was pretty funny though."

She laughed, "That was Emily's idea."

Chapter 49

Cesari and Melissa took a cab to her apartment where he dropped her off. Before she left, he asked her for Feinberg's pillowcase. She looked puzzled but was in too much of a state of shock to ask why. She thanked him again and he watched her enter the building. He then had the driver take him to a liquor store on Third Avenue, a block north of St. Matt's. It was almost 9:00 p.m. and the place was getting ready to close.

He bought six, one-liter bottles of vodka, a couple of cheap lighters and threw everything into a box, including the pillowcase. He then walked to the hospital and around the back to the parking garage where he found a couple of Vito's guys sitting in a Suburban with a pair of binoculars keeping watch. There was no one around and no trucks backed up to the loading dock.

They saw him coming and the driver rolled down his window. The engine was running and the air conditioning was on high. He knew them both from the Kit Kat and greeted them.

"Hey Fat Tony, Big Eddie. How are you guys holding up?"

Fat Tony was in the driver's seat and pushing four hundred plus pounds, his nickname was an understatement. The other guy clocked in at a mere three hundred pounds and was svelte in comparison.

Fat Tony looked at the box he was carrying and said, "Nothing doing here, Doc. All quiet on the western front. You having a party?"

"Something like that. What's the guard situation?"

"Light and amateurish, mostly. Every hour on the hour a couple of hardhats walk around with big wrenches and crowbars and then duck back in. Once in a while a more professional type wearing a suit comes out to take a sniff. He's probably packing judging by the way his jacket fits. He glances around, gets bored and takes a powder like the others. They don't seem overly concerned."

"Good. Can you guys take orders from me or do you have to call Vito?"

They looked at each other and Tony said, "What kind of orders?"

"First, please tell me you have a full tank of gas."

"It's full."

"Good. Now I need your gun, I need the Suburban, and I need you two to leave before the police come."

Fat Tony raised his eyebrows. "I better call Vito."

He dialed, told Vito what was happening and then handed the phone to Cesari. "Cesari, what are you doing?"

"Creating a distraction for you like I promised. Besides, you might need a couple more really big guys to help lift those crates. Is your truck there?"

"The truck's here and I already have plenty of really big guys at my disposal. You going to tell me what you're doing?"

"What fun would that be? Just be ready. Call me when Yorgi and Ivan vacate the restaurant. The action's going to start in about an hour give or take."

"Fine, give the phone back to Fat Tony."

Vito spoke to Tony for about half a minute and then hung up. Then both men got out of the vehicle. Tony handed Cesari the keys to the Suburban and a sleek looking .45 caliber Sig

Sauer P220 Legion with a gray finished slide and frame. It had an eight plus one capacity and good balance. Cesari liked it.

He said, "Extra clip?"

Fat Tony reached into his pocket and handed him another magazine of bullets. "Thanks, Tony. I'll see you over on First Avenue later."

Cesari loaded the box of vodka into the Suburban, got in himself, and turned on the radio as Fat Tony and Big Eddie disappeared from view into the stairwell of the garage. It was a half-mile to the restaurant, and they could use the exercise. Cesari smiled, glanced at his watch and then looked through the binoculars they had left behind. The driveway was paved and smooth with stone retainer walls on either side. The loading dock itself was cement and the large door was made of steel. There were two large metal dumpsters set to the side. So far so good. He didn't see anything particularly flammable. He settled in with the music.

At 11:00 p.m. he put the SUV into gear and drove onto East Tenth Street where the entrance to the driveway leading to the loading dock was. He parked there and hoofed it the rest of the way carrying the box of vodka. The back area of the hospital was dark and deserted except for a few overhead lights on the loading platform itself. He hid behind one of the dumpsters, took Feinberg's pillowcase out and tore it into six more or less equal strips. It was harder than he thought it would be, but he got the job done quickly. Then he opened all the bottles of vodka and stuffed one end of each strip into each bottle leaving himself a six to eight-inch fuse dangling out. In a matter of seconds the exposed fuses were saturated with alcohol.

There was only one road into the loading dock and the same road out. It was wide enough for a large truck but not two vehicles at the same time. The trucks made a complicated U-turn when they finished their business. Such was life in a dangerously overcrowded city where every inch of real estate was hotly contested. But this was perfect for tonight's exercise; dark, quiet, and desolate with low risk for collateral damage.

Just as he completed his preparations, two hard hats with crowbars came out the side door of the garage chatting and looking around for anomalies as they ambled across the thirty-foot-long platform. Cesari waited for them to walk the length of the dock and nearly reach the door again. He wanted them to be able to escape back in. When they were within five feet of the door, they turned their gaze one more time to the expanse of the driveway and away from the dumpsters twenty feet away in the shadows.

Cesari rose, flipped the safety off Fat Tony's .45 with his thumb, and fired a round into the metal garage door over their heads. The report echoed loudly in the silence of the night. The clanging of the metal so close to their heads caused them to jerk and jump away. They turned in all directions to see where the shot had come from but Cesari had already ducked back into cover. The door opened and slammed closed as the men yelled for help and fled for safety.

Cesari's next move was to count to ten, take a deep breath and think about something happy. In a minute, the door opened, and large men peeked out. Cesari lit one of his Molotov cocktails, and launched the bottle at the garage door. It hit and burst into flames which spread in every direction. The door was yanked closed again and Cesari could now hear men yelling and scrambling. They were under attack by an unknown enemy. The alcohol burned and smoldered but eventually died back down with nothing flammable to propagate the blaze. In five minutes, the door slowly opened once more and Cesari took a wild shot at it missing by nearly ten feet, pinging off the wall overhead. He threw another cocktail in their direction and watched it burn itself out.

The scene repeated itself twice before his phone rang and Vito said, "They're on their way. I don't know what you're doing but they flew out of here like bats out of hell."

"Good. What are they driving?"

"The white catering van for the restaurant."

"Okay, thanks."

Cesari threw one more firebomb at the door and emptied the rest of the clip into the garage. He threw the gun into the box with the last two bottles of vodka, picked up the whole thing and ran to the Suburban. He hopped into the driver's seat, ducked low and waited. Just a few minutes later, he watched the white catering van burn rubber up the driveway past him. As soon as it was out of sight, he started the SUV and drove it halfway up the driveway and angled it to fully block their egress. He checked behind him to make sure he was a safe distance from the street.

He opened all the windows to allow good air flow, got out of the SUV and took the two vodka-soaked strips of pillowcase out of their bottles. He tied them together and stuffed one end into the gas tank leaving him a comfortable length of fuse dangling outside. After swapping magazines, he put the gun in his waistband, and dumped all the remaining vodka over the back and front car seats. He then calmly proceeded to the back of the vehicle, took a deep breath and lit the fuse.

He sprinted to the sidewalk on Tenth Avenue and just made it when the Suburban erupted in a fireball behind him. He caught the tail end of the heat burst and felt a hard tap in the back as a small piece of glass from the SUV struck him. He turned to see the black smoke of burning oil, leather, and gasoline billowing upward. With a thirty-one-gallon gas tank capacity, he was sure the Romanescu boys weren't going anywhere for a while. Just to be safe, he dialed 911 and anonymously called in the tip, adding that there were armed men in a white van shooting the place up.

His work done, he jogged over to First Avenue to help Vito and Tierney with the weapons cache. By the time he arrived from the Avenue A side of the alley, he had worked up a sweat. Vito's men had pulled a twenty-six-foot, six wheeled box truck into the parking lot behind the tenement building. The coal chute doors were open and eight men including Tierney and Vito toiled furiously and as quietly as possible. It was no small task trying to lift six-hundred-pound wood crates and hoist them upward. Vito's men had come prepared with heavy duty nylon ropes and the guys outside would loop it around the bottom part of each crate after it was placed on the distal end of the coal chute. Then they would pull the box up and lift it into the truck. Four guys in the basement and four guys outside. From the front of the tenement building in the alley all was serene.

It was barely midnight and it appeared they were almost halfway done. Vito and Tierney were in the basement. When Vito saw him, he said, "Cesari, come down here and help us. Those guys up there got the easy job."

Cesari wanted to laugh but didn't. He waited until the men up top picked up the most recently arrived crate and removed it from the chute's opening and then sat on the edge, saying, "Catch me."

He let himself go and slid down the chute, nearly knocking Vito over. He adjusted himself and Vito scolded him. "Did you have to do that? We have a step ladder here."

He pointed at a six-foot metal step ladder that was leaning against the wall next to the chute. Cesari said, "You might have said something sooner."

Tierney shook his head. "Jesus, you two are like Abbot and Costello."

Cesari greeted Tierney noticing that he had finally taken off his tweed suitcoat, rolled up his sleeves and was drenched in perspiration. He said, "Good evening, Detective. Getting a workout I see."

Tierney grinned, "I had no idea being a crook was such hard work."

Cesari laughed, "Stick with us, Detective."

"How's Yorgi?"

"Preoccupied for a while. By the way, Vito, I think you're going to need a new Suburban."

"That's great, Cesari, now maybe you and Tierney can stop jawing and help us."

The machine-like procession of carrying the heavy crates and lifting them onto the bottom of the chute continued for another forty-five minutes. After the last weapons crate disappeared from sight, one of the men called down that there was no more room in the truck, and they were ready to go.

Tierney looked over at the last two boxes with the dead guys in them. He said, "I guess we'll leave them here."

Cesari nodded. "I agree. There's no point in coming back for them either. What would we do with them anyway?"

Vito said, "Who do you think they were? We never really talked about it."

"Probably the drivers," Cesari ventured. "Yorgi hijacked the truck after it left the hospital or maybe even bribed these guys to bring the weapons here instead of their original destination. My guess is he didn't have much use for them after that."

Vito shook his head. "I bet he bribed the schmucks or they wouldn't be down here. They probably even unloaded the truck for Yorgi. If he had highjacked the truck and killed these guys somewhere else, he would have dumped their bodies there. No, he killed them down here right after they stacked the boxes neatly against the wall for him. He even made them bring two empty boxes with them."

Tierney said, "Pretty good analysis, Gianelli. You're on the wrong side of the law. So speaking of the empty crates, where are their contents?"

Cesari and Vito shrugged. Cesari said, "We may never know. On the other hand, they did pull an RPG out of the van when they attacked us. Maybe they just helped themselves to a few of the goodies."

As they talked, the rest of the crew filed out through the coal chute with the assistance of the men outside. Vito didn't want anybody trouncing through the upstairs part of the house leaving clues. They were trying to keep as low a profile as possible. Cesari, Vito, and Tierney were standing in front of the furnace and just getting ready to adjourn when they heard a sound coming from the adjacent room.

They glanced at each other with alarm, hurriedly turned the lights out and stood by the door listening. The incandescent bulb next door flicked on and a sliver of light shone from under the door. They heard footsteps approaching slowly down the wood staircase which creaked and groaned.

Cesari was standing next to Vito on one side of the door and Tierney on the other. The door swung open and a hand reached in to turn on the lights. Out of the shadows, Tierney grabbed the man's arm and dragged him into the room, flinging him to the floor. Cesari made sure there was no one behind him in the other room and flipped on the overhead lights. Tierney jumped on the guy straddling him and pinning him to the floor.

With the lights on they saw a middle-aged Indian man in shabby clothes with a scruffy white beard, thick glasses and awful teeth. His foul-smelling breath reeked of alcohol. The man was too shocked or too drunk to speak. He had a small black bag with him that had been tossed to the side when he went down.

With his hand on the man's throat, Tierney growled, "Who the hell are you?"

The man recovered and looked at Tierney, his eyes wide with fright. In a thick Indian accent he stammered, "I am humble dentist."

Chapter 50

Tierney rose and dragged the man with him as Cesari and Vito crowded around. Tierney pushed him against a wall, "Does the humble dentist have a name?"

"It is Sanjay Sundaram at your service, and I respectfully beg you not to kill me."

"I'll think about it. Now what is a humble dentist doing down here at this hour?"

The man was stammering now and sweating, "I left one of my instruments here. I come to retrieve it and then I leave. Nothing more, nothing less."

Vito stepped into the guy's face, getting angry. "The mirror?"

"Yes, sir. You have seen it?"

"Forget about that. Did you do some work recently on a beautiful redhead?"

He nodded, "Yes, my finest cosmetic job. She wanted to look like a vampire."

Vito pushed Tierney aside and grabbed the man by the throat, practically lifting him off the floor. "You son-of-a-bitch. They killed her."

The man wheezed and clawed at Vito's hand. He pleaded through collapsing lungs, "I assure you, sir, she was very much alive when I worked on her. What they did to her afterward, I know not."

Cesari put his hand on Vito's shoulder and he relaxed a little letting the man breathe. Tierney said, "Put him down, Gianelli, and let's talk. It seems we have a new problem."

Vito was still frothing. "Like what?"

Tierney turned to the dentist. "Go sit over there on one of those crates and don't make a sound." He pointed at the two crates with the dead men in them and then faced Vito and Cesari, saying, "I believe him. I mean look at that guy. He's one bottle of booze away from being a street person. If Sofia was dead when they brought him in, they would have killed him too. No one in their right mind would leave a witness as unreliable as this to walk around talking about what he'd seen. So now we have to decide what to do with him because we can't have him walking around blabbing about seeing us."

Cesari thought hard about the dentist and finally said, "Maybe we can put him to good use here."

"Such as...?" asked Tierney.

"First, Vito tell your boys to take the truck and secure it somewhere. I assume you guys have a car somewhere?"

Vito said, "Several, one on either end of the alley and the one I came in parked a block away."

Tierney said, "And I have my Subaru."

"Vito, have one of your guys bring a car around to the coal chute and wait for us. I'm going to talk with the dentist."

Vito went to the coal chute and Tierney walked with Cesari over to the nervous dentist. They sat on either side of him. He was trembling. Cesari said, "That girl was a friend of ours."

"I am beginning to understand this, but I did not know they would kill her. A lot of people these days disfigure themselves for aesthetic reasons. I do not question these things."

Cesari thought about that. It was very plausible. "Yes, but on a bloody wood board in the basement of an abandoned building?"

"I cannot speak for the circumstances. I need money. They offer money. Girl was alive."

"Are you really a dentist?"

"Yes, from Governmental Dental College and Hospital, Mumbai."

"Okay, we're going to forgive you for what you did to our friend if you agree to do a job for us."

The man started to relax for the first time since his arrival. "I am your man," he professed.

Cesari said, "You see these crates we're sitting on?"

He glanced around and nodded.

"There are two men in them that need your services. I want you to do to them what you did to our friend."

His eyes went wide again, and he let out a deep breath but agreed. "Whatever is required of me. It won't be as nice a job. I have some tools with me in my bag but not all."

"Just do the best you can, okay? That shouldn't take too long, right? We're not looking for perfection, but time is an issue."

"Give me twenty minutes. I give you great price."

Cesari chuckled, "Great, we'll open the boxes for you. Go get your bag."

Vito joined them as they were prying the tops off the crates. Tierney said, "I appreciate your sense of karma, Cesari, but is it worth the risk of wasting more time here?"

"An extra half hour tops, okay? Maybe less, and we're doing fine timewise. With any luck, Yorgi and his brother will be sitting in an interrogation room for the next couple of hours trying to explain why they have RPG's in the back of their van."

Vito asked, "What are we doing exactly, Cesari?"

"The dentist has agreed to make two more vampires for us."

"Why? To play with Yorgi's head?"

"Life is too short not to have fun, Vito."

He snorted, "I can't believe that guy is really a dentist."

"Maybe it's the best they can get in this neighborhood," offered Tierney.

****

When Yorgi had pulled the van into the loading dock, he saw several of his men and a couple of hardhats milling about searching for an unseen enemy. He and Ivan got out and were taking report and assessing the damage when the Suburban blew up several hundred yards behind them. The driveway up to the garage curved around as it approached the loading dock so they couldn't tell exactly what happened, but they could all see the clouds of black smoke rising upward over the tree line. Yorgi instinctively knew he had been lured into a trap. He yelled at Ivan to get back into the van and for everyone else to button down the garage and sit tight.

They piled into the van and steamed down the driveway coming around the turn at an unsafe speed and then slammed on the brakes when confronted by the inferno. Less than ten feet away, they realized there was no way out.

Ivan was horrified. "Yorgi, we cannot remain here. The back of the van is filled with RPGs and assault rifles. If we are found out…"

Yorgi was pissed but stalwart. "Have no fear, little brother. I have plan."

It crossed his mind to try to blow the thing off the road with an RPG but that might not work and would attract even more attention. The van was just about the same size and weight as the Suburban, so he put it into reverse and backed it up thirty feet. Then he put it back into drive and floored the accelerator.

"Hold on, Ivan."

The impact was violent and caused the Suburban to roll over onto its side. Both men lurched forward, then backward and then forward again. Ivan's airbag deployed but not

Yorgi's. He was too relieved to be annoyed at the malfunction. Ivan slumped sideways, unconscious with a broken nose but otherwise seemed okay. The van stalled from the collision and Yorgi started it up, pressed the pedal down hard, and rammed into the Suburban again. He kept his foot to the floorboard and the tires squealed and metal scraped. Smoke and flames licked at his windshield and seeped into the cabin. He coughed and prayed and little by little the Suburban slid toward Tenth Street, picking up momentum.

The two vehicles eventually reached the sidewalk and plunged into the street together. Yorgi breathed a sigh of relief because the sounds of wailing sirens were now approaching. He pushed the Suburban as far as he could across to the other side of the road, reversed back and then turned right. In the rear-view mirror, he saw the flashing lights of police cars and fire engines stuck behind traffic way off in the distance. The burning wreck of the SUV blocked the road and drivers were keeping a healthy distance back. The front of his van was smashed and smoking and he hoped he wasn't leaking oil. This would be the wrong time for the engine to freeze up.

What to do?

He glanced at his watch. He was to meet Dimitri at 6:00 a.m. at the Roxy Hotel, and had no intention of being late. But now all hell was breaking loose and where was Tibor? He had not answered his phone all day. That in itself was very un-usual, even for a young man in love. He glanced at Ivan. Blood was streaming down his face, but he was breathing. His nose looked awful and he wondered if it could be fixed.

He let out a sigh. A lot of negatives. Who was it that had attacked the garage and for what purpose? Gianelli? But why? He had accomplished nothing. The Italian would have to be dealt with and soon, but right now he had more pressing is-sues. Shlomo was still missing, Ivan was incapacitated, and Tibor was getting laid by the ugliest woman on two conti-nents. But there were some positives too. If Shlomo stayed missing that would be a plus, the weapons were safe, and he could carry out his plan without the help of his brothers.

As he chugged along Third Avenue, the service engine and oil light flicked on. The oil pressure had dropped to near zero and the engine temp had risen sharply into the red zone. He wasn't going to make it back to the restaurant.

Shit!

C'mon...c'mon... He urged the vehicle forward, but it was starting to decelerate and he was crawling along at twelve miles an hour. He couldn't let the van stop here in the middle of Third Avenue with all the weapons in the back and Ivan passed out in the front. He turned onto Cooper Square, saw a sign for a public parking garage and breathed a sigh of relief. At least the van would be out of sight. He took a ticket and crawled to the top level, and just as he pulled into a space, the van sputtered, jerked and died with a hiss, spewing fumes out from the engine block.

Now what?

He leaned over and shook Ivan, but he was out cold. A direct hit in the face with an airbag was like being hit with a bat. He may even have a concussion when he woke up. There was no telling what condition he would be in. He dialed Tibor again for the umpteenth time and again there was no answer. He left another voice message and shook his head. You couldn't rely on men his age. Their heads were always in the clouds over one thing or another. He took in a deep breath, let it out and called one of his men, Nicolae, to bring his Ford Explorer to offload the weapons and transport Ivan to safety. It was late, the man had been drinking, and since he didn't have much use for it in the city on a daily basis, his SUV was in a long-term parking garage some distance from his apartment. Yorgi settled in. This could take a while.

Chapter 51

By 3:00 a.m. all of the weapons had been transferred to the Explorer and covered with blankets. Ivan had come around, and although he was very uncomfortable and shaky with a massive headache and double vision, he seemed mostly okay. Yorgi knew he needed immediate medical attention. Back in Romania, he had reset many broken noses in the field, but this one looked a little more complicated and he suspected Ivan was going to require some sort of surgical reconstruction. The headache and double vision were a different matter altogether and that made him worried about some sort of traumatic brain injury.

As Nicolae drove the Explorer away, Yorgi turned to Ivan in the back seat surrounded by piles of AK12s and RPGs concealed beneath their coverings. He said, "Ivan, I have to meet Dimitri in just a few hours. You know I cannot miss this meeting."

"I understand, Yorgi."

"I will have Nicolae bring you to hospital for treatment. You must be in terrible pain."

"I am, brother."

Yorgi turned to the driver. "Nicolae, drop me off at my apartment in SoHo and then bring Ivan to St. Matt's emergency room. Stay with him and keep me updated. Park car on top floor of parking garage. Windows are tinted and weapons are covered. They should be okay for short period of time."

"Yes, Yorgi." Nicolai said as he turned onto Lafayette Street.

"I will call weasel CEO and make sure you get best care possible, Ivan."

When Ivan didn't answer, Yorgi turned back to him again. Ivan had lapsed back into unconsciousness. He said to Nicolae, "Drive faster."

****

"So what happened with you and Feinberg, Cesari? You never said," asked Tierney.

They were driving in Vito's Cadillac to one of his safe houses in Little Italy. It was an apartment over one of the restaurants on Mulberry Street where the neighbors minded their own business and never saw or heard anything unusual. One of Vito's men followed them in Tierney's Subaru.

Cesari said, "It was interesting for sure."

Tierney was in the passenger seat as Vito drove. He turned and said, "Is that all I'm going to get?"

"For now, that's all I can give you."

"When will I get it all?"

"When you're retired and living the life."

Tierney laughed. "I can see it now. Me and you on a beach in Ft. Lauderdale with Gianelli serving us Pina Coladas in an orange jumpsuit and an electronic ankle monitor."

Vito scoffed, "That'll be day."

Dr. Sundaram, sitting next to Cesari in the back, said amiably, "Gentlemen, I can see you are all in excellent humor. Perhaps, this would be good time to suggest you let me go. I promise again to say nothing to anyone."

Tierney replied, "No can do, Doctor. You'll be safe, well fed and not lacking for anything, but we can't take the chance of one of the Romanescu boys running into you."

Vito added, "Relax, Doc. Tomorrow, you're going to have the best Italian food in the city."

Sundaram didn't say anything and resigned himself to his fate of home-made lasagna, Chianti and tiramisu. Cesari yawned and said, "It's after 3:00 a.m. We could all use a little shuteye."

Tierney said, "Amen to that."

"There enough room in there for me or do I have to go home?" asked Cesari.

Vito shook his head. "It's small, only one tiny bedroom and a couch. Enough room for one of my guys to keep an eye on Dr. Sundaram, but that's it unless you want to sleep on the floor."

"No, thanks," Cesari said. "How about a lift home, Detective?"

"Sure."

They pulled up alongside the curb of Mulberry and Grand where they all got out. Vito's guy handed Tierney the keys to his Subaru and took charge of the dentist. Cesari and Tierney got into the detective's car and sped away, leaving Vito to manage things.

Once they were alone, Tierney didn't waste any time. Without any enthusiasm he said, "Cesari, you do realize that if Feinberg turns up dead, I'm going to have to arrest you. I know I've gone down the rabbit hole with you and Gianelli, but I haven't gone down that far."

"Well he's dead so I'll save you some time."

He let out a breath. "What happened?"

"When I arrived at his apartment, the door was open, so I let myself in. I had my crowbar. It was my intention to teach him a very severe lesson but that was all. But I was too late, I found him on his bed with a bullet wound to the abdomen and bleeding badly. I won't lie. He was still alive but just barely so. He died within minutes of my arrival. I didn't see any point in calling 911."

He left out the part about Melissa, the gun and the pillow. Over the years, he had become a master at disinformation and deflection. He'd always thought he'd make a great asset for some intelligence service, but Tierney was too smart and too experienced for his subterfuge.

Tierney said, "And you don't know what happened?"

"It might have been an accident. He was holding a pistol in his hand. Maybe he was cleaning it or something. "

"An accident? A gunshot to the abdomen? Not likely, Cesari. Try again."

"Then maybe he was in a struggle with some guy and pulled the gun out. The other guy might have turned it on him. It would have to have been a big guy because Feinberg wasn't a shrimp."

Tierney warmed up to that idea and said, "That's a possibility but you don't know who might have killed him?"

"I didn't say that. In fact, I'm sure I do know. I just can't narrow the suspect list down to under a thousand. In less than six months, Feinberg had pissed off an entire hospital, its employees and their families. One of them obviously had enough. My guess is an angry husband of a nurse he hit on."

Tierney nodded. "Was your Melissa nurse married?"

"No, and no boyfriend either, and there's no way she would have come out on top in a struggle with that ape. I'm not even sure I would have."

"And yet you went there with nothing but a crowbar?"

"And the element of surprise. He would have been on the floor the minute the door opened and wouldn't have gotten the chance to pull out a gun let alone walk to the bedroom to get one."

He thought about that and said, "You sound like you've done this before."

"I watch a lot of TV."

Tierney snorted, "I bet… One question, Cesari."

"I'm listening."

"Am I going to find your fingerprints in his apartment?"

"Not a chance. I wiped down everything I touched."

"Isn't that a peculiar thing to do for someone who's innocent?"

"Not if you have a record like I do."

"So all I'm left with is a dead slob who liked to abuse women and lots of suspects?"

"A dead slob with lots of enemies and even more dangerous friends. He was the front man for an organization running guns, remember? Feinberg was skating on thin ice and he didn't even know it. They might have decided they didn't like the job he was doing."

"Is that the way you would like me to sell it?"

"It's possible."

"I suppose it is. It's also possible that this nurse, Melissa, got the snot smacked out of her, got understandably angry, took matters into her own hands and now you're covering for her. Should I even bother talking to her or is she going to have an alibi?"

"I'm pretty sure she's going to have an ironclad alibi."

"Let me guess, she was banging some Italian doctor all night?"

"All night."

Tierney was amused. "What are you, Cesari? Some sort of bleeding heart? Take in stray animals and that kind of stuff? You're going to protect a woman who just the other day was screaming to cut your balls off?"

"You know how women are."

Tierney laughed. "That I do. You're the one I'm having trouble figuring out."

"I have an unusual sense of justice that doesn't always involve the law but always involves right and wrong."

Tierney stopped the Subaru in front Cesari's building on Sixth Avenue. He said, "Fine... Feinberg was an asshole and got what he deserved. Who cares who the instrument of justice was? Is that the idea?"

"Isn't that the way it would have played out in Afghanistan if you ever found the men that tortured that girl, Shahzadi?"

Tierney was stung by the memory and hesitated a bit before admitting, "It would have been worse. In fact, it was worse, a lot worse because I did find them, and I didn't let them off so easy. I made it last for days. They begged me to die."

There followed an uncomfortable silence that lasted for a full two minutes. Eventually Cesari said, "I'm sorry for bringing that up."

Tierney glanced at the leather bracelet on his left wrist. "Don't be. Sometimes we all need to be reminded of who the real victims are and what we really stand for. We're worried about weapons and rightly so but look at all the other people here who have been hurt in the process like your friend, Melissa. Feinberg and Acevedo are nothing but savages just like Shlomo and Yorgi and they all need to go down hard."

"Very hard," Cesari agreed.

"Any suggestions for the next step now that we have the weapons?"

"I'm not sure there is a next step. I say we keep doing what we're doing and wait to see what happens."

He nodded. "Agreed. We keep up the surveillance. The chess board has changed, and they will have to react. By morning they'll know Feinberg's dead. Between that and what happened at the hospital tonight, we've lit a real fire under their asses. They'll have to do something."

Cesari added, "I agree, and the timeline on when this character from Romania arrives will determine a lot about what happens next. If Yorgi figures out those weapons are missing before he gets here, our gambit will have failed, although they'll still have the problem of who took them. If he doesn't figure it out before he arrives, Yorgi will have a lot of explaining to do, and we want to be right there when all the begging for his life stuff begins. Well, it's almost four. How about we meet at eight over on First Avenue."

"Okay, Cesari, a couple of hours of sleep is better than nothing. I live just over the bridge in Brooklyn, so I better get moving."

"Why don't you stay here tonight? I live in a massive loft. You can have the sofa and as much scotch as you can drink."

Tierney contemplated the offer but declined. "Thanks, but I need to check on my cat."

Cesari grinned. "You have a cat?"

"A big fat thing. Gets lonely and acts out if I leave him for too long."

"You're killing me, Detective."

Chapter 52

Yorgi arrived at the Roxy at 6:00 a.m. sharp. His head was still reeling from the night's excitement. He was tired and had slept fitfully. The constant updates from Nicolae and the CEO about Ivan had him very concerned. Ivan was still in the emergency department, very groggy and confused. His head CT scan was negative for a cerebral hemorrhage or a subdural hematoma. The neurologist was confident that he was suffering from a straightforward concussion and should snap out of it with time. Apparently, this was not an unusual complication of a head on collision with an airbag. His nose was another matter. The ENT doctor was going to take him to the operating room in an hour. The cartilage hadn't simply been displaced, it had been crushed, and Ivan may even be looking at a series of reconstructive surgeries. The airbag had struck him at an unfortunate angle and smashed his nose straight back into his face and he may be permanently disfigured.

He had roused Acevedo from bed, and he was now behaving as the dutiful flunky he was, smoothing out all the bureaucratic roadblocks for his brother. The CEO had personally woken the doctors involved with Ivan and ordered them to expedite his care. He understood he was not to leave Ivan's side, and even when he went to the OR, he was to gown up and accompany him. Nor was he to speak about Ivan's condition to anyone. Acevedo would be tied up for hours which was good because Yorgi didn't want him near the loading docks this morning.

Yorgi had cleaned up well from the night before and wore a fresh, dark gray suit, his best shoes, a crisp white shirt and subdued blue tie. He looked every bit the businessman he aspired to be. He was standing outside the Roxy on White Street, where Sixth Avenue met Church finishing his second cup of black coffee waiting for Dimitri. Dimitri wasn't the kind of guy who told you where he was staying. You met him somewhere in public where he could observe you from a safe distance and shoot you if necessary.

At 6:15 a.m. Dimitri's entourage appeared coming down Church Street. Three brand new, sleek black Mercedes-Maybach S 650 sedans in a row pulled up next to him. It was quite a display of wealth and power as each sedan started at over two hundred thousand dollars and since Dimitri only arrived several hours ago, he must have purchased them over the phone from some high-end dealership, which probably jacked up the price another thirty percent to accomplish such a rush order. He must have at least ten or twelve armed men with him.

A sharply dressed, bulky man got out of the passenger seat of the middle car and called out his name. He nodded and the man opened the rear door. Yorgi sat in the most luxurious leather seat he had ever experienced. Next to him was a gargantuan of a human being with a closely cropped beard and slicked back hair. He pressed a 9mm Glock into Yorgi's side. The man who opened the door got back into the passenger seat and the caravan lurched forward. No one spoke as Yorgi was frisked vigorously. He was unarmed but they took his wallet and cellphone anyway. He offered no resistance. He knew the routine and had been on the other end of it many times.

And he understood why.

They were in a very dangerous business with a lot of money on the line. They were merchants of death and now one of their own had either been killed or gone rogue. They had no way of knowing whose side Yorgi was really on. Maybe he had killed Shlomo, a not unheard-of scenario in any business. Not that anyone here cared about the morality of it, but if Shlomo couldn't trust Yorgi, then neither could they. And if it was decided they couldn't trust him, then he was a dead man. After the pat down, they drove for ten minutes before the cars stopped. They were idling on West Broadway a few blocks from the Roxy. His was now the lead car and he was escorted from there back to the Mercedes in the middle and let inside. Musical Mercedes, Yorgi thought. Very clever. Just because there was a remote chance Yorgi had borrowed an RPG and had someone aiming it at them. They weren't sure yet what they were getting into and they were being cautious.

Yorgi turned to see the face from the laptop. The one who called himself Dimitri. The cars started moving again and the man in the front passenger seat turned around and aimed another Glock at his chest, only this one had a long silencer on it. Dimitri was a little man, almost a head shorter than Yorgi. He was in his eighties with glasses, wrinkles and hearing aids. He had dangerous eyes and held a walking stick between his legs. Yorgi was concerned about that.

Dimitri said, "Good morning, Yorgi. Finally, we meet in person."

Yorgi stared down the barrel of the gun. "Good morning, Dimitri."

"We have a lot to talk about, Yorgi."

"I accept whatever fate you have in store for me, Dimitri."

"That is good. You will tell me everything that has been going on these past few weeks and months and leave nothing out. Any hint of a lie, half-truth or reticence on your part will not only be the end of you but of your brothers as well."

"I understand, Dimitri."

"First, are the weapons in the hospital secure?"

"Yes, they are. There have been no further incidents," he lied. "We have the whole place locked down awaiting your arrival as was requested."

"You will take me to see them with my own eyes. Our clients grow impatient."

"I understand."

"Good. Second, have you found Shlomo?"

"I have not. I have men searching everywhere. I think there is possibility that he may have fled the city."

"What about his daughter, the lovely Drusilla? I understand she has a house in the city. Is it possible he is hiding there?"

"Is not possible. Tibor is fiancée to Drusilla. He visits her at house every day and reports nothing unusual other than she is sad and worried about father's absence."

Dimitri pondered that for a minute and then continued. "What about missing weapons?"

Yorgi allowed himself to show a little enthusiasm. "Of this I can give good news. Less than twenty-four hours ago truck was found and weapons retrieved. Because of recent events, I decided to not bring them to hospital but have them stored safely in different location awaiting your arrival."

"That is good news. And drivers? What of them?"

"Unfortunately, when my men came across the truck, the drivers were already dead in back. Shlomo ambushed the shipment in order to sell weapons for private gain. I am sorry to have to tell you this, Dimitri."

"Where did this take place?"

"The truck was found in an airport parking lot in Cleveland, a city in mid-west, a half day's drive from here. One of the drivers Shlomo left for dead managed to call me with dying breath and give us location with phone's GPS. He confirmed our worst fears that it was Shlomo who was responsible."

"Why would Shlomo leave truck in airport?"

"Airport parking is great place to leave vehicles unattended, especially in long-term parking. Relatively secure and no one questions their presence especially if parked in remote area. I suspect he knew we would be hot on his trail and meant for truck to cool off for a few days before new drivers came to take away."

"All the weapons were still inside?"

"All but the contents of two crates. There was an empty RPG crate and an empty AK12 crate. I do not know where these weapons are. Shlomo may have been planning to arm his new men with them."

"You mean go to war with us?"

"I do not know what he was thinking. I can only try to explain the facts."

Dimitri thought about it all and said, "I am impressed, Yorgi. You have done an excellent job and salvaged an unsalvageable situation. Where are the bodies of the two drivers? As I mentioned, one of them is family, husband to my granddaughter."

"I remember you tell me this and am very sorry I could not save him. Out of respect for you and your family, I kept bodies and brought them to secure location with weapons. They are in the empty weapon's crates. I did not want to bring bodies to hospital. I thought it presented too much risk, but I assure you that they have been treated with the utmost respect I could provide. I hope that I did right thing."

"You did well, Yorgi. And now we must deal with Shlomo. How long has he been babbling about vampires?"

"It has been months now and he has become increasingly erratic in his behavior."

Dimitri relaxed a little and spoke in Romanian to the man with the gun. He also relaxed, put the weapon away and turned around. Dimitri said, "Tell me everything he said about vampires."

"He talked a lot about them. How real they are and that you could never tell where they were. Recently, he has been seeing vampires and their work everywhere. Of particular concern was story he told about when he was young man in Romanian village. He said he had firsthand knowledge of vampires and had witnessed a whole village slaughtered by them. He went into great detail about this and was quite convincing."

Dimitri was quiet for a minute and closed his eyes. When he opened them again, he said, "The old fool."

Yorgi didn't respond to that. There was meaning behind it that was beyond his grasp. Dimitri continued, "It was not vampires who slaughtered villagers. It was Shlomo and I. We did it for revenge of our families. They betrayed our parents to the nazis; his because they were Jews and mine because they refused to worship at the altar of Herr Hitler. When we grew up, we made them pay the price for their treachery. In the middle of the night we dragged them from their homes and stabbed them in the neck with icepicks and sharpened screwdrivers, leaving the bodies in conspicuous places to instill terror. The ignorant peasants thought it was the work of vampires. Night after night we did this until the rest of the villagers finally abandoned their homes. We then burnt the village to the ground. We learned later that at least two children who had been hiding in their basements died in the flames."

Dimitri paused to take a deep breath. "We fled to Bucharest after that to start a new life. At first, we reveled in our success, but the guilt of those innocent lives began to seep into Shlomo's consciousness. It grew and grew until he could not bear it. I could see an internal war being waged and like a tidal wave, he was eventually overwhelmed by it. Eventually he blocked out his own culpability. In his mind, it really was vampires who butchered those people and burned down the village. Naturally, I could not take him to doctors, but over time I got him to at least suppress the need to talk about it. Until now that is…"

Yorgi soaked it all in and finally understood why Shlomo was so obsessed with the undead and why his little game with vampires had worked so well. The man was teetering on the edge and he had pushed him over. He wanted to smile. Opportunity was ninety-percent timing he had heard a wise man say.

Yorgi said, "I guess Shlomo's mind is beginning to slip."

Dimitri snorted. "Beginning is an understatement, Yorgi. I have not heard him speak of vampires or what happened in that village in over sixty years. Shlomo's mind is much further gone than you think. He must be found and silenced before he begins to talk about other things. Tell me about your brothers now, Yorgi. How do they fare?"

This was tricky for Yorgi. He didn't want to tell Dimitri about the attack on the hospital last night or of Ivan's injuries. It would suggest that perhaps he did not have a handle on things. Yet to withhold the truth would be a death sentence for all of them. But if he told them Ivan was injured and in surgery, Dimitri might want to go see him, and in Ivan's condition, on narcotics for pain and confused from his concussion, he might say things he ought not. Exhausted and stressed, Yorgi forgot one minor detail...

He said, "All is well. Ivan is managing business interests in other parts of city as we speak. Tibor is in love and spends much time with bride to be, Drusilla."

"Is good to see family happily engaged, but I am sad for Tibor."

"Why is that, Dimitri?"

"Unfortunately, Drusilla will have to be terminated along with father."

Yorgi flinched.

Chapter 53

Cesari opened the back door to the Escalade and let himself in at five minutes of eight. Vito was driving and Tierney rode shotgun. Both were having their morning coffee with fried egg sandwiches. They were parked a long block away from the restaurant on First Avenue. Tierney had binoculars wrapped around his neck.

"Anything happening?" Cesari asked.

"Lots, Cesari," Vito replied. "My guys spotted a fleet of high-end Mercedes sedans pulling into the back of the hospital about fifteen minutes ago. Ten KGB looking guys got out along with Yorgi and an old man. All ten guys were bigger than Yorgi, by the way."

"Great."

Tierney added, "We're assuming the old guy is the special guest from Romania they've been anticipating."

Cesari nodded. "How many people do you have over there?"

"One in the garage behind the hospital and one in a car on Tenth Street near the entrance to the driveway."

"Did Yorgi and his friends do anything special?"

Vito shook his head. "No, they conferred for a while in the driveway is all. It looked like Yorgi was giving his boss the lay of the land and then they went inside. My guys have orders to let us know as soon as they leave and the one on Tenth will tail them at a discreet distance just in case they don't come here."

"My guess is that with all the trouble they've been having and Shlomo's disappearance, the big shot wants to personally inspect his merchandise," offered Tierney.

Cesari said, "That would make sense. Any sign of Ivan or Tibor?"

"Haven't seen Tibor in almost two days now and haven't seen Ivan yet today. I'm not too worried about either one. With this Romanian capo and Yorgi we have the head of the snake."

"Still, I wonder what they're up to," Cesari mused.

Tierney said, "I'm pretty sure Tibor's preoccupied with his lady friend, but who knows about Ivan? He may have a headache after last night. I called the precinct to find out what happened and apparently they busted their way through the roadblock you set up."

Cesari grinned. "Good for them… Speaking of road-blocks, how are we set up today?"

Vito said, "Like I said, I have a guy in a car waiting on East Tenth Street. If it looks like they're trying to move the weapons, he'll block off the driveway as best he can and Tierney will bite the bullet and call his pals. But without a decent-sized truck that doesn't seem likely at the moment."

"What if he has to follow them?"

"If he leaves to do that, the guy watching from the garage will take up his position. Over here, I have a car with two men on Avenue A ready to block the alley at a moment's notice and then there's us."

Cesari noted, "But that still leaves us with a problem."

Tierney said, "I know. We're out gunned by two to one. Don't worry, Cesari. Gianelli and I have a plan. We're going to let you go in first to draw their fire. Then, we'll sneak up behind them and make the arrests."

Vito thought that was hysterical and laughed. Cesari wasn't quite as enthralled with the joke. "I'm glad you two are having a good time but would somebody explain to me why we only have six guys."

"Because, Cesari, I didn't know they were going to bring the entire Romanian army with them and also because I thought we were strictly doing surveillance. No one said anything about search and destroy," chided Vito.

"Fine, but the question remains as to tactics against a numerically superior force."

"We're not going to duke it out with them, Cesari," Tierney said seriously. "But we have enough firepower to keep them boxed in until help arrives. All we need to do is suppress them. They don't want to die any more than we do. The minute the squad cars start showing up, Gianelli and his boys disappear, and the NYPD takes over."

"You don't want to call help now?"

"And tell them what exactly? Remember, we were never in that restaurant or that tenement building or the basement of the hospital. That would have been illegal and in direct violation of their constitutional rights, and I would never do such a thing. However, once the shooting starts, I'll have an obligation to call in overwhelming force for the public good and possibly one of them may rat out what's going on at the hospital in the hopes of saving his ass."

"What if no one rat's out anybody?"

Tierney turned around with a quizzical look, "For a guy that pulled off a move like you did with Feinberg, I thought you'd be smarter than that."

"I get it. No one has to rat about anything. That's just the cover story for sending the S.W.A.T. guys into the hospital."

"I'm glad you understand. I've already alerted certain people I can trust to be discreet and await my call. I told them something big may be going down this morning and it will mean promotions for everyone. They'll have two teams suited up and ready to go; one to the hospital to get the weapons and your CEO, the other here. I haven't told anyone the details yet, but they know I'm not one to sound the alarm unless it's serious."

"Okay, so we wait."

****

Yorgi knew danger. He had lived with it his whole life. He also knew how to mask his emotions to not betray his underlying emotions or thoughts. The Russian bastards had taught him well, but at the moment he felt a rising fear that was threatening to overwhelm his defenses. They had not returned his cellphone to him despite reassurances that all was well. It did not sit well with him and once they entered the basement of the hospital, Dimitri had lined up all of Yorgi's men and disarmed them. Dimitri's men guarded all the entrances and exits as Yorgi's men knelt facing a wall with two submachine guns aimed at their backs. Then, as if nothing at all was unusual, he reviewed the entire inventory with Dimitri. Crate after crate in exhausting and methodical fashion. It took more than an hour and Yorgi prayed that not even one bullet was missing.

When they had finished, Dimitri said, "Good, Yorgi. All is in order. We go now to inspect remaining weapons you recovered. Your men can resume their duties."

"Yes, Dimitri."

Their weapons were returned to them and Yorgi gave his men last minute instructions. Once they were on the road again, Yorgi noticed that the lead car turned left onto Third Avenue while the remaining two cars kept going east toward the restaurant on First Avenue.

He asked, "Where do they go, Dimitri?"

"To Drusilla's home in Chelsea district. I already know address."

Yorgi heart skipped a beat. "You waste no time."

"Time is too valuable to waste, Yorgi. Friend or not, crazy or not, Shlomo should have known better than to betray the council. There was only one possible outcome for such actions, but do not worry. My men have been instructed to make it a quick death."

Yorgi hesitated and then said, "Perhaps, you would allow me to call, Tibor so he does not attempt to interfere. After all, he is in love with Drusilla."

"That will not be possible, Yorgi. If Shlomo is hiding there and Tibor knows then all must die. If Shlomo is not there, then my men will make every effort to spare your brother, but in the end, Drusilla dies today as payment for Shlomo's deeds. I cannot let you warn Tibor. His loyalty or his duplicity must be revealed in their totality. I am a little disappointed you did not think to search her home yourself. Come now, Yorgi. If all goes well, you will have bright future."

Yorgi was sick to his stomach. Could Tibor possibly be that stupid as to try to hide Shlomo? Why? For love of Drusilla? Is that why he hasn't been answering his phone? He kicked himself for not even considering searching for Shlomo in Drusilla's house. He had trusted Tibor. Tibor was the last one to see Shlomo. He said he drove him to the airport and walked him inside. He watched him go through security. That part had been verified, but Shlomo could easily have retraced his steps, met Tibor outside and driven off. Why go through all that? Because it could be verified with the airport, that's why. It would throw everyone off the trail. It worked and now they would all die. If Shlomo is found in Drusilla's brownstone and Tibor knew, then all was lost. What one brother does all are responsible for, and the Romanescus would not be allowed to die quickly. Of that, he was certain.

"We are here, Yorgi," Dimitri startled him back to reality as they approached the restaurant.

"Have driver go into alley. Tenement where weapons are hidden is less than one hundred meters. There is parking lot behind building where cars will be unseen."

As the cars crawled down the narrow alley toward their destination, Yorgi's sense of doom increased. His mind raced, and with every passing minute he became convinced that Tibor's passion for Drusilla might have conquered his reason. Yorgi let out a quiet breath as he contemplated his situation. He was trapped. Not counting Dimitri, there were six very large, armed and dangerous men, two in this car and four in the car behind them. The other four had gone to Drusilla's brownstone. As well trained as he was, the odds were definitely not in his favor.

He realized that he was sweating and tried to stay calm, reminding himself not to overreact. If Shlomo wasn't at the brownstone, then all would be well and he would be a rich and powerful man, the right hand of the council in America. Drusilla would be dead, but there was no way around that one, and as long as Tibor did not try to defend her too vigorously, he would be fine. Please, Tibor, do not die for hag, Drusilla. The reality was he had no idea what was going to happen next.

He looked at Dimitri's walking stick and wondered if it was as deadly as Shlomo's. That presented possibilities in an emergency, but that would have to be as a last resort. On the other hand, if he could convince them to open all the crates, he may be able to grab an AK12 and some ammo or possibly a grenade.

The cars slowed as they reached their destination.

Chapter 54

"Where'd did the third car go?" Tierney asked as they watched the two Mercedes enter the alley next to the Ukrainian restaurant and disappear from view.

Vito replied, "I don't know. My guy said he turned left on Third Avenue right after they came out of the hospital. That's all he could say. By the time he passed through the intersection, the first car was out of sight."

Cesari said, "That's good news for us. Less guns and muscle for them."

"Maybe," countered Tierney. "Not knowing the location of your enemy is generally not considered an advantage on the battlefield, Cesari… All right, it's time to tighten the noose. Gianelli, have the guys on Avenue A block off the alley on that side. We'll block it off on this side. Have the guy who tailed them pull into the alley and sit tight. We'll park behind him as a double buffer should they try to ram him out of the way. I assume everyone on your team is armed, Gianelli?"

Vito nodded. "Pistols, shotguns, and Gaetano is blocking Avenue A with a Fat Mac. Yorgi and his pals aren't getting out on that side without permission."

"What's a Fat Mac?" asked Cesari.

Vito called his guys with instructions and Tierney turned to Cesari to explain. "It's basically a hand-held cannon. It's a specially made, bolt action rifle that uses the .950 JDJ round which is three inches long and weighs over half a pound. It's the largest hunting rifle in the world and believe it or not, quite legal."

"Sounds like a serious weapon."

"It is. It weighs over fifty pounds and each bullet costs about forty or fifty bucks."

"What do you hunt with it?"

"Nothing really. The rifle is too damn expensive and unwieldly for the average guy. It's more of collector's thing. Some guys have to own every toy out there so they can sit around the campfire talking about how big their gun is... You think Gaetano can handle it, Gianelli?"

Vito finished talking to his men and said, "Don't worry about him. Worry about Yorgi if Gaetano decides to shoot at them with it. That bullet will rip through the engine block and still probably kill everyone in the car."

Tierney grinned, "As nostalgic as that imagery makes me, Gianelli, let's hope it doesn't come to that."

Vito put the car in gear and followed his guy into the alley while Tierney watched for activity through his binoculars. Tierney said, "I don't see anybody in front of the building. They must have driven both cars into the back lot."

Cesari added, "You know the Fat Mac thing raises some interesting possibilities."

"Such as?" asked Tierney

"I like the idea of blowing up their engines or disabling them in some other way. If we could do that while they're preoccupied, then they really wouldn't be going anywhere. Somebody pops a couple of rounds in the air for effect and you call it in as shots fired. Yorgi and company are trapped."

Tierney argued, "You're assuming they're all going into the building. The smart money says they leave at least a couple of guys outside standing guard. Too much of a risk, Cesari. Going in there prematurely could turn this into the O.K. Corral. Let the men in blue do their jobs. We're just here to slow them up so the guys with the flak vests can take them down."

Vito said, "He's got a point, Detective. Why should we worry about them coming at us? Without wheels they're nothing. I hate to agree with Cesari, but I think it's worth a try."

Tierney raised his eyebrows and said, "Et tu, Vito?" referencing Julius Caesar's famous line when he realized his friend Brutus had betrayed him.

Cesari rushed to smooth things over. "C'mon, Detective. It's not that bad of an idea. I'm not saying we rush in there in full force. Let me sneak up on them. If I sense trouble, I'll just pull back."

He thought about it, sighed and said, "How would you approach them?"

"It's broad daylight so walking around to the back might not be a good idea if they're standing guard. I'll go through the front entrance like we did the other day. Like I said, I'll retreat if there's any hint of a problem."

The Detective appraised Cesari as if for the first time and said, "We could've used a guy like you in Afghanistan, Cesari. You got metal. Go ahead in."

"I'll need a weapon. In fact I'll need two weapons. Anybody have a knife on them?"

Vito handed him a sleek looking full-sized 9mm Beretta and Tierney handed him his four-inch pocketknife. Vito said, "Be careful where you point that. The safety's off. It's already chambered and loaded with one hundred and fifty grain hollow points."

Tierney said, "You better not screw this up, Cesari."

****

Yorgi was relieved that Dimitri had posted two men outside in the parking lot as sentries. Now he only had to deal with four armed men bigger than himself. The odds were still quite formidable but now improved by thirty-three percent. He turned on the light and out of respect offered Dimitri to go first down the stairs. Ever cautious, Dimitri declined, but sent two of his men in the lead with Yorgi close behind. Dimitri and the others followed in the rear.

At the bottom of the steps, all the men stood frozen. Yorgi gasped and felt his heart pound. The others pulled out handguns and took up battle stances. Sitting propped up at the table were the two dead drivers. A full week postmortem and smelling every bit of it, Cesari had strapped them to chairs with rope and had tilted their heads back exposing their filed-sharp fangs. The rats that had been feasting on their exposed parts, ran in all directions.

Despite the decay and mutilation, Dimitri easily recognized one of the men. He walked up close to the body and appearing grief-stricken, said, "This one is my granddaughter's husband, Florin, the father of my great grandson... Is this some sort of joke, Yorgi?"

Yorgi stood there surrounded and speechless. Rarely had he ever been at such a loss for words. Dimitri added, "Have you nothing to say, Yorgi?"

Blankly, Yorgi shook his head. "I don't understand."

"Neither do I, Yorgi. How am I supposed to tell my granddaughter what has become of her beloved?" And with increasing menace added, "Do you think to make fool of me?"

Yorgi didn't say anything. He wracked his brain thinking through the possibilities. Two of Dimitri's men moved close behind him sensing where this was heading. Yorgi noticed but pretended not to be alarmed.

Dimitri said, "Show me the weapons so I can at least claim some small consolation for my sorrow."

"Yes," stammered Yorgi but had a sinking feeling in his stomach as he led the way into the other room. How could he talk his way out of this mess? At whose feet could he lay the responsibility for this disaster? But if he thought things were bad, he soon found them to be a whole lot worse as they approached the wall where the weapons should have been. All hopes of snatching a grenade or an assault rifle were completely dashed as he gazed upon the barren wall.

He turned to Dimitri and mumbled, "I swear to you, Dimitri. The weapons were right here. I put them here myself."

"Then where are they? Offer me some reasonable explanation, Yorgi."

"Someone plays trick on you and me. It has to be... Shlomo. That's it. He toys with us...laughs at us...dares us to catch him. It must be him."

Dimitri curled his lip in a sinister grin. "Shlomo? You tell me he is senile old man. How could he possibly remove thirty full crates of weapons from under your nose?" He looked around the basement and went on. "There is not even a staircase leading out, Yorgi. Come now, you must try harder than that."

And he did.

"Shlomo must not really believe in vampires. He only pretended to convince us that he is crazy and now he mocks us."

As they spoke, the circle around Yorgi growing tighter, a phone buzzed loudly from inside one of the men's pockets. He took it out, read a text message and then handed it to Dimitri. It was Yorgi's phone that they had taken from him. Dimitri read the message and smiled.

He said, "It seems we have a problem, Yorgi. Would you like me to read to you?"

When Yorgi didn't respond, Dimitri read the message from Nicolae out loud, "Ivan is out of surgery and doing well. He will remain in hospital for several more days. You told me not to leave brother's side, but he is stable now. I would like your permission to move weapons before they are discovered."

Yorgi felt like he couldn't breathe. Caught in multiple lies, he felt his legs buckle, and even in the dim lighting of the basement one could easily see his face grow pale. The evidence against him was damning and incontrovertible. He would have killed for much less. In that moment, all the fire left Yorgi. All the grandiose plans of living large and powerful at the expense of others vanished into thin air. He was now on the other side and knew defeat for the first time in his life. Seeing through the eyes of one of his many victims, he understood their helplessness.

All was lost.

Chapter 55

Cesari crept through the foyer and down the dusty hallway toward the rear of the building with the Beretta in one hand and the knife in his pocket. If the cars were unattended, he planned on slashing all the tires and any exposed lines or hoses underneath the chassis. He hadn't quite come up with an alternative strategy if the vehicles were guarded. One sentry and he'd be all right. That would be a straightforward get the drop on him, smack him in the head with the butt of the pistol and then slash the tires. Two guys and it would all depend whether they were standing next to each other. If they were separated by more than a few feet or on opposite sides of the cars, he would be at a tactical disadvantage and most likely provoke a gun battle which he didn't want to do. He had to remind himself that stealth was the high priority. Let New York's finest make the arrests. Leaving dead bodies lying around would be poor form and would put Tierney out on a limb with the department. As he reached the back door, he peered out the small window to its side.

Shit.

There were two men patrolling the lot. One was ten feet from the door leaning against one of the Mercedes, and the other was at the far end of the lot taking a piss against a bush with a cigarette in his mouth. Cesari slunk back behind the door and gingerly turned the dead bolt to keep them out. He needed time to think it through, but then he heard a sound coming from the basement. He glanced at the cellar door. There it was again.

It wasn't a good sound.

He tested the knob and turned it gently. It was unlocked, and he opened it a crack. It was the unmistakable wailing of a man in great pain. It was Yorgi. He couldn't see anything from his vantage point but he could hear very well.

Yorgi was pleading for his life. "Dimitri, I would never betray you."

"Is too late, Yorgi. I cannot spare you, but I can offer you this small comfort. If you tell me where weapons are, then I will kill brothers quickly. And do not tell me you only know where two of the crates are. I do not believe you would steal just two crates with all the others at your disposal."

"I honestly do not know, Yorgi."

"Yorgi, consider your poor baby brother, Tibor. He is soft compared to you. He will suffer greatly as will his bride to be Drusilla. My men await my call as to whether their ends will be swift or slow. Is entirely up to you."

Cesari caught his breath. Now he knew where the other Mercedes went; to Drusilla's brownstone in Chelsea.

Yorgi said, "I don't know where the weapons are. I swear. It had to be Shlomo."

Dimitri sighed. "I know not what has been going on here with you and Shlomo, but I know enough that the council has been betrayed and that I personally have been betrayed by the both of you."

"No, Dimitri. No..."

The basement and stairwell filled with his screams again as some unknown torture was applied. With the noise, Cesari took the opportunity to open the door fully, lie on his stomach and ease himself down one step. He waited for more screaming and then eased himself down another step. Bracing himself with his left hand, he kept the gun pointing toward the kill-zone. After lowering himself down one more step, he had a partial view of the room. The drivers' bodies had been tossed to the side in a heap and now Yorgi was the one tied to a chair. His face was swollen and purple and one of his ears was lying on the table next to a severed finger. A belt was looped around his neck, and blood poured out of his wounds, his nose and his mouth. An old man stood close, hissing more pain and suffering into Yorgi's good ear. Two large men stood with their backs to the steps and two more were facing in his direction, but he could only see their legs from his angle. The old man held a two and a half foot extremely thin blade in his hands with a diamond encrusted handle. The guy looked like he should be in a nursing home for retired gestapo agents.

"Dimitri. I beg you. My brothers know nothing," gasped Yorgi.

"We will find out, but here let me help you. You are bleeding too much. Hold him."

One of the giants standing behind Yorgi, grabbed the belt around his neck roughly, tightened it, and held his head in a vise like grip. Dimitri took a torch lighter for cigars out from his pocket and flicked it on. The four burners sprung to life with great enthusiasm, hissing loudly. Dimitri applied the flame to the remnants of Yorgi's bleeding ear. The pain was excruciating and Yorgi shrieked and lurched to no avail as his skin blackened and blistered. By the time Dimitri was done Yorgi had nearly fainted. The stench of burnt flesh gradually replaced the smell of fear and death. Cesari was certain Yorgi wouldn't last much longer like this. That wasn't a good thing. Tierney wanted these guys turning on each other, not dying. He didn't know who this Dimitri guy was, but he already didn't like him.

But now he had a new problem. The other men had gone to Chelsea to torture and murder Drusilla and Tibor. Something about that didn't sit well with Cesari. It violated all sorts of internal codes. He needed to act quickly. Tierney was going to hate him for what he was about to do but it was unavoidable. He slowly withdrew back to the top of the stairs but remained prone on the floor. The guys outside wouldn't get through quickly enough to stop him, but they would definitely get through and then he would be toast with enemies in front and behind. He needed the guys in the parking lot neutralized. He texted Tierney and Vito.

Shots fired in the basement! Call in the calvary now! There are two men out back that require immediate attention!"

He waited one minute and then reached up with his left hand and turned the lights off. The basement went dark and suddenly quiet except for Yorgi sobbing incoherently. Dimitri calmly ordered one of his men to go see what was wrong. At this point, they were probably thinking it might simply be a burnt-out light bulb or faulty breaker. If it didn't turn on again, they could just move to the furnace room and finish what they were doing. Cesari heard heavy footsteps up the stairs and then suddenly a cellphone flashlight flicked on. Looking over him for the light switch, he didn't notice Cesari at first or at last because Cesari shot him immediately in the chest. The heavy round and close proximity caused the man to hurtle backward off his feet landing on his back at the bottom of the steps, instantly dead. The sound was deafening and now a new smell took over the room.

Burnt gunpowder.

For a moment everyone froze and then pandemonium ensued below with much cursing in Romanian. Wild shots went over him in the dark as he eased himself down three steps again. Another phone light went on near the table and Cesari fired at it causing the man to scream and fall to the floor. He quickly withdrew back up the stairs again as multiple shots were fired in the direction he had been. Cesari hoped that Tierney was racing to the back of the building to nab those guys before they broke the door down. He could already here them banging and yelling.

Almost on cue, he heard muffled gunfire outside signaling that a firefight now raged both inside and outside the tenement. He called out, "Dimitri, I know you speak English. You're trapped. There's no way out."

"Who are you?"

"I'm with the New York police department."

It was close enough to the truth. Dimitri's reply was two more shots fired in his direction followed by the lights turning on in the furnace room and then the door there slamming shut. Less than a minute later, more shots came from within the furnace room and then silence. Cesari stood, turned on the light and went cautiously down the steps. There were two dead men lying on the floor; the one from the top of the stairs and the other one by the table who had foolishly turned on his cellphone light. Yorgi was wheezing and bleeding heavily from a stab wound to the chest. Apparently, Dimitri had decided to finish him off rather than let him speak to the police. He was unconscious, face down on the table and perilously close to the point of no return.

The furnace room door opened and Cesari swung around with the Beretta to see Vito, panting and pointing a gun back at him. They both relaxed a smidgeon. Vito said, "We came down the coal chute."

Cesari nodded his approval, "Good thinking. Where's Tierney?"

"In there handcuffing two of them. He's been shot in the shoulder, but he'll be all right."

Cesari went to the furnace room to see him. He stepped over a dead man and found Dimitri and his last surviving goon sitting on the floor handcuffed to one another. Tierney, who was standing over them saw Cesari approach, grimaced in pain and said, "You've got some explaining to do, Cesari."

"I don't have time. You've got to get Yorgi and yourself to a hospital fast, and I have to go now. More lives are in danger. Are your boys on the way?"

"They should be here any minute with ambulances. We called everyone. I already told Gianelli to get his men out of here."

Cesari concurred, "Then we're all set here. I'm going to commandeer one of their Mercedes. Is that okay with you, Detective?"

Tierney nodded. "Be my guest."

Cesari looked at Dimitri and his gorilla. Both had hatred in their eyes. Cesari said, "Keys."

The goon sucked in and then spit at him. It missed but before he could regret it, Cesari smacked him in the side of the head with the Beretta so hard his eyes rolled up and he slumped forward, unconscious. For a second Cesari thought he might have killed him which wouldn't have been a bad thing. It's just that he hated to lose his temper like that.

He turned to Dimitri. "Keys."

The old man sighed with resignation. "Men outside, both are drivers."

Cesari turned to Tierney. "Detective, I'm sorry but I really have to go. Vito, are you coming?"

"No, I'll stay here with Detective Tierney."

Tierney said, "Get going, Gianelli. You don't want to be found here."

"I think you should lie down, Detective, and you might want to loosen your tie. You don't look too good. I'll be fine. I heard shots and came running to the aid of a police officer being fired upon." He handed Cesari his pistol. "I don't even have a weapon."

Tierney managed a smile but was starting to look ashen. He took Vito up on the offer and sat down on the floor, leaning back against a wall. He opened his tweed suitcoat and re- vealed a blood-soaked white shirt. As suggested, he loosened his tie and collar. He said, "You're all right. Did you know that, Gianelli?"

"I've been trying to tell you that for years. Now don't die on me, okay? I don't want to have to tell my guys I gave mouth to mouth to a New York City cop. I'd never live it down."

Tierney thought that was funny. "You'd never live it down? For Christ's sake have you looked in the mirror recently? I'd have to move out of the state if that ever got around."

Cesari thought that Tierney was going to be fine and left them. Yorgi, he wasn't so sure about as he bounded up the steps two at a time. Outside, he saw two other men on the ground, one was dead and the other bleeding heavily and gasping for air. He searched the nearest man and found the keys to one of the Mercedes as sirens wailed up and down First Avenue. He threw the pistols onto the passenger and seat and started the engine. It roared to life and he soon came flying out of the alley onto Avenue A correctly anticipating the surge of emergency vehicles would come in from the other more trafficked side.

Chapter 56

The Mercedes handled like an advanced fighter jet, from the head's up display to the six hundred plus horsepower engine which rumbled effortlessly propelling him crosstown. Cesari had the benefit of not being particularly concerned with etiquette this morning. He dodged around stalled traffic into opposing lanes and slammed the accelerator through red lights and stop signs. Most of the cops in this area were on First Avenue or raiding the basement of the hospital. He had thought about asking Tierney to send a couple of squad cars to the brownstone but had nixed the idea as too clumsy and might provoke the exact thing he was trying to prevent, a bloodbath in Chelsea.

Cesari had the advantage over the Romanians in that he knew the neighborhood. The street the brownstone was on was narrow, one way, and always congested. Parking space was at a premium, so unless they were extremely lucky, they would be double-parked outside. Which meant that at least one or two of the four men would be in the car waiting while the others were inside. Which meant that periodically, they would have to move the car to allow through traffic or else risk a confrontation with law enforcement. Moving the car meant circling the block. It was a bummer but that's why most people didn't have cars in the city.

From a couple of hundred feet, Cesari saw the Mercedes facing away as he turned onto the block. He slowed to a standstill while he considered his options. Ramming them would be fun but his own airbag would deploy potentially injuring him or worse. He had heard that the force of the exploding bag could sever the thumbs wrapped around the steering wheel, and he really liked his thumbs. If he shot at them, the guys inside the brownstone would be alerted as would everyone else in the vicinity.

Very amateurish.

He pulled his car slowly up behind them. Ten feet away he flashed his headlights. The driver rolled down his window and waved him forward. Apparently, he wasn't one of those guys who moved his car just because he was in the way. Technically, there was enough space to pass him but only if Cesari pulled in his mirrors and crawled by at one or two miles per hour. No one in their right mind in a two hundred thousand-dollar Mercedes would attempt such a feat if there was an alternative so he flashed his lights again.

The guy raised his left arm again and this time gave him the finger. Cesari smiled, untucked his shirt and stuffed one of the Berettas into the small of his back. He then got out of the car and walked up to the driver's side. The two men were well-dressed in subdued suits and ties, with large thick muscled shoulders and chests. They looked very European for some reason. Maybe it was the slick backed hair and ponytails. The driver sized him up and wasn't impressed. Cesari was wearing blue jeans, sneakers and his cotton shirt was out. In addition, he looked fairly harried from his earlier activities.

The man scowled and said, "There is plenty of room to pass. Don't be asshole."

"Sir, I am an off-duty police officer and I live right there." He pointed to the building next to Drusilla's. "You're blocking through traffic and need to move this vehicle immediately or I will have your car impounded."

"What means impounded?"

"Confiscated, seized, taken from you, and brought to a police station where you will have to pay a fine to have it returned."

The two men glanced at each other and took him a little more seriously. Cesari could see the wheels spinning. A police officer living next door to Drusilla was an unexpected complication. An arrogant, hostile police officer was even worse.

The man said, "If you are police officer, show us your badge."

"Sir, I just told you I am off-duty. My badge is in my house in a drawer, and if you make me get it, I will invite several of my fellow officers to join me. We will then arrest you and tow the car. Do you want that, or would you rather just move your vehicle around the corner where there is a parking garage?"

They looked at each other again. The driver said, "We move car."

"Thank you and have a nice day."

Before he started the engine, however, the man sneered and spit on the street next to Cesari's feet. Cesari looked down at the spot and then at the man. This was twice some euro-trash had spit at him today and according to Cesari's calculations that was twice too many. He quickly pulled the gun out from behind his back and pressed it into the man's temple.

Cesari said, "You're under arrest."

"What for?"

"Spitting on public property is against the law in New York State and carries a two-year mandatory sentence."

"You've got to be fuckeeng keeding?"

"I wish I was. Now put your hands on the steering wheel and you over there put your hands on the dashboard. Are either of you armed?"

Before they could respond, Cesari reached inside the driver's suitcoat and retrieved a Glock19 from his shoulder holster which he dropped onto the street and kicked under the car.

He said to the passenger, "What about you, sunshine? You got one too?"

The man nodded slowly, "Yes, we are private security."

"Really?"

"Yes."

"I believe you but what say we take the weapon out with your index finger and thumb and toss it out your window anyway. Move real slow and be very careful. I'm a little jumpy right now and at this range, if I shoot, the bullet will travel right through your friend's skull into your face... Once you lose the gun, we can discuss our differences in a more relaxed manner."

He did as he was told, and the gun clattered away between two Hondas. So far so good. No shots fired. Just a guy leaning into a car talking to his friends. He said, "Now drop your cellphones onto the street."

Then he said to the driver, "Pop the trunk and give me the keys to the car."

The trunk clicked open and he handed the keys over. Cesari said, "Now get out and walk to the back of the car and please don't do anything rash." He said to the other guy. "You stay there and don't make a sound."

In the rear of the vehicle, Cesari pressed the Beretta hard into the small of the man's back and growled, "Get into the trunk and don't hesitate, even slightly."

It was difficult for him because of his size but he made it in while Cesari did his best to keep one eye on his companion. Curled up awkwardly in the trunk, the man said, "You are not police. Who are you?"

"Something much worse."

Cesari looked up and down the street. It was a quiet neighborhood and although there were one or two people walking their dogs or taking a stroll no one seemed to be paying them any attention. That would soon change. Without warning, he punched the man as hard he could in the face, twice, and watched his lights go out. There was no point in leaving him conscious to figure out the emergency release mechanism that was in all modern car trunks. He closed the trunk, went to the passenger door and flicked the pistol at the other guy.

He said, "Get out, don't be stupid and let's go see how Tibor is doing."

They walked up the steps to the front door of the brownstone and Cesari positioned himself slightly to the side and behind the much bigger man who was directly in front of the spyhole. He pressed the gun into his back and said, "You have a choice. If you do what you're told, you will live. If you don't, you will die, right here and right now. Do you understand?"

He nodded. "Who are you?"

"You Romanians sure are an inquisitive bunch, aren't you?"

"Is good to know who enemy is."

"I'm not your enemy and I'm not your friend."

"Then who?"

"Death, if you don't do exactly as I say. Are we clear on that?"

"Is clear."

"Good. You are going to ring the door buzzer and tell your friend in there that you need to use the bathroom. When he opens the door you are going to punch him in the face as hard as you can. I want you to hit him hard enough to break his jaw. Are you strong enough to do that?"

He shrugged. "I will do my best."

"You need to do better than that because if you fail, I will have no choice but to kill you both, but it won't be quick. I will be angry and shoot you in the spine first. You will be paralyzed from the waist down while I do terrible things to you. Do you understand?"

"I understand."

"Where are they keeping Tibor and Drusilla?"

"Second floor bedroom. Out of sight. At least that is what I was told. I haven't been inside myself. I wait in car with driver in case of trouble."

"What kind of trouble?"

"We were told Shlomo may have new men."

"So I guess you didn't find Shlomo in there?"

"Only Tibor and Drusilla inside."

"What were your orders?"

"Dimitri say wait for call from him."

"Yes, but certainly you knew what was probably going to happen."

"Of course. Dimitri is angry. We definitely kill Drusilla and Tibor. We were waiting to hear from Dimitri how slow and how painful was to be their deaths. Is his way of doing things. Is what he will do to you too when he catches you."

"Is that right?"

"It is his way."

"Has anyone in there been harmed?"

He shook his head. "No, they are tied up but unhurt. Lucky for girl she is so ugly."

"I see... How do you know what she looks like if you didn't go in the house?"

"Men inside text picture. My eyes still hurt."

"So you were going to freelance it with her if she was attractive?"

He shrugged again. "Why not? She is dead woman anyway."

This guy wasn't holding anything back. He was a textbook sociopath. That was for sure. Cesari said sarcastically, "Well, no one could accuse you of not having standards... Okay, press the buzzer and remember what I said."

"I no forget. Break jaw or bullet in spine."

He pressed the buzzer twice and stood in full view of the peephole. Less than a minute later someone could be heard on the other side of the door. "Is everything all right out there, Kronid?"

"Everything is good, Luca. I need to use bathroom."

"Hold on."

They heard locks clicking and the door swung open revealing a slightly smaller man in the process of replacing a pistol into his shoulder holster. Cesari nudged Kronid in the back with the Beretta so as not to get any bad ideas. He didn't. As soon as the door was open enough, Kronid hurled a massive upper cut to the other man's chin. So much force and kinetic energy was behind the blow that the man was lifted off his feet and Cesari could hear the satisfying crunching of his jawbone. The man fell backward unconscious, and with all his strength, Cesari shoved Kronid into the foyer where his momentum caused him to trip over his friend. He stumbled and fell face forward into the living room and Cesari quickly leaped onto his back, hammering him into unconsciousness with the butt of the Beretta. He was confident they would both be out of it for at least an hour or more. It happened very quickly and very quietly.

Cesari glanced around for others but there were none, so he closed the front door and locked it again. He grabbed the gun from the guy with the broken jaw and hid it under the sofa and then tried to imagine what they would do if they suddenly woke up. They were injured and unarmed. The guy with the busted jaw shouldn't be a problem because he would need a doctor. The other guy may or may not have a concussion. They would both want revenge of course but would their desire for that outweigh their common sense? Cesari finally decided that both of them may fear Dimitri more than they feared him. He took a sofa cushion and pressed the Beretta into it over the back of Kronid's knee and fired once. The sound was fairly well muted. The man twitched and groaned but didn't wake up. He repeated the procedure with the guy in the foyer. They definitely wouldn't be a problem now.

As he stood up, he heard a male voice call down the stairs, "Is everything all right, Luca? Who was at door?"

Chapter 57

Cesari didn't reply to the voice but concealed himself along the side of the staircase not visible from the top. The best course of action would be to keep quiet and let the man's curiosity get the best of him. The man called out once more for his friend and waited for a response. After five more minutes, nothing happened and no one came down the stairs. Cesari decided the man was skittish and that he was going to have to go up there after him.

He glanced up the stairs and took a deep breath as he cautiously took his first step. He remembered the second-floor bedroom was huge, at least twice the size of the largest bedroom he'd ever seen and extravagantly furnished but that was all he could remember about the home. Still, that would be the most likely place to keep hostages and that's where the guy from outside said they were. What would be the point of lying about that?

The steps were carpeted and quiet. Cesari reached the top poised to attack or be attacked, but all was calm as if everyone was asleep. He approached the bedroom with great care and stood to its side while he listened. He heard nothing and knew he needed to make a decision. Why he was doing this for Tibor and Drusilla he wasn't one hundred percent certain, but he frequently relied on his instincts about people and this was one of those times.

He called into the room, "I'm coming in. There's no escape. Your friends can't help you."

A shot rang out and a bullet splintered through the door, landing in the opposing wall of the hallway. So much for that. He got on his knees, and from the side reached out and grabbed the doorknob, turned it and pushed the door open. Another two deafening shots came flying in his direction over his head. Plaster, paint and wood chips caused him to duck for cover.

Cesari tried again, "Don't be stupid. With all this shooting, someone will call the police. You'll have a chance with them. But if you keep this up, you'll die. Dimitri has already been arrested."

There was silence at the mention of Dimitri's name. "If you are not police, then who are you?"

What's with these guys and the questions?

"I'm just a friend of the family and I don't want to kill you if I don't have to."

"Why not?"

At least he had him talking. "Enough people have died today. I don't even care if you're arrested or not. I got nothing against you personally. Just leave without hurting anybody. You can go out the fire escape if you want."

"Maybe you shoot me while I climb down?"

Cesari had a feeling about this guy. His nerves were frayed, and he just needed an exit strategy that didn't involve him getting killed. "Maybe, but I won't. Like I said, enough people have died today. Look I'm going to enter the room with my hands up."

"Not good enough. Throw weapon into room where I can see."

Cesari hated these leap of faith situations but didn't see what choice he had right now. He did have his cellphone and if they weren't on their way already from all the gunfire, he could call the police, but then they'd have a desperate Romanian with hostages on their hands. Cesari was trying to dangle the hope of a clean escape in front of the man. He slid his gun into the room, slowly rose to his feet and stood in the doorway with his hands up.

He was completely surprised by what he saw. Four chairs were lined up in a row facing him and from left to right sat Zenobia with her usual sunglasses, Drusilla with her veil, Tibor and Shlomo. Shlomo was dressed impeccably in a three-piece suit with a silk breast-pocket handkerchief. He held his fancy diamond-headed walking stick in his left hand. Tibor's hands were tied behind his back and his ankles were restrained to the legs of his chair, but the others were free. Cesari assumed that because of his youth and size, Tibor was the only one that was considered a physical threat. They all looked at him with surprised recognition.

Dimitri's man was crouched behind them aiming his pistol at Cesari through the shoulders of Tibor and Shlomo. He said nervously, "Get down on knees, hands on floor."

Cesari assumed the position but kept his eyes on the guy. He was sweating and agitated. This was supposed to have been an easy jog in the park; an old man, his daughter, and her lovestruck boyfriend. Now he was in the deep end and he suddenly realized he didn't know how to swim. He probably tried calling his friends and Dimitri and realized Cesari was telling the truth. Help wasn't on the way.

Cesari said, "You're all alone up here. You should get out while you can. You haven't killed anyone. Hell, you've barely even committed a crime. You go back to Romania. In a month no one will care who you are. They got Dimitri. That's who they want."

"Shut up. I need to think." The man stepped around the row of chairs, his gun in front of him. "Do you have another weapon?"

Cesari shook his head. "No, I don't."

"I check for myself. Don't move."

As he stepped forward in front of his captives, he focused his full attention on Cesari. Now in his blind spot, Shlomo seized the opportunity and suddenly grabbed the top of his walking stick with his right hand and twisted. With speed Cesari would have thought impossible for such an old man he vaulted up from his seat unsheathing his sword and lunged forward. With incredible precision he pierced the base of the man's skull like an Olympic fencer practicing a forward thrust on melons. The force and angle of the thrust carried the blade through his vertebrae and out from his mouth. Instantly paralyzed, he had seconds to contemplate his fatal mistake of having turned his back on an extremely dangerous man. Blood oozed out of his mouth as he began to twitch and jerk. Shlomo withdrew the blade with an ugly grinding of metal on bone sound and the man crumpled to the floor in a lifeless heap.

Cesari looked on silently as the man sputtered and expired. Everyone in the room was quietly horrified as Shlomo wiped his blade on the dead man's shirt. Cesari started to rise from the floor when Shlomo whipped the blade around to within inches of his left eye.

Shlomo said, "Move very slowly, Doctor."

Cesari stood to full height as Zenobia moved to untie Tibor. Cesari said, "You're going to kill me? I just saved all your lives."

"You almost got us killed. We were in negotiations with him."

Cesari thought about that. "You were trying to buy your way out of this mess?"

"Of course. Money is the best way to make friends. Unfortunately, now that will not be possible."

"The guys outside didn't know about this. They didn't even know you were here."

"No, they didn't. The two inside were how do you say, double-dealing. They were planning to kill their friends in the car."

"How could you be sure they wouldn't have double-crossed you once they got their money?"

Shlomo smiled. "Of course they would have. That was a certainty. I only hoped to buy time to do what I just did now."

"Well then maybe you should consider thanking me."

"No, because now there is a dead body in Drusilla's house, the police are most likely on the way, and Dimitri will know I am still alive. Deal was they were going to tell Dimitri that they kill me, very painful death of course. After I deliver money, they betray me and kill for real." Sirens screeched shrilly in the distance. "We are out of time. Come everyone, we must go."

Cesari said, "Go? You're not going anywhere. None of you, but especially you, Shlomo. You killed a rabbi. Why?"

"And a priest and an Imam and so many others. But to answer your question, the rabbi disappointed me."

"That's why you're not going anywhere."

The blade inched closer to Cesari's eye and Shlomo smiled. "Aren't you forgetting something, Doctor?"

"Like what?"

"I'm the one holding the weapon."

"Oh that."

With lightning alacrity, Cesari reached up with his left hand and grabbed the sword in its mid-portion, deflecting it upward away from his eye. His grip was vise-like as he applied the greatest force he could muster. The pain was excruciating as the edge of the blade cut through his flesh and blood spurted around his fingers. Shlomo's odd-looking eyes went wide in consternation. Zenobia saw and frantically tried to undo Tibor's knots so he could join the fray. Drusilla sat there frozen by fear.

Shlomo instinctively jerked backward to loosen Cesari's grip but he held on even tighter, took a step forward and grabbed the old man by the throat with his right hand, his index finger and thumb acting like pincers on Shlomo's carotids and trachea. His flesh was soft from age and too much good living. Cesari's fingers dug deep meeting almost no resistance.

Shlomo clawed at him frantically in alarm with his free hand to no avail. Cesari was younger, stronger, and very angry. The silent struggle lasted ten seconds. Shlomo's face reddened, his eyes bulged out and he suddenly dropped the sword and went limp, collapsing to the floor, unresponsive but still breathing.

Zenobia looked up frightened and realized she was too late. Tibor was still tightly restrained. Cesari told her to stop what she was doing and sit down next to Tibor. She did as she was told and stared at Shlomo lying on the floor.

"Is he alive?" she asked, noticeably worried.

Cesari bent down and took the handkerchief from Shlomos breast pocket. He wrapped it tightly around his wounded hand saying, "He'll be fine."

She said, "What do you want from us?"

Cesari wasn't in the best of moods and said sharply, "I'm asking the questions here, all right?" Then he looked at Drusilla on the other side of Tibor and said, "You first. Who are you?"

She hesitated and then said, "You know who I am. I Drusilla."

Cesari reached over, pulled her veil off with his bloodied hand and slapped her in the face with the other. "Don't make me say it again."

The woman under the veil was not a woman at all, but a short, fat man in a wig with mildly feminine features, a bad complexion and a one day's growth of beard. Stung by the blow, he sputtered in a thick Brooklyn accent, "Hey, keep your paws to yourself, y'animal. I don't gotta tell ya nuttin."

Cesari stood over the man with clenched fists and glowered at him. "Do I look like a patient guy to you, meatball?"

The man glanced at the other two and said, "You don't gotta be rude… They call me Sunny. That's Sunny with a U on account of my sunny disposition. Sunny Basilone from Bensonhurst."

Cesari glanced at the woman he knew as Zenobia. "And that would make you?"

She looked down as if she were ashamed of herself. "Drusilla."

Tibor started to say something and Cesari said, "Quiet. Your turn's coming up soon. He turned to the real Drusilla. "You're Shlomo's daughter?"

She nodded. "Yes."

Cesari was quiet for a few seconds before saying, "I thought so. The night you lured me to your apartment so your boyfriend here could plant that evidence against me, you tripped and your sunglasses fell off. I saw your eyes and I suspected it. Shlomo told me his daughter had inherited the eye thing. At the time, a lot was going on and I couldn't wrap my head around all the subterfuge. So tell me what this is all about and be careful about manhandling the truth. I already know most of it."

She hesitated, realized that deception was no longer an option and began, "My father knew that because of who he was and the people he associated with that I would always be a target for others to get at him. So he sent me to private schools and tried as best as possible to keep me out of the public eye, but as I grew it became obvious that he could not keep me hidden forever so he decided to set trap for those who would prey on me. He created the ugly Drusilla, the creature no man would ever want, and I became Zenobia, beautiful friend of Drusilla. I could be with father and safe from enemies."

"You mean until this guy and his brothers came along?" he said turning to Tibor.

Drusilla said, "Is not that way. I fell in love with Tibor the first time I see him. I could not keep up deception with him."

Tibor added, "And I love you, Drusilla, with all my heart and soul. I would die for you."

Cesari stood up and punched him in the face so hard his chair fell backward. Drusilla and Sunny jumped up. She exclaimed, "Why did you hit him? He is defenseless."

Cesari spoke sternly, "Sit down, Drusilla. Pick him up, Sunny... I have bad news for you, Drusilla, but your boyfriend Tibor, and his brothers murdered an innocent girl and mutilated her to make her look like a vampire just to drive your father crazy. They also committed several other horrific homicides in the same vein. I took the girl's death kind of personally, Tibor. I didn't know her very well, but she seemed nice."

Tibor had a swollen, bleeding lip. He glanced downward. "You are right, but I did not want to hurt her. Was older brother's idea. Older brother's plan. I cannot resist orders from older brother. It has always been his birthright to be in charge." He turned to Drusilla. "When I met you, Drusilla, everything changed in my heart. The way I see the world changed. Everything changed. I wanted to get away from brothers and start new life with you."

Drusilla started to weep and threw her arms around him. Sunny on the other side sniffled, "That was beautiful."

Cesari rolled his eyes. "And so what happened here?"

Tibor said, "My brothers betrayed Shlomo and plotted against him, but as father of my Drusilla, grandfather to my children, I could not go along with it and watch him be killed. So I came up with plan to spare him. I revealed to him plot and hide him here hoping to make our escape, but plans fall apart today."

"Assuming you were to make it out of here alive, where were you off to?"

Drusilla said, "Shlomo has always been fond of Boca Raton. He has beachfront condominium there overlooking golf course."

They all looked up as the police sirens grew closer. Cesari said, "One more question." He looked at Sunny. "Just how in hell were you supposed to pull off being a Romanian girl with a guy like Tibor?"

He went into his routine. "Is easy to fake accent, no? More hard to fake be in love." Then he went back to his normal Brooklynese. "It worked with you. Besides, when Tibor first came sniffing around, I pretended to be too modest to ever be alone with him or speak directly to him. Zenobia would always be present to protect my honor and she would always talk for me. This way I didn't have to worry about not speaking Romanian. We really poured it on thick. The idea was to scare him off as quickly as possible. When he kept coming back, I even pretended I wanted to have a tumble with him if you know what I mean. It didn't matter. We'd only met a couple of times when Zenobia fell in love and told him the whole gig."

Cesari said to Drusilla, "Where'd you ever find this guy?"

She grinned. "The Drusilla impersonators usually only last one or two years. We pay well and most of time is boring work. We find Sunny in Bucharest. Father and I see Sunny on street corner telling jokes, play banjo and perform card tricks for money. Father like."

Sunny interjected, "I was thinking of applying to their clown school. It's top rated. I can juggle pretty good too, but Shlomo made me an offer I couldn't resist. Sit around, eat great, watch TV, do nothing ninety-nine percent of the time for six-figures. Who's going to argue with that?"

"Clown school?"

"Hey, we can't all be tall dark and mysterious. You know what I'm saying?"

"I guess," Cesari said. "Drusilla, did your father know about you and Tibor? I'm just trying to get it straight in my head."

She shook her head, "Not until the end. Originally father give Tibor permission to court me thinking he would be repulsed by Sunny and go away, but I couldn't help myself when I see Tibor. Then when Tibor drive father to airport to certain death in Romania, he tell him everything and offer him salvation."

Cesari nodded, and as she leaned over and kissed Tibor, they heard a door crashing in downstairs. Cesari said, "When your father wakes up, I suggest you urge him to cooperate to the fullest of his ability. He won't get off. Not a chance of that, but they may take it easy on the rest of you if he can nail Dimitri and any other bigwigs involved. Everybody in law enforcement dreams about catching the big fish."

Sunny said, "Hey, what about me? I didn't do nuttin."

Chapter 58

Twenty-four hours later, Gunnery Sergeant Robert Tierney USMC retired was sitting up in his hospital bed at St. Matt's, recovering from surgery to remove the bullet from his shoulder. The round had embedded itself in the soft tissue and thick muscles of his upper shoulder and chest and fortunately had not significantly damaged bone or any major blood vessels. Most importantly, it had missed his lung by just a few millimeters. A full recovery and early discharge were anticipated by the surgeon. Tierney sat there with his arm in a sling sipping on broth with his other hand and holding court with Cesari and Vito who had only just arrived.

"How do you feel, Detective?"

"Like a million bucks, Cesari. Haven't seen action like that in a long time. It felt good to be back in the saddle again."

Cesari grinned. "Thanks for calling your boys in blue and letting them know I was one of the good guys. It was getting kind of hairy at the brownstone when they first arrived."

"I heard you created quite a mess there. I'm impressed. Four Romanian mobsters and Shlomo, and not a scratch on you. That's pretty good by any standards."

Cesari held up his bandaged left hand that had required fourteen stitches and hurt like hell. "Well, not entirely without a scratch."

Tierney turned to Vito. "I want to thank you again, Gianelli, for staying with me at the tenement. The true test of the mettle of any man is how he reacts in a life and death crisis and you passed with flying colors. You are officially off my person of interest list."

Vito cracked a smile. "Thanks, I'll fire all my attorneys right away."

Cesari said, "Yorgi underwent successful surgery too, although he was in a lot worse shape than you when he arrived. My sources in the ICU tell me that he's doing well. Well enough that his room is crowded with FBI agents."

Tierney said, "And my sources in the FBI tell me he's singing like a canary. It sounds like Ivan and Tibor are going to happily spill their guts as well. I love it when a plan comes together. Now it's just a question of who is going to crack first, Shlomo or Dimitri?"

"My money's on Shlomo," Cesari replied. "He's got the most to lose if the feds go after his daughter, which they could easily do as an accessory. She made no bones about the fact that she was aware of his business. He'll want to avoid her involvement at all costs."

"I have to agree. That would be a very strong motivator. What do you think, Gianelli?"

Vito mulled it over for a moment before saying, "I think that Dimitri and whoever he represents back home will be sending as many troops here as quickly as they can to try to silence Shlomo and Yorgi."

Tierney nodded in agreement. "Probably... The FBI agent who stopped in here earlier said that they've notified Interpol about these guys. Apparently, Interpol has been hot on Shlomo's trail for some time now and would love to horn in on any action. So if we can get Shlomo to give up his people across the pond, they'll run interference over there and try to keep them occupied."

"Interpol?" Vito asked. "I wonder if that's who those shadowy guys were I told you about, Cesari. The ones lurking in the background when the feds were questioning me a while back."

"You were questioned by Interpol?" Tierney asked.

"Not by them directly. The feds brought me in for what I thought was routine harassment and there were guys standing off to the side. The feds kept asking me if I knew Markov, but they never said why. I guess now I know."

Tierney nodded. "That is interesting, but it's all water under the bridge now… I guess that wraps it up, boys."

Cesari raised his hand. "What about the CEO?"

Tierney allowed himself a chuckle. "Oh, him. They found him hiding under his desk, shaking like a leaf. He's talking faster than anyone else. Apparently, he was accidentally led to believe that his pal Feinberg was murdered by Yorgi in an attempt to tidy up loose ends and that he was next on the clean-up agenda. That was all he needed to let it rip. They're going to love him in prison."

Cesari said, "Literally I hope, but the way the system works, he'll probably be playing tennis in some light-weight federal prison or on the streets doing community service in six months."

Vito said, "Yeah, but at least his career ruining hospitals is over. That's something."

"You think so, do you?" Cesari said cynically.

Tierney was puzzled. "C'mon, Cesari, be real. What hospital would take on a loser like that?"

"You'd be surprised, Detective. You'd be surprised."

The End

About the Author

John Avanzato grew up in the Bronx, New York. After receiving a bachelor's degree in biology from Fordham University, he went on to earn his medical degree at the State University of New York at Buffalo, School of Medicine. He is currently a board-certified gastroenterologist practicing in upstate, New York, where he lives with his wife of over thirty years. Dr. Avanzato co-teaches a course on pulp fiction at Hobart and William Smith Colleges in Geneva, New York.

Inspired by authors like Tom Clancy, John Grisham, and Lee Child, Avanzato writes about strong but flawed heroes. His stories are fast-paced thrillers with larger than life characters and tongue-in-cheek humor.

His first ten novels, *Hostile Hospital, Prescription for Disaster, Temperature Rising, Claimed Denied, The Gas Man Cometh, Jailhouse Doc, Sea Sick, Pace Yourself, The Legend of the Night Nurse, and Hilton Dead* have been received well.

Author's Note

Dear Reader,

I hope you enjoyed reading *Bleeding Heart* as much as I enjoyed writing it. Please do me a favor and write a review for me on amazon. The reviews are important, and your support is greatly appreciated. I can be reached at johnavanzato59@gmail.com or Facebook for further discussion.

Thank you,

John Avanzato MD

Hostile Hospital

When former mob thug turned doctor, John Cesari, takes a job as a gastroenterologist at a small hospital in upstate New York, he assumes he's outrun his past and started life anew. But trouble has a way of finding the scrappy Bronx native.

Things go awry one night at a bar when he punches out an obnoxious drunk who won't leave his date alone. Unbeknownst to Dr. Cesari, that drunk is his date's stalker ex-boyfriend—and a crooked cop.

Over the course of several action-packed days, Cesari uncovers the dirty little secrets of a small-town hospital. As the bodies pile up, he is forced to confront his own bloody past.

Hostile Hospital is a fast-paced journey that is not only entertaining but maintains an interesting view on the philosophy of healthcare. If you aren't too scared after reading, get the sequel, *Prescription for Disaster*.

Prescription for Disaster

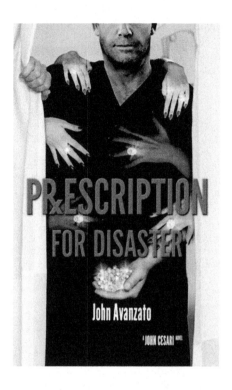

Dr. John Cesari is a gastroenterologist employed at Saint Matt's Hospital in Manhattan. He tries to escape his unsavory past on the Bronx streets by settling into a Greenwich Village apartment with his girlfriend, Kelly. After his adventures in Hostile Hospital, Cesari wants to stay under the radar of his many enemies.

Through no fault of his own, Cesari winds up in the wrong place at the wrong time. A chance encounter with a mugger turns on its head when Cesari watches his assailant get murdered right before his eyes.

After being framed for the crime, he attempts to unravel the mystery, propelling himself deeply into the world of international diamond smuggling. He is surrounded by bad guys at every turn and behind it all are Russian and Italian mobsters determined to ensure Cesari has an untimely and unpleasant demise.

His prescription is to beat them at their own game, but before he can do that he must deal with a corrupt boss and an environment filled with temptation and danger from all sides. Everywhere Cesari goes, someone is watching. The dramatic climax will leave you breathless and wanting more.

Temperature Rising

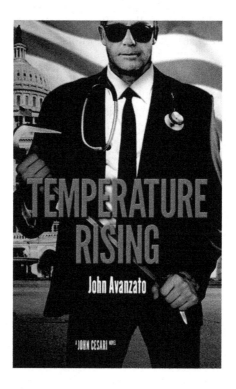

John Cesari is a gangster turned doctor living in Manhattan saving lives one colonoscopy at a time. While on a well-deserved vacation, he stumbles upon a murder scene and becomes embroiled in political intrigue involving the world's oldest profession.

His hot pursuit of the truth leads him to the highest levels of government, where individuals operate above the law. As always, girl trouble hounds him along the way making his already edgy life that much more complex.

The bad guys are ruthless, powerful, and nasty but they are no match for this tough, street-smart doctor from the Bronx who is as comfortable with a crowbar as he is with a stethoscope. Get ready for a wild ride in *Temperature Rising*. The exciting and unexpected conclusion will leave you on the edge of your seat.

Claim Denied

In Manhattan, a cancer ridden patient commits suicide rather than become a financial burden to his family. Accusations of malfeasance are leveled against his caregivers. Rogue gastroenterologist, part-time mobster, John Cesari, is tasked to look into the matter on behalf of St. Matt's hospital.

The chaos and inequities of a healthcare system run amok, driven by corporate greed and endless bureaucratic red tape, become all too apparent to him as his inquiry into this tragedy proceeds. On his way to interview the wife of the dead man,

Cesari is the victim of seemingly random gun violence and finds himself on life support.

Recovering from his wounds, he finds that both he and his world are a very different place. His journey back to normalcy rouses in him a burning desire for justice, placing him in constant danger as evil forces conspire to keep him in the dark.

The Gas Man Cometh

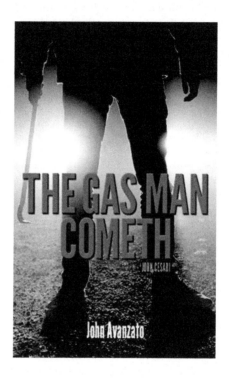

A deranged anesthesiologist with unnatural desires lures innocent women to his brownstone in a swank section of Manhattan. All was going well until John Cesari M.D. came along becoming a thorn in his side.

Known as The Gas Man, his hatred of Cesari reaches the boiling point. He plots to take him down once and for all turning an ordinary medical conference into a Las Vegas bloodbath.

Hungover and disoriented, Cesari awakens next to a mobster's dead girlfriend in a high-end brothel. Wanted dead or alive by more than a few people, Cesari is on the run with gangsters and the police hot on his trail.

There is never a dull moment in this new thriller as Cesari blazes a trail from Sin City to lower Manhattan desperately trying to stay one step ahead of The Gas Man.

Jailhouse Doc

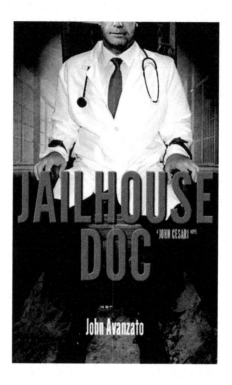

Dr. John Cesari, former mobster turned gastroenterologist, finds himself on the wrong end of the law. A felony conviction lands him in Riker's Island, one of the country's most dangerous correctional facilities, doing community service.

Fighting to survive, he becomes trapped in the web of a vicious criminal gang dealing in drugs and human flesh.

A seemingly unrelated and mysterious death of a college student in Greenwich Village thrusts Cesari into the middle of the action and, forced to take sides, his options are to either cooperate or die. Which will it be?

Sea Sick

Recovering from a broken heart, John Cesari M.D. embarks on a Mediterranean cruise to unwind and clear his head. His goals are to see the sights, eat a lot, and most of all to stay away from women.

A chance encounter in a Venetian Bar with the lusty captain of the Croatian women's national volleyball team just before setting sail turns his plan on its head. When she tells him she is being sold into a forced marriage, he is thrust into the middle of a rollicking, ocean-going adventure to rescue her.

Murder on the high seas wasn't on the itinerary when he purchased his ticket, but in true Cesari fashion, he embraces his fate and dives in.

Pace Yourself

John Cesari's former lover Kelly and her children have gone missing and her husband is found dead in an underground garage. When law enforcement fails to act, Cesari launches his own investigation. He discovers their disappearance is linked to a shady company in Manhattan called EverBeat selling defective pacemakers to hospitals.

EverBeat has ties to both the Chinese military complex in Beijing and to the United States government. Trying to unravel the web of deceit one lie at a time leads to a trail of corpses throughout the city that never sleeps. Hunted by professional killers and thwarted by personal betrayal, his only goal is to save Kelly and her family.

The Legend of the Night Nurse

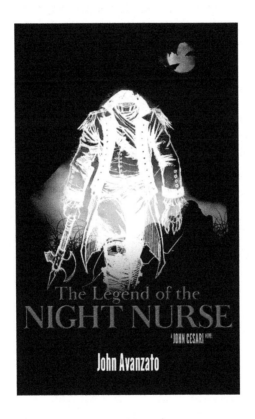

Our favorite gastroenterologist John Cesari joins a small hospital in rural New York and is beginning to acclimate to the colorful administrators who hired him when Jasmine walks into his life. Single, beautiful and just a little bit odd, he is immediately smitten by her charm. He soon discovers that she is more than just slightly eccentric and is dangerously obsessed with Halloween, witchcraft and devil worship.

Cesari is determined to help her as Halloween night approaches and everyone's excitement reaches a fever pitch. The thrilling conclusion will leave you breathless. The Legend of the Night Nurse proves once again that on Halloween night all things mischievous can and will happen.

Hilton Dead

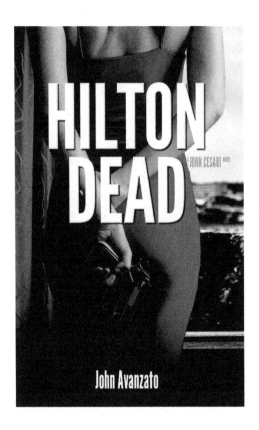

Trapped on a small island off the coast of South Carolina during hurricane season, Cesari finds himself in the company of mysterious yet collegial fellow travelers. The severe weather conditions pose serious challenges for the group, but the odd behavior and quirky dispositions of the hotel staff are even more disconcerting. And then, one by one, the guests start to disappear…

KCM Publishing
a division of KCM Digital Media, LLC

Made in the USA
Middletown, DE
15 September 2021